GARTH NIX

TERCIEL & ELINOR

HOT
KEY
BOOKS

First published in Great Britain in 2021 by Hot Key Books

This paperback edition published in 2022 by
HOT KEY BOOKS
4th Floor, Victoria House, Bloomsbury Square, London WC1B 4DA
Owned by Bonnier Books
Sveavägen 56, Stockholm, Sweden
www.hotkeybooks.com

A CIP catalogue record for this book is available from the British Library.

ISBN: 978-1-4714-0971-4
Also available as an ebook

1

Printed and bound in Great Britain by Clays Ltd, Elcograf S.p.A.

Hot Key Books is an imprint of Bonnier Books UK
www.bonnierbooks.co.uk

TERCIEL & ELINOR

The creature that stepped out through the garden gate and stood behind the line of Lesser Dead in the field no longer looked much like Amelia Hallett. The Dead spirit within had begun to corrode and warp the flesh, had stretched the body like a wax doll to make it taller and thinner. Its neck was twice as long as any human's, and its fiery mouth now extended all the way across its face, from ear to ear. The heliotrope nightgown was too short and had split into separate, trailing strands, doing little to cover the pallid, bluish flesh beneath. Its arms had also grown, and the nails on its hands were several inches long and viciously curved.

It raised one taloned hand and pointed at the small group around the bonfire, just as the roof of Coldhallow House fell into the fire and a massive eruption of flame and sparks blew up into the sky.

'The water will not save you, Abhorsen!' shrieked the creature.

Books by Garth Nix (selected)

THE OLD KINGDOM SERIES
(in reading order)
Terciel and Elinor
Sabriel
Lirael
Abhorsen
Goldenhand

Clariel (prequel)

Across the Wall: A Tale of the Abhorsen and Other Stories
To Hold the Bridge: Tales from the Old Kingdom and Beyond

Newt's Emerald

For younger readers:
THE KEYS TO THE KINGDOM SERIES

Frogkisser!

Have Sword, Will Travel
Let Sleeping Dragons Lie

To my wife, Anna, my sons, Thomas and Edward, and our dog, Snufkin; and to all my family and friends. Also to the many readers who have found the Old Kingdom over the years and keep coming back to visit.

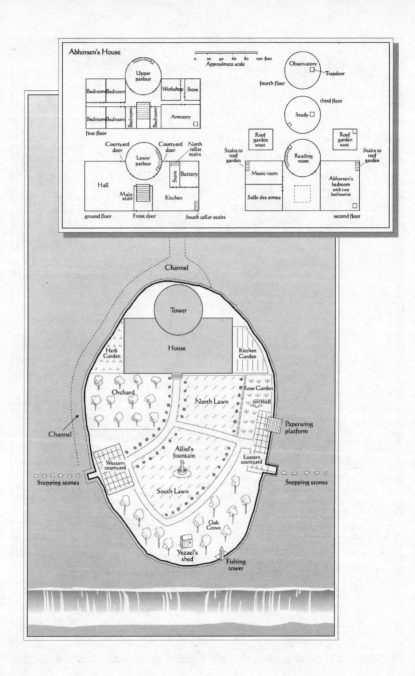

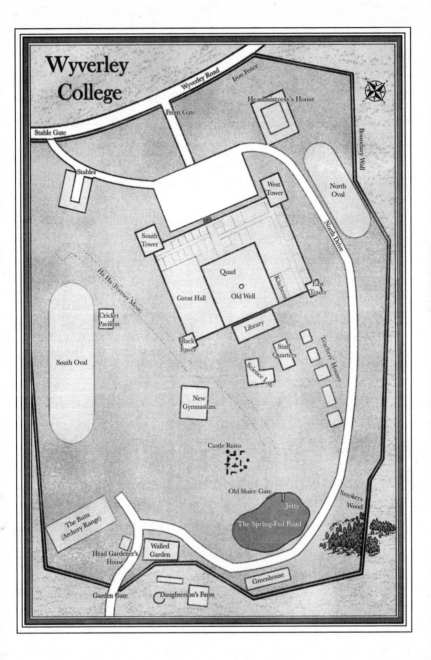

PROLOGUE

The fig tree was ancient and huge, its lower trunk buttressed by enormous roots that rose out of the lawn around it like the fins of some vast subterranean creature, while its upper branches topped out at two hundred feet, a full hundred feet higher than even the red-roofed tower of the Abhorsen's House nearby.

A boy, perhaps eight years old, brown-skinned, dark-haired, thin in the face and everywhere else from lack of food, was climbing swiftly up through the branches of the fig with fierce determination. He was wearing ragged, many-times-repaired breeches and a new linen shirt, far too large for him, that had been cinched in the middle with a silk scarf, also new, to make a kind of tunic, and his bare feet were extremely dirty.

It was very quiet in and around the tree, but the boy climbed in a frenzy, as if he were pursued. Several times he almost lost his grip or footing, but he didn't slow or falter. Finally, as he neared the top and the branches became slimmer and began to bend and creak, he slowed down. Soon after, reaching a point some twenty or thirty paces short of the crown, he stopped and straddled a horizontal branch, setting his thin shoulders against the gnarled trunk of the mighty tree.

He couldn't see much from his vantage point. The leaves were too thick around him. But there were a few spots where the foliage thinned. Through these gaps he could catch a glimpse of the red-roofed tower house below and the white limestone walls that surrounded the island it was built on, an island in the middle of a broad, fast-rushing river that only a few hundred yards to the south plunged over a massive waterfall.

The boy stared at the mist rising along the line of the cliffs, marvelling again at the quiet, the roar of the falls held back from the island by magic, or so he supposed. It had been noisy enough on the riverbank, and almost deafening when the old woman had jumped across the stepping-stones with him on her back, the boy gripping her so hard around the neck she'd told him crossly to stop choking her or they would both die.

The old woman. She'd said she was his great-aunt, but he didn't think that could be true. She'd repeated this claim to the beadle at the workhouse in Grynhold, and the mayor, so they would let him go, but they wouldn't have stopped her anyway. They were all bowing and begging her pardon and asking if she wanted wine or oysters or cake or anything at all the town might give her.

But all she had wanted was him, and they had been happy to hand him over. No one had asked what he wanted.

There was a rustle higher above, and a crunching, snapping sound. For a moment the boy thought it was a branch breaking, but the sound went on too long. A continuous crunching noise. He stood up and parted the branches immediately above him. All the boy saw was glaring green, elongated eyes and a broad open mouth full of very sharp white teeth.

He flinched, lost his footing, and almost fell, but sacrificing skin, he managed to keep his grip on the higher branches. He swung there for a heart-stopping second before he scrabbled his feet back onto a thicker, lower branch.

Branches creaked above, as if suddenly bearing more weight, and the foliage moved so Terciel got a proper look at what was above him. He was surprised to see it was a man, or sort of a man, because his first, half-seen impression was of something smaller. That said, this man was no taller than Terciel, albeit much broader across the shoulders. He had an odd pinkish nose, and there was that hideous, many-toothed mouth and the huge emerald eyes. Adding to his strangeness, his skin was entirely covered in fine, very white fur or down, which grew longer on his head and chin to give the appearance of hair and a beard. He had been eating fig-bird chicks out of a nest, crunching their tiny bones. There was a feather in the corner of his mouth and a single drop of blood on his broad white chest.

A red leather collar was fastened tight around his neck, a collar that swarmed with Charter marks to make some sort of spell, and a tiny silver bell hung from the collar. The boy

3

could see the clapper swing inside, but it made no sound, at least not one that he could hear.

'So,' said whatever this thing was, spitting out the feather. His voice was that of a grown man, and sardonic. 'You're her new one.'

The boy crouched lower on the branch, ready to drop down to the next branch below, to climb down as fast as or even faster than he had climbed up.

'Don't fret,' said the creature. 'You're safe enough from me.'

'What are you?' asked the boy nervously. He had one foot on the branch below, but he stayed where he was. For the moment. 'I mean who? Sir.'

'Many things once,' said the stranger, yawning. His teeth were even longer and sharper than they had seemed at first, and there were more of them. 'I am a servant of the Abhorsens. Or to be more accurate, a slave. I have had many names. Your mistress calls me Moregrim.'

'The Abhorsen. Her, down there,' said the boy, frowning. He gestured at the house. She'd taken him inside as soon as they arrived and handed him over to two strange magical servants she called sendings. They were like daytime ghosts, their skin and eyes and hair and everything all Charter marks, uncountable tiny marks in different colours, swarming and crawling about to create the illusion of living people. The sendings had tried to give him a bath, but he'd managed to escape and climb the tree.

'Yes indeed,' replied the dwarf, his green eyes sparkling with mischief. 'Her down there is the current Abhorsen, and you, I presume, are her latest Abhorsen-in-Waiting. Terciel, that's your name, isn't it?'

'How do you know that?'

'I listen at doors,' said Moregrim blithely. 'And windows. Both the real and the metaphorical.'

Terciel frowned again, not understanding what the strange creature was talking about.

'Tell me,' said the dwarf idly, not even looking at the boy, 'have you wielded the bells yet? Touched the handles? Worn the bandolier at least?'

'What?' asked Terciel. He still wasn't sure whether to flee down the tree or not. He had climbed it with the idea of hiding there until nightfall, and then trying to escape this island, but with this magical slave of the Abhorsen's here, that plan had already failed. He looked around, wondering if there was somewhere else he could hide. Apart from the main house and its immediate gardens, there was an orchard, and lawns, and a strange little house or shed to the south, but nowhere that would offer safety from a search.

He tried not to think even further ahead, to how he might cross the river, so swift, with the vast falls so close. The stepping-stones were too far apart for him to jump. Maybe there was a boat. He was good with boats, a true child of the fishing port of Grynhold. Launched from the northern end of the island, where the current would be weaker, maybe—

'Have you wielded the bells?'

The bells.

The sudden change in Terciel's admittedly already difficult life had started with the appearance of seven bells in a bandolier. One moment they had not been there, and then there they were, in Terciel's most secret eyrie in between the chimney stacks on the roof of the Grynhold Fish Hall. He'd been steeping a stolen piece of salt fish in a rain bucket, heard something strange, and looked away for less than a second. When he looked back, there was the bandolier, with the mahogany bell handles sticking out of the pouches that kept the bells silent, the handles and the leather crawling all over with glowing Charter marks, which slowly faded from too-bright brilliance as he watched, though they remained visible.

Terciel had left the bells and his fish, departing across the rooftop in a great rush that set the roosting gulls flying. Despite having the forehead Charter mark himself, he had never been taught magic, since he was an orphan of no account, merely a line in the register of the Grynhold Workhouse, an annoyance to the beadle who oversaw the children there, and nothing more than that to anyone else. His parents, who might have taught him Charter Magic, had drowned when he was two, and his much older sister, Rahi, who had looked after him for a while afterwards, had disappeared before he was four. Or thereabouts. He had no memory of his parents at all, and only a vague recollection of his sister.

Everything he knew about them came from rare answered questions or from overhearing people talk about him, which happened even less frequently. Mostly he was ignored, apart from a cuff to speed him out of the workhouse to the oakum-picking shed, or a cuff to get him back in again at the end of the day, with an occasional caning thrown in if his absence from the daily work was noticed.

All Terciel knew about magic was that the old healer Maralide made Charter marks appear from nowhere, sketching them in the air and on broken skin and bone, and sometimes they healed a hurt or cured a sickness, and sometimes they didn't. And what Terciel knew about magical bells came only from stories whispered at night in the workhouse dormitory, whispers backstopped by the constant gurgle of the north aqueduct close by, whose swift running water kept the town safe from the marauding Dead, terrible creatures who were brought back into the living world by awful necromancers *who used magical bells*.

Seven bells, carried in a bandolier, worn across the chest.

Three days after the bells had appeared in Terciel's eyrie, the old woman had arrived in Grynhold, and shortly after that Terciel had been called to the beadle's office and then when he had fled instead, since he had numerous petty crimes of fish theft and other misdemeanours that might have come to light, he had been apprehended by an unprecedented collegiate effort on the part of the beadle and her associates, the Grynhold Town Watch, and a large number of fisher-folk who were ashore waiting for the tide to turn before they went out again. It was the last group that had soured Terciel's attempted escape. The fisher-folk had never bothered the boy before, and he had been hiding among the drying nets.

They had dragged him before the old woman, and he had met her piercing black eyes, seen her horrendously white face, so much paler than anyone's ever should be, and then he had looked down to the seven bells she wore in a bandolier across her chest, over an armoured coat of unusual design, made of many small interlocking plates, several scored with the mark of weapons that had failed to penetrate.

Terciel had screamed when he saw the bells, and it had taken the combined effort of the mayor, the beadle, and the woman herself to convince him that she was not a necromancer come to steal his life and use his dead body for some terrible unspecified purpose. They'd explained that bells with Charter marks were special, not the usual necromancer's tools, and they also were *not* the same seven bells that had appeared in his eyrie.

Those bells had come to him specially, the woman said, and it meant he had to go and get them and then he would have to come away with her. That was when she had said she was his great-aunt and her name was Tizanael, and he could call her 'Aunt Tizzy'.

Terciel had noticed everyone else called her 'Abhorsen' and bowed low, something the free fishers of Grynhold didn't do for anyone else.

With the fisher-folk turned against him, there was nowhere Terciel could hide. He'd climbed the fish hall and carefully picked up the bandolier by the very end of one strap, carried the bells down, and handed them over to the Abhorsen. She said she would keep them until his training began, when they got to the 'House', wherever that was. They'd left soon after, walking out under the aqueduct in the late afternoon, something that filled

Terciel with terror. To go beyond the safety of running water, with the night coming on?

But nothing had happened, then or in the next three days and nights. After a while it occurred to Terciel that this was because he was travelling with someone the creatures of the night were afraid of themselves. He wanted to run away but dared not try anything, not when she was so close.

Now he was trapped here, on this island on the edge of a waterfall, and he didn't know what to do.

Moregrim asked the question again, but Terciel didn't answer.

'Could you take my collar off? It itches.'

Terciel shook his head slowly. He hadn't touched the bells and he wasn't going to touch a collar with all those marks glowing and floating upon it, not least when he didn't know what this creature was.

The strange man slid along the branch above on all fours, a curiously nimble movement. Terciel noted his fingers were very stubby and ended in claws, and were covered in the same short white hair that was all over his body. He also appeared to have a vestigial tail.

'Take off my collar!'

Terciel lowered himself to the branch below, and then the next, climbing down as rapidly as he ever had to escape the workhouse, with the beadle shouting at him from the window above.

There was shouting here too, but it came from below.

'Come down at once!'

'I am coming down!' he shouted back. He could see her now, on the lawn below the tree, one hand raised in a beckoning motion. For a second he thought there was a bright star on her finger, before he saw it was the afternoon sun catching the ring she wore at the right angle to make it flash.

'Not you!' called Tizanael, the fifty-first Abhorsen in a line that stretched back over centuries to the very first, whose name had become synonymous with the office. 'Him! Come down at once!'

A white form leaped past Terciel, too close for comfort, gripped a branch with those taloned hands and swung down further, switchbacking down the branches in swinging falls and crouching leaps, the blocky body moving with incongruous mobility. The boy followed more slowly, losing sight of both the creature and Tizzy as he entered the denser foliage of the lower branches.

When he finally reached the ground, the dwarf was kneeling in front of Tizanael, his head tilted at a very inhuman angle that obviously was no discomfort. The Abhorsen no longer wore the armour, bell bandolier, and sword, but a robe of dark blue embroidered with a multitude of tiny silver keys a golden rope in place of a belt, with a small dagger in a metal sheath at her hip. She held her left hand high, the silver ring catching the afternoon sun. The small ruby set in the ring glinted red, like a spark caught upon her finger.

'You were forbidden to leave the house, Moregrim.'

'This whole island is often termed the "House",' said the dwarf, with a yawn. 'I thought that was what you meant.'

'I meant the structure to my left,' said Tizanael shortly. 'I will now be more specific. You are to remain within the walls of the building I am indicating until I give you leave otherwise.'

She pointed at the whitewashed, red-roofed house with its sky-blue door and the door knocker in the shape of a lion's head, a ring held in its jaws.

'I also did not give you leave to change your shape,' added Tizanael. 'Whether for the purpose of climbing trees or anything else.'

Moregrim emitted a high-pitched hissing noise and stood up. For a moment Terciel thought the strange, short man was going to attack Tizanael, but instead he bowed low. As he straightened up, he changed, suddenly more humanlike. Now his skin was as pale as the Abhorsen's, his hair and beard were no longer fur-like, though still luminously white, and he was clothed in a shapeless white smock. The collar that had been around his neck had become a broader red leather belt hitched around his waist, and the small bell swung inside a large bronze buckle. The vestigial tail had entirely disappeared.

Moregrim bowed, turned away, and headed not towards the front door of the house but to an open gate in the wall on the right-hand side, which led to the kitchen garden. When he was about ten paces away, he turned and snarled, green eyes directed piercingly at Terciel.

'She killed Rahiniel!'

Tizanael raised her hand. She did not do anything Terciel could see, but Moregrim writhed and fell over his own feet, rolled twice, and yowled exactly like the cats that frequented the Grynhold Fish Hall, before he got up again and stumbled away through the garden gate.

Tizanael turned to look at Terciel. Her face, as ever, was set. Not angry or antagonistic, like the beadle's so often was. This was simply an absence of emotion. Terciel had no idea what she was feeling or thinking.

'Who's Rahiniel?' he asked.

'Your sister,' said Tizanael, watching him carefully. 'I believe she was generally known as Rahi.'

'Rahi?'

Terciel took in a slow breath. He could almost remember Rahi. At least, he had the faint recollection of someone wrapping him up in a blanket and kissing his forehead as hail clattered on the roof. It had been cosy and warm, so not the workhouse. That was more likely to have been Rahi than his mother. He had been too little when his parents died to remember anything of them.

But that was his only memory. She had left, and he had always presumed she was dead anyway. What did it matter how she died?

'I did not kill her,' said Tizanael. 'She was my Abhorsen-in-Waiting. It is a dangerous office we hold, and she did not survive one of the many tests we face.'

'That man, or whatever he is, Moregrim. He wanted me to take off his collar.'

'You would not have been able to,' said Tizanael. 'Not yet. But Moregrim lays his plans long ahead. For now, simply remember that if you take off his collar, he will kill you.'

Terciel shrugged, attempting to show he wasn't scared. But he was, and they both knew it.

'You are to be my new Abhorsen-in-Waiting,' said Tizanael. 'That is why the bells came to you.'

'Why me?' asked Terciel.

Tizanael did not immediately answer. Terciel shifted, lifting his heels nervously, as she continued to look at him, gaze unblinking.

'It is a very difficult thing to be the Abhorsen,' she said finally. 'Many different strengths are needed. These tend to occur more frequently in those descended from the first Abhorsen, who was given many gifts by her . . . mother . . . you might say. So the bells often choose one of that line, however distant. Like your sister, Rahiniel, and now you.'

'You're not my aunt,' said Terciel defiantly. He didn't really understand what she was going on about.

'No,' replied Tizanael. 'I am your great-great-aunt. You have something of the look of my brother, Herranael, your great-grandfather.'

'Where's he, then?'

'He is dead,' replied the Abhorsen. 'They are all dead now, of that line, save you.'

Her expression didn't change, nor her tone of voice. She might have been speaking of the weather, or the time of day.

Terciel scowled, and scuffed the dirt with his heel.

'Did they drown?' he asked. His parents had drowned. Most of the orphans in the workhouse had lost their family to the sea.

'No,' replied Tizanael.

'Everyone dies,' said Terciel.

'Yes,' said Tizanael. 'In the right time. And it is my task . . . our task . . . to make sure they stay dead.'

'How?' asked Terciel. He felt suddenly tired, and hungry, and overwhelmed by all things he didn't understand. His entire world had changed, and it seemed unlikely to be for the better, even though his old life had been bad enough.

'I will teach you,' said Tizanael. 'But first, you must bathe, and put on clean clothes, and then we will eat a proper dinner. No more travel bread and water.'

'Salt fish?' asked Terciel.

Tizanael shuddered, the first time he had seen any kind of human expression pass over her statue-like mask of a face.

'Definitely not salt fish,' she said.

Terciel nodded, and walked ahead of her back to the blue door with the lion knocker. It was that simple reaction that convinced him there was hope in this new life after all.

He was so tired of eating salt fish.

1

The huge greenhouse that generations before had been used to raise bountiful crops of flowers and prize marrows had been remade into a theatre of sorts when Elinor was nine years old, and constantly improved since then. Now she was nineteen, the dolls that had once provided her supporting cast had long since been relegated to being her audience, seated in two rows of garden chairs at the south end. They had been replaced as performers by life-sized plasterboard cutouts, repainted as necessary. Elinor still played nearly all the parts and did all the voices.

She was doing one now, standing behind a bright red-and-gold cavalier to deliver the most famous speech from Breakespear's *The Three Noble Kinswomen*, Sir Merivan revealing he was betrothed to all three ladies but would marry none and was in fact in love with the orphan Kit Catchpenny.

'None of thee could but be more than a sister unto me—'

'Elinor!'

The agitated voice of Mrs Watkins preceded her into the glasshouse, the tone unusual enough to wake Ham Corbin, who had fallen asleep among the audience, despite Elinor's rousing performance over the last hour as the entire cast of the Breakespear classic. He *was* eighty, so Elinor did not take it as a criticism. Besides, he had been primarily a circus performer, and loved only the parts of plays that called for tumbling and swordplay and knife-throwing, all of which he had taught her since he had first come to Coldhallow House, ostensibly as an elderly and thus inexpensive groom but in fact more of an unlikely assistant and sometime foil to his niece, Roberta – though like everyone else, he only ever called Elinor's governess 'Mrs Watkins'.

Elinor sighed and let the rest of Sir Merivan's soliloquy subside back into the lower reaches of her mind. She stepped out from behind the cavalier cutout, revealing herself to be a full head shorter than the knight, as she stood no more than five foot three in her stockings or, as was the case now, in socks. She was wearing her long-dead father's clothes, a subdued tweed suit in brown and green, which matched her eyes. They were brown with flecks of green, and her hair was simply brown, a very undistinguished brown to her own eyes. The suit had been altered somewhat to fit, but was still baggy. Her father had been no taller than her, but considerably weightier and notoriously slow-moving. Elinor was slim, strong, swift, and dexterous, and Ham had said she was the physical equal of any of the circus folk he had worked with, though he qualified this by adding she was not as strong as 'Helena, the Strongest Woman in the World' nor as flexible as a contortionist known as the 'Mirror Snake'.

She looked a drab sparrow among the bright cutouts, Elinor thought, not for the first time. But even though she played all the parts, she never dressed as the flamboyant characters in her favourite dramas. She wore her father's old clothes simply because they were more comfortable and it was much easier to do all the things she liked doing in trousers rather than in an ankle-length dress and a tightly buttoned jacket, not to mention several layers of flannel underclothing.

It had been a tactical error to step out from hiding, Elinor realised, as Mrs Watkins saw she was once again wearing her father's clothes, with a cloth cap pulled down low over her forehead to hide the unsightly brand there, rather than a bonnet or even a scarf.

'Elinor! You have to get dressed. The doctor is here.'

'I thought he was coming tomorrow,' protested Elinor.

'The pony trap from the station is halfway up the drive! It must be bringing the doctor,' exclaimed Mrs Watkins. 'Hurry! Oh, Ham, not now!'

Ham ignored his niece, throwing four wooden balls in quick succession at Elinor, who caught them automatically and began to juggle, cycling the balls around in front of her face before she threw them back with great speed and accuracy straight at Ham's nose.

He caught the balls with a coughing chuckle and slipped them back into the pockets of his shabby greatcoat. Though it was the tail end of summer and the days still had some warmth, and the greenhouse with its iron-framed glass roof caught the sun, Ham had begun to feel the cold. Great age had not so far lessened his dexterity, but it had reduced his resistance to extremes of temperature.

'You've the sure eye, Miss Elinor,' he said. 'Knives next time.'

'You'll do no such thing,' scolded Mrs Watkins, though she knew full well her uncle would pay her no heed, and that Elinor had been juggling knives for years anyway. Though not usually when Mrs Watkins could see, to spare her feelings. 'Come on, Elinor. I have put out your Sunday dress and the blue bonnet.'

Elinor hooked her arm through Mrs Watkins's elbow as they left the greenhouse, and gave her a fond smile.

'What would I do without you, Mrs Watkins?'

The governess sniffed.

'Become even more of a hellion,' she said.

'I wish I was a hellion,' said Elinor sadly. 'Wearing men's clothes and staging plays all by myself hardly counts.'

'It would be more than enough if word spread of it,' snapped Mrs Watkins. She was almost dragging Elinor across the courtyard between the greenhouse and the main house now, in her eagerness to get her out of sight before their visitor might see her, though the doctor would come to the front door on the other side.

'How could it?' asked Elinor. She paused, forcing Mrs Watkins to release her arm. 'No one ever visits. I never go out.'

She gestured at the hills around them, good grazing land for sheep, though there had been none there for years and the once well-managed woods on the heights had begun to encroach upon the fields. Elinor's father, the late Edmund Hallett, had been a very indifferent farmer anyway, and since his death eight years before, Elinor's mother, Amelia, had let everything go: the land lay fallow, all the farmworkers and most of the servants had gone, and no social calls were made or allowed.

Now Amelia Hallett herself lay close to death, up on the four-poster bed in the grand bedroom that took up a good quarter of the old house's second floor. Elinor looked up at the windows there, even now half expecting to see her mother peering down at her, the same distant figure she had always been, leaving Elinor's education and well-being almost entirely to Mrs Watkins, intervening only in usually unwelcome ways on those rare occasions when she roused herself to leave the bedroom or parlour.

Mrs Hallett had taken to her bed three weeks previously, after feeling 'light-headed and odd', and had thereafter quickly lapsed into a state closely resembling death, while not actually being dead. The local doctor having proclaimed himself entirely baffled, he had suggested telegraphing the famous Dr Branthill and that worthy had eventually agreed to make a visit.

Though Mrs Hallett was not in the window, a sudden and miraculous recovery not having occurred, Elinor kept staring up. The weather vane atop the house was screeching as it slowly rotated, the screech almost seeming to come from the bronze owl that sat atop the directionals. The winds were extremely set in their ways here, usually coming from the south or southeast. The weather vane rarely moved much, if at all.

Now it had swung all the way around, and the arrow clutched in the bronze owl's claws was pointing north.

'A wind from the north,' said Elinor softly, almost to herself.

'What's that?' asked Mrs Watkins. She looked up too, and gasped. 'No, that can't be—'

The weather vane screeched and moved again, slowly circling around to point in a more accustomed direction to the southeast. But it didn't stay still, jerking northward for a few seconds before swinging back, as if the wind from the north was simply waiting its turn.

'I don't remember the last time the wind came from the north,' said Elinor. 'The servants all think it brings trouble, don't they?'

'It does,' said Mrs Watkins. She did not sound at all like her usual self. 'I hope not here.'

'What do you mean?' asked Elinor.

Mrs Watkins was still watching the weather vane. It was twitching between south-southeast and nor-nor'-east.

'We're a good fifteen miles further south than Bain,' she said, apparently to herself, for when Elinor repeated the question, she shook her head and gripped the young woman's arm again and pulled her along.

In the end, it took Elinor fifteen minutes to dress in the ridiculous layers of flannel and corsetry, many-buttoned coat, and flounced long dress that the year-old copies of *The Gentlewoman's Magazine* from Corvere said were suitable for a young lady of middling social status and wealth. Though in Elinor's case both these things were notional. Even before Amelia Hallett had put Coldhallow House in near isolation, her parents had always kept her secluded from local society, such as it was, and she had begun to realise from the lack of upkeep to everything that while the family may have been wealthy once, it was no longer. Or her mother was even more of a miser than she had always seemed to be. As with many other subjects, money was not something Amelia Hallett would discuss with her daughter, even before she became ill and could not talk at all.

The finishing touch was an unfashionable bonnet, pulled low to hide the disfiguring scar on her forehead. Amelia always insisted her daughter keep her forehead covered to hide the brand, and did not care to hear that bonnets had been out of fashion for at least several decades, even in the country.

Elinor accepted it was a disfigurement. She was relieved it was sometimes hardly visible, but it always became more distinct when she was upset or angry, probably something to do with blood flow, and it could not be concealed with paint or powder, somehow always showing through. Elinor could often forget about it, but Mrs Hallett had an absolute horror of the brand, possibly because it had been mysteriously inflicted by her own mother, Elinor's grandmother.

Elinor wasn't clear on exactly what her grandmother had done, or how she'd done it, as her mother refused to discuss the matter. She had no memory of any traumatic pain or, indeed, anything else that might have made the mark. Mrs Watkins had already been her governess then, but she had not seen what happened, having been sent on an errand clearly to get her out of the way. She had returned to find the baby's forehead indelibly marked and Mr Hallett threatening to whip his mother-in-law off the property, forbidding her ever to darken his threshold again, a sensibility shared by his wife.

'Come along, Elinor,' urged Mrs Watkins, returning to check on her charge's progress for the third time and help her with the final buttons. 'The doctor wouldn't take tea or anything, he's already gone straight in to your mother. These city folk, always in a rush!'

Elinor followed her governess, feeling both excited at finally meeting someone new, and nervous, in case the doctor somehow discerned her disfigurement under the bonnet and cried out in disgust or whatever it was her mother was always afraid was going to happen.

But the doctor hardly spared her a glance. He seemed very eager to conclude his visit and be gone.

'I'm afraid I can offer no more promising diagnosis than my esteemed local colleague,' said Dr Branthill hurriedly, even as Elinor walked into her mother's bedroom. 'I concur with the treatment to date. Continue feeding her. It is a good sign that she can still drink. Clear soups and the like, calf's-foot jelly, tea, a little lime juice. You have done well with the nursing. There is no better course than clean linens, regular bathing and turning, and if you can take her out in the chair when the weather is clement, that I also advise.'

'Maria, my mother's maid, has been responsible for her care,' said Elinor quickly, not wanting to take credit for something she hadn't done, and in all honesty, did not want to do. Her mother had never liked Elinor touching her, had always shrugged off any attempt at a hug or a kiss. Mrs Watkins said this was because Amelia had been forcibly taken from her own mother at birth, and raised by two of her dead father's strict and judgmental aunts in Corvere, so she'd never learned how to love *anyone*, or be a parent herself. This explanation, while it made perfect sense, didn't make it any easier for Elinor.

'Do you see any hope of . . . of recovery?'

'I simply do not know,' said the great man. Many a lesser doctor would have offered some meaningless claptrap that upon close examination would mean nothing. 'She breathes, albeit incredibly slowly. Her pulse, likewise. She lives, but in a very lowered state. The pallor of her skin is curious, but her lips and fingernails blush, showing no trace of blue. Her blood is red, her breath sweet. Her temperature is normal . . . she is not cold, despite what you think you saw—'

'I have seen it several times!' protested Elinor. 'The thinnest layer of frost that forms upon her skin. But when I touch her, it disappears. It only happens at night—'

'Ah, late at night, when you are very tired and of course anxious,' said the doctor hurriedly, making quick motions with his hands as if to sweep away whatever Elinor had seen or thought she'd seen. 'You are certain she never speaks?'

'No words,' said Elinor. 'Sometimes I have come into the room and thought she was singing under her breath.

Or humming. But it is so faint I'm never really sure whether I've heard it or not.'

'While we have made many advances in medicine these last few decades, much continues to be unknown,' said the doctor. He hesitated, then added, 'Particularly when considering the . . . ah . . . oddities of this locale.'

'What do you mean?' asked Elinor.

The doctor gave her a look she couldn't decipher. It wasn't exactly suspicion, nor puzzlement. Something between the two.

'The North,' he said finally.

It was Elinor's turn for a puzzled expression to form upon her face.

'What has that to do with anything?'

The doctor glanced at Mrs Watkins.

'It's not really the North here,' said the governess nervously. 'We're miles and *miles* south of Bain. We don't have . . . the oddities . . . usually.'

'The oddities of the locale,' repeated Dr Branthill, almost to himself. He glanced out the window as he spoke, and hurried to close his bag. Elinor looked out too, and saw the tops of the poplars in the drive were beginning to sway.

Not in their usual direction.

The wind was blowing from the north again. Not fiercely, but certainly enough to set the treetops swaying.

'You are a local woman, Mrs . . . er . . . Wobkins?' asked the doctor.

'Aye,' she answered, not correcting his mangling of her name. She hesitated, then added with a touch of defiance

Elinor had not often seen in someone so concerned with social differences, 'Bain born and bred, as it happens.'

'I too,' replied Dr Branthill, surprising both women. 'Rather further north, in fact, even closer to the Wall. I do not often come back. I . . . trust . . . trust you recall the childhood warnings pressed into us all. Given the condition of Mrs Hallett, I do not think this is quite so far south as one might hope and . . . and I do not like this wind.'

He no longer looked the picture of the confident medico but rather a slightly apprehensive middle-aged man whose side whiskers were quivering.

'So I am most anxious to get considerably further south myself before nightfall. I am sorry I cannot offer you any greater certainty or any relief for your mother, Miss Hallett. Good day!'

He was out the door before Elinor had a chance to even thank him, or offer any parting words. She followed him more slowly, only half listening as he clattered down the main stairs, strode swiftly down the gallery, and went out the front door like a jack-in-the-box, shouting for his coachman, who was to take him post-haste to the station and the soonest possible train southward.

2

'What did the doctor mean by the "oddities of the locale" and "the North"?' asked Elinor as she and Mrs Watkins sat down for their afternoon tea, brought to them in the drawing room by Maria, who was the sole remaining indoor servant apart from Cook, the others all having left over the years and not been replaced, though again Elinor didn't know whether this was from miserliness or necessity.

'Oh, these city folk,' said Mrs Watkins vaguely, picking up the pot. 'I do need a cup of tea.'

Her hand shook slightly as she poured, almost spilling tea in Elinor's saucer.

'You seemed to know what he meant,' said Elinor firmly. The tea spilling was a familiar distraction technique. 'He was frightened of the wind being from the north. So are you. And what does it have to do with Mother?'

'Your mother would not like me to . . . to . . . discuss local superstitions,' said Mrs Watkins. She spoiled this firm utterance by glancing out the bay window at the leaning poplars and this time unintentionally splashed tea into her own saucer as she overfilled the cup. The wind was still blowing from the north. Not fiercely but a steady breeze.

'My mother is ... my mother ...' Elinor stopped, took a breath, and continued. 'Whatever is happening to my mother, she is not in a position to stop you, Wattie. Please, I'm no longer a child. Tell me.'

Mrs Watkins lifted her cup and took a rather surprising gulp of tea. Elinor blinked at this, as she could not count the number of times the governess had recited, 'ladylike sips, Elinor, ladylike sips.'

'Mrs Hallett told me I'd be dismissed without a character if I talked about any of this,' the older woman finally said. 'Sent away, Elinor!'

'No,' replied Elinor with considerable alarm. How could anyone send Mrs Watkins away? It was unthinkable. She reached across the table and gripped the governess's gloved hand. 'I wouldn't let her send *you* away.'

'It wouldn't be up to you,' said Mrs Watkins with a sniff. 'She warned Ham as well, and everyone else.'

'But why?' asked Elinor.

'I can't tell you,' said Mrs Watkins. She took her hand from Elinor's grasp and fidgeted with a napkin. 'And I may have done something else that will get me dismissed anyway.'

'What!'

'I don't know what came over me,' said Mrs Watkins. She stared down at her empty cup, as if hoping to see some explanation in the faint swirl of tea leaves at the bottom. 'I really don't . . .'

'What did you do?' asked Elinor slowly. She couldn't imagine Mrs Watkins doing anything that would require dismissal, or even anything that would be more than slightly annoying. Like when she fussed over Elinor's clothes.

Mrs Watkins shook her head slowly, still gazing into her teacup.

'When I went into the village to send your telegram to Dr Branthill, I remembered I'd sent another one three weeks ago, when Mrs Hallett was first taken ill,' she said. 'But I had no recollection of it until then. She must have made me do it, put it in my head long ago!'

'Who?' asked Elinor, now totally bewildered. 'My mother? What other telegram? To who? What do you mean, "put it in your head"?'

Mrs Watkins didn't answer.

'Wattie . . .'

'No, no. I can't tell you, not without your mother's permission,' muttered Mrs Watkins. 'Maybe it won't matter.'

She looked out the window again. The poplars had steadied, and the wind was ebbing, perhaps even changing direction.

'Yes, it won't matter,' she said. But she spoke in the tone of someone trying to convince themselves that some dread future would not arise, knowing full well it probably would.

They sat in silence, drinking tea for the next five minutes. Usually Mrs Watkins would crack under this treatment. She couldn't bear it when Elinor wouldn't talk to her. But this time she remained silent as well, and it was Elinor who finally broke.

'Why did the doctor say he wanted to get away before *nightfall*?'

Mrs Watkins looked out the window again.

'I'm sure it won't matter,' she said finally. 'The wind has eased and swung around.'

'But what is that to do—'

'Never mind, Elinor!' replied Mrs Watkins, in as close to a snap as she'd ever managed. She raised one fluttering hand to her temple and added, 'Perhaps it is time we attended to your autumn clothes. I think the yellow poplin will need to be recut—'

'I'm going back to the greenhouse,' interrupted Elinor. 'To throw knives with Ham.'

Even this did not provoke a response from Mrs Watkins. She merely nodded and poured herself more tea. The dregs from the pot, almost solid tea leaves, splashed into her cup because she had forgotten to place the strainer.

Elinor stared for a moment, then turned away, disturbed even more by this totally uncharacteristic behaviour from her governess than by her mother's illness. The latter had always been remote and absent. Having her upstairs in bed made little difference to Elinor's life. But Mrs Watkins behaving like this was entirely new, and very upsetting.

Perhaps Ham would tell her what his niece would not, Elinor thought. She raced up the steps to her room, intent on changing into her comfortable clothes as quickly as possible. As always, her greenhouse theatre represented a safe refuge, where she could forget her cares and lose herself in the immortal works of Charlotte Breakespear, Henry Eden, or the more recent farces of the continental playwright Tontaire.

But Ham was almost as closemouthed as Mrs Watkins.

'Nah, nah, young lady,' he said as he threw a knife underarm at her. 'We've no need to talk of the north wind and the like down here. We're more than fifteen miles south of Bain, and it's another twenty-five or maybe even thirty miles north from there to the Wall.'

'What's the distance from here to the Wall got to do with anything?' asked Elinor, who had caught the knife and sent it spinning around with two others. In a moment she would catch all three and throw them back.

She knew about the Wall, of course, from various lessons. It was some sort of ancient ruin that marked the border between Ancelstierre and the neighbouring country to the north, the Old Kingdom, which was a backwards place of little interest. Or so she had been taught . . . though it now occurred to her that the paucity of information about the place was odd. Her geography textbooks were full of information about Ancelstierre and the countries across the channel and beyond. She'd had to learn the names of the capitals by heart, and their key products and other useless facts. But she'd never heard the name of the capital of the Old Kingdom, or even seen a map that showed anything beyond the border with Ancelstierre. Admittedly, geography classes were far from her favourite, and as with many other lessons, she'd usually been reading a pocket edition of a play set carefully inside a larger textbook while Mrs Watkins read aloud and hoped her student was following along . . .

She threw the knives at Ham, following them immediately with another question.

'What's so special about the Old Kingdom?'

Ham caught the knives but didn't throw them back. He looked at her, his craggy face worried.

'Why all these questions, Miss Elinor?'

'The north wind,' said Elinor. 'My mother's illness. Mrs Watkins is behaving so strangely. I feel it's all connected. I feel . . . I feel odd. As if something is going to happen. And I don't know whether to be afraid or excited. I need to know, Ham.'

'It's not my place to speak of such things,' said Ham. 'When I first came here, Mrs Hallett was very firm. She told me then I mustn't speak of things . . . things further north.'

'My mother's dying,' said Elinor, and knew it to be true. 'Everything is going to change.'

Ham nodded. But instead of answering, he threw the knives again. Elinor caught them instinctively, sent them whirling about her head and threw them back, adding a ball from her pocket. The old man sent knives and ball back again, adding another ball, very fast, right on the edge of what Elinor was able to handle.

Forced to completely focus her mind on the rocketing, spinning projectiles, Elinor thought that Mrs Watkins's uncle was also a capable hand at distraction when he didn't want to talk.

After juggling practice, Ham withdrew immediately, muttering something about 'duties', which, since he didn't really have any now that they no longer had any horses, apart from occasionally helping out with odd jobs, was also clearly to avoid Elinor's questions.

After he'd gone, she somewhat half-heartedly entered into planning her next production, Breakespear's *Love Laments Loss*, which would require extensive repainting of her cutout characters and the addition of a new one, since the dyed sheepskin she'd used to create bear fur for *A Vintner's Tale* had got mouldy and so had to be replaced.

But her heart wasn't in it, and she hadn't got much beyond muttering and moving pieces around the stage when the bell rang in the house for supper. Hoping that it might be something nice and not merely bread and dripping, Elinor skipped across the courtyard. She paused partway to note that the weather vane continued to vacillate, and the wind, though not a true northerly, was tending to shift between southeast and northeast, which was still unusual.

Unfortunately, it was bread and dripping again. Elinor complained, and Cook answered that she'd had no housekeeping money that month and what did she expect, and Mrs Watkins tried unsuccessfully to keep the peace. In the course of this conversation, Elinor was alarmed to discover that none of the servants had been paid for two months, their salaries in arrears even before Mrs Hallett had taken to her sick bed.

The mention of housekeeping money and staff payments, or the lack of them, made Elinor thoughtful. After supper, she detached herself from Mrs Watkins and made her way up to her mother's room. She didn't like visiting, particularly now, but clearly something had to be done.

The paraffin lamp in her mother's room was lit, but it did not seem to shed the normal amount of light. The corners of the room were shadowed, and Mrs Hallett lay in gloom. Elinor thought Maria must have dimmed the lamp after she'd finished for the evening, but the wick was set to burn high. Elinor frowned. The lamp probably needed a new wick, or perhaps her mother was economising with a lower grade of paraffin.

She went to the side of the bed. Her mother lay as still as before, when the doctor had visited. Now, in the night, it felt to Elinor even more like she was looking at a dead person.

'Mother,' she said hesitantly. 'Mother. I don't know if you can hear me. I . . . we . . . need a little money for housekeeping and to pay the servants. I don't mean to be presumptuous, but I wondered if I might look in your bureau? For any ready money, I mean.'

There was no answer. Elinor hadn't expected one. She waited, though, feeling it was important to show respect. Her mother didn't move, and there was no sign of the strange, momentary frost Elinor had seen or thought she'd seen before. It was quiet, and there wasn't even a hint of the humming noise she'd heard before, or thought she'd heard.

Mrs Hallett's bureau had long ago been some merchant's travelling cabinet, a vast portmanteau that when set on its end could be opened to reveal a writing slope, a rack of pigeonholes for correspondence, and numerous small drawers. It had been set up, open, against the wall next to the much larger wardrobe, an heirloom of flame mahogany.

Elinor opened the first drawer like a thief, as quietly and surreptitiously as possible. She couldn't help but look over her shoulder, back tensing in expectation of a sudden, cold outburst from her mother, to be followed by a lecture on how Elinor was failing to meet the most basic expectations a mother might have for her daughter.

But there was no sound, no movement from the bed. The drawer was full to the brim with unpaid bills, many stamped with 'Second Demand' or 'Payment Appreciated', others with handwritten amendments insisting that at least some of the outstanding amount must be remitted or the matter would be referred to solicitors or debt agents or action taken in various courts. The bills went back several years.

The second drawer was full of letters from solicitors in Bain and Cornbridge (the closest large town to the south) and even from the capital, Corvere. Elinor skimmed through them, an awful, cold sensation rising up her stomach to clog her throat. Most referred to court judgments already *won* against her mother. 'Erris & Daughters, Seamstresses v. Mrs Hallett', 'Gordon the Grocers v. Mrs Hallett', 'Levett's Bank v. Mrs Hallett'. None were for trifling amounts.

The third drawer contained even more solicitors' letters, but these were all from Gwenyth Lord or her nephew

Barnabas Lord of Lord, Lord & Lord in Corvere, who Elinor vaguely knew had looked after her family's business affairs for generations. These letters were a mixture of calm regret and urgent calls to action, none of which appeared to have had any effect. The most recent letter, on top of the pile, contained a deadly phrase that immediately attracted Elinor's eyes.

Despite your recent, unexpected remittance in gold and its application against the first mortgage, I regret to advise your debts are still far greater than your remaining assets. We have received formal notification from Morrison's Bank, who hold the second *and* third *mortgages upon Coldhallow House, that they have begun the process of foreclosure, which will be complete within the month. You should prepare yourself for bailiffs to be placed by Morrison's and other creditors, who will take inventory and will also remove for sale all portable property in advance of any auction.*

The letter was dated slightly more than a month previously.

Elinor replaced the letter very slowly and closed the drawer. Her hand was shaking. Though she had thought about what might happen if her mother died, those thoughts had not been very deep ones. Elinor had let herself imagine that whatever happened to her mother, she would be able to continue living as she had always done. Performing plays, even if they were only staged for herself and Ham and sometimes Mrs Watkins and a bunch of discarded dolls. Hiding away from other people, keeping her branded forehead secret, avoiding the derision it would attract.

To some degree, though she did not want to acknowledge this even to herself, Elinor had thought her life might be *better* if her mother died. Amelia Hallett had only ever been a critical presence. She didn't do anything positive for her daughter. Certainly she never showed her love, or gave her any encouragement for anything.

But if the farm had to be sold . . . her home had to be sold . . . to pay the family debts, then what was she going to do?

Mechanically, Elinor opened the fourth drawer. It was full of small, empty velvet bags. She pushed them flat, and in doing so, found one in the corner that was not entirely empty. She pulled it out, undid the drawstrings, and reached inside. The bag contained two gold coins, of unfamiliar design. They were not Ancelstierran unites, or any continental currency she could identify. There was no writing on them at all, but they were very finely detailed and well struck. One side had two female figures in loose robes standing back to back, and the other a design of a dozen stars in a pattern, which looked like it was part of some larger heraldic device. The coins were heavy. Elinor, remembering a story about pirates, bit one and her teeth left an indentation. They were definitely pure gold, or close to it, and so worth quite a lot.

But not anywhere near enough to cover the debts Elinor had seen listed on the demands for payment. If all the empty velvet bags in the drawer had been full at one time, there had once been a small fortune here. But no longer.

A faint noise made her turn around in alarm.

Her mother was motionless. The house was still. Elinor kept absolutely silent, listening. For a few seconds she thought she must have imagined it. Then she heard the sound again. It was very faint, two or three sustained notes with several seconds of silence between each one.

She moved closer to the bed and leaned over. The sound *was* coming from her mother, but Amelia's mouth was closed. Elinor bent down so her ear was close to her mother's face, but it seemed to make little difference. The three notes were so faint, it sounded as if they came from far away, but at the same time were somehow emanating from Amelia's closed mouth.

Puzzled, Elinor straightened up. She looked down at her mother and leaned in again. The strange ice was forming across her skin, a layer so thin and delicate that in the dim light she might have missed it if she wasn't so close. She reached out and touched her mother's cheek with the very tip of her finger. It *was* ice; her finger came away wet and very cold.

The window suddenly rattled, making Elinor jump. The wind was rising again, gusts gripping the window frames. She walked over and looked out, but it was too dark to see which way the poplars were swaying or to get any sense of the wind's direction.

Elinor looked back at her mother and for a second thought she'd woken up. Her eyes were reflecting the lamplight, though they were strangely red, as if tiny flames burned where her pupils should be. Elinor looked at the lamp, expecting to see it smoking, the light turned red, but it hadn't. Though dim and low, its light was the usual soft yellow. Elinor slowly turned back towards the bed. The strange red light in Amelia's eyes was gone. When she crossed the room to look more closely, her mother's eyes were shut. The strange sound had also stopped, and the ice had disappeared. Elinor gingerly touched Amelia's face again. Her skin was cool, but not cold.

For a moment Elinor wondered if she simply had too much imagination. She was always pretending to be someone else, after all, performing her plays and imagining herself to be in some made-up land or historical locale that never really existed, at least not the way it was portrayed by Breakespear or Eden.

But she was sure she'd heard the low sound, and her mother's eyes had shone like fire, for a moment. And this was the third time she'd seen and felt the ice.

Frowning, Elinor left the room. She still had the two gold coins clutched in her left hand. For some reason her forehead was aching under the scarf she usually wore around the house when there were no visitors. She must have tied it too tightly, she thought as she slowly descended the stairs, looking for Mrs Watkins.

But Mrs Watkins was not to be found. Cook and Maria were in the kitchen, communing in very few words, as they usually did, over a last cup of tea before bed. Usually Mrs Watkins would join them, but she wasn't there, and she wasn't in her room.

Elinor went to her own room, which was at the back of the house, so she could look out the windows that faced the courtyard and the greenhouse and stables beyond. As she had half expected, there was a light in the windows of the room above the stables, where Ham had his abode. As he usually went to sleep at sunset, this was nearly always an indication that his niece had gone to seek the old man's counsel.

She briefly considered going over to join them, to tell them the terrible news about her mother's finances, the likely arrival of bailiffs and the consequent expulsion from her home. Their home. But she didn't have the heart to do so at night. Ham was old and probably already in bed, with Mrs Watkins sitting on the end, talking away. Neither of them needed to hear bad news right now. It could wait for morning.

Despite readying herself for bed, Elinor thought it was unlikely she would be able to sleep. Everything had been turned upside down. Where could she go? What could she do? Become a governess? That was what happened to young women like her in lots of books. But who would hire someone with a hideous scarred forehead, or at best an eccentric who always kept her head covered?

Maybe she could join a theatre, Elinor thought. Not as an actor, of course. In some sort of hidden capacity, behind the scenes. As a bookkeeper, perhaps, or to look after the wardrobe. Though she was nowhere near as accomplished a seamstress as Mrs Watkins. Maybe they could both work in a theatre on the costumes. It would be fun, far more interesting than simply repainting her wooden cutouts. Probably not well paid, but enough for Elinor and Mrs Watkins to have a small cottage somewhere, with a thatched roof and window boxes full of azaleas.

Slowly, this daydream overtook Elinor's worries. Her eyes closed and she began to drift into sleep.

She had entirely forgotten the doctor's visit, her mother's strange condition, the questions she wanted to ask about the North, the Old Kingdom, and the Wall.

High above her, the weather vane on the roof turned to the north again, before creaking back towards the south, without ever entirely getting there.

3

It was drizzling and cold the next morning, the light dim and the day already showing the signs of the oncoming winter. Raindrops were steadily crawling down the dining-room windows and Coldhallow House, with its fireplaces either unlit or anaemically fed, lived up to its name.

Elinor told Ham the unwelcome news of their impending ruin first, because they were both early risers and Mrs Watkins was not, though she was always up for breakfast by eight.

The old man was far less bothered than Elinor had expected. In fact, he seemed more disappointed there would be no rehearsal of *Love Laments Loss* that day as planned, since it was one of the plays where he got to be onstage as a jester and do some juggling and partake in a mock quarterstaff duel with Elinor.

'It's only the last little while I've settled,' he said, clearly considering the past decade no time at all. 'The road's not so bad a life, and you've the skills, Miss Elinor. Why, any fair or travelling show would take you. And Mrs Watkins, for her mending and making costumes. And I could go on as the oldest juggler alive, I expect, unless Dan Roberts is still in the business. He'd be ninety-five or -six, now, though, and I ent heard of him working these past few years.'

'Do you really think I could do that?' asked Elinor, a new dream replacing the one about joining a fixed-in-place theatre company. She imagined a charming caravan, drawn by matched donkeys of unusually friendly disposition. But this dream, too, could not stand up against reality.

She touched her forehead.

'Even with this?'

Ham opened his mouth, looked across at the house towards Mrs Hallett's bedroom, then shut it again to think for a few seconds before answering.

'Might bother some people,' he said finally. 'But show folk don't fuss so much.'

'Really?' asked Elinor, brightening. The possibility that not *all* people would be repulsed by her scar had not occurred to her before.

But her unsightly forehead was only part of the problem.

'What about Mother?' she said, almost to herself.

Ham heard, but he had no answer.

That question, and a number of others, Elinor put to Mrs Watkins over breakfast as they huddled in their coats in the fireless dining room, hoping that having to think about practical considerations would lessen the shock for her governess. It was a good tactic, but it proved unnecessary, as Mrs Watkins already had her suspicions about the economic situation of Mrs Hallett and Coldhallow House.

'Look at this,' she said, indicating the breakfast spread, which featured porridge, some day-old bread, a small portion of dubious butter, and nothing else, save tea. It would not be an absolute disaster until the tea ran out. 'When there's naught but porridge for breakfast, something is up.'

She repeated this dolefully.

'Something is up.'

At that exact moment, as if in answer to her words, the harsh rap of the bronze knocker sounded from the front door. It was something very rarely heard at Coldhallow House, and they both jumped.

'A bailiff!' squeaked Elinor. 'Already!'

'And in this weather,' remarked Mrs Watkins. It seemed in her world bailiffs did not travel in the rain.

'Whatever you do, don't accept their paper,' continued Mrs Watkins in a rush. 'Don't even touch a corner. And . . . and don't let them touch you with the paper, or with their tipstaff.'

'Do they still do that?' asked Elinor.

'Perhaps we shouldn't even answer the door,' suggested Mrs Watkins.

'Good idea,' replied Elinor. 'I'm not dressed to receive anyone anyway.'

Under her own good wool coat, she was wearing one of her father's old suits again, a loud rusty red tweed apparition, with a blue silk shirt, and one of her shabbier cream scarves wrapped tightly around her head, and two pairs of socks – a thick and a thin – inside rubberised blue boots of unknown vintage labelled as 'The Gardener's Friend'.

At that moment they both heard Maria's heavy-heeled shoes clacking on the no-longer-well-polished floorboards of the short gallery that ran through the centre of the house, connecting kitchen, dining room, drawing room, the main staircase, and the front door.

Maria, who would usually be upstairs with Mrs Hallett and had no business being so close to the front door.

'Maria!' shouted Elinor. 'Don't open the door!'

Since Maria was somewhat deaf, Elinor followed this shout with immediate action, leaping from her chair to almost broad jump into the gallery. Mrs Watkins puffed as she pushed her own chair back to come after her. But even the fleet-footed younger woman was too slow to reach Maria before the maid had turned the knob and pulled the front door fully open, with a querulous, 'Can I help you?'

The young man in the doorway, backed by grey sky and drizzle, did not have a tipstaff. He was tall, and thin, and strangely pale, though he did not otherwise look unhealthy. A damp tweed cap pulled low shadowed his face somewhat, but could not hide the deep dark brown of his eyes. His hair was as black and shiny as polished ebony. It was long, pulled back and tied in a queue behind with a dark blue ribbon, a fashion disappeared from Ancelstierre these hundred years or more.

He wore a military-looking khaki waterproof cape over a country suit in a subdued dark blue twill shot with faint traces of white or perhaps even silver, and decidedly drab

44

black riding boots, muddy to the ankles. Behind him, Elinor saw Ham holding the head of the visitor's horse, a well-set-up bay. The old man had a sixth sense for appearing when his work as a groom was needed, rare as it was these days.

The visitor did not look old enough to be a bailiff, Elinor thought. He couldn't be much older than she was, if at all. Though his eyes, those deep dark eyes, suggested some ancient weariness, in stark contrast to his clear, unlined skin and youthful posture.

She froze in the hallway, staring at him. Maria stepped aside against the wall, as ever the well-trained servant. For a moment Elinor felt as if everything else was blurring away to become a badly painted backdrop behind the principal actor who had just set foot on the stage.

He lifted his hand to show a folded paper.

A bailiff, after all.

'No!' shrieked Elinor, suddenly breaking out of her trance. Racing forward, she slammed the door in his face. It would have broken his nose if he hadn't leaped back.

'Quick on his feet,' gasped Mrs Watkins, coming up loyally behind. 'I suppose it goes with the business. You were perhaps a little hasty, Elinor.'

'Who was that, Miss Elinor?' asked Maria, for once jarred out of her stolid, almost mechanical demeanour. She had been Amelia Hallett's maid for more than thirty years, and was either genuinely uninterested in anything other than the work she had to do, or had pretended to be that way for so long it had stuck.

'A . . . a bailiff,' replied Elinor. 'I don't want Mother bothered by him. Or anyone like that. There might be others. So we won't be opening the front door at all from now on.'

'Yes, miss,' said Maria dutifully. She turned around and clomped along the gallery, heading for the stairs. She often sat by Amelia, doing some of the endless sewing to repair curtains, cushion covers, tablecloths, or clothing that Elinor occasionally felt guilty about never doing herself. Her employer's lack of responsiveness didn't seem to bother Maria at all, any more than Amelia's casual disdain had done before.

'Is it as simple as that?' asked Elinor. 'I mean, we just don't let them in?'

'It should delay matters, at least,' said Mrs Watkins. 'While you work out what to do.'

Elinor glanced at her, and was strangely reassured to see that Mrs Watkins genuinely seemed to think she would work out what to do. Against this, her half-asleep dream of joining a theatre company did not seem very realistic in the light of day, nor did Ham's notion of becoming a circus performer. The harsh reality of being turned near-penniless out of the house had come very much into focus.

'Though there isn't a lot of food in the pantry or the cellar,' said Mrs Watkins. 'Cook has said she won't stay past Friday if she isn't paid her "'rears", as she calls them, and the month ahead as well. Maria will stay on, I expect, even unpaid. As long as she can.'

Mrs Watkins didn't need to mention that Ham and she herself would not go anywhere without Elinor, though it had turned out they were both owed more than anyone. Mrs Hallett had stopped paying them a full two months earlier than the other servants.

'If you take the two gold coins I found to Cornbridge and change them at the bank, I expect we can pay Cook and Maria and get some staples—'

Another knock at the door made both women jump. They held each other and looked at the massive piece of dark-stained oak as if it might suddenly fling open.

'He won't just *keep* knocking, will he?' whispered Elinor.

Someone shouted a few words.

'That's Uncle,' said Mrs Watkins.

'Yes,' said Elinor. 'What . . . what's he saying?'

They sidled closer to the door, listening. Ham was shouting, but not in anger or fear, simply to get his message through the heavy oaken door and the thick stone walls of the old farmhouse.

'Miss Elinor! You need to see this man.'

'Don't take the paper, Ham!' shouted Elinor. 'He's a bailiff!'

There was some indistinct talking beyond the door, then the man called out. He had a strong, clear voice, a baritone much clearer than Ham's bass grumble.

'I'm not a bailiff! I've come in answer to *your* telegram!'

A piece of paper came sliding under the door.

'I'm not falling for that!' scoffed Elinor. But Mrs Watkins let out a strange noise, scuttled forward, and picked up the paper before Elinor could stop her. She unfolded it and held it flat, reading it quickly, her eyes blinking in agitation.

It obviously was a telegram, red stripe and all.

'It's the telegram *she* made me send!' hissed Mrs Watkins.

'Who?' asked Elinor.

'I told you! Your grandmother! She must have put it in my head years ago. I didn't even know I was doing it until afterwards.'

Elinor took the offered telegram. It was short and, to her dismay, was sent as if from her mother even though she could not have written or authorised it.

THE MAGISTRIX WYVERLEY COLLEGE STRANGE HAPPENINGS HERE COLDHALLOW HOUSE NEAR PARNE VILLAGE NORTH OF CORNBRIDGE PLEASE PASS ON MESSAGE TO ABHORSEN NEED HELP AMELIA HALLETT DAUGHTER OF MYRIEN CLAYR END

'Who's "the Magistrix Wyverley College"?' asked the bewildered Elinor. 'What does "Abhorsen need help" mean? And is Myrien Clayr my grandmother Myr?'

'Yes, Myrien Clayr was your grandmother,' said Mrs Watkins with an anxious glance to the ceiling and Mrs Hallett's bedroom above. 'And the Magistrix is the woman who teaches magic at Wyverley College. A school, north of Bain. I suppose your grandmother didn't know who it would be when the help was needed, or she'd have put in the name.'

'Teaches magic?' asked Elinor. She felt stunned by yet another totally unlooked-for revelation. 'Magic?'

'That's one of the Northern things,' said Mrs Watkins rather weakly, 'we've not been allowed to talk about.'

'I wish we had,' said Elinor slowly. She felt suddenly very weak in the knees, but there was nowhere to sit down and she wasn't going to collapse in front of Mrs Watkins. She might have a heart attack from the fright. 'Magic is real?'

'Yes . . . though what a young man has to do with the Magistrix and Wyverley College I don't know,' continued Mrs Watkins suspiciously. 'It's a girls' school.'

A girls' school where you could learn magic. When she was younger, Elinor had dreamed of going to an *ordinary* girls' school like the New Prospect School in the Billie Cotton books, meeting and having friends, learning more than Mrs Watkins's simple curriculum with its emphasis on needlework and outdated etiquette, and circus skills from Ham. Having access to thousands of books in a real library, instead of the mere hundreds in her father's former study. And now she learned there was a girls' school that taught magic as well, real magic . . . but it was too late for her.

If it was true. Mrs Watkins was not prone to imagining things, or telling falsehoods. But could magic possibly be real?

'I think we'd better let him in,' said Elinor, and opened the door.

The young man stood a few paces back from the front step, looking up at the sky. He ignored the raindrop that fell on his upturned face.

'Wind's swinging around again,' he said. 'That's not good. Where's Myrien?'

Elinor began an indignant reply along the lines of expecting the basic courtesies, whoever this man might be, but Mrs Watkins beat her to the punch.

'Myrien's dead, sir. Six years past. Mrs Hallett put her in a lunatic home, somewhere south.'

'What?' asked Elinor. She felt overwhelmed by all the things she didn't know, and dull and stupid for not realising she was so ignorant. 'Mother told me grandmama died at her own home when I was five! She was alive for *eight* years after that?'

'So who sent the telegram asking for help?' asked the young man.

'Mrs Watkins,' said Elinor, pointing firmly. 'And who, exactly, are you?'

'I only sent it after a fashion,' protested Mrs Watkins. 'I didn't even know I was doing it until afterwards. Myrien must have put it in my mind, sir, only it didn't come up until that north wind and Mrs Hallett being took peculiar.'

'Mrs Hallett took peculiar?' asked the young man, ignoring Elinor's question about who he was.

'My mother. I am Elinor Hallett, and I have to say—'

'So where is your mother, Amelia Hallett, Myrien of the Clayr's daughter?'

'She is lying upstairs seemingly dead, only the doctor says she isn't,' said Mrs Watkins nervously.

'Wattie!' protested Elinor. 'You can't be telling strangers—'

'Seemingly dead but not . . . Does she have the Charter mark?' asked the young man with concern, somewhat belied by the fact that he wasn't even looking at them. His head was turned towards the poplars. The tops were tilting again, the wind rising.

The wind from the north.

'No,' quavered Mrs Watkins.

The young man nodded, as if this was the expected, but unwelcome, answer. He walked swiftly back to his horse, unstrapped and took down a long case from in front of the saddle.

'That stream or burn or whatever you call it here, up there. I saw it coming down the hill, but I couldn't tell if it's running?'

'What?' Elinor asked. She was completely thrown now.

'The ghyll. It's swift, but not too wide, sir,' replied Ham unhappily. 'You think it'll come to that?'

'Best to expect the worst,' said the young man. 'I need you to build a bonfire on the other side – if you can in this drizzle – and have torches ready. Does *anyone* here have the mark?'

Ham and Mrs Watkins looked at Elinor, at her forehead. She flinched back as if struck and instinctively reached up to pull her scarf tighter.

'What are you—'

'The Charter mark,' replied the young man impatiently. He pulled his cap off and pointed to his own forehead. There, in exactly the same place as Elinor's unsightly blemish, he had the identical, shameful brand. Only his mark was shining faintly, a soft silver under the drizzling rain, bright above his dark eyes.

Elinor heard a strange choking sound. It took her a moment to realise she was the one making it. Her legs did give way after all, and she had to grab one of the hooks on the wall coatrack to stop herself falling down.

'Untaught, I take it, and thus useless,' said the man. He bulled past her, swept the dusty silver tray meant to receive visitors' cards off the card table, laid down his case, and with swift, well-trained movements unclasped the straps, opened it, and drew out a sword.

Not just any sword. The slender steel blade shone with light from illuminated symbols that moved and swirled within the metal, symbols that Elinor instinctively felt were akin to the mark on her forehead, the same mark that was on this strange visitor's head.

It had to be magic, magic from the North.

As Elinor gawped, he reached inside his coat with his left hand and pulled out a set of panpipes. Seven tubes of silvered steel, the shortest the length of his little finger, the longest twice that, joined together by two crossbars of bronze. The metal of the pipes also shone, bright symbols crawling across steel and bronze.

'I left my bells at the fort,' he said with a confidential air. 'So as to look more unprepared. For whoever has set this little trap in motion.'

'What?' asked Elinor weakly. What did bells have to do with anything? Or panpipes, for that matter? Unprepared? Trap? And his forehead mark . . .

'Your mother's upstairs? Or what purports to be her?'

'Purports to be . . .'

'Show me,' said the man. He looked at Mrs Watkins. 'You'd best get everyone else out, help Ham with the fire. He told me you're both from north of Bain. You remember the rhyme?'

Mrs Watkins bobbed a curtsy and surprised Elinor very much by singing in a little-girl voice:

When the Dead do walk, seek water's run
For this the Dead will always shun
Swift river's best or broadest lake
To ward the Dead and haven make
If water fails thee, fire's thy friend
If neither guards, it will be thy end.

She was singing to the tune that Elinor had always known as 'When Little Lambs Do Lap the Dew', but these words were entirely different.

'What are you going on about, Mrs Watkins?' asked Elinor. 'Who is this man? And I am definitely not letting you go up to Mother.'

'He's the Abhorsen,' said Mrs Watkins. 'He must be. Oh, Elinor, we should have told you—'

'A great many things, from the sound of it,' snapped the young man. 'And I'm not the Abhorsen. That's my great-aunt Tizanael. I'm the Abhorsen-in-Waiting. Terciel, at your service, Charter help me. Now, the wind is coming from the North, it's clearly been summoned to do so, the day is dark and getting darker, and there is no time to waste. Where is your mother, Elinor?'

'She is upstairs, in bed,' replied Elinor stiffly. She made one last effort to return this situation to something approaching normality. 'I . . . I fail to see how this concerns you.'

'It does, however,' said Terciel. 'Because I do not think it is your mother upstairs, not any more. There is something Dead there. Perhaps not entirely present in Life as yet, but it waits upon the threshold. I know it is there, it knows I am here, and the longer I do nothing, the greater the danger. Will you let me past?'

Elinor hesitated for a fraction of a second, trying to make sense of all this strangeness. But there was no sense to be made, save that there was something seriously wrong with her mother and instinctively she *knew* Terciel was somehow the right person to deal with it, just as Ham was the right person when a horse was injured, or Mrs Watkins when a dress was torn apparently beyond repair.

She stepped aside. Instantly, Terciel was off up the stairs, his shining sword held high.

'Wait!' shrieked Elinor, and ran after him. Ham and Mrs Watkins ran the other way, obedient to Terciel's instructions.

At the top of the stairs, Terciel slowed down and looked back at Elinor.

'Is there someone else up here?'

'Mother's maid, Maria,' said Elinor. 'Shall I call her out?'

She started forward, but Terciel pulled her back.

'No,' he whispered. 'It's too late.'

'What do you mean it's too late?' Elinor whispered back, her face close to his. She felt an almost overpowering urge to touch the mark on his forehead. It was even brighter now, as if it were made of some copper-tinged golden fire, and she wondered if her own dull scar could ever be like that.

'I'm sorry,' whispered Terciel. 'I'd have saved her if I could.'

'Saved her from—'

A terrible scream issued from inside Amelia Hallett's room. The most awful scream Elinor had ever heard, made worse because it was recognisably from Maria, clearly terrified beyond reason, or in awful pain, or both.

The scream suddenly stopped, cut off at its height. The door to Amelia's bedroom flew open, and a thick, low blanket of fog slowly began to roll out across the floor. Accompanying it, there was a horrible, breathy, stick-cracking cackling noise that Elinor doubted could come from any human mouth.

'Too late,' whispered Terciel. 'Run. Run!'

He lifted the panpipes to his mouth and blew upon the second-longest tube, the sixth in line. Elinor had half turned to flee, instinctively obeying the determination and fear in Terciel's voice. But the sound of the pipe caught her, stopping her in place. It was not a single note, but a choir of notes that blended into one, the sound overcoming all others so she could hear nothing else, and somehow mixed in with this unearthly sound she *felt* rather than heard Terciel commanding her to stop where she was, to stand still.

'Not you!' shouted Terciel to Elinor. He looked back at her and then swiftly to the bedroom door again. Elinor followed his gaze and saw her mother appear in the doorway. At least, for the briefest moment, she thought it was her mother. It was a human form of the right height, in her mother's heliotrope nightgown, with her mother's dyed-auburn hair, but the hair hung lank on a face where the flesh had caved in upon the skull, and where her mother's eyes should be there were sockets of flame, and black smoke coiled up where there should be eyebrows.

'Stop!' commanded Terciel again, and he blew upon the sixth pipe once more. Elinor felt the sound of it in her bones, but this time she did not feel its compulsion, and knew its dominating power was not directed at her but at the monster who wore her mother's flesh.

The thing that was not Amelia Hallett shuddered, but it did not stop. It took a step forward. Silver sparks suddenly burst up around its feet, eating at the decayed flesh to show the bone beneath, but still it took another step, and then another. Its jaw dropped, lower than should be possible, revealing a flickering red fire within its mouth and throat to match its eyes, and once again it cackled, the horrible, clack-clack cackle, cutting through the sound of the pipe as no other sound had done.

Terciel reeled backwards, into Elinor. He stumbled, obviously not expecting her to still be there. She caught him, feeling his muscles flex as he stopped the instant half turn and sword stroke that he'd instinctively been about to do.

'Go!' he shouted, grabbing her and accelerating into a sprint for the stair. 'It's too strong here! We have to get out!'

Elinor ran, as much from fear of what she'd seen as from Terciel's urging.

At the base of the stairs, Terciel turned and lifted his sword, sketching out a symbol in the air. As the sword point moved, it left a trail of bright golden fire that persisted in the air. Elinor instinctively knew this was another mark akin to the brand she bore, she could feel the skin on her forehead tingle, as if in response.

The creature who wore her mother's body slowly came down the stairs, one step at a time. Its legs were now little more than bone, with strips of hanging flesh. But there were no more silver sparks and it was moving faster.

The golden mark Terciel had drawn in the air had started no larger than a single handspan, but it was growing larger, and Elinor saw there were other marks within the big one, like an illusory painting where you couldn't see the dots unless you were up close.

Terciel turned again, thrust the panpipes into his pocket, and grabbed her hand, dragging her along the gallery.

'Sorry about the house!' he gasped.

'What!'

He let go of her as they staggered out into the drizzle. Elinor turned to look back through the open door and saw the creature in her mother's body step down into the golden marks Terciel had drawn, a shining pattern that had spread to be several feet in diameter. As the thing touched it, there was an explosion of golden light, like sunshine suddenly bursting through heavy cloud. But there was no accompanying blast of air as in a real explosion. Elinor flinched back, blinded, and felt Terciel take her hand again.

'Sorry again! Should have warned you. Come on.'

Elinor blinked furiously as he dragged her away, her sight returning but marred by drifting black blobs. A sudden waft of smoke hit her nostrils, and the edges of her blurred vision filled with flickering red and orange light.

The house was on fire. Elinor halted, resisting Terciel's attempts to move her.

'The fire won't stop it,' said Terciel urgently, pulling on her hand. 'Only slow it down. We have to get to the ghyll.'

Elinor stopped resisting Terciel and ran with him, around the house and through the courtyard to where the old kitchen garden had been, taking the path from the fallen gate on the far side that led through the bare field up the hillside towards the ghyll.

'I'd hoped it would be something less powerful,' panted Terciel as they ran together. He glanced over his shoulder, tripped, and would have fallen if Elinor hadn't grabbed his elbow. She was glad she was on the opposite side from his sword, which had wavered in his hand as he fell.

'Thanks.'

The ghyll cut its way down from much higher up the hill above Coldhallow. Up there it was a twenty- or thirty-foot-deep ravine with the stream rushing through in a series of small waterfalls, here it was a lesser cut, and lower down in the home field it was a steep-sided creek, currently well-lined with a great snarl of blackberry vines, which in the past would have been removed by the farmworkers. Within half a mile it reached flatter country and broadened, the water slowing to a sleepy, steady flow.

Elinor spotted Ham and Mrs Watkins where a fallen tree had long ago been laboriously dragged down from the copse higher up the hill and laid across the ghyll to form a makeshift bridge. Ham had made a bonfire of garden stakes and sticks gathered from the edge of the copse and he was trying to light it, without noticeable success. The drizzle didn't seem heavy enough to stop this fire, but it had been going most of the night, so the fuel they'd gathered was wetter than it looked.

Terciel ran nimbly across the log, with Elinor close behind.

'Stand back,' said Terciel. As Ham and Mrs Watkins scrambled away, he spoke a word, or perhaps mouthed it. Elinor wasn't sure if she heard anything or not. A glowing symbol sped from his mouth as if he'd spat it, flew through the air, hit the piled-up sticks, and the whole thing caught alight in an instant. It was a healthy yellow-red fire that had none of the awfulness of the flames in the Dead creature's eyes and throat.

'What's happened to my mother?' demanded Elinor. 'And what was that thing . . . that thing that looked like her?'

'Your mother has lingered on the very border between Life and Death for weeks,' said Terciel shortly. He looked up and down the ghyll, and then up the hillside behind them. It was darker still under the trees. The copse, like the other parts of the Coldhallow estate, had not been looked after, and the trees grew close and thick. 'She was not allowed to properly die by the entity that is currently using her body. I would say she entered into an agreement she didn't understand or more likely didn't believe. It couldn't have happened any other way, not here, so far from the Wall.'

'An agreement?'

'To arrange a situation to lure me here,' said Terciel. 'Did she suddenly come into money recently?'

'No, quite the reverse!' snapped Elinor.

'Gold, probably,' said Terciel. 'From the Old Kingdom. I suppose you wouldn't have known about it.'

'I would!' protested Elinor. But she could feel the weight of the two strange coins in her jacket pocket. She remembered all those empty velvet bags in the drawer and the line in the solicitor's letter about 'the unexpected remittance in gold'.

'It doesn't matter now,' said Terciel. 'For her, anyway.'

'To lure you here . . .' muttered Mrs Watkins nervously. 'But I thought it must be Elinor's grandmother who made me send the telegram.'

'No compulsion could hold that long. It must have been someone much more recent, I fear, though they've made you forget,' said Terciel. 'Have you had any strange visitors?'

'No,' said Mrs Watkins and Elinor together. But Ham frowned and shook his head.

'There was the man brought your wool from the post office three weeks back, instead of Mrs Killick,' he said slowly. 'But I only saw him going away down the road. Scraggly and bald.'

'What are you talking about?' asked Mrs Watkins. 'Mrs Killock brought my wool as usual. I remember . . . I remember . . .'

She shut her eyes and stood completely still, evidently *not* remembering.

'There you have it,' said Terciel. A raindrop blew against his forehead and slid into his eye, making him blink. 'Is there any other way to cross the ghyll close by?'

'Not afore the flat,' said Ham. 'Matter of a mile or so. But it's not so deep cut from here. You could climb down and wade across.'

'The Dead won't cross fast running water,' said Terciel. 'They don't like rain either, it's uncomfortable for them. Though this drizzle hardly counts as rain.'

'So we're safe here?' asked Mrs Watkins.

'Safer than over there,' replied Terciel, which did not comfort the others at all.

'Where's Cook?' asked Elinor suddenly.

'She wouldn't leave her kitchen,' replied Mrs Watkins very slowly. 'You know what she's like.'

They all looked at the burning house.

'There'll be no stopping that fire with the wind up,' said Ham. The wind wasn't that fierce where they were standing, but the house was less protected, and it was well ablaze. 'Not that the brigade from Cornbridge will be in any hurry to come. Not with the wind as it is.'

'The wind from the North,' said Elinor. 'Though no one will tell me why that's important.'

'It brings magic with it from the Old Kingdom,' said Terciel. 'Free and Charter Magic.'

Elinor wanted to ask him what on earth that meant, but he wasn't looking at her. He was gazing back across the ghyll to the field. Though there wasn't much rain, the clouds were very dark and low, slowly scudding southward above them but never moving apart enough to create a gap. There was no hint of the sun, and the dull, diffused daylight was augmented by the red glow of the burning house. That glow was steadily getting brighter as the fire spread, and a vast plume of deep black smoke was rising above it to join with the low white cloud.

Elinor saw something come out of the garden gate. Not her dead mother, or whatever animated her. This was something else. Her eyes couldn't make sense of it for a moment or two, before she realised it was or had been a human, but it was so twisted and bent it was barely recognisable. It scuttled on all fours, and one arm was cut off at the elbow. It was not clothed, but its flesh or whatever passed for flesh was cracked and broken like dried mud and split wide enough to show white bone beneath, which glinted red in the light from the burning house.

Another Dead Hand came out of the garden gate and joined the first. This one was mostly intact, but it had a corroded sword through its middle, which it was trying to pull out and wield, but the blade was too well lodged in its rib cage. Both Hands moved out slowly, as if uncertain of their way, or unused to movement. The spirits that animated the decayed flesh had long been absent from Life.

More Dead came behind the first two, a lot more. Dozens and dozens of them, moving aimlessly at first, before in answer to some command inaudible to Elinor they spread out into a rough line by the garden wall. Most were obviously bog creatures, but there were some so malformed it was hard to discern whether their original forms had been humans or animals, or something in between.

'It is making Dead Hands already,' said Terciel. 'In quantity. There must be a graveyard close by. Which isn't on the map I borrowed.'

'There's no graveyard that I know of, sir,' said Ham. He had a dagger in his hand now. Not one of his normal throwing knives. This one looked very sharp. 'Closest is the village cemetery at Korbeck, and that's three miles away.'

Elinor and Mrs Watkins exchanged a fearful glance, the older woman leaving it to Elinor to explain.

'We studied the local history for a term when I was fourteen,' said Elinor. 'There are some references to a battle here, in ancient days, between the tribe of the Baineri and the Parrell. The dead of both sides were supposedly buried somewhere between the house and the village.'

'In a bog, I would say,' said Terciel professionally. 'They're very well-preserved.'

'We're safe from them here,' said Elinor nervously. 'Aren't we? You said they can't cross running water.'

'I spoke truly,' said Terciel. He hesitated, then added, 'But if that Greater Dead creature directs them, it is likely they'll try to dam the ghyll upstream.'

'A Greater Dead creature?' asked Mrs Watkins. Elinor could see from the set of her jaw and the tone how much effort it took to keep her voice from trembling.

'Something powerful from the far reaches of Death, a Fifth Gate Rester or the like,' said Terciel grimly. 'Come into Life again, which it should not. It is the thing inside your mother's corpse. And there it is.'

The creature that stepped out through the garden gate and stood behind the line of Lesser Dead in the field no longer looked much like Amelia Hallett. The Dead spirit within had begun to corrode and warp the flesh, had stretched the body like a wax doll to make it taller and thinner. Its neck was twice as long as any human's, and its fiery mouth now extended all the way across its face, from ear to ear. The heliotrope nightgown was too short and had split into separate, trailing strands, doing little to cover the pallid, bluish flesh beneath. Its arms had also grown, and the nails on its hands were several inches long and viciously curved.

It raised one taloned hand and pointed at the small group around the bonfire, just as the roof of Coldhallow House fell into the fire and a massive eruption of flame and sparks blew up into the sky.

'The water will not save you, Abhorsen!' shrieked the creature. There was still a faint, horrible echo of Amelia Hallett's speech in its otherwise otherworldly voice. It gestured to its servants, commanding them. In answer, the Dead Hands moved like a tide, swarming up against the garden wall, ripping the stones away wherever they were loose. With a thundering crash, a good third of the wall came down all at once, head-sized stones tumbling and smashing down among the creatures. Long-dead flesh was crushed and bones splintered, but they did not care. Gathering up the loose stones, the Hands turned to stream across the field towards the ravine. Some, the most badly crushed, crawled or hopped behind, each still lugging a stone in obedience to their master.

Elinor felt sick to her stomach, but she also couldn't look away. She noted that the Greater Dead thing did not advance with its minions, but stayed back close to the wall, and she felt grateful for that. The lesser creatures were bad enough.

Terciel drew his panpipes and stepped forward to the edge of the ghyll. The water below moved swiftly, but it was not deep. There were several dozen Dead Hands coming, and though they were dropping as much earth as they carried, were generally stupid, and several would probably fall in, he figured they would be able to dam the watercourse quite quickly.

'Come *on*, Auntie,' he muttered desperately as he considered which pipe to blow, and wished he had his bells.

4

As the line of Dead Hands reached the other side of the ghyll and began to throw the stones into the stream below, Terciel blew upon the shortest and least of the pipes, the one corresponding to the bell Ranna. The Sleeper, the bell who brought quiet rest. He tried to direct its power forward, so as not to catch Elinor and the two old folk, but he dared not look back or break his concentration as he blew. Like the bell, the pipe imbued with Ranna's power could send *him* to sleep if he got distracted.

The pipe's sweet lullaby sounded across the field, surprisingly drowning out the crackle and bang of the fire. There was an enormous blaze now, the house fully alight and the fir colouring all the clouds above with angry red. The drizzle continued to fall, but it was not heavy enough to extinguish or even to slow the flames.

Several Dead Hands crumpled at Ranna's sound, the guiding spirits within the ancient bog flesh sinking into unconsciousness. Three of them tumbled down the side of the ghyll into the water, but though the running water sent the spirits within into Death, this actually made things worse, as the remnant bodies washed up against the stones to speed the building of a makeshift dam.

This unexpected result distracted Terciel for a moment. A wave of weariness came over him, his knees buckled and he almost fell, but he managed to still the pipe, snatching it away from his mouth and catching his fall by leaning on his sword, sticking it point first in the dirt like some ordinary walking stick. No way to treat a blade, particularly one so old and redolent with Charter Magic. It was a named weapon too, Rorqualin. He hoped it would not take the mistreatment amiss, as he hastily stood upright and pulled the tip free.

Elinor rushed to his side.

'What can we do?' she asked. 'Shouldn't we run away?'

'No,' said Terciel. 'The Dead are swift in pursuit. And we have a part to play here.'

'A part?' asked Elinor. She heard the near panic in her own voice and took a deep breath. She was always playing heroes in her greenhouse theatre, or coolheaded competents at the least. Sir Merivan would not falter here, nor Queen Rosalind from *The Siege of Thrame*. She had to be like them. 'What do you mean?'

'You'll see,' said Terciel hurriedly. He thrust the panpipes into his pocket. 'Take up the torches. Most Dead fear fire, for their flesh is dry and will kindle easily. These bog creatures may be more difficult . . . but in any case, stand by me and try to force them back. If we're lucky, the dam will not hold, and we should . . . may have help soon.'

'Miss Elinor and I can throw knives,' said Ham. 'I've brought the sharp ones, miss.'

Terciel shook his head.

'The Dead feel no pain. They do not bleed,' he said. 'Knives are useless. Take up the torches.'

Ham had prepared several torches, wrapping sackcloth around dead branches gleaned from the fringe of the copse. Elinor took one and thrust it in the fire, turning it so it caught well alight. She was pleased to see her hand was not shaking.

'Spread out. Push them back,' instructed Terciel.

The Dead had worked quickly to build their dam, and the stream had begun to back up and pool behind it, leaving little more than a trickle downstream, though even this appeared to deter the Dead from crossing. Some were going back across the field to collect more stones, but at least a dozen crouched on the opposite side of the ghyll, like dogs waiting to be unleashed.

'You're not going to use those pipes again?' asked Elinor.

'They aren't strong enough,' said Terciel. 'There are too many Dead. Stand ready!'

The Dead rushed down into the now dry stream below the dam and started clambering up, many on all fours, scrabbling at the ground and pushing one another aside in their eagerness to take the lives of those opposite. Lives that would help them stay in Life longer, sustain them for a few more deeply desired hours in the living world.

Terciel hacked at their hands and legs, the Charter marks on his sword blazing, silver sparks streaming wherever he struck. Ham had a flaming brand in each hand, and he spun them around to deliver ferocious blows against two Dead creatures at the same time. Mrs Watkins thrust with her torch as if it were a stout umbrella, pushing the flaming end into a Dead Hand's face. It recoiled and fell back on the wrong side of the dam, where the water swirled as it rose higher and higher against the blockage. The Hand squealed like a stuck pig and thrashed, but the spirit was banished and the corpse left behind curled into immobility. But the stream picked it up and pushed it against the rocks, to make the dam more secure.

Elinor swung her torch two-handed, like the chieftain Ruhan Ard-Ruhan in Treedmuir's *Last King of the West*, complete with the bloodcurdling yell she'd used when playing the part. She smacked one Dead Hand down into the ghyll, ducked under another one's attempt to grab her, and kicked it in the kneecap as she scuttled back. As it lurched forward, she executed a perfect thrust to its chest that sent it into the ghyll, arms windmilling and teeth gnashing the air.

A second later, the first five Dead Hands that had crossed the ghyll were down, their motivating spirits either banished into Death or their physical forms so badly dismembered they could not get back up. But there were many more already charging across, and they had spread out along the ghyll so they would outflank the few defenders almost immediately.

'Get behind the bonfire!' shouted Terciel, stepping back even as the Dead raced up the side of the ghyll. Elinor and Ham obeyed instantly, but Mrs Watkins stumbled and fell to one knee.

'Eli—'

Her cry was smothered as a Dead Hand leaped upon her, slamming her flat. A moment later all the closest Hands were worrying at the fallen governess, teeth snapping and taloned hands rending. Killing the living gave them the strength to stay in Life, and they were all greedy for it.

Ham yanked Elinor back as Terciel drew more symbols with his sword in the air and his left hand, a long chain that he threw upon the bonfire, even as Elinor struggled to get free of Ham and charge forward to do something, anything, for Mrs Watkins, even knowing it was already too late.

The chain of marks fell on the bonfire and exploded back out again as dozens of brilliant, shining red-gold spears, thrusting up to make a palisade between Terciel, Ham and Elinor, and the Dead. The creatures shied back from this fence as if they feared the spears even more than fire, though Elinor could feel no heat from them, only from the bonfire, which still burned beneath the magical fence.

But the palisade extended no more than a dozen feet in a straight line, and the Dead were already swarming around each end.

'Back to back!' commanded Terciel. The three survivors stumbled together, shoulders touching. Elinor held her torch high, ready to strike. Terciel lifted his sword, and Ham spun his two flaming brands.

They all knew they could not last long, not against so many Dead.

I'm going to die, thought Elinor. Thoughts were racing through her mind like panicked mice discovered in the pantry, fleeing in all directions. In the next half a minute, perhaps even less, and I haven't managed to really do anything and there is so much I don't know, including all the things I've just discovered I didn't know, to do with the North, and the Old Kingdom, and the magic, and that girls' school, and who was Grandmother anyway—

The Dead charged forward, and every thought vanished, every part of Elinor's being focused on swinging her torch, on keeping the terrible creatures that rushed at her away.

'Auntie!' shouted Terciel, which Elinor thought was a very odd thing to be someone's choice of a final word.

But his shout *was* answered. Not with a human voice, but the sudden, immensely powerful toll of a deep bell. Elinor felt it through her entire body as much as she heard the strange, multilayered voice that was akin to the pipe Terciel had blown in the house as a great wave upon the sea is to a ripple on a lake.

The Dead creatures who had been about to attack stiffened and stopped in place. Elinor looked wildly around her and saw that all the Dead Hands – those close by, those crossing the ghyll, the ones in the field – all of them were motionless, bizarre statues backlit by the flickering red light from the burning house. Held in place by the implacable force of the bell known as Saraneth, the Binder.

Another bell sounded, even as the first bell's tolling still echoed. This one was lighter, and livelier, and Elinor felt her feet do an involuntary little dance. A sudden urge to walk came upon her, to stride out, somewhere, anywhere.

She resisted, but the Dead did not, or could not, and they were being given very specific directions as to where they were to go.

The second bell was Kibeth, the Walker, and the one who wielded it used Kibeth's power to make the spirits inside the ancient bodies walk into Death, there to be gathered up by the swift waters of the river and tumbled through the gates to the Ninth Gate and beyond, to final death.

Only the Fifth Gate Rester, the Greater Dead, was strong enough – and far enough away – to resist the compulsion. But it fled, leaping across the fallen garden wall to run back through the courtyard, skirting the great fire. It ran northward from there, its legs growing longer and more muscular, and its feet broader, the talons shrinking to become mere claws.

The palisade of golden spears vanished, leaving only a few shining marks that slowly drifted to the ground like feathers from an over-plumped pillow, and vanished. The bonfire flared up once, twice, and then fell into itself and went out, sending up a stream of smoke to join the great pall that was spreading overhead from the burning house.

Elinor ran to where Mrs Watkins lay and knelt by her side. The governess was clearly dead, her neck chewed almost through, her dress sodden with blood. She had a surprised expression on her face. Ham knelt slowly by Elinor, his knees clicking. He reached over and gently closed his niece's eyes.

'It was quick,' he said quietly, almost to himself. He looked back past Elinor at Terciel. 'She won't . . . she won't become one of . . .'

He gestured at the fallen Dead about the place.

'Her spirit too was caught by Kibeth's call,' said Terciel. He was quite matter-of-fact, like Ham explaining to Elinor how a particular knife trick worked. Purely mechanical, with no emotion. 'She will safely die the final death. And we will burn all the bodies, so they cannot be used as they have been.'

'She should be buried properly, with a gravestone and . . . and all that,' said Elinor dully. She wanted to look away from the governess's face, now so slack and strange without the animating force of life, but she could not. Mrs Watkins was . . . had been . . . her dearest, closest friend and companion. Closer to her than her own mother. Who was also dead.

The realisation struck Elinor with renewed force.

Her mother was *dead*.

Mrs Watkins was *dead*.

She took a long, shuddering breath and forced herself not to burst into tears.

'No,' said Terciel. 'You have seen what can inhabit buried corpses. Even here, if the wind comes strongly from the North. There is a Charter spell to ensure complete immolation, a simple one. You would have learned it yourself if you'd been taught properly.'

'Have you tested her mark?'

Elinor flinched and snapped around to see who had spoken. A woman stood by Terciel. She was taller than him by several inches, older by many decades at the least, her face cold and hard, her skin even more strangely pale than the young man's, her hair as black, but cut very short.

Like Terciel, this woman had the same mark upon her forehead. It was glowing, golden, and somehow comforting. Elinor wondered if her brand was glowing like that too. It never had before. Or not so she'd noticed.

The old woman also wore a military-style waterproof cape, but the clothing under it was out of the history books – a coat of armoured plates, and over it a leather sash or shoulder belt arrayed with flapped pouches or holsters that clearly contained handbells, the mahogany handles hanging down and exposed, a curious arrangement that meant the bells had to be drawn up and out by opening the flap and gripping the clapper inside the bell. Charter marks, shadowy, faint ones, moved across the handles of the bells.

She had a sword in a scabbard at her side, a battered old weapon with an emerald in the pommel. The scabbard and the weapon also crawled with faint Charter marks, marks that changed shape and melded together and spun out as new marks, and as Elinor watched, one or two briefly shone brighter before dimming back to a faint glow. She wanted to touch them, to know about them. But at that same time she felt this attraction, Elinor instinctively knew they could be dangerous.

Much like the old woman, and to a lesser extent, Terciel. Everything about them spoke of power and violence. Contained and controlled, but there, ready to be used.

Elinor shivered, and found it hard to stop that turning into the full-blown shakes. But she managed it, though she had to look away from Mrs Watkins, up to the smoky sky. No drizzle fell upon her face, but her cheeks were wet.

'No, I haven't checked her mark yet, Tizanael,' said Terciel evenly, in the voice of a student who resents being told what to do all the time, to a teacher.

This had to be the Abhorsen herself, Elinor realised. Whatever that meant. And she was Terciel's aunt. Or great-aunt.

'Do so, at once,' ordered Tizanael. 'We have no time to waste. You are too trusting. Some mortal accomplice has been at work here. It could be her.'

'What?' asked Elinor indignantly. 'Me?'

'It's not painful or anything,' soothed Terciel. 'I simply need to touch your baptismal mark, and at the same time, you touch mine. If they are unsullied, not false marks set to deceive, then we feel the presence of the Charter. Weaker here, of course, so far from the Wall, even with this wind. But there will be no doubt.'

'There will be plenty of doubt!' snapped Elinor. 'I have no idea what you are talking about! What is the Charter, to begin with? And how can touching the scar on my forehead do anything?'

'It isn't a scar,' said Terciel. 'And the Charter . . . the Charter describes the world, and everything in it. It underlies all things. The mark on my forehead, the marks you saw me use to change some part of the world, to bring fire or deny the Dead, all these are part of the Charter. If you know the marks to call, to draw or describe, then you can order or change almost everything, within the constraints of what the Charter wills. That is Charter Magic.'

'My scar is magic?'

'Terciel has already told you it is not a scar,' said Tizanael impatiently. 'Hurry up. We must dispose of the bodies here and get after Urhrux.'

'You already know its name?' asked Terciel, surprised.

'I went into Death to examine who had passed through here. That was why I was a little late,' replied Tizanael grudgingly. She paused, then added, 'Urhrux was not acting of its own volition. So hurry up.'

Terciel nodded, looked around carefully as if he might see some hidden enemy, then looked at Elinor. She stood up slowly and glanced at Ham, who nodded gently, as if to say this was all right. Tizanael looked around, sniffing the air, her hand resting on the pommel of her sword.

Terciel strode close to Elinor and lifted his hand, forefinger extended, stopping an inch from her forehead. She grimaced, seeing him looking there. It was hard to fight the years of her mother telling her to keep her forehead covered, that the brand there was a scar, a particularly unsightly one that would disgust people.

'Just the lightest touch,' said Terciel. 'You do the same to me.'

Elinor raised her own hand, her finger half curled, and gingerly reached up. An inch from the glowing mark on his forehead, she stopped.

'Yes,' said Terciel. 'Now.'

Elinor hesitantly touched his mark, expecting to feel soft skin, and to be awkward about that, to be touching a young man in any way and any place, no matter how lightly, and to be touched so herself.

But it wasn't anything like she expected, or could have expected. She didn't feel the touch at all, or Terciel's fingertip against her forehead. Instead, all her senses were overwhelmed. The world disappeared, all sight and sound cut off. She saw only Charter marks, millions and millions of brilliant glowing marks all around her, stretching into infinity, and she heard sounds that did not exist, and she felt an astonishing mixture of excitement, fear and a sense of contentment all at once, and she knew, she knew to the very marrow of her bones, that she was part of this vast, limitless Charter, and so was everything and everyone else, Terciel and Ham and the woman who must be the Abhorsen, and the little fish in the ghyll, and the ghyll itself, the rocks and the water, and the field beyond and the weeds in the garden and the sky above and the stars and . . . everything . . . everything . . . everything . . .

5

Terciel snatched his hand away and jumped forward to catch Elinor as she fainted. He laid her carefully on the ground, using her scarf to make a pillow.

'Unsurprising,' said Tizanael coolly. 'It would be a great shock to have borne the mark so long but never felt the Charter proper. She will sleep for some time, I judge. Come, Terciel. We must immolate the bodies and get after that Fifth Gate Rester.'

'I should carry her to . . . um . . . shelter,' said Terciel. He looked over to the burning house and did not need to add that there probably would not be any shelter if the fire continued.

'Can you do anything to stop the fire?' asked Ham anxiously. 'The house is done for, but the stables should still be safe for a little while. My room is there. I've heard you can shift the wind and make rain . . .'

Terciel cocked an eyebrow at Tizanael.

'The wind is already changing,' she said. 'Whoever summoned it has lost or relinquished their hold.'

'Even I could probably encourage this drizzle to do more,' said Terciel. 'But you could do it best, Great-Aunt.'

'Always "Great-Aunt" when you want something,' said Tizanael, with a swift glance down at Elinor. 'These people are not in our charge. We are south of the Wall.'

'But we let them be bait for the trap against us,' argued Terciel. 'I think we owe them something. More rain is not so much, surely?'

'Do not become sentimental,' said Tizanael. 'An Abhorsen cannot afford it.'

'It would be practical too,' said Terciel quickly. 'If you can bring a heavy rain and extend it northward, it will hamper that Fifth Gate Rester. Urhrux. Or any other Dead that may have been raised.'

'Your horse is in the closest box in the stable to the house,' Ham pointed out. 'If it hasn't kicked the door down and fled. Though mebbe you don't really need horses.'

'We could ride double, Aunt—'

'Hmmph,' said Tizanael. 'Begin upon the bodies. I will see what I can do with the rain.'

She lifted her arms above her head and whistled, strange notes that Ham had never heard come from a human mouth, and he was no mean whistler himself. With the sound came glowing Charter marks that spilled from her lips and sped into the air, shooting up into the sky like festive rockets, disappearing into the smoky cloud.

A few feet from her, Terciel drew several marks upon the body of Mrs Watkins. The last one he cupped in his hand and held, turning to Ham.

'She was a relative of yours? I thought I saw a likeness.'

'My niece,' said Ham heavily. 'Roberta. Though she liked to be called by her husband's name. Watkins, he was, Theodric Watkins. I suppose the name was the only thing he left her. She remembered him more fondly than he deserved.'

'Farewell, Roberta Watkins,' said Terciel. 'Do not look back.'

He let the last mark fall from his hand. It landed as a glowing ember in the bloodied hollow of her neck, there was a whoosh, sparks flew, and then she was entirely consumed in fire, all of her – clothes, flesh and bone – reduced to fine ash in a single second, and in another second, the fire winked out as if it had never been.

A moment later, the rain suddenly intensified, from a faint drizzle to a heavy, beating fall, coming down fast and cold. Tizanael grunted in satisfaction and strode over to the nearest Dead Hand, and began to sketch the marks that would immolate the body so it could not be used again.

This did not stop her from looking at Terciel with a glare that could only mean 'hurry up!'

Terciel had been about to bend down and pick up the girl. He sighed and stepped back from her, acknowledging to himself an odd feeling of protectiveness, not something he had ever felt before. He wanted to take Elinor to safety, to wake her up and tell her everything would be all right, to talk to her and try to make her smile. But Tizanael was quite right. There was no time to waste.

'Can you take the girl?' Terciel asked Ham. He eyed the old man doubtfully. Ham was still gazing at the thin layer of ash that was all that was left of his niece. It had already mixed with rain and earth to form a greyish rivulet that was flowing down into the ghyll.

'Aye,' said Ham. He bent down slowly, but lifted Elinor easily enough, cradling her in his arms. 'There's not so much of Miss Elinor. All wire and gumption, but no weight. You sure she'll take no harm from this Charter business?'

Terciel didn't answer for a moment. He stepped closer, wiping the rain from his face. It had already begun to quench the fire, but even more smoke billowed up from the house.

'Not physically,' he said at last. 'But now that she knows what she was meant to be part of . . . she may yearn to know the Charter again.'

'More to worry her,' said Ham regretfully. He resettled Elinor to be sure he held her securely, and stepped onto the log bridge. There was a flash of sudden light off to one side, refracted by the rain, as Tizanael immolated another bog corpse.

Terciel glanced at his great-aunt, who had moved on to another corpse and doubtless was on the verge of a caustic comment to get him to attend to the task, then stepped closer again.

'If she needs assistance in that particular,' he said quickly and almost too quietly for Ham to hear over the drumming rain, 'tell her to go to Magistrix Tallowe at Wyverley College and say her grandmother was Myrien of the Clayr. Tallowe is also of that descent. They would be distant cousins, of some sort.'

'Aye,' said Ham. 'I'll tell her.'

He strode across the bridge. Terciel watched for a second, then went to the closest Dead Hand and began to call out marks for fire, sleep, cleansing and peace, sketching them in the air above the ancient bog-preserved corpse.

When Elinor woke up, she was momentarily bewildered. She was lying on a narrow bed, not her own; there was a strong smell of smoke, and she was fully clothed, missing only her shoes. It took her a few seconds to realise the bed was Ham's, in his loft above the stables. She was lying under a patchwork quilt, one Mrs Watkins had lovingly sewn over many months from various odds and ends of unsalvageable clothing.

Mrs Watkins. Elinor felt a sob rising up from deep inside. She buried her face in the quilt and let it capture a short, barking cry of grief. She didn't want to wake Ham up. He was asleep in his big armchair near the sole window of the loft, which looked out over the courtyard. Rain drummed on the tiled roof and peppered the glass. The curtains were drawn but not fully closed, and a single, slippery ray of sunshine slid through the gap, though it was hard to tell the time of day.

Elinor slid off the bed. Her legs felt weak, and she tottered a few steps before she steadied herself. Her first thought had been to look out the window, but on the way there, her eye had caught her own reflection in Ham's small shaving mirror, which hung on a nail from one of the exposed posts, above the stand that held his washbasin. He got his hot water from the kitchen in the metal can that was stashed below the washstand. Or he had, Elinor thought. The kitchen must have burned along with the rest of the house.

She stepped closer to the mirror and pushed her hair back from her forehead. The scar . . . no, the Charter mark . . . was different now. It shone with a soft golden light, and Elinor wondered how she had ever been convinced it was a scar or burn, something ugly to be hidden. She sniffed back more tears. Angry ones this time, at what her mother had done to her.

Ham stirred in his armchair, and looked over. Elinor had never seen him look like he did now. Beaten down, and showing his true age. But he smiled fondly at Elinor and started to lever himself out of the chair. It was cold in the room, the small iron stove in the corner lit but the fire within almost burned out, only a few glowing coals visible through the grille. Ham always moved slower in the cold.

'Don't get up!' said Elinor swiftly. 'You shouldn't have given me your bed, Ham.'

'Nowhere else to put you, Miss Elinor,' said Ham, ignoring her protest. He got himself upright and stretched, reaching for the ceiling, flexing his clever juggler's hands. 'The house is completely gone.'

Elinor crossed to the window and twitched the curtains open a little wider so she could see out. It was near sunset, she saw now, though the sun was mostly obscured by drifts of rain and cloud. Individual tendrils of smoke still rose from the house from small buried pockets of fire, but no great billowing column, and she saw no visible flames. Eventually the rain would get in everywhere and put out whatever embers remained.

'Yesterday all I was thinking about was *Love Laments Loss*,' said Elinor. 'And now ... Wattie is dead. And Mother. And Maria. And Cook. And my home is destroyed. Not that it was much of a home in some ways, I suppose. Wattie did her best to make it one for me, but ... and all the time, my mother telling me the mark on my forehead was a horrible scar!'

Ham shifted uneasily behind her.

'We should have told you about that,' he said. 'Only Roberta never would go against Mrs Hallett, your mum. And I wouldn't go against Roberta.'

'I know, Ham,' said Elinor sadly. 'I don't hold it against *you*, or Wattie.'

She looked at the house again.

'I suppose I should be doing something. I should tell someone what happened. Or at least tell them about the fire. I suppose ... I suppose I'll have to say that's what killed everyone—'

She bit back a sob.

'Constable Goodwin will be up from the village soon enough,' said Ham awkwardly. 'He'll have been waiting for the wind to change. Even down here they know not to go out when the north wind blows.'

'The north wind, bringing magic with it,' said Elinor, almost to herself. She touched the mark on her forehead, and felt an echo of that incredible connection, the joining she had experienced when she had touched Terciel's mark and been drawn into the Charter. 'So much to know . . .'

Ham cleared his throat.

'The young one. That Terciel. When you keeled over, he said summat about if you needed help with the magic, the Charter and all that, then you should go to Magistrix Tallowe at Wyverley College and tell her you're the granddaughter of Myrien of the Clayr. She's a Clayr too, Tallowe. You're some sort of cousins.'

'Cousins?' asked Elinor, surprised. She knew her father had a pair of ancient, estranged aunts in Corvere, but had never heard of any other relations on either side of the family. 'And what does "of the Clayr" mean? I thought it was Grandmother's surname.'

'I don't know, Miss Elinor,' said Ham. 'I'm only telling you what he said. Terciel.'

'Terciel,' repeated Elinor. He lingered in her mind, a sudden, vital presence who had changed everything. Or maybe he had simply coincided with it. 'He's . . . they've gone, I suppose?'

Ham nodded. 'North, after they burned up all the bodies. Going after that . . . that thing. He said it would try to get back to the Old Kingdom, because it couldn't exist here once the wind changes.'

'Has the wind changed?'

'It's winnering about,' said Ham. 'Slowly turning southeast, I reckon.'

'But unlike the wind, everything else can't go back to how it was,' said Elinor dully. 'I wonder—'

She stopped, mid-sentence. Several drops of rain had pooled together on the lower-right pane of glass in the quartered window, and the setting sun hit this limpid circle in such a way that it filled with colour and for a few seconds it seemed to be a picture, or a photograph, though Elinor knew there were no colour photographs and this was certainly glorious colour. She realised with a shock that it was herself she was looking at, but not as she was now. It wasn't some kind of reflection. She looked older somehow, and was wearing strange clothes, some sort of leather armour, and her hair was shorter and . . .

Another raindrop ran down the glass and exploded the temporary pool, the picture fragmenting, water and sunshine once more separate things. Elinor blinked. She'd occasionally had visions like this when she was small, seen pictures in water, on the frosted lawn, in an icicle that hung from a punctured gutter, but not for years. Mrs Watkins had called them 'fancies' and chuckled at Elinor's imagination. When Mrs Hallett had heard it mentioned, she had made Ham go and break off all the icicles, and the gutter had been mended. Elinor had forgotten. It had been a long time ago.

Something else caught her eye, something outside, not on the glass. A flash of movement, breaking through the haze of rain.

'There's someone by the corner of the house,' she said to Ham, lowering her voice even though there was no chance anyone outside could hear her over the rain.

'Probably that Constable Goodwin or someone from the village,' replied Ham. He came over next to her and pulled the curtain back so he could see as well.

'I don't think so,' said Elinor. Her forehead twitched, and she touched the mark there again. 'Why would they skulk by the corner like that?'

Ham didn't answer for a moment, staring out the window, his old but bright eyes intent. Then he opened his coat and took out one of his sharp throwing knives and handed it to Elinor, before taking out another himself. He had four altogether, two on each side in special lined pockets.

The skulking figure must have seen the movement, or sensed their presence. A man, a thin, balding man, his scalp all shiny from the rain. He stepped out into the courtyard and looked straight at them. He was an unprepossessing figure physically, in a sodden military overcoat over a farm labourer's serge jacket and trousers, with heavy boots. But somehow he made Elinor shiver, a shiver that intensified as she saw a heavy raindrop slide down his forehead and, as it did so, reveal a mark that had been hidden until that moment.

Not a warm and glowing Charter mark, this *was* a scar – a scar like a segmented worm half-buried in the flesh. As Elinor stared in horror down at the man, the scar moved and writhed.

The man smiled, an unfriendly smile, and reached inside his coat. His hand snapped out with a revolver.

Ham pushed Elinor roughly aside. Falling, Elinor heard the bang, the window shattering, and the thud of a heavy bullet striking flesh. Instinctively she did as Ham had taught her long ago, tucking in her head, relaxing into the fall and turning it into a roll that not only dissipated the force of the fall but also took her away from the window. She held on to her knife, turning it outward so she would not stick herself.

Ignoring various pains, she rolled over, looking anxiously for Ham. He was lying on his back by the window, not moving. There was a bullet wound above his nose, a sharply delineated hole where no hole should be. His head lay back at a gross angle, because much of the back of it was missing, and there was already a pool of blood beneath him, spreading fast. He still held his knife, but there was no more life in his hands, those dexterous juggler's hands that could catch and throw anything back.

Anything except a bullet.

Swallowing down a sob, Elinor crawled over on her elbows and took another knife from inside Ham's coat, then slithered towards the rough staircase that led down to the stable proper. At the top she stopped to listen. If she saw the man, she would throw one knife and charge with the other, she thought. He might have some magic that protected him from thrown knives, and the wind might not have changed enough.

At first all she could hear was the steady drumbeat of the rain on the roof. Then she heard soft footsteps on the cobbled floor of the stable below. The man – or whatever he was – must be sneaking in through the barn doors at the south end, which had been ajar for years.

Elinor took a breath to steady herself, readied her knife and kept listening. He would step into the stair cautiously, no doubt, at the corner there . . . and she would put a knife in his eye. If she could do it before he shot. He had been very fast.

The faint scuffing sounds continued below, but the man did not appear. Suddenly, the Charter mark on her forehead stung her, and the scuffling noises vanished, to be replaced by another noise, right behind her. She spun around, but the thin man was already upon her, gripping her wrists with hands that burned like fire. She kicked him, as Mrs Watkins had taught her, aiming straight for the groin, but he turned sideways and took it on his hip and he twisted her wrists until she had to drop the knives and effortlessly he threw her down the steps.

She rolled again as she hit the steps a third of the way down and kept rolling, and when she landed at the bottom she instantly sprang up and ran, not taking a moment to catalogue her hurts or scream protests or lie sobbing or any of the other things a young woman who had not had the benefit of Ham's circus training would presumably do.

She was halfway across the courtyard when she heard him jump from the window of the loft, hobnailed boots shrieking on the pavers. He must have climbed up before, though it would not have been easy. Elinor didn't pause to look. She accelerated instead, heading for the conservatory. She didn't stop there to try to bolt the door either. She knew her attacker would simply break the glass. Instead she went straight to the ancient oak coffer she used to store her stage weapons, flipped it open and took out the two-handed sword she'd used to play the part of Ruhan Ard-Ruhan. Lifting it up, she turned to face the door, ignoring the stabbing pains in her wrists. They felt like they'd been burned where he'd held her.

The sword was blunt, but it was heavy, and she knew how to use it. Ham had always been careful to teach her both the stage-fighting techniques and the actual combat moves for the weapons they used in the plays. He said it was how he had been taught, that it was necessary to know both in order to orchestrate a believable-looking fight for an audience.

Elinor remembered something else too. She could almost hear Ham telling her, 'Now remember, Miss Elinor, if you do ever have to fight in earnest, don't pull your punches – but don't lose control neither. Strike hard, recover fast and strike again.'

The iron-framed door screeched on stone as the man pulled it open, past the point where it caught on a slightly raised paver. Elinor and Ham never opened the door that far.

He didn't come in. He stood there, in the rain, looking at her, and he didn't have the revolver in his hand. He seemed ordinary enough. Thin and wiry, middle-aged, balding. Save for the writhing scar on his forehead, and the odour of hot, worked metal that rolled off him, as if somehow under his skin there was a forge.

There was a red glint in his eyes. It wasn't a reflection.

'Were they both here?' he asked. His voice was scratchy and uneven, as if he had injured his throat. 'I cannot see how else the plan would fail.'

'Who?' asked Elinor. She kept the sword high and ready, though her wrists felt as if they had been pierced through with hot needles, and it was hard to hold the weapon up. She was also starting to feel other hurts. Bruises down her side, perhaps a cracked rib or two. She had experienced those before. It hurt to draw breath.

'The Abhorsen and her apprentice,' said the man easily. He never stopped looking at her with those red eyes, he never looked away, and he never blinked. 'We only wanted to take the lesser of the two. I think they were both here. Odd that she would come so far south of the Wall. She never has before.'

'I don't know what you're talking about,' said Elinor. She felt the weight of the sword increasing and knew she could neither hold it nor wield it for long. So she stepped forward, intending to bring the fight to him.

'Yes, you do,' replied the man. He tapped his forehead, the roiling scar spreading like a squashed raisin, re-forming as his fingertip moved away. 'But where do you fit in, I wonder? A great-niece or something of that nature?'

He smiled as if she had offered a gift.

'How *useful* if you should happen to have the blood—'

He didn't finish his sentence, the revolver suddenly in his hand again, and he shot Elinor even as she lunged forward. Something scored her left side like fire but she kept going and swung at him. He ducked back and the sword struck the iron frame of the door with force enough to make it ring like a bell, and the six panes of glass all shattered at once.

Elinor fell back and tried to lift the sword to strike again, but the pain in her side was too great. She stumbled backwards and almost fell, having to use the sword as a crutch to stay upright. All the time she expected the man to shoot again, to feel a moment of intense pain and then it would all be over.

But the man didn't shoot. He put his revolver in the pocket of his coat and from the other pocket took out a length of rope and started towards her, muttering, apparently to himself.

'A chance made from a chance lost, helps me avoid a greater cost.'

Elinor made a supreme effort, standing as straight as she could with the pain in her middle trying to bend her in two, and raised the sword halfway to her shoulder.

The man stopped and turned his head. He hesitated for a moment, then sprinted away, out of the greenhouse and across the courtyard and over the fallen garden wall, into the obscuring rain.

For a moment Elinor thought he ran from her, but then she heard the jangled bell, the clatter of harness, and the drumbeat of hooves on the metaled road, and she saw the fire engine from Cornbridge come around the corner of the house, drawn by six horses, the pump boiler on it belching out gouts of steam and smoke. Behind the engine were several police officers on horseback, and behind them a bunch of breathless villagers who had run up the hill.

The pain in her wrists spread to her elbows, and Elinor found she *really* couldn't take in a breath because something was quite wrong on the left side of her torso, more than just a cracked rib. She dropped the two-handed sword, doubled over, and took three staggering steps out to the courtyard, to fall down in front of Constable Goodwin, who was already feeling guilty he had delayed investigating until he was sure the wind was going to change.

6

It was late autumn in Ancelstierre, cool but not cold, and the sun had not yet begun to set. But Terciel and Tizanael, with their companion, crossed the Wall to enter the tail end of winter and full night in the Old Kingdom. A matter of thirty paces to walk the Charter mark-infused tunnel through the ancient stone structure. Looking back, Terciel could still see sunshine, but when he tilted his head to look up here, there was no sun, only the black night leavened by a great swath of stars, for the night was clear and very cold.

Terciel shivered and pulled his fur-lined woollen cloak tighter. He was back in gethre scale armour again, and wore his bandolier of bells, with a sword at his side. The blue-and-silver tweed suit had been packed away in the big chest kept for the Abhorsens at Fort Entrance, the headquarters of the Crossing Point Scouts who patrolled the Ancelstierran side of the Wall. Most of them were Charter Mages, like Major Latimer, who accompanied them now, and those who were not were still very familiar with the nature of the border and the Old Kingdom beyond. Latimer was close to retirement, and had not stopped complaining to Tizanael about the changes that were coming, a topic that he had maintained all the way from the Fort to the Wall.

'They've never wanted to know before. They've let us "irregulars" take care of everything,' he said. He had not left the tunnel, for he would almost immediately go back, and was surrounded with a golden nimbus from all the shining marks that lined the stones within, still active from the passage of three Charter Mages. 'Now there's talk of posting a regular division here and building a trench line from west to east to face the Wall, as if this was some sort of continental border! Can you imagine how ordinary troops will fare against the things that come over the Wall?'

'I can,' replied Tizanael. She did not look at the Ancelstierran officer, instead gazing off into the dark ahead of them. 'But we have more immediate concerns.'

'It might seem a distant problem now,' said Latimer, not cowed by Tizanael's stern response. He had known her for more than three decades, since he had come to Fort Entrance as a pink-cheeked subaltern. 'But you know you can't ignore things on our side. Take what's just happened! The boy lured over here to finish him off.'

Terciel grimaced. He didn't like being described as 'the boy'.

'Yes,' admitted Tizanael. 'It was a well-organised plan. And it would have succeeded if I had not been there.'

Terciel shuddered, thinking about what would have happened if he had been alone. Initially, she had said he should go alone. When the message-hawk had brought the word from Magistrix Tallowe saying help was needed so far south of the Wall, Tizanael had thought it would be good training for Terciel to go by himself, that he needed experience being separated from the Charter and they were overdue to liaise with the Crossing Point Scouts in any case.

But she had changed her mind, though she had not deigned to tell Terciel why, other than to say that her reluctance to cross the Wall might have become known, and an enemy could have planned to make use of this.

'Even so,' she said to Latimer. 'I regret the diversion. That message-hawk who came to me at the Fort. It was from the Regent in Belisaere—'

'More Dead in the palace again?' asked Terciel eagerly. He had only been to Belisaere once, when he was sixteen, but the visit had been memorable, thanks to a young woman he had met. He had forgotten how troubled Tizanael and the Regent had been, for it should not have been possible for any Dead to be within the grounds of the palace, the whole city being kept safe by the swift-flowing waters of its massive aqueducts.

'Not this time,' said Tizanael, with a quelling glance. 'A village has been attacked in the Upp river valley, to the north of Uppside. All the villagers slain or taken and the village's Charter Stone broken – something not easily done, for it needs the fresh-spilled blood of a Charter Mage and a powerful Free Magic sorcerer to do it. There was only one survivor, a girl who hid on the butter shelf of the well. She said the attackers named themselves the Servants of Kerrigor.'

'Kerrigor?' asked Latimer. He frowned. 'I vaguely recall the name. You and Prentice talked about him one time, when Prentice commanded the Scouts and I was still wondering what on earth I'd got into. Wasn't Kerrigor some enemy you dealt with, oh, years ago—'

'So I thought,' said Tizanael grimly. 'As other Abhorsens before me have also thought, and also been mistaken.'

'You've not mentioned this Kerrigor to me,' said Terciel indignantly. 'Who is he?'

'Who or what. I am not sure – we have never been sure – exactly what he is. A Dead creature of great power, who was most likely once a Free Magic adept and necromancer, or some hybrid Free Magic entity. He is powerful and clever, and in the past at least, had many followers. Lesser necromancers and common bandits, border reavers and the like. They called themselves the Servants of Kerrigor. If they are abroad again, I must assume Kerrigor has also returned. He has always had allies south of the Wall. He was probably behind the plan to lure you to your death. Or to take you prisoner, use your blood to break a Charter Stone.'

Terciel grimaced. He didn't like the sound of that at all.

'Allies on my side of the Wall, in Ancelstierre?' asked Latimer. 'That's all I need. These "Servants of Kerrigor", are they mortals? Dead? Free Magic creatures?'

'All of these. But I doubt any but the mortals could cross the Wall, or venture very far south. They would be trouble enough, of course. Lesser necromancers, Free Magic sorcerers and the like. Disguised, and perhaps with long-established identities in your country. All of Kerrigor's plans look far ahead.'

'This is very troubling,' said Latimer. He sighed. 'I suppose I'll have to look into the events at Coldhallow House more closely, which means stirring up some enemies of my own. By which I mean various bureaucrats in Corvere, who are expert at covering up and obfuscation and not much else. I would have liked to have been told about this before, Tizanael.'

'I had thought Kerrigor gone forever, the Servants dispersed,' said Tizanael. 'Twenty-three years ago, I surprised Kerrigor in an attack upon a village near High Bridge. He fled, sending many Dead against me to slow my pursuit. But I destroyed them and found him in the body he then wore. I forced him from that flesh, and followed him into Death. Unlike most, he had no fear of going deeper, and we fought a running battle through to the Fifth Precinct. There, Saraneth took him and Kibeth made him walk from the dark bridge. He fell into the river and was taken, swept through to the Ninth Gate, to return no more to Life. Or so I presumed. The Clayr did warn me, but I discounted their visions. They see so many futures, and so often confuse themselves . . .'

Terciel began to say something but stopped himself. Tizanael did not welcome him supporting the Clayr. She had some long-held problem with the women who saw futures in the ice, up in their fortress town under the glacier, far to the north of the Old Kingdom.

'If these "Servants" are about again, how can we identify them?' asked Latimer.

'They bear a brand upon their brows that mocks our Charter marks – an ugly, moving scar that proclaims their allegiance.'

'Oh good! That should make it—'

'The adept among them can disguise this, of course. Usually as a Charter mark.'

Latimer emitted something between a growl and a sigh of exasperation.

'How has Kerrigor returned from Death anyway? How is that possible?'

'He is clearly even more powerful than I suspected, or has some secret anchor in the living world,' said Tizanael. 'But Terciel and I will hunt him down again.'

'We will?' asked Terciel, amazed. Tizanael usually kept him away from the most dangerous tasks and opponents the Abhorsens took on, venturing forth by herself.

'Yes,' said Tizanael. 'I fear it will require both of us, and all our strength and cunning, to deal with Kerrigor. And something else, which I hope to learn more about when we reach the House.'

'We're going home?' asked Terciel eagerly. He loved the Abhorsen's House, not least for its safety from the Dead. The House occupied an island in the middle of a massive waterfall where the river Ratterlin went over the Long Cliffs, providing wide, deep and very fast running water all around. He could relax there, climb the ancient fig as he always did, go fishing, soak in a hot bath supplied by the slightly sulphurous waters from the subterranean hot spring . . . it was the only place in the entire world where he didn't have to be constantly on guard and ready for anything.

'We will go to the House first,' said Tizanael forbiddingly. 'But as soon as we can, we will begin the hunt for Kerrigor.'

She paused, noted Terciel's head hang lower in disappointment, and added without a change of expression, 'I expect we will be in the House for a week or two.'

Terciel's head came up and he smiled. Even one week at the House was a great luxury.

'Do you think this young woman, Elinor Hallett, had anything to do with the trap set for you?' asked Latimer, who had clearly been brooding on Tizanael's comment about Kerrigor having agents in Ancelstierre.

'She wasn't involved,' said Terciel quickly. 'Her mother was paid to provide a situation where we might be asked for help, but I don't think she understood what that really meant. For herself, or anyone else.'

He hesitated, then added, 'If you do make inquiries, Major, can you tell Elinor I hope she is all right? And if she needs—'

'We cannot offer people on the other side of the Wall assistance willy-nilly,' interrupted Tizanael sharply. 'Put the girl out of your mind, Terciel.'

'She's not in my mind,' grumbled Terciel, but even as he said it, he knew he was lying. There was something about Elinor's earnest face, those surprised brown eyes . . . They lingered.

'We must go,' continued Tizanael.

'Good hunting, then,' said Latimer. He gave Terciel a slightly quizzical glance, having seen the young man only a few times before and never having wondered about what kind of life he must lead. Now he did, a little. 'I'd best go back before my patrol comes through, wondering where I've got to.'

He stood at attention and saluted, his mail coat jingling. His uniform was entirely usual for the Scouts, though it would attract stares of wonderment and official abuse from the regular army down south. In addition to a short mail coat over his green regimental tunic, he wore leather breeches and heavy, hobnailed, handmade boots rather than the striped trousers and shiny patent-leather ankle boots of the usual Ancelstierran officer. He had a sword at his side, a proper medieval-looking cross-hilted straight blade, not a ceremonial dress sword or sabre. He did have a holstered revolver on his other hip. Sometimes modern firearms would work in the vicinity of the Wall, even on the Old Kingdom side. Mostly not, but it was always worth a try.

Terciel and Tizanael bowed in response. Latimer turned on his heel and strode back through the tunnel. Charter marks brightened further as he passed, merging with the sunshine still streaming through from the south, so it seemed that he disappeared into a doorway of pure light.

Unlike the Ancelstierran side, the region near the Wall in the Old Kingdom was mostly uninhabited and generally dangerous. Consequently, there was nowhere safe to leave a horse, nor any shelter to be had nearby. Terciel grimaced as he thought of the journey ahead.

'Moonrise soon. We will walk through the night,' said Tizanael. She looked up at the star-filled sky for a few seconds. 'There is a need for haste, and it will not snow.'

Terciel nodded. He was already tired, and cold, but there was no point complaining. Though she was so much older, Tizanael was seemingly made of iron. She was also far more adept at the fine art of using Charter Magic to bolster her strength and endurance without wearing herself out from using the magic. Casting the spells was such an effort for Terciel that it hardly ever worked out positively. It usually took more out of him than he got back.

'You go ahead,' said Tizanael. 'Take Uallus as your guide once the road turns to the northwest. I will follow a hundred paces behind.'

'So I am to be bait once more,' said Terciel. He looked up and fixed his eye on Uallus, the red star. It seemed to him to have a baleful aspect this night.

'Yes,' agreed Tizanael. She paused for a moment, thinking. 'Be watchful, though if there is some danger, some prepared ambush, it will more likely come as we approach the Long Cliffs, when we are tired and close to home. Or even on the riverbank, though no Dead will go near the House save under great compulsion.'

'Which something like this Kerrigor you mentioned could provide,' said Terciel. He took two paces and touched the stones of the Wall, revelling in the connection to the Charter, fully restored now they were back in the Old Kingdom. He had not liked the absence of the Charter in Ancelstierre, or even the lessened presence that came when the wind blew in from the north.

'You don't think he will face us himself?' he asked, attempting nonchalance.

'Not yet,' said Tizanael, not making Terciel feel any better. 'The attack on Far Upp took place yesterday. He could not be here so soon unless he shucked whatever body he has been using, and I can see no advantage for him to do that. In any case, this is neither the time nor the place to speak of it.'

She gestured for him to go, an emphatic 'get a move on'.

As always, Terciel obeyed, stepping out into the darkness, his boots thudding on the hard-packed earth of what had once been a road. There was enough starlight to see the way, and already a hint of the moon promised more light to come.

Even with sufficient light, Terciel did not walk as fast as he might, pausing every now and then to look about and listen. He heard Tizanael from time to time, some distance behind, though she stopped when he did, so her footsteps were like an echo of his own. There were few other sounds, for this was a barren heath, with no branches to sway or leaves to rustle. Once he heard an owl call in the distance, a falling, high-pitched scream, and once he stopped for some time to listen to something moving up ahead, before he determined it was a small predator, a fox or a vatch.

Well after midnight, with the ice-ringed moon high above, he heard Tizanael closing the gap between them. He stopped and edged off the road to watch and listen. He could see his own moonshadow now, long and threatening, sprawling across the blank parchment of the road like spilled ink.

'Dinner,' said Tizanael, with no trace of irony. Dinner in this case meant a few minutes' rest, hard biscuit provided by the Crossing Point Scouts, and a gulp or two of water from the bottle at Terciel's side.

'We have made good time,' said Tizanael. She looked up at the sky, noting the position of various stars, and she sniffed the air as well. Her ability to fix their position seemed another, even more inexplicable, magic to Terciel, though he believed her when she said it simply came from long experience traversing every part of the Kingdom, and a superb memory. He had a good memory too, but he wasn't sure it would ever be so well-filled as Tizanael's, no matter how many years he spent adding to it. 'Another two hours will see us at the seventeen-mile marker. We will be at the House by dawn. All being well.'

Terciel nodded, crumbs of the exceptionally tough biscuit falling from his lips. He washed down what he was able to chew off with a drink of water, slinging the bottle back over his shoulder as Tizanael indicated he should go on. It was too cold to stay still for long anyway. Terciel considered a Charter spell for warmth, but instead chose to pick up his pace, hoping movement would regain the warmth he had lost so quickly when he stopped.

He did cast the Charter spell for warmth, and one for invigoration, when they passed the seventeen-mile marker and found the Charter Stone a hundred paces behind it. By placing his hands on the obelisk that swam with tens of thousands of marks, Terciel was able to access the Charter more easily, effortlessly calling out the particular marks he needed, linking them together to make the spell and drawing them in a line from the stone into his arms and legs. Warmth blossomed from the glowing marks, spreading through every part of him, eventually making his fingers and toes and the end of his nose tingle with renewed heat. The spell for invigoration he drew in the air, a dozen marks coming easily from the stone. He breathed them in, breathing deep, sending the spell to the bottom of his lungs and thence into his blood.

Tizanael did likewise, though Terciel noticed she cast a different invigoration spell than the one he had used. Which she had taught him, along with all his other magic. He resolved to ask her about it when the opportunity arose. Tizanael did not like 'chatter', as she called it, when they were travelling. That had been drummed into him very early, right back to the dimly remembered time when she had brought him from Grynhold.

Reminded of this, Terciel spat out a crumb that had lingered too long in a corner of his mouth, before he walked on. The Scouts' travel biscuit was awful, its consistency worse than its taste, but he still preferred it to salt fish. Even now, years later, neither he nor Tizanael had ever eaten salt fish again.

He was glad of the respite offered by the spells and the Charter Stone, for they had left the remnant road behind and the path that led onward was harder, climbing up the stony slope, soon becoming a series of steps that switchbacked up a steep hillside. Long, broad steps, cut directly from the stone in ages past. Here and there, strange symbols could be seen in them, when the moonlight fell just so, but they were not Charter marks, neither the active marks nor the drawings that were used to represent them. Tizanael did not know the meaning of these symbols either.

When Terciel had first passed this way with her, she had bitterly lamented the loss of so much knowledge when Hillfair was destroyed, the vast but insecure palace on the riverbank the Abhorsens had inhabited, back in more peaceful centuries when there were rarely any Dead to deal with, Free Magic creatures slumbered, and the House in the river was a forgotten relic of bygone times.

That was before the Queen and her daughters had been mysteriously slain in Belisaere, probably by the treacherous Prince Rogir, and the royal line destroyed. Ever since, various Regents had fought a losing battle against the rising forces of anarchy and disruption, born out of whatever had happened to the Charter itself with the death of the Queen and the princesses. It was something that all Charter Mages could feel without being able to identify, an absence or a void in the Charter itself, that defied investigation or even attention. No one could think about it for very long, and attempted discussions always faltered into unwilling frowns and diversions.

Halfway up the steps, Terciel felt the strange, icy tingle in his mind that indicated the presence of the Dead. He stopped at once. He heard Tizanael below, not stopping as she usually would when he did, but climbing up faster. She would have sensed the Dead too. The Abhorsen was even more finely attuned to the presence of the Dead in Life than he was, a consequence of far more time spent in Death, as could be seen by the pallor of her skin, which was entirely leeched of pigment. Terciel had deep brown skin before he walked in Death, but he was pale now too, the only trace of his original skin tone on his chest, around his heart. That had never changed.

He could sense only one entity. There was something odd about it. He couldn't tell whether it had originally been human or not. Then he felt it shift and move, and realised that what lurked in the dark higher up the hill was a Dead human spirit spread among the bodies of several dead animals, probably weasels or stoats. A single, animating force occupying five or six corpses, who would move and think and act as one. Like a flock of Gore Crows, with a similar purpose, to serve as scouts or sentinels.

Tizanael came up behind him.

'Stoat fingers,' she whispered. 'Not newly come into Life. I cannot feel the presence of any other Dead.'

Terciel nodded, still listening. He could hear the stoats every now and then. As far as he could tell, they were keeping to the higher steps.

He and Tizanael stood in silence for several minutes, both listening for movement, minds questing for any more signs of the Dead out in the living world.

'Eight stoat fingers,' said Tizanael. 'But I can sense no guiding power behind them. There is no necromancer nearby. Can you hear anything save the stoats? My ears are too old for this.'

'Only the scrabbling of small animals,' whispered Terciel.

'They have been sent to watch us,' said Tizanael. 'They will not dare to close. But be on your guard.

There may be other dangers here, these minor Dead set to distract us from more powerful foes, perhaps even mortal enemies lying in wait. It is an old technique for ambushing Abhorsens. I will go ahead. Stay close.'

She drew her sword and unlatched the strap on the bandolier cup that held the bell Saraneth, the binder. But she did not take it out, for a stumble in the darkness might prove more disastrous to the bell-wielder than any Dead. After a moment, Terciel drew his sword and undid the strap that covered Ranna. The Sleeper was generally a more forgiving bell, and powerful enough to overcome most opponents.

Charter marks glowed faintly on sword blades and bell bandoliers, soft, faint light that would not impinge on their night-time sight.

Tizanael stepped up, and Terciel followed, close at her heels.

7

Elinor woke slowly and muzzily, constrained by sheets and a blanket that were drawn taut across her body and tucked well in. She could smell carbolic soap too, something she hadn't encountered for a long time, ever since she'd complained to Mrs Watkins she didn't like it, whatever her governess thought of its disinfectant properties.

Mrs Watkins. Elinor's eyes snapped open and filled with tears. Pushing her arms out from the restraining covers, she brushed the tears away and looked around. As she'd already guessed from the carbolic smell and the practically lashed down red blanket over her, she was in a hospital ward. As she realised that, she felt a stabbing pain in her side, accompanied by several lesser aches along her left leg.

There were six beds in the ward, but the others were all empty. A nurse's desk at the far end was unattended, and the big blue door beyond it was shut. There were several windows, but the curtains were drawn, and the ward was lit by gas lanterns on the wall, though only two of the four Elinor could see were lit, so it was not as bright as it could be.

She rolled over, grunting a little at the pain, and gratefully drank from a glass of water on the bedside table. There was also a handbell there. Elinor eyed it for a few seconds, thinking of Tizanael's bells, the Dead Hands stopping in place and then moving as one, and everything that had happened. It hurt to stretch out her arm, but she reached for the bell and was about to ring it when the blue door at the end swung open and a nurse hurried in. Elinor let go of the bell and gratefully rolled onto her back. Her side hurt less that way.

'Miss Hallett! It is good to see you awake.'

The woman was some sort of superior nurse, Elinor knew from the commanding way she spoke and the splendour of her uniform. Her starched white hat had particularly broad wings, her red tunic had epaulettes with silver stars on them, and the watch pinned to the white apron over the tunic was gold with little diamonds on the face that winked in the gaslight.

'I am Matron Parkness,' said the nurse. She sailed over to Elinor's bed and hauled the bedclothes tight again. 'You must lie still. You have been sadly bruised with some nasty abrasions, several ribs cracked, and your wrists quite burned. All of which you will recover from perfectly well, but you must do as you are told.'

'What about the bullet wound?' asked Elinor. She remembered the shock of that sudden pain, greater than any of the other hurts.

'Bullet wound?' asked Parkness brightly. 'You must have imagined that, dear. One of the abrasions is quite deep, perhaps a stone or something similar when you fell. But no bullets, fortunately.'

Elinor was about to protest this obvious falsity, but she held it back. There was something about the way Parkness was talking, a kind of flummery that she recognised from her own mother when she had been determined not to acknowledge the existence of some unpleasant reality.

'Where am I?'

'The county hospital, dear.'

'Which one?'

'Bainshire, of course. Where did you think?'

'Oh,' replied Elinor. 'Cornbridge is closer . . . I thought it would be there.'

'It was considered better to bring you here,' replied Parkness obscurely. 'Dr Bannow will see you soon. Do you need the bedpan?'

'No . . . yes,' said Elinor, suddenly aware she did. 'But I can go . . . I can go to—'

'No, you must stay in bed,' said Parkness. She drew the covers back and flourished a bedpan like she'd performed an amazing conjuring trick, though she'd simply picked it off the stand at the end of the bed.

Several minutes later, a thoroughly humiliated Elinor swore to herself that she would recover in record time, though Parkness had treated the whole process no differently than Mrs Watkins would sewing on a loose button while Elinor stood still.

'And here's the doctor,' declared Parkness, holding the bedpan up like some sort of sacrificial offering as she sailed majestically away, passing the doctor near the door with a breezy, 'Good afternoon, Doctor. The patient is awake and has passed water.'

The doctor, an older woman wearing a nondescript white coat over a drab blue dress with a ruffled collar, nodded. She had two pairs of glasses stuck high on her grey hair, which was bundled on top of her head, but neither fell off with the nod.

Far more interesting from Elinor's point of view was the Charter mark on the doctor's forehead. Faint, and not currently glowing, but definitely the same as her own, and Terciel's, and Tizanael's.

Dr Bannow saw her looking.

'Yes,' she said easily. 'I too bear the mark, though I have few claims to being an actual mage, apart from some small knowledge of healing and prophylactic spells. That's why you have come to my ward. The hospital authorities do not officially admit to the peculiarities that occur in Bain and other parts close to the Wall, but in fact must be prepared for them at some level. I represent that slight capacity to deal with magically induced wounds and the like.'

'But I was shot and bruised,' said Elinor. 'Not hurt with magic.'

'The burns on your wrists suggest otherwise,' said Dr Bannow.

Elinor lifted her arms so the sleeves of her hospital gown fell back. Her wrists were heavily bandaged, the bandages impregnated with some sort of yellowish paste.

'Oh,' she said. 'Where the . . . the man . . . held me.'

'Not an ordinary man,' said Dr Bannow. 'A Free Magic sorcerer, I would guess. I found it very hard to force a spell of healing into those burns. But you helped me, even while unconscious.'

'I did?'

'Yes. Your own Charter mark is very strong, I suppose refreshed by the recent north wind. I found if I touched it I could access the Charter more easily. I don't know why. I wish I knew more about Charter Magic in general. Often I can't do any at all, unless I go up close to the Wall. Or when the north wind comes, which isn't all that often.'

'Why don't you go across the Wall, into the Old Kingdom?' asked Elinor. 'Learn more?'

Dr Bannow gave her an odd look before replying.

'Because I am too afraid, an entirely sensible emotion, I believe. I content myself with learning odds and ends, on the rare occasions someone who knows more than I do crosses my path.'

'Like the Abhorsens?'

'Oh, I wish! They are on another, higher plane entirely, when it comes to Charter Magic. I did meet Tizanael once, but she did not deign to teach me anything. She told me folk south of the Wall should simply move further away and not meddle with matters beyond our ken. But that was years ago. I did hear she and the young Abhorsen-in-Waiting came south with the wind these last few days, but I did not see them. No, I have had to learn what little I know from the few Ancelstierrans who have the mark. Not counting the Crossing Point Scouts. They also do not teach what they know, not to civilians.'

'What about Magistrix Tallowe, at . . . at Wyverley College?' asked Elinor.

Dr Bannow smiled ruefully.

'Abigail Tallowe took an immediate dislike to me and refused to share any of her knowledge,' she said. 'I don't know why. Perhaps she thinks she is special because she keeps message-hawks for some Old Kingdom folk, and passes on telegrams and messages, and so will not deign to fraternise with lesser people such as myself. Lie back now. I must examine your wounds.'

Elinor obediently lay back. Dr Bannow drew a Charter mark in the air with her right forefinger. It hung there, glowing, and she tried to draw another mark next to it, but nothing happened and the first mark winked out of existence.

Dr Bannow sighed and wiped her forehead. Even trying the spell had obviously wearied her.

'Oh well, I'd hoped it might work. A small spell, to make my hands aseptic. I will have to resort to carbolic soap. I won't be a moment.'

She went to the nurses' station and washed her hands to the elbow carefully in the tin basin there, the stench of carbolic acid strong in the air. Taking a clean towel from the shelf, she dried her hands and returned to Elinor.

As Dr Bannow pulled back the covers and lifted Elinor's gown, the young woman peered down at herself. Her left side was a mottled blue-black, and there was a bandage taped over what she knew was a gunshot wound. It ached but not unbearably so. The doctor carefully undid the bandage around her middle, peeled back the dressing, and bent close, sniffing.

'That's healing very nicely. I managed a spell to clean and close it up, so it's days ahead of where you would be otherwise. If only I could get the other doctors here to . . . well, that's another story. I'll replace the dressing.'

'It is a bullet wound, isn't it?' asked Elinor as the doctor pulled the rest of the dressing off.

'What? Yes, of course. A big, slow bullet. An army revolver, I'd say a .455. You were very lucky it only grazed your side. A few inches over and you'd be dead.'

'The matron said I didn't have a bullet wound.'

'Parkness? Yes, officially you don't, so she has to go along with that, though she's not as hidebound as she seems. She's one of the few nurses who will help me with the "unusual" cases.'

'Why "officially"?'

Dr Bannow was painting the wound with a purple concoction and didn't answer immediately. When she had finished, and replaced the dressing and bandage, she stood back and said, 'Because the unacknowledged policy in Bainshire is to never officially acknowledge anything troublesome related to magic and certainly not to make any permanent record of it. I am curious how a bullet wound comes into that category however, and as I haven't been told very much, would you care to tell me exactly what happened to you? I can fetch us some tea.'

Over several cups of tea, Elinor told Dr Bannow what had happened at Coldhallow House. She cried when she got to Mrs Watkins's death, and sobbed so hard describing Ham's murder that she couldn't breathe and had to stop talking for a while. Dr Bannow sat next to her on the bed and held her shoulders until the sobs diminished.

'I should not have asked you so soon,' she said apologetically. 'Your wounds have healed very quickly. I forgot it is not simply a matter of the physical hurts.'

Elinor nodded, still unable to speak.

'Rest now,' said Dr Bannow. She helped Elinor lie back, arranging the pillow under her head. 'You're safe here. If you need anyone, ring the bell.'

Elinor nodded again, wearily. The talking and the crying had exhausted her, her limbs felt leaden, and the pain in her side had risen from a dull ache to a sharper one. She let out a gasp as it twinged again.

'I'll give you a shot for the pain before I go,' said Dr Bannow. Through half-closed eyes Elinor saw her pick up a hypodermic needle.

'No, I don't need it,' she muttered, remembering the biography she'd read of the poet Adrasson and her morphine addiction. Mrs Watkins had given her Adrasson's collected poems for her sixteenth birthday, she suddenly remembered, and began to weep again.

'It will help you with the pain and calm you—'

'No!' sobbed Elinor. 'Adrasson.'

'The poet? Oh, I see. But addiction doesn't happen with one or two shots.'

Elinor managed to hold her breath for six seconds, and stopped sobbing. She took another, slower breath, centring herself as Ham had taught her to do, to enter the calm, focused zone required for intensive juggling.

'The pain isn't so bad. And I am . . . I am . . . I will manage.'

Dr Bannow hesitated for a long moment, then said, 'Very well. I'll be back to check on you soon. If the pain worsens, don't hesitate to ring the bell.'

'I won't,' whispered Elinor. She shut her eyes again, and focused on her breathing, drawing in slow breaths, holding them for the count of six, then exhaling as slowly. Darkness crept in with each breath, the pain of her wound ebbing, while the pain of her loss was put aside for later.

Eventually, Elinor slept, a troubled, waking sleep, but nevertheless welcome for what it was.

A week later, Dr Bannow declared Elinor well enough to leave, in terms of her physical health at least. She had doubts about how Elinor was otherwise, despite the young woman outwardly having enormously improved. She didn't cry any more, but to the doctor, Elinor's set face was not necessarily an improvement.

But she had weathered the last few days in particular without breaking down. This included two unwelcome visits: the first from several rather embarrassed senior police officers and an entirely unembarrassed and slimy functionary from the Chief Minister's office in Corvere. The police officers asked her to tell them everything that happened that day, the least senior taking it all down carefully in his notebook.

Then the functionary told her to forget everything she had told the police officers and insisted she sign a document agreeing that the rushed inquest – which had already been held without Elinor's evidence – into the deaths of Elinor's mother, Cook, Maria, Mrs Watkins and Ham had been properly conducted, though it attributed all of the deaths to 'a house fire of accidental ignition'. It also demanded she not discuss the events with anyone at all, but most particularly newspaper reporters. Elinor had resisted at first, only signing when she realised the oblique language in the document was actually a very definite threat she would be put in a mental institution if she didn't sign.

The second visit had been from her family's solicitors in Corvere, represented by the stately Mrs Gwenyth Lord herself, senior partner of Lord, Lord & Lord. In between shallow expressions of sorrow at the deaths, remarks on how handsome Elinor's father had been in his prime, how successful her grandfather, and how reputable her mother's aunts, Mrs Lord managed to convey the key facts that Morrison's Bank had foreclosed on what was left of Coldhallow House and the estate; agents acting for other creditors had seized any portable properties of value; and there was nothing left. Or almost nothing, for it turned out Elinor's grandmother, the mysterious Myrien Clayr, had left a small – a very small – annuity for her granddaughter. Amelia Hallett had tried to seize the principal, several times, but had failed.

Elinor was surprised that Mrs Lord had apparently supported her mother in these attempts. It became clear through the conversation that the solicitor was one of those people who feared and distrusted anything from the Old Kingdom, and considered Amelia's aunts to have done entirely the right thing in taking her from her mother, and that Myrien Clayr should never have gained even a brief release from the asylum she'd been put in, said release having resulted in her encounter with Elinor as a baby and her engaging other lawyers who had secured her money away from Amelia.

This did not endear her to Elinor, and the interview was concluded in a very cold and businesslike way, with Mrs Lord announcing she could not wait to get on the train and 'return to civilisation'.

'What are you going to do?' asked Dr Bannow when the visitors had left and Elinor was ready to depart herself. In a turnabout, the doctor was sitting on the bed in the otherwise empty ward, and Elinor was standing dressed in clothes given to her by Matron Parkness, who said they were her sister's, who was much of the same size as Elinor. As the clothes were entirely new, from undergarments to a many-buttoned coat, Elinor doubted this, but she could not refuse the charity. Her grandmother's annuity would ensure she didn't quite starve, but little more than that, and apart from those quarterly payments, she had only the two gold coins that had been in the pocket of her father's coat. The coat itself was in the cupboard by her bed, but despite the kind attentions of Matron Parkness and the hospital laundry, it was too stained and torn to be worn anywhere except perhaps while working in a garden, digging compost or the like.

'For the *immediate* future, I will have to seek employment,' said Elinor.

Dr Bannow looked at her with knowing eyes.

'And beyond that?'

Elinor hesitated. But she knew no one else who bore the Charter mark, anyone who might have some inkling of understanding.

'I am going to prepare myself to go to the Old Kingdom,' she said defiantly. 'I want to find my . . . my family there. Learn more about the Charter and Charter Magic.'

'I am glad you said "prepare" yourself,' said Dr Bannow. 'I wasn't joking when I said I wasn't brave enough to cross the Wall when I was young. It is a very dangerous undertaking.'

'"A foolish fool knows not the foolish things they undertake, but a wise fool knows the wisdom of the foolery they make",' quoted Elinor.

'What is that from?'

'*The Court of the Sad Prince*,' replied Elinor. 'Act Two, Scene Four.'

'Oh, Breakespear,' said Dr Bannow. 'Not one I've seen. Or read, for that matter.'

'It's one of the Obscurities,' said Elinor slowly. Ham had always considered the group of three lesser-known and very rarely performed plays termed the Obscurities as the best of all Breakespear. They had the most clowning and ridiculous fights. Elinor didn't share Ham's opinion. Her favourites were unexceptional, the plays whose popularity had endured for centuries, like *The Three Noble Kinswomen* and *A Stone Shall Speak*.

'What exactly do you have in mind in terms of preparing yourself?' asked Dr Bannow.

'I do need to seek employment first,' repeated Elinor. 'But once that is sorted out, I hope to have some time to learn more about the Old Kingdom and, most particularly, more Charter Magic. I may be able to do both these things at Wyverley College.'

'Wyverley College! You mean from Magistrix Tallowe? I doubt she would help you in any way, the woman's a—'

'We're related,' interrupted Elinor. 'Apparently. I'm hoping that will help. And the school must employ servants.'

'Servants? But surely *you* can't be—'

'What else can I do?' asked Elinor. 'I have no qualifications to be a teacher, which I'm sure a proper school like that would require.'

'Yes,' agreed Dr Bannow. 'But a school servant! Scrubbing floors and serving schoolgirls!'

'Only until I am ready to go to the Old Kingdom,' said Elinor. 'Six months, or a year, perhaps. I'm sure I can cope with that.'

'Have you considered university?' asked Dr Bannow. 'My old college has scholarships, as do others. And if you don't object to being a servant, some of them still have places for sizars, so there would be some point to being a servant, since you would end up with your degree. I could help you.'

'You're very kind,' said Elinor. 'But I know what I want to do.'

'You're very young,' said Dr Bannow. She sighed. 'And like I said, far braver than I am, or ever was. If you're set on it, I can help you with some of the formalities. You will need to get official permission from authorities on both sides of the Wall. I looked into it when I thought I might go myself, before the coming of wisdom or perhaps the caution that grows with age. If you do manage to get a place at Wyverley College, I hope you will write, and perhaps visit me from time to time. I do not often have the company of others who bear the mark.'

'I will,' said Elinor. Impulsively, she embraced the doctor, who hesitantly stood up and returned the gesture.

'I can't say I've ever hugged a patient before,' she said. 'But then you are unusual, Elinor. Good luck with everything. Do let me know how you get on. I must confess I am very curious how you will be received by Abigail Tallowe!'

8

The stoat fingers retreated up the steps as Terciel and Tizanael advanced. Soon it became apparent they were set to watch from as close as they dared, never coming near enough to be within the influence of the Abhorsen's bells or a Charter Magic spell that might destroy their decayed flesh.

The steps became steeper and narrower as Terciel climbed, and the moonlight was bright enough to see the dark shadow of the Long Cliffs ahead. Before they reached the top of the steps and the foot of the cliffs, the Dead creatures streamed off to the north, leaping from ledge to ledge along the lower part of the cliffs. They would find some deep crevice to gather in, to hide from the day, and unless reinforced by the necromancer who'd brought them from Death, the spirit inside the small dead animals would erode the flesh away and in a matter of days retreat into Death once more, there to be carried away forever.

'Mere watchers, as I thought,' said Tizanael, pausing to regain her breath as they left the last step and stood on the carefully chiselled expanse of flat rock at the foot of the escarpment. It always reminded Terciel of a sort of overgrown step, as if it were parent to all the much smaller steps that wound their way below. 'But who for? You remember how to open the door here?'

Terciel nodded, and carefully removed the bell Mosrael from his bandolier. Mosrael, the Waker, whose full-voiced call brought the listener into Life and cast the wielder into Death. But in well-trained hands, a mere whisper from Mosrael could also be used to reveal the hidden, to open locks and ways, and indeed, wake those whose sleep was not of the ordinary kind.

But always Mosrael wanted to serve its primary purpose, so it was a particularly dangerous bell. Terciel rang it once, very cautiously, with the merest flick of his wrist, and he stilled it immediately, grasping the clapper. Even so, he felt the sudden, icy presence of Death, and for a moment saw the river, felt the current clutching at him, trying to take him in its grasp. It gripped him for a second as the single, short note of the bell echoed along the rockface, only to loosen and fade as silence returned.

A moment later, a door bloomed into visibility, lines of bright Charter marks speeding up and across to draw the outline of the portal in the formerly featureless grey stone.

'Good,' grunted Tizanael, stepping forward. The door opened, drawn back by a tall figure clad in silver mail, a naked sword brandished in its right hand, head shrouded by a hood. At first glance a powerfully built human, it was not actually a mortal at all. Its hands gave it away, for they were not living flesh but made up of thousands of tiny Charter marks, moving and glowing faintly to create the illusion of golden-hued skin. It was a Charter sending, a created servant of limited sentience and ability, this one made and set here centuries ago as the doorwarden of the steep, subterranean path that ran up to the western bank of the Ratterlin, high above.

The sending closed the door behind Terciel. The Charter marks faded, the doorway once again becoming solid grey stone. The doorwarden saluted with its sword. Terciel tried not to look at its face, or faces. He always found it disturbing, particularly as some sendings did not have human features at all. This one had several visages, flickering between male and female. Distinctive faces, full of character.

Not for the first time, he wondered about how sendings were made. This one seemed based on several real people, but every part of it was Charter Magic: flesh, armour, sword. Tizanael said he was not yet ready to learn how the sendings were made, or more particularly there were other things he needed to learn first, and he had not had time to try to find a book about it in the library of the House. He never had time for anything beyond what Tizanael immediately wanted him to learn. As far as he knew, Tizanael had made only one of the sendings in the House or its close environs, like here. They were nearly all creations of past Abhorsens.

'Not long now,' said Tizanael as she strode up the steeply slanting passage. She trailed her fingers against the wall as she walked, Charter marks rising up from the stone like small fish rising to bait. There were ancient Charter spells in this passage, spells to light their way, and to lend strength and fleetness to those who might need it. Tizanael was drinking them in. Terciel put his hand against the wall too, and felt his fatigued muscles become a little less weary as the glowing marks left the stone to enter skin.

Other marks sprang up overhead, simple ones to provide illumination, which faded behind them as they passed by. Under their light, Terciel saw that Tizanael was looking very weary, her back not so straight as usual, her feet scuffing the floor a little. He had never thought of how old she was much before, but in recent months he'd slowly become aware that she was very old indeed. She was still considerably more capable than he was in almost everything they did, but it seemed to Terciel that it was taking more of an effort from her, and it was taking her longer to recover from their excursions and alarums.

He almost said something as she stumbled and recovered, but he didn't. Tizanael never welcomed inquiries about her health, or how she was feeling, or in fact anything that wasn't directly related to whatever task they were currently engaged with. Instead he focused on keeping himself going. Despite the artificial bolstering provided by the Charter spells in the passage, his legs still ached and he felt very tired. Only the thought of his comfortable bed in the House kept him going. That and Tizanael's scorn if he suggested they rest so close to their destination.

Finally they reached the upper end of the passage. Another doorwarden waited there, this sending smaller and slighter than the one below. Its Charter-created clothing was a cowled robe that hid its face, if it had one. It opened the door and then raised a delicate portcullis of silver wire that lay beyond, a fragile-looking thing that seemed less like a proper barrier and more like a fishing net left too long on the shore, made stiff with salt and sunshine. Yet it too was a creation of Charter Magic, and much, much stronger than it looked.

'All well below?' Tizanael asked the sending. It bowed to her, indicating nothing had disturbed its post.

Even so, Terciel advanced out cautiously onto the ledge that stood high above the riverbank. The rumble of the falls hit his ears, so he looked quickly around, the noise loud enough to cover any enemies who might be about to make their move. But he couldn't see any danger. The moon was almost directly overhead, the sky clear, the landscape laid out below in silver clarity. There was the enormous plume of spray where the Ratterlin, four hundred yards wide at this point, went over the cliffs in the truly massive falls. The House, their island home, stood on the edge of the waterfall, in the middle of the river.

There was no colour to see under the moon, but his mind supplied the details. The red-tiled roof of the main house, the whitewashed perimeter walls surrounding the island, the green of the lawns, the yellow-green of the orchard. In daylight, the sun would glint from the windows of the tower, though they were not glass but some unbreakable crystal known to the artisan Charter Mages of long ago. The Wallmakers, whose bloodline had vanished, at least as a separate lineage, much as the royal line had done.

There were steps down from the ledge to the riverside, the descent testing muscles differently to the climb up from the plain below. Then the last exertion, jumping across the stepping-stones ironically known as the 'Abhorsen's Bridge'. They were spelled to help those who wore the mark to not fall off, but even so were always wet and somewhat slippery, the river incredibly swift and the lip of the waterfall almost unbearably close. If you did slip and fall, there would be no chance of survival.

It was like that other river, Terciel thought. The cold river of Death. He shivered, thinking of his spirit being tumbled through the Gates, spirit flailing, until the Ninth Gate and the final death beyond. If the current took you there, that was it.

Except, it seemed, for the thing called Kerrigor.

'There is a Paperwing on the platform,' said Tizanael, pointing to the platform high on the eastern wall, a temporary structure that the sendings put in place to launch one of the Abhorsen's own Paperwings, or in this case, to relaunch a visitor's. It was easier to land on the lawn, but difficult to take off from there, so the platform was necessary. There was a Paperwing on it now, a magical aircraft with a canoe-shaped body and long, swept-back wings. Terciel couldn't see its colour scheme, but it had to be the green and silver of the Clayr. No one else flew Paperwings now, with the royal line gone.

'We must have a visiting Clayr,' confirmed Tizanael. 'That was very swift. I trust it means they have actually done what I asked for once.'

'Which is what?' asked Terciel. He started down the steps, grunting as his calf muscles complained. He shivered again, this time from the cold. The spell for warmth he'd cast at the Charter Stone had long since worn off, and the wind was biting. There was ice on the Ratterlin, chunks of it floating downstream from the north, where the river would be partly frozen, only the deep, swift-moving central channel remaining clear year-round. There would be more ice floating down soon as the riverside sheets began to thaw and break up with the coming of spring.

'Find a book in their vaunted library and bring it to me,' said Tizanael. She paused, looked around, and added, 'Don't get careless. Those stoat fingers might not be all that's around. The sendings in the passage are old, and not as sharp as they might be.'

'Yes, Great-Aunt,' replied Terciel, but he didn't slow down or lift his head to look around.

'I mean it,' said Tizanael sharply. 'The Abhorsen Keramitiel was killed on the riverbank, shot by an archer hiding in the reeds in that little corner upstream by the big boulder.'

She pointed at a spot a hundred yards away, though the reeds were invisible in the night, only the boulder standing out in the moonlight.

'Depending on your sense of the Dead isn't enough, and my eyes, like my ears, are not what they were either. Even if your ears are better, the waterfall is noisy enough to cover even the clumsiest of assassins. So be alert.'

'Yes, Abhorsen,' repeated Terciel. This time, he meant it.

They reached the river without incident, though Terciel had stopped three times to stare at deep drifts of moonshadow, until he was certain they did not contain enemies and he had jumped and half drawn his sword in response to the sudden passage of an owl overhead.

The river seemed particularly swift and rough in the night, and the stepping-stones smaller and wetter than they did in daylight. But there was no other way to reach the House, and the deep, swift water, while threatening to Terciel, was also comforting, as a most powerful defence against the Dead.

'What are you waiting for?' asked Tizanael. 'You've crossed a hundred times or more. Get on with it. I need my bed.'

Terciel nodded and jumped to the first stone. As always, once committed to the crossing, it was better than anticipating it. He let his momentum carry him forward and jumped to the next stone and the next. Though the stones looked slippery, they were crosshatched for grip as well as spelled for safety, and soon he was in a familiar rhythm, jumping from stone to stone with practised ease. The roar of the waterfall was so loud it blanketed everything else out, and the spray rolling back from the waterfall drenched him from head to foot. But it was familiar, and he welcomed it, for it was also a sign that a hot bath, a good breakfast and a proper bed awaited just up ahead, behind the whitewashed walls of the island in the river.

The last jump was to the landing stage that thrust out from the rocks. He made it, gripped the rail and turned to look back. Tizanael was further back than he'd expected, jumping with slow deliberation, pausing on each stone for several seconds rather than adopting Terciel's continuous movement.

When she neared the landing stage, he stepped back, but stayed close enough to lunge forward if she fell. He'd never done that before, but he'd also never considered it might be possible.

Tizanael did not fall. She immediately strode along the landing stage, taking the lead. The gate in the wall swung open ahead of her and she marched in, her hobnailed boots striking sparks on the redbrick path. Terciel followed, hurrying to catch up. Whatever magic controlled the gate, it was either breaking down with age, or had been imbued with a sense of humour, for it had shut in his face more than once when he had not followed close enough on Tizanael's heels.

Once through the gate, the roar of the waterfall vanished. The quiet peacefulness of late night replaced it. Terciel looked up at the moon, which was no longer so high, nor so bright. Soon the first flush of dawn would start to fill the eastern sky, slowly spreading across the river.

Tizanael looked back at him.

'We will not have your usual lessons in the morning,' she said. 'I am very weary. We will meet whoever the Clayr have sent at noon. You should rest too, Terciel, though I suppose you must first perform your strange ritual.'

'Um, yes,' said Terciel, a little embarrassed. As Tizanael walked slowly to the front door of the House – which a sending had already opened, standing by to take Tizanael's pack and boots – he walked across the lawn to the great fig tree. Dropping his own pack, he divested himself of cloak, bell bandolier, sword, stockings and boots, and he started to climb.

It was stupid, he knew, particularly when he was so tired from the long walk through the night, and without his heavy cloak the sweat was already freezing on his skin. But it was something he had always done, ever since that first time, when Tizanael had brought him here as a small boy. When he returned to the House, he climbed the great fig. It had started as some sort of rebellion, an act of independence. He wasn't sure why he continued with it, now that he had basically completely acquiesced to Tizanael's plans for him. He was the Abhorsen-in-Waiting. He would be the Abhorsen.

But climbing the tree, he could forget that, at least for a little while. He was just a boy again, leaving his problems behind him on the ground. Revelling in the height and solitude, completely separate from the world—

'Welcome back.'

Terciel stopped climbing and peered up through the branches, his heart suddenly hammering. Bright emerald eyes peered back down at him. Moregrim, the strange white-haired dwarf, was sitting on a higher branch, his stubby legs dangling.

It was a shock. Terciel had seen Moregrim only twice since that first time, and at that only fleetingly, and within the House. Tizanael had never explained what Moregrim actually was, other than to say he was a servant of the

Abhorsens, but not bound as tightly as one might want. She also always reminded Terciel he must never remove Moregrim's red belt or collar, whichever it was, and whatever shape he was in, without explaining how it was he had different shapes or what they were. It was one of many subjects where Terciel wished she was more forthcoming.

'What are you doing here?' asked Terciel crossly. 'Tizanael ordered you to stay in the House. The actual house part of the House. I remember it distinctly, the day I came here.'

He did too. His arrival at the House was seared in his memory.

'I can usually slide out of an order that is not repeated,' said Moregrim, peering down. 'Eventually. You're not going to tell her, are you? I could be very useful to you.'

'Of course I'll tell her!' snapped Terciel.

'I know things,' said Moregrim. He grinned, showing off those too-sharp teeth. 'Far more than you Abhorsens. You've lost so much. I can answer all your questions. Tizanael doesn't, does she?'

'I'm not interested in your answers,' said Terciel. 'Do as you're told, and go back into the House. The house proper, I mean.'

Moregrim hissed, an unnerving sound from something that at least looked like a man.

'Go,' ordered Terciel. 'You're a servant of the Abhorsens. I am the Abhorsen-in-Waiting. Go!'

Moregrim hissed again. White fire flared inside his mouth, and the Charter marks on his collar suddenly blazed up. He dropped down, and for a second Terciel thought he would fall, but he gripped a branch below and swung down to another, crouching on it in a very inhuman way, before descending further. Terciel watched him swing from branch to branch to the lawn, there to stalk away towards the house, luminously white in the gloom, his red belt still bright with many golden Charter marks. The miniature bell, Terciel now knew, was Saraneth. The Binder. Which was a very disturbing thing to see swinging freely, whatever sound it made heard only by Moregrim, all the bell's power directed inward.

Terciel slowly started climbing again, his limbs leaden.

Somehow, the House did not feel quite like the refuge it always had before.

9

Elinor begrudged spending five shillings on a horse and carriage to convey her from the railway station at Wyverley Halt to Wyverley College, but she knew it was necessary. Walking there would disorder her neat clothes, and though she wanted employment, most likely as a servant, she thought it would be best to initially approach Magistrix Tallowe as a gentlewoman, so she needed to look the part.

'You want me to wait, miss?' asked the driver as they wheeled past the open wrought-iron gates and up the drive towards the front of the school, an imposing structure of some antiquity, being built almost three hundred years ago according to the sign at the gate. The main building ahead had four towers, two large ones at the front and two somewhat smaller ones at the rear. The central core was five stories high with some sort of open quadrangle in the middle, and there were numerous outbuildings. Over to the east, Elinor could see teams of girls in blue-and-white sports uniforms playing cricket on the oval. She felt a momentary pang at that. She had played cricket, of a sort, with Ham. They had often used cricket balls in their juggling.

'Um, I'm not sure,' she replied, handing over the two half crowns agreed in advance and a threepenny bit as a tip. 'I can't afford to pay you to wait . . .'

'That's all right, miss,' said the driver easily. 'The head gardener here is a friend of mine. I'll nip around the back to his cottage and have a jar with him. One of the school servants will know where to find me. Send one when you're ready to go.'

'Yes, thank you again,' replied Elinor hurriedly, stepping down from the carriage. It was both odd and unsettling to think she might soon be one of those servants, at the beck and call of even visitors to the school.

The front steps were marble-faced brick, giving a suitable impression of stolid prosperity. The heavy front doors looked somewhat out of place to Elinor, being oak and massively reinforced, both leaves heavily peppered with iron bolts, the heads green with verdigris. They looked more like the doors to some ancient castle than a school.

The right-hand leaf was slightly ajar. Elinor looked through the gap and saw a broad hall, wainscoted in mahogany, with a decorative plaster ceiling and dark floorboards showing lighter paths on the left and right sides, the timber polished by the passage of many girls. There were numerous plaster or perhaps even marble busts of significant persons lining the walls, on stands evidently procured at different periods of the school's history. One of the closest was a bust Elinor knew well, the depiction of Breakespear's head, which featured as an engraved frontispiece of her own copy of the *Collected Plays*.

Closer to the door than Breakespear's bust, a schoolgirl sat upright in a wicker chair under a sign that read in gilt, mock Gothic script, 'Hall Monitor'. She looked about sixteen to Elinor, and apart from wearing a rather ugly pale lavender beret with the school badge pinned on it, was dressed in much the same way: a long full skirt and a many-buttoned jacket of navy blue over a pale cream blouse whose collar and cuffs were ruffled. A scholar's robe of dark blue edged in red hung over the back of the chair.

The girl saw Elinor looking in, sprang up like a jack-in-the-box, and got herself in a bit of a tangle trying to get her Fifth Form scholar's robe on far more quickly than was sensible, at the same time gabbling out a stock welcome.

'Good afternoon and welcome to Wyverley College. I am . . . curse it . . . oh, I'm sorry, don't tell . . . please . . . I am the hall monitor, my name is Miss Congrove, please state your business.'

That last was said with a flourish as she settled the robe properly on her shoulders, stepped forward and pulled the partially open door back towards her. It moved very easily despite its weight and size, clearly set on most superior hinges.

'Hello,' replied Elinor. 'My name is Miss Elinor Hallett, and I am here to see Magistrix Tallowe.'

'Magistrix? You mean Mrs Tallowe?'

'Yes,' agreed Elinor hastily.

The girl frowned and looked up at the ceiling, as if hoping for inspiration.

'Perhaps you could direct me to Mrs Tallowe?' asked Elinor. 'Or . . . or send word that she has a visitor?'

'I'm not sure,' replied the girl anxiously. 'I mean, I've been hall monitor before, but the visitors at the front door are always for the headmistress.'

'What do you do with them?' asked Elinor. She had expected to feel shy and overawed coming to this large and imposing school, not knowing any more of such places than she'd read in the Billie Cotton books, which began with *Billie Cotton New Bug* and concluded with *Billie Cotton Rules the Sixth*. But instead she felt so much older and more collected than this blushing girl who didn't know what to do with her.

'They sign the book and I take them to the school secretary,' said the girl.

'Let's do that,' replied Elinor. 'Then I will become the school secretary's problem, Miss Congrove, rather than yours.'

'Oh, good idea!' said Miss Congrove, very much relieved. She pointed further along the hall to a table with an inkstand, several quills and an enormous leather-bound ledger.

Elinor signed her name and gave her address as Coldhallow House. That was still true, for another month or so, when the sale would be finalised. For a moment she wondered who might have bought the property from the bank, but quickly dismissed the thought. That part of her life was over, and she did not want to think about the house, for this invariably led to thoughts of Mrs Watkins and Ham, and Maria and even her mother. Thoughts she had to keep at bay or she would be overwhelmed by them.

Miss Congrove read over Elinor's shoulder, and led her along the hall to a room with an open door, adorned with a sign in the ubiquitous mock Gothic gilt letters 'School Secretary'.

Inside, a thin, elderly lady wearing a gold-rimmed pince-nez was working behind a long green leather-topped mahogany desk that would not have been out of place for a senior partner at a bank or solicitor's firm. An electric lamp shone brightly on her desk, making Elinor realise the light in the hall had also been electric. The only place she'd seen electric lights before was the railway station in Bain.

'A visitor for Mrs Tallowe,' announced the girl. 'Miss Elinor Hallett of Coldhallow House.'

'Good afternoon,' said the woman stiffly, rising from her chair. 'I am Mrs Harmer, the school secretary. Is Mrs Tallowe expecting you, Miss Hallett? I had not had word, and the staff do not generally entertain visitors during the week.'

Elinor inclined her head.

'I am sorry to say that it is a family matter that brings me to see Mrs Tallowe,' she said. 'A death, in fact.'

'Oh!' exclaimed Mrs Harmer. A slight intake of breath from behind Elinor made the secretary glare through the gold-framed eyeglasses. 'Return to the front door, Wilhelmina.'

Elinor was unable to stop herself exclaiming 'Wilhelmina!' though she did manage to lower her voice.

'Those silly books,' said Mrs Harmer with a heartfelt sigh. 'We have a dozen Wilhelminas currently at the school. We do not allow them to use "Billie", of course.'

'Of course,' muttered Elinor.

'I will have someone inform Mrs Tallowe you are here,' said the secretary. 'Would you care to wait in our visitors' drawing room? I will have tea sent in. Tea is calming when bad news must be imparted.'

'Thank you,' replied Elinor. 'You are very kind.'

'Not at all,' said Mrs Harmer. She walked out from behind her desk to give a surprisingly hefty tug on a bellpull in the corner of her office. 'The drawing room is to the left as you go out, the second door on. It has a sign.'

Elinor nodded and went out. Wilhelmina had returned to her seat by the front door, and was sitting stiffly at attention. Other than the hall monitor, there was no one else about, but Elinor could hear the susurrus of a large number of girls reciting something somewhere deeper inside the school, perhaps mathematical tables.

She walked past the next door, which bore the sign 'Deputy Headmistress', and stopped before the one after, which was indeed marked as 'Drawing Room – Visitors'. Someone at the school liked everything labelled, Elinor thought. The signs were all uniform, written in the same hand, and didn't look that old.

The drawing room was rather dim, lit only by a single electric lamp and what light made its way in from the lone window. There were several armchairs and, surprisingly, a piano in the corner. The walls were not wainscoted as in the hall, but painted plaster, in what Elinor considered a slightly bilious green. There was another door, which surprisingly did not have a sign on it. Unable to help herself, Elinor went to it and tried the handle, but it was locked.

A slim bookcase in the corner proved of little interest, containing only dusty volumes of classic works Elinor had either read or knew enough about that she would never willingly read them. Apart from that, there was a single moderately good painting on one wall, of the school itself at some earlier date, which bore a bronze plate engraved with 'The School, by a former student'. It was signed in the bottom right corner, but Elinor couldn't make out the name. Judging from the clothing and the parasols of the girls promenading down the front drive, it had been painted a hundred years ago, or thereabouts.

The door opening behind her drew Elinor away from the painting. A maid in a white pinafore over a very plain brown dress came in with a teapot, cups and saucers, milk jug and a battered sugar bowl on a tin tray.

'Tea, miss,' she said, putting the tray on a side table by the chairs.

'Thank you,' said Elinor. The maid ducked her head and hurried out again. Elinor watched her go, and wondered how she would perform even such basic tasks. She could make and serve tea, of course, but there was the ducking of the head, the not meeting people's eyes, the being humble and not joining conversations and so on. Mrs Watkins hadn't been like that, or Cook, or even Maria. But Elinor knew Coldhallow had not been a normal household.

She sat down, but thought she'd better wait for Magistrix . . . no, Mrs Tallowe, before pouring the tea. It was interesting 'Magistrix' was not a word recognised by Wilhelmina and obviously not used in the school, or not used widely. Perhaps even though magic was taught here, it was not talked about, Elinor considered. She remembered what Dr Bannow had said about officialdom turning a blind eye to magic in the North. Likely it was the same here at the school. Thinking of this, she pulled her straw hat down a little lower at the front, making sure her Charter mark was hidden.

She sat alone for a few minutes more, trying not to think about what had happened and what her life might become now. Her side ached, though the wound had healed and Dr Bannow was happy with her recovery and said this pain would pass in time. Her wrists ached too, though there was only the faintest sign of hot, burning fingermarks. Dr Bannow was less confident about that pain ever disappearing. She simply didn't know.

There was a knock on the door, a polite rap before entry. The woman who came in was neither tall nor short, and was not distinctive, other than the dark green scarf she wore. Concealing her forehead, Elinor noted. Apart from that she looked to be in her forties and was sensibly attired in several layers of unfashionable grey flannel. The scarf was the only touch of colour about her. Even her eyes were grey.

'Miss Hallett?' she asked, her voice anxious. 'I am Abigail Tallowe. Is it my sister? Has . . . has she passed away?'

Elinor stood up and inclined her head.

'No,' she said quickly. 'No one close. In fact I am not even sure you knew my mother, Amelia Hallett.'

'Amelia Hallett? I don't think so . . .' faltered Mrs Tallowe. She walked to the closest chair and sat down in it, rather too swiftly than could be comfortable. Elinor thought perhaps she wasn't so much relieved her sister hadn't died as disappointed. There was something in the set of her mouth.

'Her mother, my grandmother, was Myrien Clayr,' said Elinor. 'Or Myrien of the Clayr, if you will.'

Mrs Tallowe looked swiftly around the room and back at the still-open door. Elinor watched, waiting for her to speak.

'It is best to speak quietly of any matters to do with . . . the North,' said Mrs Tallowe finally, her voice low. 'Myrien? I believe she was my grandmother's cousin. No close connection. Nevertheless, thank you for letting me know.'

She stood up and took a step towards the door.

'That's not all,' said Elinor. She felt a surge of recklessness well up inside her and removed her hat. Mrs Tallow saw the mark on her forehead and stopped.

'I believe it is customary for us to touch each other's mark,' said Elinor.

Mrs Tallowe hesitated for a long second.

'Oh, very well,' she said crossly. She went to the door and closed it, before turning back and removing her scarf.

143

'You do understand that most people around here prefer to not be reminded of the Old Kingdom and all that comes from it?'

'I do indeed,' said Elinor, thinking of her mother.

They both reached out at the same time, and touched each other's marks. Elinor had done this with Dr Bannow several times in the hospital, and had not fainted, learning to accept the sudden immersion in the immensity of the Charter. But the experience had also not been as intense or powerful as when she'd touched Terciel's mark. Perhaps because even though she was closer to the Wall by many miles, the wind was not blowing from the north.

This time the experience was even less significant, and in fact could almost be described as pallid. Elinor felt the presence of the Charter in the other woman, but it was distant, not the all-encompassing immersion she'd had before. The Charter was not corrupted inside the teacher. It was simply less present.

Mrs Tallowe, for her part, drew her finger back very quickly, and her face paled.

'There,' she said. 'Both of us true bearers of the Charter. As I said, thank you for visiting, and I am sorry for your loss—'

'I want you to teach me Charter Magic,' said Elinor, rather more bluntly than she'd planned.

'What? Teach you . . . No! I only teach girls here at the school, from the old families who want it. They all know it is not to be spoken of elsewhere. Who told you I teach magic here?'

'Terciel,' replied Elinor, stretching the facts a little. 'The Abhorsen-in-Waiting.'

Mrs Tallowe stepped back and looked from side to side, as if fearing an ambush.

'That's . . . that's . . . anyway, I cannot. It is a long tradition of the school, and so allowed, provided it is done discreetly. A student from outside would attract attention the school authorities would not welcome, not at all. I absolutely refuse.'

'What if I was here at the school, in some capacity?' asked Elinor.

'We do not take new students after the Fourth Form,' said Mrs Tallowe. 'Certainly not straight into the Sixth. How old are you, anyway?'

'Nineteen,' replied Elinor. 'But I was not thinking of becoming a student—'

'You are too old in any case,' interrupted Mrs Tallowe. 'Now, you must go!'

'I was thinking of obtaining a post as a school servant,' said Elinor, halting Mrs Tallowe's rush to the door.

The older woman positively shrieked and held a fist to her mouth, before managing to cough out, 'No! No! I cannot possibly have even a distant relation as a servant here! Think what the girls would make of it! And my colleagues! I positively forbid it!'

'I doubt you will be able to stop me,' said Elinor, drawing herself up to her full height, which still left her several inches shorter than Mrs Tallowe.

Mrs Tallowe drew in a long breath and deliberately refastened her scarf, pulling it low on her forehead. Her nails were bitten to the quick, Elinor noted.

'I have been a teacher here for nineteen years,' she said, very stiffly. 'Nineteen years of dedicated service. If I go to the Head and ask her to not hire a servant, or indeed to dismiss one, I believe she would do as I ask.'

Elinor believed her too and sighed.

'I am sorry I offended you,' she said, conscious of a bridge burned and no other river crossings anywhere in sight. 'I did not mean to do so. I need to learn Charter Magic, so I may go into the Old Kingdom.'

'You will not learn it from me!' snapped Mrs Tallowe. 'And if you go into the Old Kingdom you will likely die, and quickly, making you even more foolish than you now appear. Good day!'

She flung the door open and stormed out.

Elinor waited a full minute, breathing slowly, centring herself. She had handled Mrs Tallowe badly, she knew, badly enough it seemed unlikely a recovery was possible. She would not be learning magic from Magistrix Tallowe, to add to the few small spells she had already learned from Dr Bannow, all that the good doctor knew.

Sighing, she went out into the hall. Wilhelmina watched her from the front door. Elinor smiled at her, to hide her own disappointment and to try to put a brave face on matters. As she reached the bust of Breakespear, this forced optimism welled to the surface.

Elinor stopped, turned to face the poet playwright, and in a loud, confident voice said:

Come the flood up the river, bearing boats
Home, deep laden with the spoils of the sea

Wilhelmina stood up and clapped. Elinor bowed as Ham had taught her, and then effortlessly turned that into a series of cartwheels along the hall, ending with a full twist and perfect landing in front of the astonished schoolgirl.

'Who,' said a strong, authoritarian voice behind her, 'are you, to declaim and cavort in *my* school!'

Elinor spun around. A broad-shouldered, silver-haired woman dressed all in black save for the fine lace at her throat and wrists had emerged from one of the doors along the hall, the sign on it not visible, and unnecessary in the circumstances. This could be none other than the headmistress, who Elinor had heard about when first making inquiries in Bain about Wyverley College. The redoubtable Professor Kinrosh, champion of women's education, who had helped found not one but two of the women's colleges at Inglesham in Corvere and in her 'retirement' had come here to Wyverley, where she had long ago been a student herself.

'I'm, I'm Miss Elinor Hallett,' replied Elinor, bowing. She didn't know why. It was a very old-fashioned thing to do.

'Know your Breakespear, do you?' asked the woman. She strode towards the door, her heavy, sensible shoes sounding like the drumbeat for an execution to Elinor. 'What's that from, hmm?'

'*The Nets of Thetis*, Act Four, Scene Two,' replied Elinor. 'Duke Esperosa's speech on the battlements, watching the fishing fleet come in.'

'Not knowing they carry his drowned daughter with them,' replied Professor Kinrosh. 'And the acrobatic display?'

Elinor hesitated, not sure for a moment how to answer. She felt there was opportunity in this conversation, but she also felt she could mess it up. She couldn't tell whether this woman was a bastion of proper behaviour and so she had already put herself beyond the pale, or . . .

It didn't matter, Elinor decided. She would never be ashamed of Ham, or what she had learned from him.

'I was taught by a master juggler and acrobat,' she said, very clearly. 'Ham Corbin.'

'Ham Corbin.'

The name stopped the older woman in mid-stride. She smiled at Elinor, but her eyes looked past her, back into time.

'There's a name I've not heard for many years,' said Professor Kinrosh. 'I saw him first as a child, several times, when the Great and Wonderful Circus came through. Never frequently enough for us, a year or two or three apart. Something never to be forgotten, and he was a wonder among wonders. Is he still performing?'

'No,' said Elinor, choking up. She wiped a tear from her eye. 'I'm afraid not. He's dead.'

'He was a relative of yours?'

The old woman was close now, bending her head to look down at Elinor. She was taller than she'd seemed from a distance. Older too, her face very wrinkled under heavy powder. But her eyes were a brilliant brown, the same as they'd been all her long life.

'No,' whispered Elinor. 'He was my governess's uncle, and a dear friend.'

Surprisingly, Professor Kinrosh reached out and carefully, slowly pushed the brim of Elinor's hat down. It had ridden up when she did the cartwheels and the twist, revealing her Charter mark, which was now hidden again.

'Why are you here?' asked the headmistress. It was not an aggressive or judgmental question.

'Oh,' said Elinor. 'I . . . I came to see Mrs Tallowe. I . . . she is a distant cousin . . .'

'And?' asked Professor Kinrosh. She had the sort of gaze that defied any attempt at falsehood or misdirection, as many a schoolgirl, teacher and fellow academic had found over the years.

'I had hoped she might teach me magic,' whispered Elinor. 'And I hoped to secure work of some kind at the school. As a servant.'

'Really?' asked the professor. 'Where is your home? Your family?'

'I have none. My father died long ago,' said Elinor. 'My mother recently. And our home is gone. Burned and repossessed.'

'There is a story behind all that, I'm sure,' said Kinrosh. 'But, perhaps to our loss, we do not take on young women of your class or background as servants here. Why come here in particular?'

'I do have relatives in the Old Kingdom,' said Elinor. 'I want to prepare myself to go there. Nowhere else teaches magic, and in the meantime I have to find some way to make a living.'

'I see,' said the professor thoughtfully. 'You know your Breakespear. You can tumble and juggle. Do you act?'

'I have done,' replied Elinor, surprised. 'Privately. Not . . . not to an audience.'

'And sing?'

'Passably.'

'Instruments?'

'Piano, reed pipe, mandolin, drum,' replied Elinor in a daze. 'Ham said I was adequate, "good enough for the fair", to be exact . . .'

She wiped another tear away.

'Hmm,' said the professor. She reached out and took Elinor's arm, urging her back down the hall, not out the front door. 'The school play this year is *The Court of the Sad Prince* and it is not coming along well. The comic fights are distressingly bad and the fooling worse. Madame Lancier – our drama teacher – and I have been wondering what to do, and now you are here! A disciple of Ham Corbin, who played the Prince's Fool for two years at the Birdcage in Corvere! The tickets were impossible to get, you know, the most sought-after things in the capital. But Corbin would throw a dozen to the crowd before each performance, and once . . . once one of those tickets landed in the hand of an undeserving student who thus was able to see one of the most incredible theatrical performances of her long life. I will never forget it.'

'He never told me *that*,' said Elinor. The tears were coming fast now, faster than she could brush them away. 'Neither did Mrs Watkins. But what . . . what do you mean about your play, and me a disciple . . .'

'I am offering you employment, my dear,' said the professor as she ushered Elinor into yet another drawing room, this one more palatially furnished, better lit and clearly more frequently used. 'As a temporary teacher's assistant to help with the play, to assist Madame Lancier with the staging and direction, most particularly with the fooling. Lodgings at the school are provided, and twenty-seven pounds a year, paid monthly, though I fear we can only take you until the end of next term, when the play will be performed. But if your intention is to go into the Old Kingdom, perhaps that is time enough.'

'Thank you,' muttered Elinor. She dried her eyes as elegantly as she could manage with two fingers as Mrs Watkins had taught her, rather than the back of her hand. 'You are very kind.'

'Nonsense! We will have tea, and you can tell me all about what has happened, and your plans,' said Professor Kinrosh. 'For I can see that there is a great deal more to your story. Take the yellow chair, child. The green one is mine.'

10

Terciel slept almost until noon, and then had to hurry. He had several sendings attend on him. Brusque, ancient servitors who hustled him into his bath, which was delightfully hot and welcome. There were hot springs far below the House and the water was piped from there. He had long since got used to the slightly sulphurous smell that came with it. One of the sendings shaved him, a strange sensation when its Charter-spelled fingers touched his face, lifting his chin or pulling on one ear. A sending would have dressed him as well, but he waved it away, putting on the soft shirt, loose trousers and slippers that were his usual comfortable garb when he was home. He tried to avoid putting on the heavier surcoat embroidered with the silver keys of the Abhorsens, but both sendings joined forces to slip it over his head and it was easier not to resist them. A supple leather belt and a jewelled dagger in a silver-banded scabbard completed the ensemble, and he managed to duck the sending who tried to fit a velvet cap on his head as he left.

A sending in a blue-and-silver tabard preceded him to the hall, the biggest and most impressive room in the house, which took up half the ground floor. Terciel sighed, because this meant Tizanael was in an unforgiving mood and was going to be all ceremonial with the visiting Clayr. If she was feeling more relaxed, the meeting would have been in her study, upstairs in the tower, or maybe even in the kitchen.

As usual, when there were distinguished visitors, the sendings had brought out all the trappings. The hall was dominated by a very long table of a bright, lustrous wood and it was laden with silver. Ornaments and decorations of uncertain purpose lined up with salt cellars and candelabra and chafing dishes all the way down the middle of the table, and each of the three settings at the end was arranged for a dozen courses, with seven different drinking vessels. For some reason, the hall sendings always set out massive drinking horns banded in gold and amber along with the more usual glasses of fine Belisaere crystal, even though no one ever drank from them and Terciel didn't even know what you might fill them with.

Tizanael was standing at the western end, in front of the floor-to-ceiling stained-glass window, which was a creation more of Charter Magic than iron and coloured glass. It mostly depicted the building of the Wall, though sometimes it changed to show other scenes from far-off days. It was the Wall today, with stonemasons labouring with the actual blocks of stone and rows and rows of Charter Mages, the long-gone Wallmakers, who were engaged in some sort of vast cooperative spell, surrounded by a storm of marks. At the far end, those mages appeared to be actually disappearing into the half-built wall, merging with the stone. As per usual it was hard to remember what you had seen when you looked away.

The Abhorsen was dressed more formally than Terciel, and he felt her gaze of disapproval at his relatively casual attire. She wore a deep blue robe stitched with thousands of silver keys, high-collared; a five-tiered necklace of cascading moonstones; a sash of silver under a velvet-covered leather belt, and her sword. A plain weapon, apart from the emerald in the pommel and the play of Charter marks on every part of it. The sword was a symbol of her office, as much as the bells.

A sending hammered the suspended bronze gong by the door, making Terciel jump. They only did that for visitors and it always surprised him. He tried to turn the nervous jump into a more planned about-turn to meet the visitor, but knew he looked clumsy. The Clayr always made him nervous, ever since he'd first visited their glacier a few years before and had encountered their very straightforward approach to sex. He was considered a suitable partner for the young Clayr who simply wanted to enjoy themselves and the generally somewhat older Clayr who wanted to have a baby and considered him as a potential father. Or to be more accurate, he thought, a sire in the same way a stallion might meet a mare and then the two would never meet again.

Terciel, who had limited social experience anyway, was unsettled by both approaches. He found the ubiquitous keenness of the Clayr to talk about why he found it unsettling even worse, including from Clayr who he'd not had intimate relationships with and never would. Nearly all of them talked about everything with each other, as far as he could tell, and after his first few excited encounters as a sixteen-year-old man sowing his wild oats, he had quickly decided the safest thing was not to give them anything to talk about. When that did not really work, as they then wanted to talk about his newfound celibacy, staying away from the Clayr's Glacier and the Clayr in general became attractive, and not difficult to achieve, as Tizanael – for her own, quite different reasons – was not keen on the Clayr.

Then there was the whole business of them being able to see the future. Or *possible* futures, as they always said. Any individual Clayr might get glimpses of times to come, usually visions in ice, glass or water, but there was no certainty what they saw would come to pass. Over millennia the Clayr had refined the process, joining together in cooperative groups to refine these visions and work out which futures were most likely. They collectively called this grouping the Nine Day Watch, which ranged from a small group of forty-nine to a watch of one thousand five hundred and sixty-eight, which included almost all adult Clayr who possessed the Sight. This largest group was only ever called to try to pin down a particular future event or danger of extreme importance, and even then, couldn't always do so.

For Terciel, it was the small, everyday foretellings that made him nervous. A Clayr seeing where he would be in several hours and meeting him there. One getting him a drink in the refectory of the Clayr's Glacier because she'd seen what he'd be drinking, and she was right, it was his favourite, a Belisaeran ale he would have chosen.

The Clayr who came into the Great Hall did not lessen Terciel's nervousness.

Like nearly all of them, she was brown-skinned, with pale blue eyes and blonde hair. She was not wearing the white robe and circlet of silver and moonstones that was the Clayr's formal garb. Instead she was in leather armour reinforced at the shoulders, elbows and knees with mail, without a surcoat, though the star of the Clayr was embroidered in gold thread directly on the breastplate. It was the uniform of the Clayr's Rangers, Terciel knew, those who patrolled the Glacier and the close approaches. Most Clayr never left their vast underground fortress; the Rangers were among the few who did. But even they rarely went much further than the foothills around the two great mountains that cradled the Glacier between them. It had been a long time since the Clayr were more actively involved in shaping the future of the Old Kingdom, rather than trying to discern what it was to be, amid many contradictory visions.

'Greetings, Abhorsen,' she said, inclining her head to Tizanael and then Terciel. 'And Abhorsen-in-Waiting. I am Mirelle, lieutenant of the Rangers of the Clayr.'

Terciel bowed in return. He hadn't met Mirelle before, and from her introduction, neither had Tizanael. She looked to be about ten years older than he was. Not one of the younger Clayr who had looked upon him as an enjoyable but transient sexual partner, but she was of an age with some of those he'd encountered who wanted a baby fathered. And she was bound to want to talk about how he felt about that, at length. So he was still nervous.

'You are welcome,' replied Tizanael. She didn't move from in front of the huge stained-glass window. In the lighter portions of it, depicting the sky, it was possible to see through to the outside, blurred shadows indicating that it had started to snow. 'Did you find it?'

'Yes. In fact, we Saw you needed it before your message-hawk was received. The librarians started the search days ago,' replied Mirelle. She held up a small iron box that so crawled with Charter marks it was hard to make out its exact dimensions, its edges blurred in gold light.

Tizanael did come forward then, eagerly.

'The box has been warded as strongly as the librarians could manage,' said Mirelle. 'They told me the book inside is very dangerous, heavily laden with Free Magic, and warded against all but the Abhorsen. They didn't even *try* to read it themselves, so I believe this is true.'

'Then it is the book I have sought,' said Tizanael, with grim satisfaction.

'What book?' asked Terciel.

'One that should never have left our own library,' replied Tizanael, taking the box from Mirelle. 'I had thought it lost, till I found a letter confirming that a number of books salvaged from the ruins of Hillfair were not brought here, but taken to the Clayr instead.'

'What book?' repeated Terciel. He was used to Tizanael's reticence. It was unhelpful, he thought, but it appeared to be an enduring habit she was unable to break.

'It is called *On the Making of Necromantic Bells and Other Devices*,' replied Tizanael. 'By the Abhorsen Lerantiel. One of the earliest in the line, the fourteenth.'

'The Clayr are pleased to return it to the Abhorsens,' said Mirelle, bowing.

'Thank you,' said Tizanael. She hesitated, then started towards the door, holding the box. She called over her shoulder, 'Continue your lessons tomorrow, Terciel. Entertain our guest today. I must study this book carefully, and I cannot do so without the proper precautions and preparation, and I hope it will also lead me to something else long lost, which is possibly within the House. You may not see me for some time.'

'Why do you have to read it?' called out Terciel.

'To deal with Kerrigor once and for all,' answered Tizanael without turning around.

A sending opened the door, the Abhorsen whisked out, and Terciel was left with Mirelle, who looked at him and raised one expressive eyebrow.

'Is she always like that? I had heard tales, but . . .'

'She is,' confirmed Terciel awkwardly. 'Um, would you like some luncheon? The sendings have put out a variety of things.'

'Enough to feed a dozen or more,' said Mirelle, casting her eye over the dishes laid out on the table.

'They always do that when we have guests,' said Terciel.

'Though one dish has been sampled already,' said Mirelle, pointing to a silver platter that had half a salmon laid out on it. Not an artfully split fish, bisected from head to tail, but simply the tail and about two inches of the body, the rest torn away.

Terciel dropped to one knee to look under the table, just in time to see the white-furred dwarf scuttling away, down on all fours, the other half of the salmon in his mouth. He did not stand up when he reached the end of the table, but raced through the open kitchen door.

'Moregrim,' he said, surprised the strange, white-furred man had been in the hall with Tizanael. 'I hope you didn't want fish, Mirelle.'

Mirelle was still looking out the kitchen door.

'Moregrim? I have heard other names,' she said. 'An ancient spirit, a servant of the Abhorsens?'

'Yes,' said Terciel. 'Tizanael says he is safe enough, if he is firmly directed.'

'I hope so,' said Mirelle, her eyes narrowed. 'That is a Free Magic creature of a high order. Something we would do our best to kill or banish if we encountered it anywhere the Clayr hold sway.'

'Moregrim is tightly bound,' repeated Terciel. He tried to sound confident, though he had his own doubts about the dwarf, and the red belt with its miniature version of the bell Saraneth. 'Would you care to eat? Wine?'

'I will eat,' said Mirelle, pulling out a chair and sitting down before the nearest sending could do it for her. Forestalled, it sidestepped and drew out a chair for

Terciel before he could do so himself. 'As it happens, I wanted to talk to you, Terciel, as well as bringing the book to Tizanael.'

'Oh,' replied Terciel cautiously, sitting down. He couldn't help but shift uneasily across his chair, to be somewhat further away. 'What about?'

'We have always Seen you, off and on,' said Mirelle easily, once again thwarting a sending by pouring her own wine. 'As we tend to have visions of the prominent persons of the Kingdom. But nothing of significance or at any distance in time, until recently. But twice now the Nine Day Watch has Seen you.'

'Oh,' repeated Terciel. He took an overly large swig of his own wine, just poured by a sending, and almost choked.

'Yes,' said Mirelle. 'Unfortunately not as clear visions as we would wish. Nothing is, of course, these last few hundred years.'

Terciel nodded. He knew about that, at least in essence. About a hundred and eighty years ago, the son of the ruling Queen had slain his mother and his sisters, and something else had happened that he felt he almost knew about but could never pin down or remember had happened, something that affected all Charter Magic. He kept meaning to ask Tizanael about it, but somehow never did. Prince Rogir had been killed, but the aftereffects of whatever he had done continued.

'And, of course, we have Seen only some of the possible futures. But a number of them indicate that you will father two children with women of the Clayr.'

Terciel did choke on his wine this time. He clutched at a linen napkin, coughing into it as a sending smacked him between the shoulder blades.

'Not soon, I should add,' continued Mirelle, reaching over to spear several slices of saffron-crusted beef with her fork. She appeared to be enjoying herself. 'In fact, it looks like the two will be many years separate, and born to different mothers.'

Terciel choked again, after having just managed to get his breath.

'These are only possible futures, but there are indications your potential children will be very significant to the Kingdom,' said Mirelle. 'Naturally, this makes you of even more interest to us than you were already.'

'I . . . I don't want to have any children,' rasped Terciel. He took a sip of wine and tried to clear his throat.

'Why not?' asked Mirelle.

Terciel grimaced. This was why he avoided the Clayr.

'I don't want to discuss the matter,' he said.

'But I do,' said Mirelle.

'It isn't anything to do with you,' mumbled Terciel, even as the horrible thought came into his mind that maybe she had Seen herself as one of these two possible mothers. The Clayr were very ready to make futures they had Seen and liked to come about, if they could do so. Though how she could imagine she might seduce him here—

Mirelle laughed.

'The look on your face! You are so transparent, Terciel. I have not come here to take you to bed, young man. My hearth-mate back home would not be happy, for one thing, and for another, we have not Seen the individual Clayr you may lie with, only . . . symbology . . . that indicates they are Clayr. Also, in our visions you are older, in one of the visions much older. As for it having nothing to do with me, it does have a great deal to do with the kingdom we both serve. So tell me, why do you not want to have children?'

Terciel stared into his wine.

'I am an orphan,' he said, after a long silence. 'My parents died when I was very young. I cannot remember them. My sister, Rahiniel, left me and died before I ever had the chance to see her again. I have only the vaguest memory of her. Tizanael took me in solely because she needed an apprentice, and I was more likely than most to survive, because of my heritage, my blood.

'I have become the Abhorsen-in-Waiting, knowing more of Death than Life. I have nothing but this. Nothing but the work we do, the necessary work, I acknowledge that. How can anyone love me, knowing what I am? How can I love anyone else? And why would I want to bring a child into this world, an Abhorsen child doomed to follow in my footsteps?'

Mirelle did not laugh this time. She looked directly at Terciel, who did not meet her gaze.

'We See many futures,' said Mirelle at last. 'The awful and the bright, mixed sometimes beyond any unravelling. But we can never be absolutely sure what will come. We can only See the good that might be and work towards making it come about, or we can try to turn back the evil happenings. A child brought into the world has no more certain future than anyone else. We strive to make them safe and loved and equip them to both withstand the bad things and to make the most of the good.

'To be an Abhorsen is to carry the weight of terrible responsibility, but your life can be more than that, and you can both love and be loved. You can make space for love in your life, for happiness, for peace, even if they are but fleeting moments of sunshine and calm amid the ongoing storm.'

'Make the best of it?' asked Terciel sarcastically.

'I do not know a better philosophy for living,' answered Mirelle. She hesitated. 'You are young. I know, only in some ways! You know death and dying, none better. But I think you need to set your mind more upon how you will live and love.'

'I follow Tizanael, and do as I am told,' said Terciel bitterly. He took another deep draft of wine, emptying his glass and quickly poured it full to the brim, before a sending could give him a more conservative portion.

'Tizanael has found her own way,' said Mirelle. 'One of endurance, with no room for anything save duty. It works for her, but is that what you want? Other Abhorsens have found different ways to live, to love, to have families and still to do what they must for the Kingdom.'

'I don't want to be like Tizanael, that's for sure,' muttered Terciel, surprising himself. He'd never really thought about his own future much. He was always so focused on learning, following Tizanael's strict instructions, defeating their foes . . .

'Does the walker choose the path, or the path the walker?' asked Mirelle softly.

'What?' asked Terciel. He knew the phrase well, for it was the last line of *The Book of the Dead*, the dread volume he had studied since he was a child, with its ever-shifting text, the bone-penetrating tingle of Free Magic in every page, held back by the Charter marks that were infused throughout. Only a necromancer could open *The Book of the Dead*, and only an uncorrupted Charter Mage could close it, at least the copy the Abhorsens held.

'The final line of the Abhorsens' principal book,' said Mirelle. 'I know that much, though I have never read it.'

'I've never understood what that line means,' said Terciel. 'Tizanael has typically never explained it to me.'

'I doubt it can be explained,' said Mirelle. 'But it is a good question to think on.'

'I'm not having a child with a Clayr or anyone else,' said Terciel, draining his glass again. He let the sending fill it this time. He was never much of a drinker, and he was feeling the effects of the wine already, not in a good way. He felt angry and belligerent, not relaxed at all.

'You must do as you see fit,' said Mirelle. She turned away from him to select various other foodstuffs to put on her plate, and changed the subject. 'As must we all. I, for example, must fly back to the Glacier this afternoon, and despite the warming spells, it will be cold, so I take on fuel against it. Try the saffron beef. It is very good.'

Terciel nodded, and reached over, glad the conversation had turned to ordinary things.

But his thoughts had not.

11

The forcefulness of Professor Kinrosh could not be resisted. Elinor took the job, signed an employment contract, and within an hour of having tea with the headmistress was being shown her room by one of the school servants and shortly after that was watching a rehearsal of *The Court of the Sad Prince* and was immediately called upon by Madame Lancier to choreograph six courtiers falling down in a line like ninepins when the fool tumbled into the leader of the file.

Within a week, Elinor loved being at Wyverley College, and though she tried not to, resented her mother even more. She would have loved to have been a student at the school. Being a teacher's assistant, though still in many ways wonderful, was not the same as having been there for years, growing up with other girls and finding lifelong friends. She was also, for the first time in her life, suddenly aware that she had missed out on learning things the girls took for granted, though she did not begrudge the peculiarities of her own circus-based learning from Ham, interleaved with the very old-fashioned curriculum taught by Mrs Watkins, using the textbooks she'd had herself as a young girl, which even then had been fifty years out of date.

She loved being part of a proper theatre troupe, or as close to it as could be. Madame Lancier had in her younger life been a professional performer in Corvere, and she was an inspired teacher. Elinor had been worried she would not like having an assistant with no experience thrust upon her by Professor Kinrosh, but she took to Elinor immediately and put her in charge of all the clowning, fighting and horseplay of *The Court of the Sad Prince*, which, as the headmistress had said, did need attention. She had to particularly work with Corinna, the Sixth Former who played the Prince's Fool, to help her with the juggling and tumbling and conjuring, much of which they had been about to cut out for lack of a proper tutor, Madame Lancier's skills being more in voice and dancing.

Magistrix Tallowe ignored her as much possible, so that learning Charter Magic seemed out of reach, but Elinor found there *was* another teacher at Wyverley who could help her with her preparations to journey into the Old Kingdom even if it was not with Charter Magic. She had no idea Wyverley College continued to offer the old-fashioned and generally long-vanished subject called 'Fighting Arts' until one of her juggling rehearsals for the cast of the play went overtime in the gymnasium.

The Fighting Arts teacher, a whip-thin, hard-faced woman from the distant south of the continent, where she had been a soldier, police officer and hunting guide, was Miss Sargraya, or 'Sarge' as the girls called her, apparently with her permission. One afternoon she came over to watch Elinor demonstrate juggling a knife, fork and spoon as her own class assembled with their practice swords.

A discussion on throwing knives led to Elinor explaining and then demonstrating the swordplay Ham had taught her, both the theatrical and the real, and this led to her being immediately co-opted as Sarge's assistant in Fighting Arts in addition to her work with Madame Lancier on the play.

Somewhere along the way, Elinor told Sarge of her ambition to go into the Old Kingdom and was immediately dragooned into individual classes to help her improve her swordplay, particularly to overcome her tendency to default to the showier, theatrical techniques. She was already a fine archer, but Sarge helped her with shooting multiple times fast, and targeting weak spots in armour or hide. Though she did not have the mark, and did not talk about it, Elinor got the impression that Sargraya might have visited the Old Kingdom. She certainly did not discount its dangers.

Apart from her quickly all-consuming work, Elinor found her new living arrangements not markedly different from what they had been at Coldhallow House. There was a row of houses for the teachers behind the main school building. She shared one of these with two other teachers' assistants, both of them much older and set in their ways. She ate her meals in the junior staff room, her place allocated and changed weekly by some unknown formula. It may have been intended to help the junior staff mix, but it did not help Elinor. She was well aware that news and gossip moved mysteriously but swiftly in the school, and she was not only an unknown newcomer but also one who had the Charter mark but was not welcomed by Mrs Tallowe.

Nor was she allowed to make friends with the students. This had been drummed into her by every teacher, that she could not earn and keep their respect if she was too friendly. Even though she was only a year older than the Sixth Formers, she must act as if there was a great void of years between them.

'Otherwise they will take advantage,' said Madame Lancier knowingly. Sarge more bluntly on a separate occasion said, 'The girls can be very cruel, and most consider the teachers as a form of common enemy, yourself included.'

It was very hard to remember this advice, particularly as Elinor liked most of the students she worked with, and she enjoyed their company working on the play. She particularly liked Corinna, and had felt an unusual sense of kinship for her, something that was explained when they were alone late one evening practising the very difficult bushel of apples, bottle of wine and loaf of bread in the coracle scene, where the Fool had to paddle the coracle, drink from the wine, eat the bread and catch spilling apples while rowing across to the island bower where the Prince awaited Lady Heartsease, only to be told by the Fool she'd gone to the other island.

The coracle, for this performance, was a papier-mâché construction on a wheeled platform that would be drawn across the stage behind an illusion of the sea, created by sawing backwards and forth three lines of waves. Moving the waves and the coracle would require a grand total of nine stagehands according to the plan devised by Elinor and Madame Lancier, but that was all to come. Tonight, the coracle sat in the middle of the gymnasium, surrounded by padded mats for the inevitable stumbles and falls.

Elinor was helping Corinna practise juggling the short paddle, the bottle, the bread and an apple, kneeling and then standing up in the coracle. While juggling, the Fool delivered a soliloquy on why she shouldn't drink the Prince's wine, or eat his bread, or his apple, or misdirect Lady Heartsease, all of which she was doing. Corinna had learned the lines, but she couldn't yet manage the very difficult juggle and talk at the same time.

'You make it look easy!' protested Corinna, dropping the apple and then the paddle. Attempting to catch them, she fell over the side of the coracle with the ominous sound of torn papier-mâché and a thump as she hit the mats. 'Gosh! I've busted it!'

'Are you all right?' asked Elinor, hurrying to help her up. As she pulled the taller girl up, she saw her beret had slipped back, revealing a Charter mark, glowing in the dim light. 'Don't worry about the coracle, it'll be easy to patch up.'

'I'm . . . I'm fine . . .' faltered Corinna, seeing Elinor's surprised stare. She tugged her beret back down. 'I hope you're not one of the people who—'

'No!' exclaimed Elinor. She pushed back her own scarf, worn as a bandanna. The students had to wear the rather ugly uniform berets inside, and straw hats outside. Many of the teachers adopted similar if less uniform headgear. But everyone seemed to take Elinor's own bandanna as a suitably theatrical affectation.

'Oh!' exclaimed Corinna. She scratched her ear and hesitated. 'Er, my parents insist, if I meet someone who has the mark . . .'

'We must both check our marks are uncorrupted,' said Elinor. 'Yes, I know.'

They both reached out, and touched their forehead marks at the same time. Elinor smiled as she felt the Charter wash over her, a welcome experience even if it was not the all-consuming rush she'd felt when she'd first touched Terciel's mark. It was also a sharp reminder of her plan to go to the Old Kingdom. She wanted to fall into the Charter again, to learn how to do magic properly . . . the school was lovely, but she had to be careful not to get too accustomed to it. The Old Kingdom beckoned to her.

'That's all right, then,' said Corinna with relief, pulling back her hand and pulling her beret down again. 'Are you going to teach us magic instead of Mrs Tallowe?'

'No,' replied Elinor, surprised. 'I had hoped to learn from her myself, but she wasn't interested.'

It was Corinna's turn to be surprised.

'I thought you must be from the Old Kingdom! Your mark feels very strong.'

'No,' said Elinor. 'Though my grandmother came from there. I didn't even know what the Charter was a few months ago. My mother always told me the mark was a hideous scar.'

'Really?' exclaimed Corinna. 'I guess there is a lot of prejudice and stupid talk. From Southerners, I mean.'

'Are you from the Old Kingdom yourself?' asked Elinor awkwardly. She was uncomfortably aware that this was the sort of personal question she was not supposed to ask the students.

'Oh, no. But we live . . . my family has a farm only six miles from the Wall,' said Corinna. 'We all have the mark, and learn Charter Magic. At least, my brother and sister learned quite a lot and I'm supposed to, but it's a bit hard when your teacher hasn't got a clue . . .'

She stopped and put her hand over her mouth, and then mumbled through her fingers, 'Sorry, Miss Hallett. I momentarily forgot myself.'

Elinor frowned, but couldn't stop herself continuing the conversation.

'You mean Magistrix Tallowe?'

'Yes . . . no . . . I won't get in trouble for badmouthing a teacher?'

'No,' said Elinor, aware she was making a decision that might have very negative consequences. But she needed to know. 'Tell me.'

'Tallowe's a terrible Charter Mage. She's afraid of the Charter, I think. All we ever do in class is practise the same safe, basic things over and over again. Nothing very useful. I mean, I know more spells than Tallowe has ever shown us!'

'I asked her to teach me,' said Elinor ruefully. 'I wondered why she was so hostile. I didn't even think it might be because she doesn't want to teach magic at all. We're even some sort of cousins, of an Old Kingdom family, but she wouldn't help.'

'She shouldn't be called Magistrix,' said Corinna. 'The old one, Mrs Nestor, she was wonderful. Nestor taught my oldest sister, but she retired, too soon. Tallowe doesn't even look after the message-hawks properly. Hazra has to do it for her.'

'Hazra Callot? She's in my backstage crew. Is she one of the girls who are learning magic?' asked Elinor. 'How many of you are there?'

'I guess there's about sixteen of us who are *supposed* to be in magic classes – I mean, our parents pay for it. But since Tallowe's been so useless, most of the Sixth Formers skip it. Tallowe never reports anyone. We're not supposed to talk about it anyway, so I guess it's easy for her to get away with not teaching. I mean, obviously since you've got the mark, we can talk, but not . . .'

'I wish it was talked about,' said Elinor. 'It would have made a great difference to me. Anyway, we should get on with this practice. You're doing very well with the paddle and the apple, Corinna.'

'Not as well as you,' said Corinna. 'You should play the Fool. I mean the part of the Fool, I didn't mean—'

'I know!' laughed Elinor. 'But very wisely, every part must be played by a student.'

They practised in silence for some time, Elinor adjusting Corinna's stance and giving her tips. When they stopped again to let Corinna take a breather, the student shyly said, 'You know, Miss Hallett . . . even though Tallowe doesn't teach us anything useful, we . . . the senior students . . . we sort of have our own lessons. Independently. I mean we practise, and Hazra has a family grimoire. You could come along too.'

'It might get all of us in trouble,' said Elinor. Then, somewhat wistfully, 'What's a grim-wah?'

'A book of spells,' said Corinna. 'There's a way to write down Charter marks, or the most common ones anyway. Obviously there's too many in general. You should come. I mean, if you really want to learn magic.'

'Mmm,' said Elinor, trying to sound as noncommittal as possible. Inside, she felt an almost irresistible urge to shout 'yes, please' and 'let's start at once'.

'We meet every Thursday, after second prep,' said Corinna. 'Tallowe plays bezique with Miss Amarand every Thursday night, and she never goes to the magic room out of the official class time anyway.'

'The magic room?'

'We call it that,' said Corinna. 'It's a kind of old cellar. There's stairs down from the East Tower basement. It's kept locked, but we have keys. It's safe if anything goes wrong. Or safer, anyway.'

'Safer . . . what do you mean?'

'Oh, every magistrix – except Tallowe, of course, cos she's useless – set spells of warding and so on in the place,' said Corinna. 'Some of the old ones have worn out, but there are plenty still working. They're interesting spells, though beyond anything any of us know.'

Elinor nodded thoughtfully, picked up the paddle and handed it to Corinna.

'We'd better get back to it.'

'So you'll come along?' asked Corinna.

'We'll see,' said Elinor. 'Now, put the paddle in your left hand and take up one apple. That's it, have the basket by your knee. That's it. Go!'

Elinor slept badly that night, wondering what she should do, the temptation of magic classes constantly intruding in her thoughts and behind that the lure of the Old Kingdom. This was exacerbated in the morning, when a letter came for her, an official communication in a red-striped envelope, with the 'O.T.A.S.' for 'On the Arbiter's Service' stamp in the top left corner. It was a reply to an inquiry she'd sent on her first day at the school, as advised by Dr Bannow, the necessary first step to entering the Old Kingdom.

Dear Miss Hallett,

Re: Miss Elinor Hallett File 026/845

Your application to pass the Border as defined by the Geographical Limitations (Northern Ancelstierre) Act of 1747 has been approved, subject to the approval of the Officer Commanding Fort Entrance at the time of your travel. This letter must be presented and be countersigned by OC(FE) before onward travel or you may not be permitted to re-enter the Commonwealth.

You also must present OC(FE) with proof of permission to enter our neighbouring state, typically a letter of passage from the appropriate authority.

A receipt for your application fee of £1.3.6 is enclosed.

I remain yr obedient servant
[an indecipherable signature in purple ink]
Assistant to the Second Personal Secretary (Adjustment)
Chief Minister's Office
Corvere

Elinor read the letter after breakfast, in the half hour she had before first lesson, which that morning for her meant attending a full run-through rehearsal in the Great Hall. She'd been looking forward to this, because the Great Hall was the closest to a real theatre she'd ever been in, though the actual stage was still to be built, and it wouldn't be constructed at the western end until closer to the opening night, on Midwinter's Eve.

But even without the stage, the vast hall with its high ceiling and wonderful acoustics was thrilling, and it was going to be the first complete rehearsal where the play would be eventually performed, albeit without final costumes and most of the technical stagecraft like the moving coracle and so forth.

She managed to forget the letter and what it meant in the intense rehearsal, with everyone involved forgoing a proper lunch and making do with sandwiches brought in by several disgruntled servants, a rare concession to the usual routine of the school.

It wasn't until Madame Lancier clapped her hands and dismissed everyone at five o'clock that Elinor's mind turned once again to the Old Kingdom. She hurried to her room to sit on the end of her bed, and forced herself into the inward focus taught to her by

Ham, fighting back the relentless intrusion of memories. Mrs Watkins tumbling down under the Dead, Ham thrown backwards, slain in a single terrible moment. But she could make these memories subside only so far. They were always there, and she supposed they always would be, and she had to overcome them somehow or perhaps simply hold out long enough that they would begin to fade.

She did press them back far enough to clear her mind to think about the big question that faced her. Should she really leave this new life at the school for the uncertainties and dangers of the Old Kingdom? It was true she felt an incredible yearning to connect more strongly to the Charter. In part she knew that this was because it offered her peace, a refuge from what had happened, and as Mrs Watkins always said, wanting something didn't necessarily mean it would be good for you. Against that, Ham had argued that enjoying something was not a sin, and a passion for something was energy to be exploited, not thwarted.

Nothing needed to be decided soon, Elinor thought. She was only employed until the play finished its run, some eight weeks away. She thought there was a reasonable chance Madame Lancier or the Sarge or both together would want her to stay on, and Professor Kinrosh continued to be kind and supportive whenever Elinor crossed paths with her, which was not often, the headmistress having many duties.

But now she had the letter allowing her to leave Ancelstierre, it was a reminder she needed the other side sorted out as well. As the Assistant to the Second Personal Secretary said, 'a letter of passage from the appropriate authority', which meant, Dr Bannow had told her, a letter from the Regent in Belisaere; or one from the Abhorsen; or one from the Clayr, who Bannow didn't really know anything about.

Elinor wondered why the Ancelstierran letter didn't refer to the Old Kingdom, or Belisaere, or use any actual names. It was probably part of the official pretence that there was nothing of importance to the north, the denial of magic and so on, but it was even more odd in an official document.

Seeking such a letter from the Old Kingdom meant sending a message-hawk, which in turn meant getting Mrs Tallowe to do it. Or, Elinor supposed, sending a telegram from the nearest post office, which in practice meant the postal alcove at Wyverley Halt. But would Mrs Tallowe even send it on, if Elinor's name was on it? She never spoke to Elinor at all, and would look the other way if they happened to pass each other in a corridor, or were in the common room at the same time.

Then there was the tantalising possibility raised by Corinna, who had mentioned Hazra was the one who actually looked after the message-hawks. Perhaps she knew how to send one as well? Elinor wasn't sure how message-hawks worked, but it might be an alternative.

Amid all of this thinking, Elinor's mind kept circling back to the central question. Whether she went to the Old Kingdom or not, she could learn Charter Magic from Corinna and her friends. But if she joined them, it would be against the rules, even if not written-down ones, and would put her employment in jeopardy . . .

Elinor sighed and scratched her head, her hand unconsciously trailing down so her fingers rested against her Charter mark. Professor Kinrosh had given her a wonderful chance. What would she think about Elinor sneaking off to join a group of students who were learning magic without a teacher?

Mrs Watkins would tell her not to go, Elinor knew. But she thought Ham would say she should. She missed them both terribly, and for the thousandth time fought back tears.

They were gone. She had to decide for herself.

It was Wednesday. Tomorrow night Corinna and her companions would be gathering in the magic room. Elinor had already gone and looked at the locked door at the foot of the tower. Several times. If she went through it, there would be no going back, and the unexpected haven of Wyverley College might be lost to her forever.

Through Wednesday night and Thursday the decision weighed upon her. She vacillated one way and another, but through it all, had the uncomfortable feeling that she would be unable to resist the temptation. Several times during their practice in the afternoon she thought Corinna was looking at her strangely, and some of the other girls she'd never paid particular attention to also seemed to be watching.

She started to wonder if it was all a schoolgirl prank, that Corinna was setting her up for something, that Madame Lancier and the Sarge were right. Against that, Elinor had felt the true Charter within Corinna, and did not doubt what she had said about Mrs Tallowe – that all rang true.

When the bell tolled in the Scholars' Tower to mark the end of second prep, followed a few seconds later by the clock in the West Tower chiming nine times for the hour, Elinor went to the magic room, knocked on the door, and when it was opened, went in.

12

Tizanael was absent for almost three weeks, or rather Terciel kept missing her. He was fairly sure she was sleeping in her bedroom, but not for long, going to it after he was in bed, and rising before he got up. Whatever she was up to, it did not coincide with regular mealtimes or the schedule they normally followed when they were at the House. Nor could he find her in any of the usual places.

Puzzled by this, he searched all over for her without success, eventually concluding she must be somewhere below, in the subterranean levels she had not yet seen fit to share with Terciel. He knew two ways she might have entered this underworld, though there were probably more: a trapdoor in the kitchen storeroom that was spelled shut beyond his ability to open (and he didn't even dare try); and a slanted door with strange silver hinges like spreading tree roots, in the cellar of the cottage known as Yezael's shed on the south of the island. But this too was barred with strong spells, most of the marks unknown to Terciel.

During this time, three message-hawks came to the mews in the tower. Two brought routine missives seeking the Abhorsen's help for suspected depredations by the Dead but which might in fact be caused by mere mortal or animal activity. The third would not give its message to Terciel, or anyone save the Abhorsen herself, and sat hooded and grumpy on its perch, the sending hawk-mistress stroking its breast feathers in a failed attempt to soothe its impatience.

A rider also came to the western shore, a woman in the red and black of the Regent's service. She did not linger but carefully dropped a bronze scroll case on the shore stone where the 'bridge' began. A sending rose from within the stone, took the case, and leaped to the next stone, and the next, eventually bringing it to the dragon-footed desk in the Abhorsen's study. The scroll case was sealed, with magic and black wax, so Terciel had to leave it unopened as well.

For the first few days he rested, apart from searching for Tizanael, but after that he resumed his studies, spending hours in the library and the study, learning new marks and spells and practising them over and over again. He climbed the great fig tree twice, as high as he dared, and stayed up there for hours, watching the river and the sky and, most particularly, the low hills to either side.

Several times, at dusk, he saw stoat fingers slinking down to the riverbank, growing bolder as the sun faded. He thought about going out in the daytime to find their hidey-holes, but Tizanael had told him to stay in the House, and he was not overeager in any case. The stoat fingers had not been overseen by a necromancer before, but there might be one out there now.

It was disturbing they were keeping a close watch on the House. He had not known any of the Dead to be so bold before. Seeing them also fed into his anxiety about eventually facing Kerrigor, and indeed, his future in general. He doubted he could ever be as competent an Abhorsen as his great-great-aunt, and he hoped it would be long before he had to take her place. He tried not to think of the alternative, that constant echo down the years of his sister Rahi's fate.

Tizanael returned on the evening of the twentieth day, as the sun set. Terciel had just sat down to dinner in the kitchen, which he preferred to the formal setting of the hall. Light snow was falling again, and it was warmer than it had been, though the day had begun with a cold frost. There were fewer lumps of ice coming down the river, a sign that spring was on its way.

The Abhorsen looked her usual steely self. She sat down next to Terciel at the end of the table closest to the great kitchen fire, and gratefully took the cup of some hot spiced concoction immediately proffered by a sending. As was usual, more of them appeared when the Abhorsen herself was about, ranging from faded, ancient apparitions who couldn't do anything save linger in the corners, to the more robust, relatively newer servants who bustled about finding tasks, as if it was important to them to be seen doing work. There was only one sending Terciel knew for sure Tizanael had created herself, a deeply hooded, slighter and smaller figure more reminiscent of a child than the other sendings. This one knelt and removed Tizanael's boots.

'Welcome back,' said Terciel. 'Some messages came in your absence. A message-hawk from I know not where, and a rider brought a scroll case from the Regent. And a couple of other message-hawks with garden-variety "Old Krom has gone missing can you look into it" sort of things. And there have been stoat fingers on the western shore, watching.'

Tizanael nodded, her eyes hooded, and she continued to sip at her drink, steam from the cup wreathing her face.

'There is soup,' said Terciel, indicating his bowl. 'Split pea and ham speck. It's good.'

Tizanael nodded and pointed at the table in front of her. Her particular sending rushed to the great iron stove and slipped in front of one of the hall sendings to take the bowl of soup that had been immediately filled by the cook. Another sending rushed over with a palm-sized oval loaf from the morning's baking.

When he had first arrived, all those years ago, Terciel had thought the food was conjured up, but he soon learned boats brought supplies down from Qyrre and Chasel and some of the villages on the banks of the Ratterlin. Admittedly, the boats had sendings for crew and never missed the special channel that let them safely come to the island and leave again, even against the inexorable current. So magic was still heavily involved.

It *was* possible to create food with Charter Magic, but as with warming spells, it often took more effort than it was worth, and so was a last resort.

Tizanael ate mechanically, still not speaking. Terciel finished his own bowl but did not leave. He had got used to Tizanael's silences and could discern the difference between 'I have forgotten all about you' and 'I am thinking and will shortly tell you to do something, probably difficult and/or unpleasant.'

He was right. Immediately after Tizanael had placed her spoon carefully in the empty bowl and it had been whisked away by her sending, she shifted on her chair to look at him.

'I had hoped to be swifter, far swifter,' she said. 'Time speeds away, when I feel we can least spare it. I have been looking for something. And studying the book that Clayr brought.'

'*On the Making of Necromantic Bells and Other Devices,*' said Terciel.

'Yes. It is the other devices I particularly wanted to know about. What have you learned about the casting of the bells?'

'Uh, not very much,' said Terciel, flustered and defensive. 'You haven't taught me . . . you didn't tell me to read—'

Tizanael gestured for him to move on. Terciel took a breath, forcing down a strong feeling of ill use. It was typical of Tizanael to expect him to already know something she had never taught him or indicated he might need to know.

'The bells are cast in Death. Neither you nor your predecessor felt it necessary to make any new bells, there being a store of them . . . here . . . somewhere. Underground, I presume, in the places I have not yet been allowed to see.'

'Everything in its time. There is good reason to limit the knowledge of a young Abhorsen,' said Tizanael. 'I should not want to drive you mad. Or did not. I think you are now past the point where that might occur.'

'I am?' asked Terciel. Tizanael was usually very sparing in her compliments.

'You apply yourself to the necessary studies,' said Tizanael. 'You have done well against the Dead, in all our forays.'

'Better than Rahiniel?' asked Terciel. He didn't know why he asked that. He had no memory of Rahi at all any more. But he still felt a slight stab of pain to say her name aloud.

'She was not with me long enough to gauge her potential,' said Tizanael.

'How did she die?' asked Terciel. He had never asked this before. It was that Clayr, he thought, Mirelle. Talking about families and children, and Abhorsens who'd managed to have both. That, and too much mulled wine.

Tizanael frowned and looked at the glow of the fire through the bars in the door of the iron stove.

'It was in the far north,' she said slowly. 'A sorcerer came across the Greenwash, with some nomads for guards. He was looking for something, probably some dormant Free Magic entity he hoped to bind to his will. We came across their camp sooner than expected. Our guide was confused. A local woman, but there was a raised fog . . . and we were among them before we knew it. Rahi took an arrow under her arm in the first few seconds, straight to the heart. Her death was very swift.'

Terciel nodded and drank the last of his mulled wine. He wished he hadn't asked the question. Now he had quite a clear picture of his sister's death, as opposed to some blurry notion of it. But in his mind's eye, the Abhorsen-in-Waiting with the arrow in their chest had his face, not his sister's.

'Why did you ask that now?'

'I don't know,' replied Terciel.

'Put it aside,' said Tizanael. 'We have work to do. As I was saying, the reason I wanted the book was for a chapter on the making of chains.'

Terciel raised his eyebrows querulously.

'Chains,' repeated Tizanael. 'I knew it was possible, but I did not know the detail. They are for use against the greatest of the Dead, those who have managed to anchor themselves in Life, so even when forced to the very precipice of the Ninth Gate, they will not pass it, and in time can sneak back. The Abhorsen Lerantiel fought one such, long ago. Lerantiel made a chain, akin to the bell Saraneth, infused with its power, and with it he succeeded in immuring the creature in the Eighth Precinct, beyond the Seventh Gate. Stuck there, whatever link it had to Life was eroded and its power was washed away by the cold river. Two hundred years later, it was made to die the final death by the Abhorsen Soraniel.'

Terciel nodded. He could see where this was going.

'So you're going to make a chain? To imprison Kerrigor in Death?'

'No,' replied Tizanael. 'I doubt that I have the strength to forge such a chain. Not now. Fortunately, I don't have to. I needed the book to learn how the chain is used, the spells required to wield it and make it fast. Soraniel brought back the chain Lerantiel made. It is somewhere in the House, in the lower levels. That's what I have been looking for, without success. Until I finally realised I had neglected an obvious source of information regarding its location.'

'Oh?' remarked Terciel. He lifted his cup again, but there was no wine left. 'What source would that be?'

'We will ask someone who was here at the time,' replied Tizanael. She raised her left hand, the silver ring with the small ruby sparkling in the warm light from the Charter marks that dotted the vaulted ceiling. 'Moregrim! Attend upon me!'

'The ring controls him?' asked Terciel.

'After a fashion,' said Tizanael. 'As with much other knowledge lost when Hillfair burned, complicated by the break in the succession of Abhorsens sixty years later, the exact nature of Moregrim is unknown. Even his name is uncertain. I believe he has also been called "Errale" and "Greeneye" and "Mogget", presuming there is not more than one of him. His ability to take various shapes confuses the matter, of course. There are a number of theories about him. He is certainly a Free Magic entity of great antiquity and has served us since the earliest times. This ring is one of three, related to the collar that binds him. It can be used to summon him, and inflict some slight punishment.'

'That ring is a cruel and entirely unnecessary accessory to my already vile captivity,' said a voice from under the table. Moregrim's voice. 'The Abhorsen who made the rings was a greater monster than anything he ever sent back into Death.'

'Who was it?' asked Terciel.

'I can't remember,' said Moregrim. He slid out from under the table on all fours and slowly stood upright. He was shorter than when Terciel had seen him up the tree, only coming up to his elbow, but more broad-shouldered, a disturbing reminder of his physical fluidity. His skin was like bleached sheepskin, strangely crumpled, and his hair and beard seemed to have a pale white light of their own.

Moregrim faced Terciel and yawned, displaying all his small, sharp teeth. His emerald eyes glittered with disdain. 'It is good two of the three are lost. Hopefully this one will go the same way soon. And the greater one too, this accursed collar—'

Terciel frowned. The dwarf did not wear a collar. Presumably he meant the belt around his waist.

'Answer Terciel's question,' said Tizanael, and touched the ring. Moregrim yelped and jumped back. Twisting around, he fell on the floor, landing on his hands and feet. Terciel frowned, for Moregrim moved very strangely for all his bulk, far more like some small animal than a man.

'Torture me all you like,' he said. 'It was a thousand years ago or more. How can I remember? You're all the same anyway.'

'You will need to wrack your memory further, Moregrim. I need to know where Lerantiel's chain is,' said Tizanael. 'I know it is stored somewhere beneath the House.'

'Ask the sendings,' replied Moregrim. 'Some of them are old enough to know.'

'Those old enough are no longer present enough. A lingering ghost I can barely see will not help,' replied Tizanael. She made a fist with her left hand and touched the ring with two fingers from her right. 'And I am asking *you*. Tell me where I can find Lerantiel's chain. I order it.'

Moregrim did not answer immediately. He sat up on the floor and licked the palms of his hands, a very unsettling sight. His tongue was narrower than any normal man's and a much brighter pink.

'Tell me,' commanded Tizanael.

'It's hard to remember,' said Moregrim with a sigh. 'Below. As you thought. In an ironwood chest with silver edges and a ruby set in the lockplate. Or maybe it was a garnet, an Abhorsen being cheap. On the sixth level. If I recall correctly, the second room on the left.'

'Good enough,' said Tizanael.

'You want to be careful with that chain,' said Moregrim, directly to Terciel. 'I bet she's going to make you carry it.'

'Enough!' said Tizanael. 'You may go, Moregrim.'

'I don't suppose there's anything but soup?' asked the dwarf. 'Fish, for instance?'

'Go! Get out of my sight!'

'I hear and obey,' said Moregrim silkily. He went down on all fours again and scuttled disturbingly away through the kitchen door.

'It *is* dangerous,' said Tizanael, a moment after Moregrim's departure. 'The chain, I mean. It resonates with the bells, and so cannot be held by someone who carries them, and if the bells are used near it, it will wake and must be kept under control until it is used, no easy task. After Lerantiel made it, the chain was borne into battle by his Abhorsen-in-Waiting.'

'What was their name?' asked Terciel.

Tizanael didn't answer, which was answer enough. With so many records lost, an Abhorsen-in-Waiting who never became the Abhorsen would not figure in any history that had come down to the present day.

'Like the bells, the chain is also an artefact of Free Magic and the Charter,' continued Tizanael. 'But unlike the bells, it is not in equilibrium. The Free Magic is more dominant. You will need to be warded against the effects of that, and there are gauntlets—'

'So I am to carry it?' asked Terciel.

'Yes,' replied Tizanael. 'And use it. I will hold Kerrigor in whatever body he currently occupies, you will throw the chain over him. It is persistent in Life and Death, like our swords and bells. We must then drag his spirit form deep into Death, and at a suitable point we will fix him in place. Probably the Eighth Precinct, as that was what was chosen by Lerantiel.'

'I have not been so far into Death,' said Terciel. He did not feel tipsy any more, and his mouth was strangely dry. 'Not past even the Sixth Gate.'

'It is time you did, then,' said Tizanael. 'You are ready.'

Terciel nodded.

'How will we even find Kerrigor in the first place?' he asked.

'Given the stoat fingers watching us, and the attempted trap for you in Ancelstierre, it is possible Kerrigor plans to move against *us*, when he has gathered a sufficiently large army of the Dead,' she said. 'But we will forestall him. Judging from those villages we know have been destroyed already, and the fact the villagers are missing entirely, not simply slain, he is mustering this army somewhere in the mountains north and west of the Red Lake. I have asked the Regent's guards and borderers, and all the mayors of the western towns, to search for indications of such a muster. The Clayr too, for all the good that will do.'

She took a swig of her drink, set down her cup and beckoned to the sending to fill it again.

'I expect the Regent's message might already bear such news. Or the message-hawk.'

'But if Kerrigor plans to attack us, he might already have a great force, and we would not be aided by the defences here,' said Terciel uneasily. 'Wouldn't it be better to await such an attack? The House has held out before—'

'No,' said Tizanael firmly. 'He is an enemy we must face, and the sooner the better. What, we should let him destroy more villages, break more Charter Stones, slay more people? We are here to protect them from the Dead, not skulk behind walls and water.'

She took another long drink, a cinnamon and ginger tang in the air. Terciel watched her, wondering what else they could do, other than confront Kerrigor directly.

Surely there had to be some cleverer course of action? Or was he simply more cowardly than Tizanael?

'We will go and fetch the chain tomorrow morning. Meet me in the south cellar, armed and armoured, at dawn. With bells, though we may have to set them aside if we do find the chain. The book says they cannot be closer than four paces to each other, lest the chain be awoken in an untimely fashion.'

'The south cellar?' asked Terciel, surprised. 'Not the trapdoor in the kitchen storeroom? Or the door in Yezael's shed?'

'There are a number of ways to enter the lower levels,' said Tizanael. 'But I have been using the stair from the south cellar, so it will be easier to pass that way again. There are numerous warding spells and guard sendings, as past Abhorsens had a tendency to put dangerous things below. There are Free Magic entities held in durance, and other dangers. They cannot escape, but going there is something of a risk.'

'Much like the Library of the Clayr,' said Terciel.

'Hardly the same,' said Tizanael dismissively. 'The Clayr gather up everything without discernment. We have always been more focused. You will be ready at dawn?'

'I will,' confirmed Terciel.

'Good,' said Tizanael. 'Once we have found and mastered the chain, we can prepare to go in search of Kerrigor.'

Terciel nodded, not trusting himself to talk.

Tizanael lifted her voice, speaking to the sending at her side.

'We will likely be going to the mountains. Prepare everything necessary, for me and the Abhorsen-in-Waiting. Ask the Paperwing if she will allow me to fly her to the northwest. I do not think we will have any time to waste, walking, or even to go by horseback.'

The sending bowed and rushed away. Tizanael pushed her chair back and rose stiffly, holding her back just above her left hip.

'I will hear what the recalcitrant message-hawk has to say, and read the Regent's missive,' she said. 'I will see you with the dawn.'

13

There were only four young women in the deep cellar. Corinna, Hazra and two others who Elinor didn't know, though from their silver-edged robes they were Sixth Formers. They were gathered together in a huddle in the middle of the room, which did not immediately look like anything special, certainly not a place of magic. It was a cellar, carved from raw stone so it was basically a cavern, without adornment, though the walls and ceiling were whitewashed. A single electric bulb dangled from the ceiling, and she could see where the newfangled flex had been fixed with iron staples into ceiling and wall, before disappearing up through a hole in the top corner of the door frame. The door was more akin to the massive oak portal at the front of the school than any of the more usual interior doors.

It was a curiously pleasant temperature. Elinor had expected it to be cold, like all the other parts of the school that lacked the temperamental steam radiators that, installed some twenty or thirty years previously, could be cajoled into providing either too much heat or not quite enough. The senior common room and some of the school offices still had the far older fireplaces instead, which usually erred on the side of not enough heat, but provided something to look at. There was no visible sign of any fire or radiator here, but it was warmer than the steps or the ground floor of the tower.

'There are only four of you?' asked Elinor. They had all removed their berets, and she saw their baptismal Charter marks shining. She removed her own bandanna. 'I am Elinor Hallett, as I guess you probably know. I've tested Corinna's mark, and she has mine, but I suppose we all need to do so?'

'We do,' said Corinna, with a swift glance around at the others, who all nodded decisively. 'But first you have to agree to our rules.'

'That seems fair,' said Elinor. 'Hello, Hazra.'

She looked at the other two. 'I'm afraid I don't know . . .'

'Oh,' said the very skinny, curly-black-haired, exceedingly tall Sixth Former. 'I'm Angharad Tramonte.'

'And I'm Kierce Waller. Corinna shouldn't have invited you,' said the other Sixth Former, who had very distinctive red hair and was probably beautiful but at this moment only looked cross. Elinor recalled seeing her playing cricket, belting balls high over the oval to shouts of approval from her teammates. 'But since she has . . .'

'What are the rules?' asked Elinor.

'There are only three,' said Corinna.

'Go on,' said Elinor.

'The first rule is you mustn't talk to anyone about what we do here, especially the teachers,' said Kierce. 'So Corinna has already broken that one, telling you, Miss Hallett.'

'No I haven't, it was never "anyone"—!'

'I'm only a temporary teacher's assistant, not actually a teacher,' interrupted Elinor, hoping to forestall an argument. 'Please, call me Elinor. Here, at least.'

'How old are you anyway?' asked Hazra.

'I'm nineteen.'

There was a chorus of gasps at this, and Angharad looked absolutely astounded.

'Gosh! Nineteen! *I'll* be nineteen in eight months. I thought you must be at *least* twenty-five. Where did you go to school?'

'I was taught at home,' said Elinor, smiling at the thought of being presumed to be twenty-five 'at least'. 'And I won't tell any teachers about this. I want . . . I need to learn Charter Magic, and if this was found out we would all be stopped. What are the other rules?'

'If any one of us says to stop what we're doing, because they're worried about how safe it is, or it feels like a spell is going awry, then we must stop immediately. No argument. Just stop.'

'That seems very sensible. And the third?'

The girls looked at one another again. Hazra made a face.

'The third one is a bit silly,' said Corinna doubtfully. 'I mean we were only in Fourth Form when we started this. Hazra was a Second Former.'

'And we only added it in because Kierce—' Hazra began.

'That is beyond not true,' interrupted Kierce. 'It was because Angharad—'

'No, it was Hazra going on about that boy on the train—'

'It was you positively . . . positively *adulating* Robert Whitakre,' said Hazra hotly to Angharad. 'And showing us that photograph portrait your sister got signed!'

'Robert Whitakre? The actor?' asked Elinor. 'What does he have to do with anything?'

All four girls started talking at once, until Corinna managed to talk louder than the others, leaning in close to Elinor.

'Rule three is that we mustn't talk about our latches.'

Elinor frowned in deep puzzlement.

'Your what?'

'Latches. It's school slang here. They say crushes at Enderby's and Yarven.'

'Infatuations,' added Corinna, not without embarrassment. 'Requited or otherwise.'

Elinor nodded, remembering *Billie Cotton and the New Best Friend*. She'd thought that one was rather unbelievable, but evidently real schoolgirls did have such obsessions . . .

'That will be easy,' she said. Unbidden, an image of Terciel rose in her mind, but she resolutely banished it. 'I don't know any men.'

'It doesn't have to be a man,' said Kierce, with a sideways glance at Corinna.

'Though there are more men around than you might think,' said Hazra seriously. 'That new gardener is quite the dish—'

'Rule three!' shouted the other girls.

Everyone laughed, Elinor somewhat cautiously.

'I don't suppose anyone can hear us up above,' said Elinor into the sudden quiet when the laughter stopped.

'Oh no,' replied Corinna. 'We've tested it.'

'I don't think it's magic either,' said Hazra. She seemed the most thoughtful of them all, even though she was the youngest. 'Simply we're quite a way down. Did you count the steps? Fourteen, and solid rock all around.'

'But there is magic here,' said Corinna. 'Like I said, all the former magistrix . . . or is it magistrixes? Anyway, they put spells in the stone to make practising magic safer. Touch the wall, you'll see.'

'No, we have to confirm her mark is uncorrupted for ourselves first,' said Hazra.

They quickly confirmed this was so. Elinor noticed that as they touched each other's foreheads, other marks glowed briefly around them, in the air and on the walls, ceiling and floor. Many marks, some so small they were like floating dust caught in sunshine, but others as big as candle flames. Often they were joined in patterns, from simple lines of marks to complicated whorls within whorls and other shapes that broke apart and faded before Elinor had a chance to take in their pattern or structure.

The other girls' marks were true, and Elinor felt the immensity of the Charter behind each mark. But it was not the intense immersion she'd felt when she'd touched Terciel's mark. The Charter was there, and uncorrupted, but it was also distant, less all-encompassing. It was like wading in the shallow waters of an immense, wondrously refreshing lake, but being unable to go deeper, or even cup the water up to drink.

Hazra must have noticed Elinor's expression as they let their hands fall and stepped apart.

'I know, it's not as strong as when you're closer to the Wall,' she said. 'Imagine what it must be like actually in the Old Kingdom!'

'Yes,' said Elinor quietly.

'We felt it when we had that north wind a month or so ago,' said Corinna. 'Though of course that can bring other things too.'

'Yes,' whispered Elinor. She looked away, trying hard to banish the memories of that terrible day. A bright Charter mark drifted out of the wall nearby, one unknown to her, and she watched it as it disappeared again back into the stone, a welcome distraction.

'Since you're new, Elinor,' said Hazra brightly, 'we had better find out what you know already.'

'Dr Bannow in Bain taught me a dozen marks. She called them "twig" marks,' replied Elinor. 'Because they are small and easy to grasp, but they connect to more marks and it helps to visualise how they are connected, as if they are all part of some enormous tree . . .'

'Yes,' said Corinna. 'That's one way Charter Magic is taught. I was. Twig, branch, bough, bole – or trunk if you like, the so-called master marks – though of course we haven't got up past the twig ones.'

'And for marks that never stand alone but must be used with others, there are those classified as leaf, blossom, flower,' said Hazra. 'It does make it easier to remember them.'

'Sometimes,' said Kierce. 'My mother doesn't think much of the tree thing. She says the only sure way is to practise finding or calling the mark you need over and over again. The same with spells, putting marks together and repeating it over and over again. Like cricket. I must have hit a cricket ball a hundred thousand times since I was five.'

'Kierce is the school's champion bat,' said Hazra unnecessarily. 'And the great hope when we go up against the boys.'

'When they deign to allow us,' said Kierce, with a grimace. 'They won't let us play in the main competition. Afraid we'll beat them, I think.'

'Probably,' agreed Elinor, who had no idea. She'd only seen village cricket played before she came to Wyverley, and then only when she was much younger, when her father was still alive. Her mother wouldn't have anything to do with the village. Or any of the neighbours, even the ones her father had been friendly with. Mrs Watkins had blamed this on Amelia's aunts as well, who were of the old nobility and didn't consider anyone outside Corvere worthy of their notice, an attitude Elinor's mother had fully shared. This was probably the root cause of her dissatisfaction in her marriage, that her husband's ineptitude with money had forced them to retire from the capital to Coldhallow House.

'So let's go through the marks you know first,' said Hazra. 'Do you draw them roughly to find them in the Charter, or speak their use-names?'

'Um, I don't even know what use-names are,' said Elinor. 'I visualise the mark I need and reach for the Charter, and if it works I see it and I suppose I sort of feel it, but to get the one I want to come out I have to draw it with my finger or my hand or whatever, and I have to really concentrate so it doesn't slip away or I get the wrong one. Or nothing.'

'That's fairly typical,' said Hazra. 'Some people find the marks they need by speaking or subvocalising the mark's use-name. It isn't actually their name, the marks don't have names, but some of the ones that get used a lot have been given names that have stuck. The system of symbology used to write down lists of marks and spells is similar. The drawn symbol is not the same as the mark, it isn't how it looks when it manifests. I mean otherwise there'd be the danger of calling the mark when you're simply recording a spell or making a list. But knowing the use-name and even sometimes drawing it in place can make the actual mark easier to bring forth.'

'I see,' said Elinor.

'Hazra was taught much more comprehensively at home before she even came to Wyverley,' said Corinna. 'Luckily for us, since old Tallowe just goes over and over the same forty or fifty marks and has never taught us anything about use-names or the written symbology.'

'My grandparents came from the Old Kingdom, and they taught my mother,' said Hazra. 'They went as far south as Corvere to begin with, but they couldn't bear the absence of the Charter. So they came back. We've a place near Lylleford. That's about ten miles east of here.'

'Oh, I'd love to meet them,' said Elinor. Actual Charter Mages from the Old Kingdom! They would have so much knowledge. They would know so much Elinor wanted desperately to learn.

Hazra shook her head. 'Me too. They both died before I was born. They were old when they came here.'

Elinor nodded, not hiding her disappointment. She didn't ask how they had managed to come to Ancelstierre, and stay here. According to Dr Bannow it was even harder to get permission to come south than it was to go north. The Ancelstierran authorities were deeply suspicious of anyone from the Old Kingdom. Only people like the Abhorsens, on official business, were allowed to cross. Though of course there were also those the army was unable to stop . . .

'Why don't you take us through the marks you already know well?' asked Hazra. She stepped back a moment before Corinna and Kierce did the same, opening the circle. 'And don't forget, if anyone shouts stop, you stop.'

'I will,' confirmed Elinor. She drew a breath, steadied herself, and focused her mind on the Charter, willing it to become apparent to her, a sea of shining marks with just the one she needed held on the topmost point of a great wave so she could swoop in and pluck it out like an osprey taking a fish . . .

The mark came into her mind, and she drew it in the air, her finger leaving a trail of golden light.

'A simple mark for illumination,' she said, her fingers swirling. She let the mark roll back down into her palm and, lifting her hand to her mouth, blew on it so it drifted across the room and stuck itself to the wall. Other marks rose from the stone, shimmering ghosts that sank away again as the protective magics laid by generations of past teachers recognised there was no threat, no miscast spell or mistakenly conjured Charter mark.

'Very good!' exclaimed Hazra. 'Now, on to the next!'

Over the next month, Thursday nights became very important to Elinor. She revelled in learning Charter Magic, but it wasn't just that, or those seemingly endless but in actuality very brief connections with the Charter that swept away all the terrible memories that lurked and festered in her head. It was having friends her own age, something she had never experienced before.

But she had to be careful not to reveal her newfound friendships outside the magic room, while at the same time not alienating those new friends. Corinna seemed to find this balance without difficulty, but then she was the one Elinor spent most time with, rehearsing the part of the Fool, so they had already established an equilibrium. Angharad and Hazra were also quite adept at changing from being friendly cooperative peers in the magic lessons to suitably respectful students when she encountered them about the school. Kierce, on the other hand, often went out of her way to be too familiar and Elinor on several occasions had had to reprimand her. It attracted attention she didn't want, particularly when she noticed Mrs Tallowe had seen Kierce waving when Elinor passed her in the corridor.

But these were small flaws in what to Elinor seemed a much happier life than she could ever have expected. She still woke sometimes in the night, crying in fear, and she still wept when she was reminded of Mrs Watkins by some small sign, like the careful mending of a costume in the play; or of Ham when she found herself channelling his wisdom and patience while teaching Corinna how to juggle.

The play was hard work, but also tremendous fun. In addition to training Corinna, Elinor also helped stage several of the set-piece fights and the ancillary clowning, including the famous feast scene that incorporated both things, with the duel between the Fool and Roger Cardamom, the former armed with a long loaf of bread and various pieces of fruit snatched from the table, and the latter his dagger. And she helped in many other ways too, assisting actors with their lines as a prompter since she knew the entire play by heart, and helping sew costumes. Everything she had been taught by Ham and Mrs Watkins was put to use.

Elinor even tidied up the theatre after everyone had left for the day, often skipping supper. It was a quiet time, with everyone else away, and for Elinor, one of the few times she was alone. But not on this evening. She was on her hands and knees picking up dropped sequins from the Prince's cloak for later reattachment when she heard her name called from the stalls.

'Miss Hallett!'

Elinor stood up like a jack-in-the-box, recognising the voice as Mrs Tallowe's. What could she possibly want?

'Yes?' she asked doubtfully. Most of the lights in the Great Hall had already been turned off, save the end where she was working. A dim figure was bustling self-importantly down the central aisle between the lines of pews, waving something above her head.

'How dare you use my message-hawks without permission!'

Elinor straightened up to her full, not all that imposing, height.

'I don't know what you're talking about!' she snapped back. She had *thought* about circumventing Tallowe by getting Hazra to send a message-hawk to one of the authorities in Belisaere, but she hadn't done it.

Mrs Tallowe strode into the light, and thrust the paper she was holding at Elinor.

'How do you explain this?' she spluttered, her words coming out so fast they got caught up in her mouth. 'Complaining about me behind my back to the Regent! I'm going to . . . I'm going to . . .'

'What will you do?' asked Elinor, genuinely curious. 'And what exactly do you think I've done?'

'As if you don't know!' spluttered Mrs Tallowe. She dropped the folded paper at Elinor's feet and turned around to flounce back down the central aisle to the great arched doors.

Puzzled, Elinor picked up the single sheet. It was school notepaper, nothing special. Written on it, in what was presumably Mrs Tallowe's reluctant hand, was a message. The writing got messier and angrier with every line, indicating Tallowe's frustration as she wrote down the message-hawk's words, which Elinor knew would have been delivered in the voice of the sender. In this case, the Regent of the Old Kingdom. It would be quite scary listening to someone like that, Elinor thought as she read, particularly a letter like this one.

Magistrix Tallowe,

We have been told you are not teaching Charter Magic as per the long-standing agreement and consequently the annual stipend will not be paid until this matter is investigated, and we may undertake other measures.

The application from Elinor Hallett for permission to enter the Old Kingdom is granted. A writ of admission will be delivered by a representative of the Clayr, who will guide and guard her, as the Voice of the Nine Day Watch has expressed a desire for this woman to come to the Glacier, the Watch having Seen her. Inform the said Elinor Hallett of this decision.

The representative of the Clayr will also investigate your reported malfeasance. She will be with you near midwinter (yours, that is). Ensure you and Elinor Hallett are ready.

Do not fail us.

Faruille
Regent
In Belisaere

'But I didn't send a message!' called out Elinor, even though Mrs Tallowe had already left the hall. 'Really, I didn't send . . .'

This was true. But she had a good idea who had. Elinor started down the aisle and had taken several steps before she stopped herself. She couldn't barge in on Corinna,

Kierce or Angharad in their exclusive Sixth Form studies, and even less so visit Hazra in her Fourth Form dormitory, shared with three other girls.

No, she would have to wait until the rehearsal tomorrow, when she could ask Corinna.

Elinor sat down on the end of the nearest pew and read the letter again. What or who was the Nine Day Watch? What did it mean that the Clayr had Seen her?

The words 'near midwinter' struck Elinor in the heart, though she didn't understand the added 'yours, that is'. The play was to open Midwinter Eve. The school hosted a Midwinter Gala, inviting all the notables of Bain and the North. Many parents and guests came, some from as far as Corvere. Elinor herself had invited Dr Bannow. In addition to the play, there would be exhibitions of archery and dancing; a debate; the demonstration of the steam engine the Sixth Form advanced science class had been building all year . . .

Elinor did want to go to the Old Kingdom. She even felt she *needed* to go. But now it seemed likely to happen sooner rather than later; she wished it might be later, because of *The Court of the Sad Prince*. There was still so much to be done. Corinna needed much more training; there was the stilt-walking pickpocket scene they hadn't started at all; so many of the actors required prompting . . .

But most important, Elinor wanted to *see* the production. She wanted to see it with the stage built, with the pews packed to bursting, the curtains drawing back to a glorious show with all the bright costumes, and the stage machinery and the actors fired up and the coracle scene and the duels and Charlotte Breakespear's wonderful words . . .

Were there plays in the Old Kingdom? There must be, she thought, and leaned back, ignoring the discomfort of the hard wooden pew. She shut her eyes and imagined a play in the Old Kingdom, thinking of all the things you could do onstage with *real* magic, allied with the ordinary stagecraft that was still somehow magical as well.

14

It was cold under the House, quite unlike the building above, which was heated with hot water pipes from the deep springs and additionally warmed by layers of magic set in walls and floors by generations of Abhorsens who sought even greater comfort. But down below, the winter beyond the walls of the Abhorsen's House had settled into the rough-hewn rock.

Tizanael went down the steps first. The sloping corridor from the cellar was quite narrow at first, but it soon broadened out to become a circular stair that went down past several landings and, for all Terciel knew, might continue on for many, many more. It certainly went on past the sixth landing, where they stopped. Guard sendings emerged from the iron-banded oak door there, heavily armed and armoured sendings with closed helmets of blackened steel, more forbidding than any others Terciel knew.

'Stay still,' warned Tizanael. She stepped forward and announced them: 'The Abhorsen Tizanael and the Abhorsen-in-Waiting Terciel.'

Tiny Charter marks tumbled from her mouth, to be lifted by her breath like glowing dust motes, sparkling in the air. The guard sendings leaned forward and took them in, the marks of Tizanael's breath merging with the marks that made up the sendings. For a moment longer they were still, before they bowed deeply and edged back, themselves fading into invisibility as they entered oak and iron and stone. The door groaned open, the hinges protesting, as if it had been a very long time since anyone had last passed this way.

The passage beyond was dark, until Tizanael stepped through the door and Charter marks in the ceiling sprang to life. Not brilliantly, as a new-cast spell for light would do, but with a soft illumination, not much better than having a candle in a sconce every few feet. But it was enough to see that this passage continued for at least sixty feet, and there were three doors on the left side, and four on the right. Heavy, iron-bound doors.

'The second on the left,' mused Tizanael. 'Or so says Moregrim.'

She strode to the door, but did not move to open it. Instead she passed her hand across the face of the door, without actually touching it. Charter marks flared in the timber and the iron bolts, many marks joined in patterns within patterns. Tizanael studied the marks carefully, and beckoned to Terciel without turning to him.

'What do you make of the spells upon this door?'

Terciel looked carefully, identifying the marks he knew. There was one spell he was sure of, and several others where he knew from the marks used the basic idea of the spell without being sure of its exact use. But there were half a dozen more where he simply didn't know any of the marks.

'There is one spell to make the door strong,' he said slowly. 'As if it were all tempered iron, and much thicker than it actually is. I can also see marks for blinding and deafening, but I do not know the spells or how they might be unleashed. Most of the marks I do not know at all.'

'You must study more,' said Tizanael. 'Though I confess there are marks here I do not know either. But one of the spells I do know is to keep this door shut against any opening. It has been permanently closed, or as permanently as may be if the spells are not unravelled. Which to be done safely would take a great deal of time and careful study, and even then I am not sure I could do it. I would need help from one of the Clayr librarians or someone like that.'

'So we can't get the chain?' asked Terciel. He felt relieved, but it was coupled with disappointment. He did not want to carry the chain, or go on a hunt for an old and cunning enemy who had evaded numerous other Abhorsens. But he also knew it had to be done, and Tizanael would probably insist they pursue Kerrigor anyway, even without the chain. Which would be worse.

'Perhaps,' said Tizanael thoughtfully. She turned around and looked at the door on the opposite side of the corridor.

'Moregrim is a creature of mischief and ill intent. He is compelled by his collar to serve us, but he has had many years . . . many centuries . . . to learn how to subvert commands. You recall he prefaced his directions with "I can't recall exactly"?'

'But that was about it being a garnet or a ruby, wasn't it?' said Terciel, and then, 'Ah. Clever.'

'Moregrim would enjoy us stumbling back up above, blind and deaf for weeks, perhaps even longer,' said Tizanael. 'Time we cannot afford, in any case. The Regent's missive concerned another village in the Upp river valley, the Charter Stone broken, the villagers gone. It has to be the work of Kerrigor. Come, let us examine the door opposite. I do not want to grow too suspicious, but there may be even more to the dwarf's double-dealing.'

The other door was not so ferociously spelled. Even so, Tizanael took her time studying the marks that swirled and rose in the surface, and typically pointed out one spell in particular for Terciel to research later, as it utilised a master mark he already knew, but in a different way.

'The master mark here is not the central part of the spell, with the other marks arrayed around and upon it,' said Tizanael. 'Instead, it has been used as a kind of capstone to hold down a group of very . . . excitable . . . marks that would not otherwise endure. This spell will last a very long time, years or even centuries, rather than mere weeks or months. Do you know what the spell does?'

'Something to do with water,' said Terciel, peering close. 'The water in living flesh? I don't understand. I've seen something of the like in a much simpler spell to dry plums for storage, but that seems . . .'

'It is not for drying, but quite the reverse. It is a spell to run water through the desiccated veins of a Dead creature,' said Tizanael. 'At least one clothed in flesh, however decayed. It would destroy any Lesser Dead, and cause great agony to a Greater one. And it would discomfit a Free Magic entity, at least one of the minor varieties.'

'Clever,' said Terciel admiringly. 'But it must take a long time to cast.'

'Several days,' said Tizanael. 'So it is only of use to trap a door or something similar. The other aspect you may have missed is that it would work both ways. That is, on either side of the door. So it may have been cast to keep something in. Are you ready?'

Terciel nodded and drew his sword. Tizanael did not ready sword or bell, but simply raised her hand.

'The Abhorsen wishes to enter.'

Charter marks glowed around the door. Dust puffed out from the seams as the door slowly creaked open, moving inward, not out. Warm, moist air rolled out, and bright light, like afternoon sunshine. Tizanael stepped back and to the side, and Terciel quickly followed suit. But the warm air and the light was not an attack. After a moment, they both carefully edged closer and looked through the doorway.

There was no small room beyond. Instead Terciel found himself looking up into a vast, narrow cavern. It was easily a hundred feet wide and at least as high, and it stretched back several hundred feet. The light came from a truly massive Charter spell made up of thousands and thousands of marks arrayed in a tight spiral so they formed an enormous sun disc on the arched ceiling high above. The light that fell below was not sunlight, but it was a close approximation and Terciel had to shield his eyes with his hand to look up at the disc.

The sides of the crevasse were terraced, a narrow terrace at the top only ten or twelve feet wide with four progressively wider terraces below. The two lowest terraces almost met in the middle of the cavern, but did not, for this was a deep drain full of fast-moving water, about six feet wide. Essential hydraulic engineering, because each terrace had a meandering stream that zigzagged along its length and then overflowed via outthrust gutters into a stream on the next terrace below, and then finally to the central drain.

The reason for the meandering streams and the sun disc above was immediately obvious. Every terrace was a riot of green, interspersed with brighter colours. There were several varieties of tomatoes and yellow squash, cucumbers and beans, and at the far end of a middle terrace, a profusion of flowers. sendings worked among the plants, weeding and pruning and harvesting. It seemed there was some sort of rotation system at work, for each of the terraces had patches of bare earth here and there, as well as the carefully tended crops.

'The Garden of Ulamael,' said Tizanael. There was a faint wistfulness in her voice, something so extraordinary Terciel snatched a glance at her and then looked away again very quickly so she wouldn't notice. 'I had read of it, but I didn't think it was still in existence. Imagine being an Abhorsen with so much time on your hands you could build such a garden! She was fortunate to live in an easier age.'

'Look! There's one of the sendings who served us dinner. And there's a stair beyond that gateway, high on the top terrace, at this end.'

'Leading to the kitchens, I expect,' said Tizanael. 'I admit I have occasionally wondered where the sendings got fresh vegetables in winter. There is little alive in the kitchen garden above right now.'

'I thought they got them from the villages up the river,' said Terciel. 'Like with the other stuff.'

'I do not think Qyrre or Chasel or anywhere on the Ratterlin or indeed in the Kingdom has such a garden as this, one for all seasons,' said Tizanael. 'Except the Clayr, under their mountain. Maybe that was where Ulamael got the idea. And perhaps help. It must have taken dozens of Charter Mages years to create that sun disc, and for it to last so long—'

'What in the Charter's name is that?' interrupted Terciel, pointing at a massive stand of fungus growing at the far end of the middle terrace, where it was darker, by chance or the arrangement of the sun disc high above. There were a dozen human-high stalks made up of brown-and-yellow roundels, with brown gilled undersides, which looked rather like a badly piled-up stack of plates heavy with leftover gravy.

'Siege fruit,' said Tizanael. 'It is an edible mushroom. Edible in that it is possible to eat it and it will sustain life. It's very chewy, and resists flavouring. You might find it is even worse than salt fish.'

'I doubt it,' replied Terciel, with a shudder. He looked around again, up and down and along the peaceful, golden-lit terraces, with the sendings working between rows of vigorous plants. 'The chest with the chain can't be here. Maybe Moregrim told the truth after all, and we'll have to work out how to open the other door.'

'No, I think it is here,' replied Tizanael. 'Look there.'

She pointed at the central drain. At the far end of the crevasse, the drain split in two and ran around a small rectangular island before rejoining on the other side to plummet down a sinkhole, one easily twelve feet in diameter. There were several objects sitting on this island. It was hard to tell exactly what they were from this distance, and the artificial sunlight was weaker at that end, but there were definitely several chests or boxes.

'Follow the drain,' said Tizanael. 'Don't fall in. It looks very deep, and the water is swift.'

Terciel nodded. Tizanael didn't need to add that the level of the water was about three feet below the lowest terrace, so if you did fall in, it would be impossible to get out by yourself and there was no sign of any ladders or ropes or anything like that.

They walked alongside the drain, past neat rows of plants Terciel didn't recognise. They had lots of vibrant green feathery foliage, but didn't grow much past knee-high. Tizanael brushed her hand through the top of one plant and said, 'Carrot,' so he presumed that was what they were, though Tizanael had never given any other indication she was a gardener.

In the next garden section of the lowest terrace there were taller, more substantial bushes, set more apart. They had small green berries forming on the branches, which again Terciel did not recognise until Tizanael muttered, 'Cloudberry, not ripe.' He liked the small, often slightly tart berries, which turned pale blue as they began to ripen, and then as they became fully ripe, wisps and swirls of white would spread over the skin, perfectly mimicking clouds in the sky. The sendings, or perhaps one particular sending, made them into jam and used the jam as a filling in excellent small cakes.

The section of the lowest terrace nearest to the island had no plantings on either side, not even weeds. The bare earth extended for about forty feet. There was the drain making a kind of moat around the island, which was perhaps ten feet square, the sinkhole behind it and the stone face of the crevasse rising up beyond.

Tizanael did not jump across the narrow drain to the island. Instead, she slowed and looked carefully at what was on it. Terciel looked too, unsure of what exactly he was looking for. There were three chests – two large ones and a smaller one between them – a glazed green urn and a silver bottle. The bottle was lying on its side and its stopper and the wire that had held it in place were several feet away.

Tizanael took a few more steps and looked across again, from a different angle.

'I don't like the unstoppered bottle,' she said. 'Abhorsens of old used them to imprison Free Magic entities and store them.'

'Why?' asked Terciel, suddenly more alert than he had been.

'I don't know,' replied Tizanael. 'It hasn't been done for hundreds of years. But there is at least one other place I know beneath the House where a number of such bottles are kept. All securely stoppered.'

'Surely if it once held a Free Magic creature, it would have long since fled?' asked Terciel. 'Or gone into the swift water and been destroyed?'

'Some Free Magic entities can resist the effects of running water, to a degree,' said Tizanael. 'Though that sinkhole undoubtedly leads into the waterfall, and few could resist the force of that. But they are ancient, and cunning, and I know far less of them than I do the Dead.'

'I can't see anything,' said Terciel. 'Or sense anything.'

'And smell?' asked Tizanael. 'Like my ears and eyes, my nose is no longer what it was.'

Terciel sniffed vigorously.

'Nothing like hot iron,' he said, meaning the distinctive, metallic stench of Free Magic. 'Only the garden smell everywhere. Earthy and . . . and green.'

Tizanael jumped over the central drain and paced around to the other side of the island, kneeling so she could see between two chests. She stiffened, and Terciel's hand leaped to his sword hilt.

'The smaller chest is ironwood, has silver edges and a ruby inset in the lockplate,' she said. 'It is the one we seek.'

'Shall I fetch it, then?' asked Terciel. The chest was half the size of the others. Smaller than he expected, perhaps eighteen inches long, twelve deep and wide.

Tizanael scratched the side of her nose, pondering.

'I mislike the empty bottle,' she said. 'And if that chest does contain the chain, it is also potentially dangerous.'

'Even from inside the chest?'

'No, but it may be designed to spring open or something like that,' replied Tizanael. She took a deep breath and walked back and forth along the drain again, looking over it to the island. 'Take off your bells, leave them a dozen paces back. Then jump across, but do not immediately pick up the chest.'

Terciel did as he was instructed. Everything seemed peaceful, with the beautiful gardens above and the Charter-made sunlight streaming down. But Tizanael was worried, and that made him worried. Worse than that, it made him scared.

Returning to the island, he stood for a moment next to the drain, looking down at the fast-rushing water, listening to the gurgle of the sinkhole on the far end. Then he jumped across, and stood near the chests, every sense alert, ready for something to happen.

Nothing did. The water kept rushing by on either side and disappearing into the sinkhole. Tizanael stood by, sword in her right hand, her left hand cupped, lit from within by the Charter marks of whatever spell she held ready.

Terciel touched the chest with the toe of his boot and gave it an experimental push. It moved slightly, sliding a few inches over the stone surface, but was heavier than he expected. He bent down and picked it up, using the bronze handles on each end, and turned towards Tizanael, ready to jump back across the drain with it.

But as he did so, he felt something grab his ankle and then almost immediately his shin and knee, and his nose and throat was flooded with the acrid, hot-metal stench of Free Magic. Whatever held him was not a hand. It was something singular and stronger, like a living rope. He couldn't see what it was because he was holding the chest, so he dropped it and tried to back away. The chest smashed into the stone and bounced towards the drain, but Terciel was held fast. Looking down, he saw his leg was encircled six or seven times by a snakelike creature with glass-like hide, so clear he could see through it. But where internal organs should be there burned the white fire of Free Magic.

It had a head like an eel rather than a snake, a diamond-shaped affair with a long mouth lined with several parallel rows of teeth, and its eyes were slits of darkness. Terciel grabbed it just behind the head as it struck at him, teeth screeching on the gethre plates of his hauberk. It reared back to strike again. It was so strong Terciel was unable to stop it moving, and the coils about his leg tightened again. He screamed and tried to move his thumbs to press into those hideous dark eyes, but he lost his grip and this time it went for his throat and he only just interposed his right forearm so it fastened on that, crunching down with ferocious force. Its teeth couldn't get through the gethre scales, but it felt like his arm was broken.

Then a cloud of Charter marks more blinding than the false sun above blew across snake creature and Terciel, doing him no harm but shattering the glassy hide. Free Magic burst out like gouts of steam from volcanic vents, scalding and poisonous. Terciel turned his head away and kicked his bound leg like an enraged donkey trying to throw off its hobbles. He fell hard on the stone, dangerously near the drain. The long body of the snake thing shattered, but the head remained clamped on his arm, the black eyes still shining, and it ground down on his arm again.

Terciel screamed again and scrabbled at the hilt of his sword with his left hand. But he was lying down and the sword was under his leg and he couldn't get the leverage to draw it, and then a glowing blade sheared through the snake creature's head, entering its right eye and exploding out the left. Golden fire blazed around the sword, and a tongue of white fire exploded out of the creature's mouth and lashed at Terciel.

Tizanael left the blade in place and called forth a master mark of binding from the Charter, letting it slide along the blade and into the thing's head. She followed this with another, and another, marks so powerful they had to be used in the instant, they could not be held in hand or mouth, or placed in stone or wood.

The tongue of fire shrivelled back into the creature's mouth, trammelled by the marks. The darkness of the eyes ebbed to leave only glassy sockets. The teeth that scraped upon gethre plates broke like chalk, no longer sustained by magic. Terciel ripped his arm free and scuttled away on his backside, almost falling into the drain in his haste to get away.

The creature's head, suspended on Tizanael's sword, cracked. All over, all at once. Hundreds of tiny shards fell, leaving a line of white fire rather like a pulsating slug on the tip of the sword. The Abhorsen picked up the silver bottle, tilted her sword, and the core of the Free Magic creature slid down into the container.

'Fetch the stopper,' said Tizanael. 'Quickly.'

Terciel jumped to where the stopper lay, picked it up in his left hand – his right arm, if not broken, was so badly bruised he could not use it – and shoved it in the top of the bottle as Tizanael set it down. He stepped back at once, as Tizanael summoned a fourth master mark and let it fall upon the stopper. A column of silver sparks six feet high blew up around the bottle, and a sudden wind swept around the two Abhorsens, a fresh wind, redolent with salt, as if it had come off the sea. Then both sparks and breeze were gone, and the bottle was securely closed, the stopper wound about with silver wire.

15

'We thought it would be a nice surprise for you,' whispered Corinna as she stood off stage left with Elinor, waiting for the bridal feast scene to finish before they could go on to rehearse the coracle piece, which Corinna understandably had still not managed to completely master. 'It was Kierce's idea to get you your permission thing. But Hazra must have put in the complaint about the teaching.'

Elinor was about to say something about it being very stupid of Hazra, but she bit her tongue. Hazra might be the most accomplished Charter Mage of them all, but she was also just turned sixteen.

'Well, what's done is done,' she said instead. 'I know you all meant well. And I did say I would probably have to ask Hazra to send a message-hawk, so I guess I gave her the idea in the first place.'

'I was wondering why Tallowe sent us all notes about attending magic class,' said Corinna.

'I expect she's going to try to pretend she was teaching properly all along,' said Elinor. 'I wish I knew how long we've got until the Clayr person arrives. "Near midwinter" could mean weeks before, couldn't it, and the Midwinter Gala is only a month away now . . . How long do you think it would take for her to get here? I mean, where would she have to come from? And what does "yours, that is" about midwinter mean?'

'Time and season change over the Wall,' said Corinna. 'I mean, it's probably already spring there or something. From the hill behind our house we can see night and day split as if with a knife along the Wall. Only we tend not to look, because it's rather unsettling.'

'I'd like to see it!' said Elinor. 'Speaking of seeing things, what does the Watch Seeing me mean? With a capital "S".'

Corinna looked sideways at Elinor.

'Don't you know? I thought your grandmother was a Clayr?'

'I never knew her,' said Elinor. 'I mean, not when I was old enough to remember.'

'The Clayr have visions of the future,' said Corinna. 'At least, that's what my mother says. They see things in ice or water, what's going to happen, though not always visions that come true.'

'They see things in ice?' asked Elinor.

She had an uncomfortable feeling in her stomach as she recalled that huge, clear icicle at the end of the greenhouse and the things she had seen in its icy depths, like waking dreams. She wished she could remember them now, and that they had not been dismissed as fancy, or Ham made to break the icicle and mend the gutter.

'Apparently. They even live in a city made of ice.'

'That can't be true,' said Elinor. 'It wouldn't be practical.'

'Who knows? Don't you think it's exciting they've had a vision of you? I wonder what it could be?'

'They live in the far north?' said Elinor, turning the conversation. 'So it might take a long time for one to even get to the Wall?'

Corinna shook her head.

'They can fly,' she said earnestly.

'What!' exclaimed Elinor, loud enough to attract a stern glance from both Madame Lancier and Tegan, the fierce Fifth Former who was the stage manager.

'In a balloon?' she continued, far more softly. She'd seen pictures of balloon ascents, though never the real thing.

'Oh, no,' whispered Corinna. 'Much better than that. A kind of flying boat, one with wings. My brother saw one. Charter Magic, of course, so they land at Fort Entrance, close to the Wall. I expect the flying craft wouldn't work further south. Or would stop working, when you were really high up . . .'

They were both silent, imagining a magical flying boat losing its feathers or its wings folding up or whatever would happen when the magic failed, and the subsequent long fall to certain death.

'So the Clayr could be here quite soon,' said Elinor. 'And I suppose I'll have to go with her.'

Corinna touched her arm, but drew back again immediately, a little flustered.

226

'I . . . we don't want you to go at all,' she said.

'Thank you,' said Elinor, a little distractedly. The bridal feast scene was finishing and the actors were about to come rushing past.

'I bet the school would keep you on,' continued Corinna. 'So you don't have to go.'

'Maybe,' agreed Elinor. In fact, both Madame Lancier and the Sarge had already told her they wanted her to stay on, and would speak on her behalf with Professor Kinrosh.

She hesitated, looking around the dim backstage area, out to the brightly lit action where Madame Lancier had stepped in to adjust the blocking, and up to the panoply of rigging and lights. 'But I think I do have to go. I love the theatre, but I realise . . . I realise growing up I used what I could have of it to disguise the other things I lacked, to paper over the gaps and tears. And now I am part of a wonderful, a wondrous play, but it . . . it isn't enough by itself. I need to find the other pieces that are absent. When I felt the Charter for the first time, I felt . . . no, I knew . . . that it was a missing part of me, a part I must bring home to myself. Also, I have no family now, save for whoever I may have in the Old Kingdom, who I do not yet know. So I do have to go. But I hope not until after we have opened the play!'

Corinna was about to say something, perhaps something difficult, for her mouth was open with no words coming out, but before she could gather the breath or the courage or the thought, a great rush of giggling, talking, prancing and preening actors came between them, forcing them apart like the tide splitting a bridge of sand.

They did not have an opportunity to talk again until the next Thursday evening, when all five gathered for their clandestine magic class. Elinor, as was often the case, was the last to arrive. As she cautiously opened the heavy door, she heard the girls giggling, and found them clustered together to look at a book Kierce was holding open. Not Hazra's grimoire, which would never incite laughter, but some well-worn tome that looked like it had lost its binding and been recovered in newsprint, of all things.

'What's that?' she asked.

'Oh, it's a book I confiscated from a *First* Former, if you can believe it,' said Kierce, who was not only a prefect but vice captain of the school.

'A funny book?' asked Elinor, leaning so she could peer over Hazra's shoulder. But when she caught a glimpse of the page, she drew back in shock, with a sudden, involuntarily intake of breath.

The picture, drawn in scientific exactitude, was of a man and woman engaged in what Elinor understood from Mrs Watkins's rather roundabout talk when she was thirteen or fourteen was termed 'copulation'.

'What is this?' she asked.

'I think the actual title is *The Physical Aspects of Love*,' said Hazra. She took it from Kierce and started flicking through the pages. Elinor blinked at some of the things she was seeing, albeit very briefly. 'It's in some obscure continental language. The pictures are very detailed though.'

'Diagrams, really,' said Angharad, with a sniff. 'Nothing *I* didn't already know.'

'There's always a few copies floating around the school, handed down from older sisters and so on,' said Kierce. 'But *not* for First Formers.'

'This copy still has the chapters that usually get torn out,' said Hazra with fascination. 'Look, all the positions for men and men, and women and women, and the . . . gosh . . . what is that with the feathers—'

Kierce took the book back and closed it with a snap.

'Perhaps not for a Fourth Former either,' she said.

Elinor bit her lip, almost spoke, stopped, then took a breath and did so.

'May I borrow it?'

She felt herself blushing as she added, 'I . . . I am rather uneducated in this regard. I only know what my governess told me, and she was . . . she was wonderful, but a bit old-fashioned.'

'It's all covered in Fifth Form Health,' said Angharad helpfully. 'Well, not the extra chapters, but the other stuff. You could sit in on their lessons, maybe.'

'No she couldn't,' said Corinna scornfully. She took the book from Kierce's hand and gave it to Elinor. 'There you are.'

Elinor looked at Kierce, who smiled her always somewhat sardonic smile and said, 'Yes, we wouldn't want even a teacher's assistant knowing less than we do about anything.'

'I know there are many things where I know less than all of you,' said Elinor. She put the book down by the door and came back to the circle.

'Um, possibly you don't know the spells for contraception either?' asked Corinna. She seemed rather embarrassed to be bringing this up.

Elinor shook her head. She wasn't really sure what Corinna meant by 'contraception', except that it had something to do with a vague talk Mrs Watkins had given her about 'coverings' employed by men.

'There are two main spells to ensure you can't get pregnant,' said Angharad, without any embarrassment. 'One you cast before lovemaking, which will endure until the next sunrise, and another which is more long-lasting, that you have to cast with every new moon. Of course, they won't work much further south of the Wall than Bain, so you need to be careful.'

'There are other methods,' said Kierce with a shrug.

'Not as sure,' said Angharad knowingly.

'There's a chapter in that book on *them*,' said Hazra helpfully. 'Though it's a bit tricky not being able to read the names. That cap thing, what's that actually called?'

No one answered her.

'I have a lot to learn,' said Elinor quickly, resolving that she would get Dr Bannow to go over the basics when she saw her next. Asking schoolgirls younger than herself to explain such things did not seem wise.

'We can teach you the contraception spells now,' said Angharad. 'Hazra as well.'

'I already know them,' said Hazra scornfully.

'I would like to learn the spells,' said Elinor. She was always grateful to learn any new spell. No matter how many new marks she learned, and new spells, she always wanted to learn more. It was a thirst she could never quench.

They were tired afterwards. The two spells were a little more complex than anything Elinor had tried before, each made up of more than a dozen marks, and there was something particularly wearying about casting a spell upon oneself. All of them sat down cross-legged when they were done, despite the cold stone floor.

'I'm sorry about the kerfuffle with old Tallowe,' said Hazra apologetically. 'I should have sent a separate message about her being useless, but I thought she might notice two message-hawks gone at once from the mews.'

Kierce rolled her eyes, which Hazra ignored.

'Has she said anything about me in the resumed magic classes?' asked Elinor.

'Ha! Resumed magic classes my foot,' said Kierce. 'All she's done is make sure everyone attends again. She's still going over the same old marks, the same old spells.'

'And no, she hasn't mentioned you,' said Corinna.

'I wonder how much they pay her to be the Magistrix,' said Hazra. From the look on her face it was not hard to tell she was thinking she might be the Magistrix of Wyverley College herself one day.

'And why would they bother paying anyone?' added Angharad. 'We're not in their kingdom.'

'My mother always says to me, "To aid one's neighbours is to aid oneself",' said Corinna. 'I think it's a quote.'

'*The Warden of Lormantil*, Act One, Scene Two,' said Elinor automatically. 'The Warden.'

'Breakespear?' asked Angharad, her brow furrowed.

'No, a contemporary, Anne Penikan,' said Elinor. 'Her plays aren't very well known now, but she was as popular as Breakespear in their time.'

'It makes sense,' said Kierce. 'If troubles from the Old Kingdom come across the Wall, at least they've helped us have Charter Mages who might be able to deal with them.'

'Preventative diplomacy,' said Corinna. 'Though there have been no real troubles from across the Wall for a long time.'

Elinor almost said something about her own experience, but did not. She wasn't sure why. Perhaps a desire to keep these untroubled schoolgirls free from the fears she had herself.

'Since it seems I will be off to the Old Kingdom myself in a month, or thereabouts,' said Elinor, 'I want to thank you all for your teaching. If I am ready at all, I mean as a Charter Mage, however pitiful, it will be due to the four of you.'

No one spoke for several seconds. Corinna looked away, the suspicion of tears in the corner of her eyes. Kierce looked at Corinna. Angharad frowned, as if she doubted Elinor would survive long. The silence was broken when Hazra clapped her hands together and jumped up.

'We haven't taught Elinor the ankle-winding spell. She has to know that one. It could be very useful.'

Everyone groaned, and no one else stood up.

'You can't be that tired,' said Hazra, but there was no force in her voice.

'I think we are,' said Elinor. 'I am.'

'Me too,' said Corinna. 'Next week, Hazra.'

The magic lessons had come on top of a full day's work, in Elinor's case including not only rehearsals with Corinna and several other cast members, but also two periods of swordplay with the Sarge's senior classes. Now that she was sitting down, the full extent of her weariness hit her. She had to push against the stone with her hands to get up, and tottered as she did so.

Corinna steadied Elinor, and Hazra picked up the book and handed it to her. They started for the door, with Angharad close behind, when Kierce hurried to get ahead.

'Let me go first,' she said.

'Why?' asked Corinna.

'Tallowe's probably watching the door,' said Kierce easily. 'I'll distract her.'

'What?'

The question came from all the others, speaking together.

'Why would she be there now?' asked Elinor. 'When we started you said she always plays cards on Thursday nights . . .'

'I saw her earlier,' said Kierce unapologetically. 'She was lurking on the first landing of the tower. So she could see anyone going in or coming out. I'm surprised none of you noticed.'

'What!' exclaimed Elinor. 'But . . . why didn't you tell us?'

'The others were already here, it was too late. Besides, it won't matter. I have a plan.'

'A plan! We're out of bounds, practising unsupervised magic, when even the supervised magic is barely allowed!' said Corinna. 'Tallowe probably thinks she can get the four of us suspended or expelled, and Elinor fired, so we'll be out of the way when the Clayr woman comes to check up on the lessons.'

'I expect so,' said Kierce calmly.

'There's no other way out,' said Hazra. 'I can't be expelled! My parents—'

'I told you, I have a plan,' replied Kierce. 'She's not going to catch us coming out. In fact, I don't expect she'll stick around when *I* go out. You all wait a full minute after I go, then follow.'

'But *you'll* be in trouble—' Elinor began.

Kierce shook her head and smiled, a wolfish smile, and growled.

'Oh no,' said Corinna.

'Brilliant!' exclaimed Hazra.

'Good thinking,' added Angharad, with approval.

'What are you going to do?' asked Elinor, with some trepidation.

'Tallowe's a coward,' said Kierce. 'She's frightened of Charter Magic, of the Old Kingdom and most particularly of things that come from the Old Kingdom . . .'

She took a breath and with clawed fingers began to trace Charter marks in the air above her head. They came shimmering into existence, golden light falling on the faces of the other young women, in part horrified, part fascinated. The marks joined to become a circle that slowly spun above Kierce's head. She plucked a final mark from the Charter, manifesting it in front of her face. The circle of marks fell to join it and slowly descended to the floor. As it sank, Kierce *changed*.

Hair, skin, school uniform swirled and shifted, becoming horny hide and stiff bristles. Her clear grey eyes became half-shuttered roundels of reddish murk, her hands taloned paws, her mouth and jaw stretching out into a tusked snout. Within a few seconds the transformation was complete, and where a young woman had been there was now a monster, a boar-headed thing that stood upright on hooved feet, russet-bristled over crosshatched skin like a lizard's, dull and red, arms hanging down past its strangely jointed knees.

Elinor gasped and reached out, as if to somehow snatch the human Kierce back into existence. But Corinna grabbed her arm and Angharad her shoulder.

'Don't touch her, it will break the spell. It's only an illusion.'

'Oh,' said Elinor. She took a deep breath. 'Is it safe to do this?'

'She wouldn't have been able to complete the spell here if it wasn't,' said Hazra confidently.

'What . . . what are you?' asked Elinor to Kierce.

The monster shrugged, lifting long, yellow-taloned hands, and growled. The growl made Elinor flinch; it carried with it terror.

'She can't speak while under the seeming,' said Hazra. 'The spell is from my grimoire but it doesn't say what the creature is, simply that it's for the frightening of enemies. Don't do the howl, though, Kierce. You'll wake up the juniors and panic the whole school.'

The monster bowed its massive head and turned to the door. Corinna stepped past and opened it, and Kierce shambled through, picking up speed as she started up the steps.

The others shared a glance.

A moment later there was an awful scream up above. It rose and fell, the echoes bouncing down the stairwell. Hazra started for the door, but Corinna held up her hand.

'We need to wait a little bit, for Kierce to chase Tallowe up the tower. Another thirty seconds. Then straight back to our rooms.'

There was more screaming. It sounded further away.

'What about Kierce?'

'She'll drop the illusion and then she'll be a prefect investigating the scream,' explained Corinna, with a smile. 'Rank hath its privileges. Let's go.'

They went up the stairs more hurriedly than usual, all of them pretending not to be in a hurry. At the base of the tower, without the need to speak, they took different doors, the privileged Sixth Formers Angharad and Corinna into the main north corridor; Hazra the western door into the shadowed quad; and Elinor the southern door to the strip of garden that lay between the school proper and the row of teachers' houses.

She could not hear any screaming outside. Either it had stopped or was simply muffled by the thick walls of the old tower, which had no windows on this side. But she half imagined she could, and it worried her as she hurried along the path, frost crackling under her feet, moving quickly between the pools of light surrounding the lampposts that were now electric, but had once been paraffin, the province of the school's own lamplighter.

Her breath puffed out in a fog around her as she walked, for winter had firmly settled in.

Tallowe was unkind, lazy and possibly vindictive, but did she deserve the kind of fright that scream suggested? Elinor frowned and lowered her head in thought. Kierce's methods typically were to aggressively attack any problem, be it a spin bowler's ball in cricket or a troublesome teacher. But perhaps they should have tried to deal with Tallowe's threats in a different way. Or rather, Elinor, as the notional adult of the group, should have worked out a way to do so.

Elinor sighed and rubbed her wrists. They were hurting again, as happened on and off, but it was far worse tonight than it had been. At least there was no pain in her side any more, she thought.

She reached her house, dutifully wiping her feet on the doormat. Ice cracked, the sound echoing. She heard laughter and looked back. A big group of teachers was leaving the school and heading her way, intent on their own beds. There had been a party for something or other in the senior common room, and clearly considerable sherry had been imbibed.

Someone moved hurriedly from the shadow of a tree to slip behind the neighbouring house. A student out of bounds, Elinor thought, probably a Sixth Former coming back from an illicit cigarette in what the girls called Smokers Wood, the copse in the northeast of the school grounds, an extension of the wood beyond that had lapped over the old stone wall that bordered Wyverley College, save along the front, where it had been replaced fifty or sixty years before with a fence of spiked iron railings.

She went inside, locking the door behind her. The two other teachers she shared with must have already retired. The light was out in their shared sitting room. Elinor went through her nightly routine, a quick wash and brushing of teeth, and visit to the toilet, then climbed up to her room, the smallest of the three. It was little more than an attic, but she liked it.

Her wrists had stopped hurting but now she had a headache, probably from simple weariness. But Elinor did not immediately turn off her light. Instead she opened the newspaper-covered book and began to look at the pictures and try to puzzle out the possible meaning of the words.

The world beyond Coldhallow House was so much more complicated than she'd ever considered, there was so much of *everything* to know . . .

16

'It was within the stone, under the chest,' said Tizanael.

'How did it get out of the bottle in the first place?' asked Terciel. His voice was hoarse from screaming, and he was supporting his injured arm up against his chest. It hurt marginally less that way.

'I think it was released on purpose,' said Tizanael thoughtfully. She used the point of her blade to touch the slightly discoloured area of stone where the chest had stood. Charter marks answered, fading marks that rose to the surface but were already dissipating and broken, so the nature of the spell they had made could not be discerned. 'But it was constrained under the chest, so the creature could not escape unless someone moved it. The empty bottle was a clue for some future Abhorsen that the creature had been put to such a use, though I did not read it right. Our distant predecessors worked far more with Free Magic and its creations than the Abhorsens of the last few hundred years.'

'So, it was set to protect the chain,' said Terciel.

'I presume so,' replied Tizanael. 'Let us step back across and I will look at your arm, before we do anything else.'

'You think there are other traps?' asked Terciel anxiously. He winced as he jumped across the drain, the jar of landing sending a bolt of savage pain from wrist to elbow, and a lesser ache flaring up his leg. He would have some nice symmetrical rings of bruising there, he thought.

'Perhaps,' said Tizanael. 'We will go slowly. Can you straighten your arm?'

Terciel couldn't straighten his arm, and he had to swallow a sob when Tizanael pushed gently against his fingers. With her help and considerably more pain, he got out of his hauberk and the leather jerkin and linen shirt beneath. Tizanael examined his forearm, and made a disappointed clicking sound with her tongue against her teeth.

'It is broken, and there is Free Magic contamination, so it will resist healing spells. I will do what I can to ease the pain and knit the bone, but you are going to have to rest. This is an ill chance. I do not want to let Kerrigor have more time to break Charter Stones in the north!'

'I didn't break it on purpose,' said Terciel sulkily. 'If it wasn't my arm it would have been my throat.'

Tizanael nodded, acknowledging this truth, though she did not offer an apology. Instead her eyes lost focus as she reached for the Charter, and she began to trace marks in the air above Terciel's arm. He recognised several marks of healing, but not the spell, and once again felt the inadequacy of his own skill. He studied all the time, and practised, but there were so many marks, so many spells . . .

The marks moved into a new configuration. Tizanael gestured with the palm of her hand and they sank into Terciel's arm, slowing as they met the already darkening, bruised skin. Tiny silver sparks flashed around the marks, but they had no heat. This was a sign the Free Magic of the creature had already leached into his flesh, and Terciel felt his heartbeat rise with that anxiety. But the sparks receded and the spell did not fail, the marks sinking further in until they disappeared. He felt a warm glow spread up to his shoulder and down to his fingertips, and the pain was greatly lessened.

'I will still have to set it straight,' warned Tizanael, promising great pain to come. 'But it should be easier now, and will get no worse. Keep holding it up. I am going to examine the chest more closely.'

'Shouldn't we wait and come back when my arm is healed?' asked Terciel anxiously.

'I need to know if the chain is here,' said Tizanael. She walked over to where Terciel had laid his bell bandolier earlier and divested her own before jumping back over the drain to the island and approaching the chest. She bent over it, looking at it closely, running her hand an inch or so over the lockplate and the reinforced corners. Charter marks flared under her palm and she watched them carefully, before moving on.

'There are many spells in the wood and metal, but they all are to lessen the effect of that which lies within,' she said after several minutes. 'And it is locked to open only to the Abhorsen. I judge it is safe enough.'

'I can't draw my sword,' warned Terciel. He knew if he dropped his broken arm he'd probably pass out from the pain, despite Tizanael's healing. 'Or focus on a spell. I can't even stand up properly!'

'I am not incapable myself,' replied Tizanael. Nevertheless, she edged back before extending her hand to touch the ruby on the lockplate with the tip of her index finger.

The lid sprang open. Terciel flinched, but Tizanael didn't move. There was a faint waft of hot iron, but not the overwhelming stench the snakelike creature had given off.

Using the tip of her sword, Tizanael shifted what looked like a piece of heavy leather. As it slid over the side, Terciel saw it was a pair of gauntlets made from some strange cloth, tied together with a silver cord. As they flopped onto the stone, Charter marks in the gloves and the ground beneath flared up for a moment, then faded into quietude.

'Protective gauntlets for handling the chain,' said Tizanael. She reached with the sword again, moving it about. 'There's some sort of bag. I think I can flip it open. The chain may be inside.'

There was a flurry of silver sparks, and she lifted up a length of a surprisingly flimsy-looking chain. Each black iron link was no thicker than Terciel's little finger, and they were not directly joined together, but rather connected with odd-looking fringed roundels of gold or something plated or finished with gold. It took a moment for Terciel to realise they were metal daisies, beautifully made to look like the real flowers. Charter marks swarmed on the daisies, thick as bees in high summer, but he couldn't see any on the black iron links. There was a faint shimmer in the air about the links, as if they were hot from an oven or a forge, but he could feel no heat and Tizanael did not lean back.

'It *is* Lerantiel's chain,' said Tizanael with satisfaction. She let the chain fall back into the chest, and used her sword point again to gently lift the gauntlets back on top, and then to push the lid closed once more. She picked up the chest carefully and tucked it under her arm. 'We'd best get you back up top and see to your hurts.'

They took the stairs from the middle terrace, which did not lead to the kitchen as expected, but actually came out in the chicken shed of the garden, a ramshackle lean-to that might have been built entirely to disguise the door that led to the subterranean regions of the House. Hens squawked and waddled out of the way as Tizanael and Terciel emerged, bowing their heads under the low ceiling.

'Interesting,' remarked Tizanael. 'This is not mentioned anywhere I have read, nor is it shown on any of the many plans we hold in the library.'

Terciel turned back to look at the door they'd exited, but there was no sign of it now. Only what seemed to be one of the whitewashed exterior walls of the House, rather the worse for years of close proximity to the chickens who roosted either side on various perches up the lean-to's wooden walls.

'An exit only,' said Tizanael. 'The kitchen sendings must have another way down. Drat!'

The 'drat' was because she'd stepped in a heap of chicken shit. Muttering, she wiped the sole of her boot on the door sill and strode out of the coop, between the fallow rows of the vegetable garden, which were currently lightly dusted with snow.

Terciel limped behind her, cradling his arm. His leg ached and was stiffening up. The spells Tizanael had cast below to take away the pain had mostly worn off and he felt ill and weak. He had almost fallen on the many steps a few times, and once had been forced to let go of his broken arm to use his left hand to brace against the wall, and even though he had tucked his right hand into his belt so the wounded arm didn't completely drop, the resultant blinding stab of agony and an awful grating sensation in his arm suggested the broken ends of the bone had moved.

'Once I set your arm and place a few higher-order healing spells upon it, I expect you will need three or four days to fully recover, perhaps a week,' said Tizanael as they went in through the kitchen, comfortable warmth enveloping them both. 'We will not waste that time however. You can learn the spells needed to reinforce yourself against the corrosive effects of carrying the chain. It would be wise if you are conversant with them, rather than simply having them cast upon you.'

Terciel nodded, not speaking. He really needed to lie down, but Tizanael kept talking. He hardly noticed the sendings who came to lift him up and carry him bodily away.

'Take him to his room,' said Tizanael to the sendings. 'I will follow shortly.'

Half an hour later, Tizanael set his broken forearm. Despite spells to dull the pain, Terciel almost passed out, gripping the side of his bed with his good hand so hard he thought he might break those fingers too. But when it was done, the height of the pain lessened, and as Tizanael splinted the arm and set even more spells at work, it faded to a constant ache. Then she set to work on his leg, once again making the tsk-tsk sound with her tongue against her front teeth.

'What is it?' asked Terciel. He was familiar with that habit.

'Burns from Free Magic are dangerous,' said Tizanael. 'And must be cleansed well, lest they become a weak place for Free Magic to enter once again. It is both insidious and corrosive to living flesh, and given I want you to bear Lerantiel's chain, I must ensure not even the slightest hint of Free Magic remains. Hold still.'

Terciel tried to see the marks she was summoning and linking together, but he didn't have the strength to lift his head. He felt the spell sink in, a welcome, calming warmth, but it changed quickly to a lancing pain that travelled from his toe to his hip and back again, again and again, each time increasing in intensity. He cried out and began to thrash reflexively, but the sendings held his legs down.

The fourth time the wave of pain reached his toes, Terciel passed out.

When he came back to himself, Terciel was surprised to see sunshine through his window. Weak winter sunshine, but when he'd been put on his bed, it was late afternoon.

Now it seemed to be morning. He edged himself upright and found his broken arm was splinted and strapped to his chest, and his bruised leg was loosely wrapped in some sort of herbal poultice.

A sending who had been sitting on the end of the bed got up as he moved, bowed and exited. A few minutes later, it returned, and a minute or two after that Tizanael came in, several sendings behind her, one with a breakfast tray.

'I'll take off the poultice now,' said Tizanael. 'Then you will be able to move around. Try not to jar your arm.'

Terciel nodded. Tizanael expertly lifted the poultice, which appeared to be made of layers of cabbage leaves sewn together, interspersed with a herbal decoction of which a major ingredient was honey. It smelled nice. It had also been heavily spelled. There were still fragments of short-lived marks fading away on every part of it.

'There's a stick by the headboard,' said Tizanael. 'Used to belong to the Abhorsen Bannatiel, I believe. If you lift and twist the head anticlockwise, there's a dagger in it.'

Terciel craned his head around to look. A heavy bog-oak stick with a bronze handle in the shape of a marsh bird's gently curved beak leaned against the back of his pillow.

'After you've had breakfast, I want you to study this spell,' continued Tizanael. She snapped her fingers, and a sending stepped forward and placed a sheaf of papers on Terciel's lap. It was the good, very white linen paper, and carefully written on it in Tizanael's familiar hand was line after line of symbols, representing Charter marks and the shorthand for how they should be joined together.

Terciel saw at a glance he only knew half of the marks, or less. He sighed, leaned back, and shut his eyes.

'I'm wounded, Aunt,' he said. 'And I don't know most of these marks. You'll have to show them to me. What's this spell for anyway? And yes, the pain is less but still present, thank you for asking.'

'The pain would be no less for my asking,' replied Tizanael. 'And I would not trouble you with this if there was time to spare. A message-hawk came this morning. The Charter Stone at Middle Upp has been broken, the villagers slaughtered, the bodies missing. Kerrigor is gathering an army and we cannot allow him to grow any stronger. The spell is one of those to armour oneself against the effects of Free Magic. I wish you to study the marks you do know so when I come to teach the rest of them tomorrow, the learning will go faster. I do not expect you to master the spell by yourself. I think you also should study the book on how to use the chain. I will bring that tomorrow.'

Terciel opened his eyes again and forced himself to sit up completely, ignoring the pain in his leg and arm. He gestured at the sending with the tray to come forward.

'What do I get for breakfast? Sweet rolls and fruit?'

'Porridge,' said Tizanael. 'Simple fare for the hurt.'

17

Elinor woke in sudden fright, sitting up straight in bed. For a moment or two she was disoriented, not knowing what had woken her. It was early in the morning, before dawn, and though there was some moonlight coming through the window, not enough for her to see the face of her alarm clock. She reached over and clicked on the bedside lamp, relieved by the comforting light. It was a nightmare, she thought, and hoped it didn't mean they were going to start their regular appearances again.

Then she heard the noise that had woken her repeated, and it was definitely not a dream. A quick tap-tap-tap on her door, followed by a hushed voice.

'Miss Hallett!'

A man's voice.

Elinor leaped out of bed and rushed to her wardrobe, flinging it open to grab the leather scabbard that held three of Ham's really sharp throwing knives, the ones they didn't practise juggling with. She slung it over the shoulder of her flannel nightdress and drew one of the knives, holding it ready to throw or stab.

She was glad she always locked her door, though it was only a small comfort. She knew it could be kicked in easily enough.

'Who is it?' she whispered.

'Albert, the assistant gardener. Only I'm actually a Crossing Point Scout. Major Latimer put me here to guard you.'

'What! Who?'

'We think Hedge is here. You have to get somewhere more secure. Edric's gone to telephone, our troop is in the village, but it'll be half an hour before help comes.'

'I don't know what you're talking about!' snapped Elinor.

'Hedge! The Free Magic sorcerer who shot you at Coldhallow House. We saw him.'

Albert sounded frightened. Elinor retreated to the far side of the room, the knife in her hand, her heart hammering. She pulled back the cuffs of her nightgown and looked at her wrists. The scars had faded before to near invisibility, but they were vivid again now, looking more like fingerprints done in red paint than ever, though they didn't hurt like they had the night before.

The night before. The shadowy figure slinking away, and her wrists burning. Was that in response to the sorcerer's proximity?

'I'm going to unlock the door,' she said. 'Wait a second and then step in, one step, but no more than that. I am armed.'

'Yes, miss,' came the loud whisper. 'Hurry!'

She crossed the room, flicked the key and stepped back again, knife ready to throw.

The young gardener who came in was the new one Hazra fancied. Though Elinor would not have called him handsome, he did have a cheerful, capable face. A tall, broad-shouldered man in his early twenties, wearing a rough brown suit, with a revolver thrust through his belt, and a scabbarded sword bayonet on his hip. His flat cap was in his hand and he was indicating his forehead, where a golden Charter mark glowed.

'Test my mark, miss, you'll know I'm all right.'

Elinor looked at him warily. She felt no new pain in her wrists, and his mark looked as it should. She slid her left foot forward and turned her body, reaching out with her left hand as she kept her right hand with the knife back, ready to strike.

Albert reached forward too, very slowly, with two fingers extended. They both touched foreheads at the same time, and sighed together with relief and relaxed as they made contact with a true mark and felt the Charter beyond.

'I don't understand,' whispered Elinor. 'The Free Magic sorcerer's name is Hedge?'

'That's what I've been told, miss,' whispered Albert.

'Why would he be after me?'

'Don't know, miss. We was told to keep an eye out for him and given his description, that's all.'

'Scarecrow thin, but neither tall nor short,' said Elinor, remembering. 'Forty or so, and the top of his bald head shone in the rain.'

'Yes, that's him. Me and Edric, we were put on the duty. Do a walk-around every four hours at night. It was Edric saw him first. We need to get inside the main school. Safer there.'

'Let me put on a coat and my boots,' whispered Elinor. She returned her knife to the sheath and laid the case of knives on her bed, before quickly shrugging on an overcoat, socks and boots, and a fur hat she'd succumbed to from a catalogue one of the Bain women's outfitters sent to the school every month. She slid a very small knife, another one of Ham's, into her boot top, slung the throwing knife scabbard over her shoulder again, and drew one of the blades to hold ready.

She was afraid, but she was surprised to find that fear was not the primary emotion inside her. She felt determined, the knife in her hand light, as if it wanted to leave her hand. Next time she saw the sorcerer, Elinor swore she would throw first, and not miss.

'After me, please,' muttered Albert. 'Stay back a few paces.'

He grinned at her, a grin that she felt was as much to bolster his own courage as strengthen hers, and added 'At least there's no wind from the North' before drawing his revolver to carefully creep down the stairs.

Elinor followed, wondering what her housemates in the other bedrooms would think if they happened to open their doors and look out. The mere presence of a man might be more shocking to them than the fact he was armed.

For a moment, she wondered why she was not shocked herself. But she wasn't. Everything changed that day at

Coldhallow House, that last day, not least Elinor herself. She wasn't sure what she was to become, but it was not someone who would be shocked by the unconventional.

It was cold outside, though the air was still. There was a frost on the grass, spreading on the edges of the paved path. Albert paused outside the house, listening, looking up towards the great dark bulk of the main school building. The lampposts spread small pools of illumination, but there were swaths of darkness in between. The moon above was a slim crescent, providing little light, and there was high cloud dimming the stars.

Albert gestured for Elinor to follow and moved forward, hunched over, walking off the path so he was more shadowed. At the corner of the larger house, where those school servants who lived in were housed, he paused. Elinor crept up closer to him.

'Where did you see this Hedge?' she asked. For an instant she almost giggled at that. Asking a gardener where he'd seen a hedge. But she suppressed it. It would be too easy for laughter to become hysteria. She had to hang on to her resolve, not let the fear that underlay it come to the surface.

'He was watching your house earlier,' whispered Albert. 'Then he went back to the cricket pavilion. We think he's been hiding there. I had to wake you in case he came back.'

They moved together to the northern wall of the library, slinking along it. Elinor's shoulder grazed the brick and she felt strangely comforted by the solidity of it, something familiar in this strange night.

From there they crossed the quad, walking on the forbidden grass rather than the path. Light spilled out from the windows at the eastern end of the northern wing, where the kitchen was and the bakers must have already begun their predawn preparations. It was enough to see the way. One of the windows in the Great Hall to the south was also lit from inside, presumably so the quad would never be truly dark. The girls were not allowed outside after ten o'clock, but teachers occasionally worked very late or had to go into the school very early.

Albert was heading for the main doors from the quad into the central building when Elinor felt a sudden pain in her wrists, that awful burning pang.

'Stop!' she hissed. 'He's here!'

Albert crouched very low, sidling into the deeper shadow by the wall, into the soft earth of the fallow flower beds. Elinor followed him. She had to breathe through her nose to stop herself audibly panting with sudden, short panicked breaths.

'Where?' whispered Albert. He had his revolver up, elbow locked to his side, his left wrist under his right in the approved fashion.

'Close,' whispered Elinor. 'I don't know exactly. The burns he made on my wrists, they ache when he is close.'

They stayed still, both listening intently. Albert moved his head very slowly from side to side, staring into the darkness on the far side of the quad.

They both heard the heavy door begin to open before they saw it. The left-hand leaf of the great oak-and-iron doors, a twin to the front doors of the school. Light spilled out from the corridor behind, silhouetting a man who stepped out a few paces. Backlit, it was hard to make out what he looked like, but he was shorter than the sorcerer Elinor remembered, and broader, and he had sandy hair.

'Albert?' he said in a low voice, but still above a whisper.

Pain spiked in Elinor's wrists. She started to grab Albert's coat as he rose up and stepped out, but missed. He took one more step forward, calling out with no attempt to keep his voice down.

'Edric!' replied Albert. 'Look out, he's here somewhere!'

The man in the doorway shimmered and changed, becoming suddenly taller, thinner and more menacing. It was not Edric. It was Hedge, who had sorcerously taken on the soldier's shape.

His hand flashed up, and something like a fire arrow sped from it and struck Albert in the chest, hurling him back. He smacked into the wall and fell to the earth, oily flames licking over his torso. The awful hot-metal stench of Free Magic assaulted Elinor's nose and throat.

Elinor threw her knife and while it was in the air drew another and threw that and the next, the first striking as the other two followed. She heard the meaty thunk of it hitting flesh, and thought the sorcerer staggered under the impact, but the two following either missed or were dodged or somehow misdirected.

Hedge did not fall down, though Elinor was sure she'd hit him in the chest, with one of Ham's most dangerous knives, which were made from a single piece of steel. They looked like particularly long and heavy arrowheads, with a short handle, the steel diamond-hatched for grip.

She lost a couple of seconds scrabbling for Albert's revolver, but couldn't find it and instead drew his sword bayonet, snatching it away as the flames spread further across his body. He had been killed instantly, she knew, because there was a dinner-plate-sized hole where his heart should be, the void filled with fire.

When she looked back, Hedge was no longer in the doorway.

Elinor dropped onto her stomach and crawled backwards along the wall. The sword bayonet couldn't be thrown, and the knife in her boot surely wouldn't do anything if one of the much larger knives had failed to wound him. She would have to get close and stab him, somehow avoiding the spell that had killed Albert, and the sorcerer's burning grasp.

For a moment she thought about screaming for help, but immediately realised she mustn't do that. The most likely people to respond would be the First and Second Form girls in the dormitories above her, and they would be killed en masse. Even if teachers came, what could they do? They would also be killed.

Albert's fellow soldier, Edric, must already be dead. But if he had managed to make his phone call first, there was a chance proper help was already on the way. All she had to do was hide long enough, Elinor thought. If Edric hadn't got through, surely the dawn and exposure would make Hedge withdraw, even if it was only for the time being.

But what if he didn't? What if he killed whoever got in the way? Innocent schoolgirls, or teachers, or gardeners?

Elinor thought of Ham, and Mrs Watkins, and Cook, and Maria, and even her mother. She gritted her teeth and slowly rose up to a crouch and started towards the open, well-lit back doors, her body tensed to duck aside or dive to the ground if Hedge appeared.

She was halfway across the quad, just past the covered-over well, when she heard a noise behind her, the rattle of a latch. She whirled around as a baker leaned out of the kitchen window she'd just opened, her nose sniffing, and saw the body of Albert and the fire still burning in his body.

'Oh! Oh! Fire! Fire!'

A chorus of voices inside the kitchen answered her, soon shushed by the senior-most of the kitchen staff present, shouting matter-of-fact orders about fire buckets and the 'newfangled alarm'.

Elinor ran to the back door, the sword bayonet ready in her hand. More lights were coming on along the north wing. The kitchen door slammed open and bakers hauling fire buckets of sand rushed to Albert's body. Bells began to jangle throughout the school, not the calm toll of the tower bells to mark lesson periods, but the harsh rattle of the newer electric alarm.

The cry of 'Fire alarm! Fire alarm!' began to echo everywhere, and lights sprang on in every building.

Elinor ran down the main corridor. There was a body by the front door, which was open. A young, sandy-haired man in clothes like Albert's. There was a revolver on the floor near him. As she ran closer, she saw he was not burned, but he lay in a huge pool of blood, his throat cut from side to side.

The door to the school secretary's office was open. Elinor sneaked a glance in, saw nothing, and jumped in on a diagonal, to surprise any ambusher. But there was no one there. The candlestick telephone that usually sat on the desk was on the floor, and a noise like a warbling bird was coming out of the earpiece. Elinor shut the door behind her and locked it, then picked up both parts of the telephone and retreated behind the desk before holding the earpiece to listen, positioning the receiver in front of her face. She'd used a telephone only a few times before. Coldhallow House did not have one.

'Porrock! Is anybody there? Anyone? Porrock! Is anyone there?'

It was a man speaking, loud and slow. This was followed by an ear-piercing whistle as whoever was at the other end tried to make a sound loud enough for a chance passer-by to hear and pick up the telephone.

'I'm here,' said Elinor, too fast. 'We need help, the two soldiers are dead—'

'Slow down,' said the man. 'Help is on the way. Who am I speaking to?'

'Elinor Hallett. I know you won't believe me but there is a Free Magic sorcerer—'

'We know, Miss Hallett. This is Major Latimer of the Crossing Point Scouts. You said Albert and Porrock are dead?'

'Albert is, and Edric I think, I don't know Porrock.'

'Edric Porrock and Keren Albert ... Are you safe where you are?'

'I don't know. I'm in the school secretary's office, I've locked the door.'

'What is that racket I can hear?'

'The fire alarm bells. Albert was set on fire by the sorcerer.'

'Fire alarm? Are the pupils evacuating?'

'Yes,' said Elinor. 'What will . . . what will Hedge do?'

'I don't know,' said Latimer, his voice redolent with apprehension. 'My first troop should be there very soon. Once he sees them he should run. I have other units coming, and the police, but from further away. I'm in Bain myself. Has the fire brigade been called?'

'I don't know,' said Elinor. She was shaking now. It was difficult to hold the telephone steady in front of her mouth. 'The fire . . . it was magical, it stuck . . . it stuck on him.'

She heard Latimer quickly ordering someone to do something about the Bain Fire Brigade, before he came back to her.

'I want you to stay in that room until my troopers get there,' said Latimer. 'Ensign Macoll and Sergeant Rourke. Are you armed?'

'I have a bayonet and a knife,' said Elinor. 'I hit Hedge with a throwing knife, but it didn't . . . I don't think it did anything.'

She heard Latimer's surprised intake of breath.

'Uh, well done. Well done. Stay in the room. Do not open it for anyone except my soldiers. Best you get off the telephone now, keep your attention focused. I believe Hedge is most likely to have gone, but stay alert. Good luck. I will be there myself in a few hours.'

There was a click as the call disconnected. Elinor set the candlestick part down on the desk and put the earpiece back on its hook. She contemplated sitting in the chair for a moment, then looked down at herself. She was covered in dirt. Instead she retreated to the corner and sat back on her heels, laying the bayonet in front of her so it could be easily snatched up.

Elinor had never considered the sorcerer who'd hurt her at Coldhallow House might be after her, or that she might not be safe at the school. She had thought all the danger was to come when she crossed the Wall.

She was still in the corner when the Crossing Point Scouts came, and it was only when Elinor heard Professor Kinrosh as well as the lieutenant and his sergeant that she got up and opened the door.

Major Latimer arrived several hours later. In that time Elinor had bathed and dressed and packed her single suitcase with her few clothes, juggling balls and practice knives. She knew, even without Professor Kinrosh actually saying so, that she would have to leave Wyverley College. Even now, her house was ringed with Crossing Point Scouts and policemen. The school was similarly infested with troops searching every building and every part of the grounds.

The fire had not spread, but the Bain Fire Brigade and multiple engines from the south had responded. Some were still showing up only to be turned away again. The police had removed the bodies of Albert and Edric, doubtless to another coroner's inquest that would say they died in a straightforward fire.

Sergeant Rourke found Elinor's knives and returned them to her. Two of the weapons had been found on the grass near the back door of the main building. The third, which was strangely blackened, had been picked up in the search of the ha-ha, the sunken ditch that had once been the moat around the castle, which had been demolished when the school was built. Elinor hadn't wanted to take the blackened knife at first, but Rourke showed her a Charter spell that would reveal Free Magic taint, and it was clear. So she sat on her bed and sharpened the knives and put them back in the scabbard and when a messenger came to get her, slung it on her shoulder before she put on her coat, which, despite a damp cloth and brushing, still showed streaks of dirt.

She was escorted to the headmistress's waiting room by Sergeant Rourke and three troopers, for what she presumed would be some sort of handover to the military authorities, to be taken as if she were a prisoner or a parcel. She hadn't met Major Latimer yet, but she'd been told of his arrival. The Crossing Point Scouts had all been very nice to her, and admiring that she'd managed to get a knife into Hedge, who Sergeant Rourke told Elinor was a turncoat who had once been a Scout himself, become a most capable and feared Free Magic sorcerer and necromancer.

Elinor was surprised as she approached the waiting room to hear the faint sound of a piano, though Rourke and her escort did not react. Someone was teasing out a slow version of 'When Little Lambs Do Lap the Dew' and with that tune came an almost overwhelming memory of Mrs Watkins singing in her little-girl voice, that day, that terrible day . . . and now Elinor had failed to avenge her when she had the chance. She should have thrown the knife at his face, she thought, not his torso, even if it was the bigger target.

She stopped and slowly breathed in, and out, wiped her eyes, and when Sergeant Rourke knocked on the door and opened it, she strode straight into the waiting room.

'Miss Hallett,' said Professor Kinrosh gravely. She was standing with another woman, both drinking sherry from ludicrously small crystal glasses. The other woman was much younger, perhaps thirtyish, and was wearing an army blue greatcoat several sizes too large for her, disguising whatever she had on underneath, save her very sturdy-looking boots, which had steel plates at the toe and heel. She was blonde and blue-eyed, with deep brown skin, a very beautiful combination that sparked a faint memory in Elinor of Mrs Watkins again, telling her how beautiful her grandmother had been with her skin like the rich loam of the south field and eyes like sapphires – and her slightly regretful addendum that neither Amelia nor Elinor looked like that.

She wore no hat, bonnet or headscarf, and there was a Charter mark on her forehead. Elinor knew instantly who the woman must be. She had come earlier than expected, but she was certainly the messenger of the Clayr.

It was the soldier who had been playing the piano. An officer who looked to be in his fifties, in bottle-green regimentals. His low shako, dark grey overcoat, and one of the medieval-looking swords used by the Scouts were on a nearby chair, and he had a holstered revolver on his belt. His hair was a stubbled white and when he turned around, Elinor saw he also had a Charter mark on his forehead.

'Good morning, Miss Hallett,' he said. He got up from the piano stool. 'We spoke on the telephone. I'm Major Latimer. I command the Crossing Point Scouts.'

'And I am Mirelle,' said the woman with the Charter mark. She tapped her forehead and gestured at Elinor's. 'I am a Ranger of the Clayr. May we test your mark? And you do likewise, of course.'

Elinor glanced at Professor Kinrosh.

'Go ahead, Elinor. I do not have the mark myself, but Magistrix Nestor was a close friend, and no headmistress of Wyverley College can be ignorant of the Charter and the Old Kingdom. We are too close to the Wall. If I had my way, we would be more open about the study of magic and all it entails, but the board is mostly composed of southerners, so we must all pretend there is no magic and do our best to hush up anything that suggests otherwise. As will be done after the events of last night, no doubt.'

'You are of course correct,' said Latimer. 'As with my superiors, the first instinct of our governmental authorities is to hide things under the carpet and hope they go away.'

'Have you found Hedge?' asked Elinor.

'We'll talk in a minute,' said Latimer. 'First, let us be sure of each other's mark.'

Elinor slipped off her bandanna and reached for the major's forehead. It was a strong connection, stronger than she usually felt with the schoolgirls. He had, Elinor realised, come from closer to the Wall, closer to the Old Kingdom, closer to the Charter she yearned to know better.

'Your mark is true,' said Major Latimer.

'And yours,' whispered Elinor.

She turned to Mirelle and they both reached out at the same time. The Clayr's mark was stronger again than Latimer's, and Elinor felt herself sway and almost lose her balance as she experienced the sudden onrush of the Charter. Mirelle grabbed Elinor's shoulder with her left hand to steady her, a grip that felt like it could crush skin and bone if the wiry ranger wanted to. She let go as they broke contact.

'True, again,' said Elinor.

'And you *are* a Clayr, cousin,' said Mirelle, with a slight smile. She had somehow found more from that brief contact than Elinor had, something the younger woman noted for future research. She looked Elinor up and down. 'It is very interesting that children born to us outside the Glacier physically take after the other parent, whereas those of us born there nearly always come out looking all too similar.'

She gestured at her own face.

'I know practically nothing about the Clayr,' said Elinor. 'I never really knew my grandmother.'

'Myrien,' said Mirelle. 'I looked her up. We're only fifth cousins, but your great-grandmother is still alive and so is one of Myrien's sisters – your great-aunt – and Charter knows how many closer cousins than I.'

'What?' stammered Elinor. 'My great-grandmother!'

'Some of us live a long time. Rappanne, your great-gran, she can't be over a hundred and ten. She's a Deputy Librarian now, very important, though she was the Chief

263

Librarian before I was born, she stepped down to let someone else have a turn. And your great-aunt Ylsen, she's probably eighty or so—'

Latimer cleared his throat, very loudly. Mirelle stopped talking and gestured for him to speak.

'There'll be time for family catching up later,' said Latimer. 'For now, you need to come with us.'

'Come with you where?'

'Ultimately, south, far south,' said Latimer. 'Though Mirelle has complicated matters by arriving with another option.'

'Why would I go *south*?' asked Elinor.

'To be safe from Hedge,' said Latimer.

'Who exactly is this Hedge?' asked Professor Kinrosh.

Latimer looked embarrassed.

'A deserter from the Scouts, before my time, who became a Free Magic sorcerer. I have been told the scar on his forehead is a sign of allegiance to a powerful Dead entity called Kerrigor. His followers call themselves Servants of Kerrigor. They can disguise it as a Charter mark, but not from close inspection.'

'And not from the rain,' whispered Elinor. 'Why did he come after *me* again?'

Latimer looked at Mirelle.

'It is possible for a very powerful Free Magic sorcerer to break a Charter Stone with their magic and the fresh blood of a Charter Mage,' said Mirelle. 'That of the five bloodlines works best: Abhorsen, Clayr, Royal, and the two strands of Wallmaker. Of these, the Wallmakers are gone, as is the Royal line. We Clayr are numerous, but we rarely go far from the Glacier, which is heavily defended. Which makes a stray such as yourself very tempting for a sorcerer who wants to break Charter Stones. Even if they have to cross the Wall to fetch you away.'

'What is a Charter Stone?' asked Elinor.

'The Wallmakers made them,' said Mirelle. 'They are like a gateway to the Charter. It is easier to cast magic around them, even easier if you are touching the stone. And they inhibit Free Magic. That is why the sorcerers destroy them, wherever they can. But it is not a simple task. Only the most powerful can manage it. If they also have the blood to spill.'

Elinor nodded, and absently rubbed her wrists. Becoming aware she was doing so, she stopped, pushed her cuffs back, and looked at the skin. The scar tissue was red again, and could be clearly seen to be made by fingers hot as fire.

'It's where he grabbed me, back at Coldhallow,' she said quietly. 'I thought it was completely healed, but it began to pain me again last night, and it grew worse when he was close.'

Professor Kinrosh looked at Latimer and Mirelle.

'Is there a continuing danger?' she asked. 'There is no north wind. This Hedge is surely without his sorcerous powers?'

'Weakened, definitely,' said Mirelle. 'But not *without*. We can reach the Charter here, which means he will also have some sorcery.'

'He killed Albert with his magic. A bolt of fire,' said Elinor. She looked at Latimer again. 'Do you know where he is?'

'We haven't found him,' admitted Latimer. 'But he will be very cautious now. The police are bringing dogs, we will continue the search. But the fact of the matter is *you* are the object of this sorcerer. If you are out of his reach, I am sure he will try to return to the Old Kingdom. We will escort you to the station, and I'll organise others to safeguard you on the train and get you quickly south.'

'I am sure you can provide a similar escort northward, to Fort Entrance, where I landed my Paperwing,' said Mirelle. 'From there, we can fly to the Glacier. Home, to your family.'

'The Glacier . . . you don't really live in a city made of ice, do you?' asked Elinor.

Mirelle laughed.

'No! I suppose we call it the Glacier because it is the prominent landmark, but the city is actually within the mountain that cradles the ice. But it is no dark maze of holes or anything like that, as I see from your face you are imagining. We have many windows and skylights and Charter-spelled ceilings in great caverns, with gardens and great halls and plenty of air and light and space. We are not really a subterranean folk, for all we may inhabit a mountain. We live in light, not darkness.'

'So will it be to the north or south?' asked Latimer.

'I had hoped to stay long enough to see the play open,' said Elinor. 'Another two weeks, that's all. I guess that's impossible now.'

'A play?' asked Mirelle.

'*The Court of the Sad Prince*,' said Elinor. 'I don't suppose you know it. Do you have plays in the . . . the Glacier?'

'Of course I know it! Charlotte Breakespear was from the Old Kingdom. You got her works from us, not the other way around. And we certainly do have plays. There's always a couple of productions underway. Music too, and dancing.'

'Charlotte Breakespear was *not* from the Old Kingdom,' said Professor Kinrosh with great authority. 'Her history is well known, despite those people who claim the work was done by the Arbiter's nephew who was the patron of her troupe—'

'Something to discuss another time, Professor,' interrupted Latimer. 'We should take Miss Hallett away at once.'

'What is your decision?' asked Mirelle. 'North or south?'

'Oh,' said Elinor. 'North. With you, to the Glacier. I was always going to the Old Kingdom.'

She looked at Professor Kinrosh.

'Thank you for everything you've done for me,' she said. 'Could you say goodbye from me to Madame Lancier and the Sarge, and everyone in the play, and Corinna and—'

'The girls in your magic class,' interrupted Kinrosh. She smiled. 'Yes, I knew. I told Hazra it could continue as long as she followed your own rules. The first two, anyway.'

Elinor shook her head ruefully. 'I should have guessed.'

'You'll always be welcome here,' said Kinrosh, taking both her hands and drawing her into a hug. 'To visit, or to help us with a play. And I know we all wish you good fortune in the Old Kingdom.'

She did not need to say that Elinor would need it.

18

The third day after finding the chain, Terciel's arm was much less painful and healing well. But his leg wasn't. It continued to hurt, and Terciel was frightened to discover that he couldn't feel his toes, even when Tizanael first pinched them and, when that didn't work, stuck him with a pin.

'The Free Magic contamination is insidious,' said the Abhorsen, casting yet another healing spell over Terciel's leg. The marks lingered on his skin as if reluctant to go further, but eventually sank in.

'But you can . . . you can make it better,' said Terciel. He tried to sound calm, but he was already imagining the Free Magic contamination spreading from his leg up through his entire body, until he was completely paralysed.

'No,' said Tizanael thoughtfully. She sighed and sat back in the chair a sending had carefully placed by the bed for her to sit on while making her examination.

'What!' gasped Terciel. He had never known Tizanael to acknowledge anything was beyond her, and he certainly didn't want to be hearing it now about his leg.

'I cannot,' repeated Tizanael. She scowled and added, 'I have asked the Clayr to send Filris, their Infirmarian. She is older even than I, and has greater experience with this sort of thing. But I will have to put up with her advice, and not simply on the healing you need!'

'That seems a small price to pay,' muttered Terciel, the panic that had surged in him still making his heart race.

'The Clayr are too ready to tell everyone what they should do,' grumbled Tizanael. 'They always have been. But do not fret. The spells I have set should hold back the contamination. I have already sent a message-hawk, urging Filris to come at once.'

'She might not come?' asked Terciel. He was unable to keep a tremor from his voice.

'As ever, it depends what they think they've Seen in the ice,' said Tizanael. 'Curse this delay! Every day lost is a gift to Kerrigor, and we will still have to finish reinforcing you to bear the chain. At least you have learned the last of the spells.'

'Well, almost,' said Terciel defensively. 'It is the most difficult.'

'Learn it,' snapped Tizanael. 'We must get on.'

She stood up very forcefully, her chair tilting backwards. It was caught and whisked out of the way by the sending as the Abhorsen marched out of the room.

Terciel sat up and drew his leg in so he could poke himself in the foot. He tried to move his toes back and

269

forth, but they did not respond. He had no sensation at all in the front half of his foot, though he could still feel a pinch at his heel. Everything looked normal enough. The skin was not discoloured; it didn't feel hot. It was simply completely insensitive.

The ringed bruises higher on his leg were still very much apparent, though less livid than they had been. Terciel pressed his finger against them, and felt the kind of pain you would expect from poking three-day-old bruises.

He slid his legs out, got his stick ready, and stood up, very slowly. When he had tried this earlier he'd fallen backwards onto the bed, so he was even more careful this time. One of the sendings who'd been nursing him moved forward, but he waved it back and took a tentative step forward, supporting himself with the stick. He had to pause to regain his balance immediately after he'd done so, but it meant he could move, albeit with difficulty.

Very slowly, he limped over to the large eight-paned window that overlooked the orchard: the apple, orange and apricot trees were bare and stark, branches skeletally white, pruned back for the season. It had been clear earlier but it was snowing now, and getting heavier by the minute, obscuring the view. He looked out, glad to be inside the well-heated room. Even the glass here was not entirely what it seemed, being heavily laced with Charter marks that surfaced as he touched a pane. He couldn't quite identify the spells – most of the marks remained hidden within the glass – but one was for reinforcement to make it as strong as or stronger than stone, and one was not exactly for warmth but something to do with insulation, preventing the transfer of heat or cold.

If he hadn't been injured, he'd probably be out in that snowstorm now, Terciel thought with a shudder, hunting down Kerrigor. Though even that would be preferable to this slow paralysis that crept up his foot . . .

He was about to turn away when movement caught his eye. He looked up and saw the snow suddenly swirl and separate, and the white, low-hanging cloud parted to admit a shaft of weak sunlight. Down through this beam of unexpected light a dark shape swooped. Too big to be a bird. Terciel thought it was some sort of monster for a second, till it turned and stood up on its tail, and he saw it in full profile.

'A Paperwing!' he cried. It had to be piloted by someone extraordinarily skilled, both at weather magic and directing the craft, for the sun was already vanishing, the corridor down through the storm closed up, and the aircraft was now in a tight spiral, turning back almost on itself, tail still down and head up, airspeed dropping.

For a moment he thought it was going to try to land on the wall platform, miss, and tumble into the river, those on board to surely drown. But the Paperwing shot over the wall, missing it by inches, and in an incredible display of bravura flying did an impossibly tight turn and came down almost vertically to rest on the snow-covered north lawn.

Sendings swarmed out of the House to hold the Paperwing down and then carry it into the hangar below the eastern courtyard. It was already folding its wings but the wind kept trying to pick it up. Terciel couldn't see the colours of the craft. The snow was swirling down again and the Paperwing was so dusted with snow it looked a kind of dirty white-grey anyway. Nor could he make out the pilot and passenger, they were too rugged up, but he figured it had to be Filris and another Clayr. They had come so quickly they must have already Seen his need for a healer before they even received the message-hawk sent by Tizanael!

He limped in a stop-start fashion back to bed and climbed in, suddenly feeling very much better.

'That was astonishing!' exclaimed Elinor to Mirelle, undoing her straps and leaning close over the pilot's shoulder. 'I have never been so frightened *and* exhilarated at the same time. But where are we?'

'The Abhorsen's House,' said Mirelle. She spat a snowflake out of her mouth and continued, 'Closest safe place once the snow really hit. I'd hoped to follow the Ratterlin north longer, but this storm is only going to get worse. No choice but to land.'

She shrugged and climbed out of the aircraft, waving away the sendings who rushed to help her. Elinor was not so quick, because she was staring at the magical beings in amazement.

'What . . . what . . . are they?' she stammered as they held her up under the arms, the myriad Charter marks that made up their hands glowing bright where they touched her. All were deeply hooded or veiled, so she could not see their faces.

'Sendings,' said Mirelle. 'Charter constructs. Servants. Past Abhorsens must have made a lot of them – there are scores of them about the place. Come on, let's get inside.'

Elinor hurried to catch up with her, almost slipping on the icy ground. Again, a sending steadied her. She looked at it, saw that it was all Charter marks, even the simple smock it wore, and what she could see of its face under a deep hood moved between several visages.

'Are they alive?' she asked. 'I mean, do they have emotions and think, like we do?'

'No,' said Mirelle. She was walking fast to the big front door, which looked very blue with all the white snow in front of it. 'They have a limited range of actions depending on what they were made to do. Some are more complex than others, of course, so it seems like they actually think. It depends on who made them, and how much care they took.'

A sending opened the door. Elinor saw a brightly lit hallway with wood-panelled walls that were somewhat reminiscent of Wyverley College, and she felt the warm air streaming out.

'The Clayr seek shelter from the storm from the Abhorsens,' intoned Mirelle before she stepped across the threshold. It had the feel of a ceremonial statement, not exactly a question.

The sending who had opened the door, who was dressed in a kind of blue-and-silver tabard, considerably more stately than the smocks most of them wore, bowed low and stepped aside.

'Are they at home?' asked Mirelle as she went in, with Elinor close at her heels. The door swung shut behind them, cutting off the cold air, and the errant snowflakes that had chased them in were swallowed up by the luxuriant carpet, a long blue runner that was dotted with silver keys of many different sizes.

The sending nodded and pointed to the right corner and slightly up, and then directly behind her where the tower was, and up.

'Terciel's in bed at this hour?' asked Mirelle. 'And the Abhorsen is in her study?'

The sending nodded, and mimed cradling a wounded arm and hopped on one foot, the other hanging.

'I see. Terciel's injured.'

The sending nodded.

'Terciel's injured?' asked Elinor, alarmed.

'It can't be too serious,' said Mirelle dismissively. She had several visible scars, on her throat and the backs of her hands, and from the little Elinor had gathered, being one of the Rangers of the Clayr was like being a soldier, and Mirelle was clearly a veteran of many battles.

'We need hot water and clothes, please,' continued Mirelle to the major-domo sending. 'Particularly Elinor; she'll need everything. I expect Tizanael will let us know when she wants to see us?'

The sending nodded again and gestured. Several indoor sendings in rather less ornate versions of the same tabard came forward, as far as Elinor could tell emerging from the walls.

'They'll give me new clothes?' asked Elinor. Mirelle had made her leave almost everything behind, because it was machine-made and would fall apart in the Old Kingdom, or so she said. Only Ham's knives and the scabbard would be all right, she'd decided, after investigation. The weapons had been forged by a master smith, and the scabbard cut and stitched by Mrs Watkins.

Elinor had trouble believing what Mirelle had told her, but it was already borne out by what was she was wearing. The sleeves of her coat had come almost completely undone at the shoulder, and she was uncomfortably aware that her underwear was fraying.

'They will,' said Mirelle. 'There's an awful lot of stuff stored here. And a bunch of sendings whose job it is to look after guests. They don't get much practice, so they're always very eager to help. See?'

A sending in a less fancy long blue-and-silver tunic – but still finer than the outdoor sendings in their smocks – was tugging at Elinor's sleeve to lead her away. Unfortunately this resulted in the entire sleeve coming off. But the sending was not dismayed. It rolled up the material and disappeared it into its tunic before taking Elinor's hand. She felt the warmth of Charter Magic with its distant echo of the Charter itself, a comforting welcome.

'Go with it,' Mirelle called out as she strode down the hall to the main staircase, as if she was in her own home, a sending scurrying close behind. 'Have a bath – the water stinks at first, because it's from hot springs, but you'll soon not notice it – get warm, get dressed. Some other sending will bring you down when Tizanael wants us. If you need anything, just ask. They understand, even if most of them can't speak.'

'Some of them can?' asked Elinor, following at a somewhat slower pace. She could feel her skirt falling down and had to hold on to the waistband.

'Apparently,' replied Mirelle, disappearing around the top of the stairs. 'Never met one myself.'

'Oh,' cried Elinor, but this wasn't in answer. It was because her stockings had failed entirely and collapsed around her ankles, and the heel had started to come off her right boot and had twisted around and was hanging there. As she bent down to pull it off, her skirt fell down as well.

'Curse it!' swore Elinor. She yanked her skirt back up and almost fell over backwards, only to be caught by a trio of sendings who had silently come up behind. Led by the first one, who clearly was her own superior servant, they gently picked her up and carried her onward. Elinor struggled for a second or two, then relaxed, and started to laugh.

This was not how she had imagined her arrival in the Old Kingdom.

'You wanted to talk to me alone?' asked Mirelle, bowing before Tizanael, who was seated at the head of the redwood table with the dragon-carving legs. The Abhorsen wore a simple robe of dark blue, without the silver key motif. A glass with a herbal tisane was on the table before her, steam rising from it. Several books were next to it, open, and the casket Mirelle had brought from the Library of the Clayr on her previous visit.

Tizanael gestured for Mirelle to take one of the lesser chairs that surrounded the table. The Clayr did so, with a slight grimace. The chairs were old and the black upholstery with the silver key motif had lost its padding so the internal ribs beneath poked through, making them extremely uncomfortable to sit on.

'Why are you here?' asked Tizanael.

'The storm, we had to land—'

Tizanael interrupted her with a snort of disbelief.

'A spring storm, not at its height, and you the most experienced Paperwing flyer in centuries? You could have flown on to High Bridge before nightfall,' she said. 'You're meddling.'

'The Voice of the Nine Day Watch commands me,' said Mirelle stiffly. She pulled down the cuffs of her robe, which had ridden up as she sat. The sending had given her a Clayr's white garment with a golden star stitched upon the breast, but it was slightly too short in the arms, possibly because the magical servants were channelling their mistress's irritation. 'I do as I am told.'

'I meant all you Clayr,' said Tizanael crossly. 'Why have you brought the young woman here?'

'She has been Seen here,' said Mirelle. 'She is important.'

'Bah!' protested Tizanael. 'How can some long-lost cousin of yours from south of the Wall be significant? She has only been woken to the Charter a matter of months!'

'It is not clear,' said Mirelle. 'I was not part of the Watch, I did not See anything myself. But I have been instructed to leave her here for a time, and to tell you two things.'

'Tell me, then,' said Tizanael. She took a sip of her tisane, and grimaced.

'First, this Elinor is not only a Clayr. She is also something of an Abhorsen. Myrien's grandfather was Jeremiel, the Abhorsen who preceded Herranael, of your own line.'

Tizanael's eyes narrowed and she glanced directly at Mirelle for the first time. 'That is of interest, given the situation. Though there are at least a dozen others with as close a connection, in Belisaere and elsewhere, having her at hand could be . . . useful.'

'It is important,' said Mirelle carefully. 'Most likely, as far as we can See.'

'As far as you can See,' grumbled Tizanael. 'Why is it none of you ever Saw my daughter's fall? All your useless visions, all your meddling, what does it amount to?'

Mirelle did not answer. This was a long-held hurt of the Abhorsen, sixty years or more ago, that the Clayr had not warned her of her daughter's accident, so she might have forestalled it. Yet Tizanael knew as well as the Clayr that they Saw only some of the myriad possible futures, and sometimes the very acts taken to prevent a particular future were the ones that ensured it. Everything they did had to be weighed carefully.

'And the second matter?' asked Tizanael, glowering over her cup. She took another sip and coughed, a stuttering cough that she seemed unable to stop. It went on for some time, Tizanael holding the back of her hand against her mouth.

'Your servant, the Free Magic entity, variously called Moregrim, Mogget, Erril, and other things,' said Mirelle.

'He has been Seen far more than in the past, and in a number of futures he has escaped his servitude and wreaks vengeance upon the Abhorsens and destruction in general. There is concern the binding laid upon him is fading, and should be renewed in its totality.'

'I wish it were so simple,' said Tizanael. She looked at the silver ring on her finger, the small ruby clasped in its centre. 'So much of our learning has been lost. All I know is that Moregrim is at his most helpful and obedient when a new Abhorsen comes to power. The binding is somehow renewed in this transition. Then, over time, it fades and he grows more fractious and disobedient. As he is now, for I have been the Abhorsen a long time. A long, long time. I may use the ring to command him specifically, but I do not know any way to fully renew the binding save my own death. Or is there something else you have Seen you are not telling me?'

'I am a ranger,' said Mirelle. 'I rarely serve in the Nine Day Watch, nor do I have many visions outside of it. I believe it was hoped you did know a way to reinforce the binding on Moregrim.'

'I don't,' said Tizanael.

'Hmm. What has happened to Terciel?'

'He has been wounded,' said Tizanael. 'By a Free Magic entity. There is some contamination in his foot that I cannot force from the bone. I have sent a message-hawk to the Glacier, asking Filris to come.'

Mirelle's eyebrows rose. She bent her head to hide her surprise, knowing Tizanael still noted it.

'I may hold a grudge,' admitted Tizanael. 'But not so tightly I would risk Terciel's life over it.'

'How bad is it?' asked Mirelle. 'When I left, Sazene had not returned from Estwael in our second Paperwing, though she may have by now, I suppose. Our third, as you may know, is old and will now not fly save in high summer. Filris might have to come by boat. A few days at least, and if the spring floods have started, problematical.'

'You haven't Seen this?' asked Tizanael sarcastically. 'Terciel is affected by a sly and subtle expression of Free Magic, but fortunately it is slow. I missed it at first. It could not have come at a worse time. We need to move against Kerrigor, and I need Terciel to bear the chain. Do you bring any word of futures Seen with regards to that? I have word from the Regent of three villages lost now, all in the Upp river valley. Kerrigor will not waste the deaths of so many villagers. He gathers an army to strike at Uppside or Edge. From there . . . he could strike here. With enough Dead to bridge the stepping-stones with boxes of grave dirt, even this House could be at risk.'

'Nothing of use has been Seen,' said Mirelle. 'You know the lands about the Red Lake are often clouded to our Sight, from long before this Kerrigor was first heard of. That may be why he chooses to attack the villages there.'

'Perhaps,' agreed Tizanael. 'It may simply be that those mountain valleys are so isolated, news of any attack takes days to reach Ganel or Uppside, and help even longer to get back. If there is any to give. The Regent's mind wanders. She has not paid proper attention to the town garrisons, and I have heard of villages that lack even a single healer or some other Charter Mage.'

She shook her head and took another sip of her tisane.

Mirelle watched her, wondering how old the Abhorsen actually was, and how ill. The ranger was not an infirmarian, but she had learned from them, for wounds and sickness and injuries were very much part of the ranger's lot. Some of the longer patrol routes around the Glacier took them away for weeks at a time. In addition to learning a great deal of healing magic, Mirelle had also been taught the use of various healing herbs and plants.

She knew from the smell alone that Tizanael was drinking a tisane made from star-arrow flowers and the sticky sap of the bentwhorl plant, a recipe used for the relief of lingering pain.

'Yes,' said Tizanael. She lifted her cup. 'It is what you think. I am old. My eyesight fades, I grow deaf, and my joints stiffen and ache, particularly in this weather. But I am still capable of wielding sword and bells.'

'I did not think otherwise,' said Mirelle.

'Tell me about the girl,' said Tizanael abruptly. 'This Elinor.'

Mirelle told her what she knew, from Elinor's encounter with Hedge immediately after the Abhorsen had left Coldhallow House up to their landing an hour or so ago, here at the House. Tizanael listened, sipping her tisane. Occasionally she wiped her left eye, which was watering, and not from the steam of the drink.

When she had finished, Tizanael sighed and stared down at her empty cup.

'I would spare her, if I could,' she muttered. 'She reminds me of my Gweniliel. But I cannot.'

She fell silent, resting her chin on one gnarled, ancient hand.

As the silence stretched on, Mirelle pushed her uncomfortable chair back and stood up.

'May I go and see Terciel?'

Tizanael nodded and waved her away. A sending came from a corner and refilled the Abhorsen's cup, and another drifted out after Mirelle.

19

Elinor's bedroom was exactly what she had always wanted and never had. It was warm and light, both provided by Charter Magic. An unnecessary but very pleasing blaze crackled away in the redbrick fireplace, some aromatic wood that gave off a faint, subdued scent. There was a writing desk and chair of simple but elegant design in a pale, slightly reddish wood; a rather more massive wardrobe of greater antiquity in dark mahogany; and the walls and ceiling were a pale blue, dotted with faded silver keys. The curtains were a dark blue but not closed even with the snowstorm outside, because the window glass was infused with magic and did not admit the cold. Though there were shutters, Elinor noted, so perhaps in the deeps of winter it was necessary to close up against hail or the like. Despite the snowstorm, Mirelle had told her it was already spring in the Old Kingdom, and the weather should soon improve.

As soon as she'd arrived, the sendings had brought up a full-sized tin bath and filled it from the taps in the corner, which did emit a waft of rotten egg stench at first, so Elinor was glad she'd been warned. She had trouble with them wanting to soap her all over and brush her hair, but eventually she'd managed to fend them off and enjoy a soak and they had dedicated themselves to bringing in all kinds of clothes and equipment, as if they were determined to outfit her for life, or a long expedition.

Elinor didn't know how to stop them, so she simply let them dress her in soft, loose undergarments that she thought might actually be silk, so much more comfortable than the flannel she was used to, even if Mrs Watkins had always said silk underwear was no better than it looked, which still made no sense to her. Following that, they had put her in a gorgeous wraparound dress of heavier silk in dark blue that tied at the side with silver ribbons and was fastened at the top with a beautiful silver-and-moonstone brooch.

A suit of leather armour was laid out on the bed, a knee-length tunic of supple light leather reinforced with breast and back plates of thicker boiled leather and bands at the shoulders and elbows, and matching trousers with armoured kneecaps and shin plates. Next to it was a neat pile of linen shirts, light undergarments, an oilskin cape, and a leather backpack that one of the sendings was preparing to stuff with smaller leather bags and pouches containing useful items for travel, though it insisted on displaying the things inside before they were repacked. Elinor had tried out a clockwork firestarter at their insistence, and a compass-type instrument that was entirely magical and as far as she could tell did not point north. She wasn't sure what it did point to, but supposed Mirelle could tell her in due course.

Another sending showed her a pair of heavy hobnailed boots, but was quickly shouldered aside by the one who seemed most superior, and this one offered fur-lined slippers of red-dyed doeskin and gestured for her to sit at the chair by the writing desk. As it put on the right slipper and tied its silver ribbons around her ankles, Elinor glanced over at the books lined up in the small bookcase at the rear of the writing desk. A sending had brought them in a few minutes before, carefully lining them up in the case.

It took Elinor a long moment to fully comprehend that the name in ornate type on every spine was 'Breakespear', and the titles all very familiar, save one. Realising this, she shot out of the chair, making the sending fall over backwards with the left slipper in its glowing Charter-mark-woven hand.

'*The Wise Woman!*' cried Elinor, snatching one slim, leather-bound volume out of the row. 'The lost Breakespear play! Oh, I'm sorry. I'll sit back down.'

She started to read the play immediately. The sending put on her left slipper and tied the ribbon, and silently moved away to stand by the door. Two others continued with their packing while a fourth stood patiently next to Elinor, holding a belt of gold plaques that supported a bone-handled narrow-bladed dagger in a scabbard of gold and ivory, waiting for an opportunity to put it on their guest.

Elinor was so intent on the play she didn't register the knock on the door at first, but the sending there opened it. Mirelle came in, saw Elinor reading, and smiled.

'You've found something interesting?' she asked.

Elinor looked up and blinked, returning to the world.

'Yes! A Breakespear play we don't have in Ancelstierre!' she exclaimed. 'I mean, it's known to be missing, there are parts of it, but this is complete! It's wonderful.'

'Can you tear yourself away for a little while?' asked Mirelle. 'To visit Terciel before we join Tizanael for supper?'

'Um, I suppose, yes,' said Elinor, conflicting emotions at war inside her. She desperately wanted to keep reading, but she also wanted to see Terciel in circumstances different from their last meeting.

She stood up, and the patient sending immediately knelt and put the golden belt around her waist, snicked its buckle shut, and settled the scabbard on her hip.

Elinor moved the scabbard back a little, drew the dagger and weighed it in her hand thoughtfully, before sliding it back home.

'Do we need to go armed?' she asked, pointing to the poniard on Mirelle's own far less ostentatious leather belt, which was studded with black iron pips. 'Even here?'

'It is a good habit in the Old Kingdom,' said Mirelle. 'And like most such habits, is best remembered if it is always followed. We are in a safe haven, here, Elinor, but you need to understand there are not many such. The towns, guarded by walls as well as the swift water of aqueduct, river or canal; the villages similarly, but less well defended. In between these places there is no safety; most of the Kingdom has long been in a perilous state.'

Elinor nodded thoughtfully, her hand on the hilt of the dagger.

'I fought the Dead at my home,' she said. 'And the sorcerer Hedge at the school. I know something, at least, of the dangers here.'

'You do,' agreed Mirelle.

'The sendings seem to think I will come to know more,' continued Elinor. 'Judging from all the stuff they keep bringing me. Armor and weapons and useful things for long travels.'

'The sendings like to anticipate different possibilities,' said Mirelle easily. 'And they tend to know things before they could possibly be told. Like your fondness for Breakespear. I think it may be because they are more deeply connected to the Charter than even we are. The Charter is in our blood and bone and flesh, but they are entirely part of it. At least, that is how I have heard their anticipations explained.'

'When do we go on to the Glacier?' asked Elinor. 'It looks like the storm is weakening.'

'I am not sure,' said Mirelle. 'There are some matters we must discuss with Tizanael, and others who are coming here. Shall we go visit Terciel? It isn't far.'

'You remind me of some friends of mine,' said Elinor, her eyes looking beyond Mirelle to her former life, which at that moment seemed so far behind her it might as well be a dream. 'Who were very adept at avoiding answering questions. But yes, I would like to see Terciel.'

Terciel's bedroom was next to Elinor's. Mirelle knocked on the door, and a sending opened it. Terciel's glad cry of 'Welcome' stuttered out in surprise as the ranger and Elinor came through the doorway.

'Oh,' continued Terciel, a frown of deep puzzlement on his forehead. 'I . . . er . . . was expecting Filris. The Infirmarian. Certainly not *you*, Miss Hallett. What I mean is, welcome.'

He was propped up in bed with several pillows, his arm splinted and bound but no longer in a sling. The bedspread in front of him was covered with sheets of paper bearing Charter-mark notations, evidently the workings of a very complex spell needing a great many marks. There was a high-necked green glass bottle of water and a silver cup on the side table next to him, and a polished wooden bowl of small, sweet apples, very wrinkled from having come out of some winter store.

'Thank you,' said Elinor cheerfully. 'I'm not surprised you're surprised! I am, myself. Before I met you I had no idea I might come to the Old Kingdom. Or about the Charter mark on my forehead, or anything, really. And we only stopped here on the way to the Glacier because of the storm.'

Terciel looked out the window. The snow had stopped falling a little while ago, and the cloud cover was rising. There were even a few errant rays of sun striking through.

'It is definitely clearing,' agreed Mirelle. 'So I expect we may see Filris and whoever will fly the Paperwing by nightfall, or perhaps some time tomorrow.'

'Filris? Who's that?' asked Elinor.

'She is the Infirmarian of the Clayr,' said Mirelle. 'Our most capable healer. Speaking of this, may I inspect your wound, Terciel? I have some small skills in dealing with the hurts of Free Magic myself.'

'Is it your arm?' asked Elinor. She was relieved to see that he looked perfectly fine, apart from the splint. More, she was surprised by her own sense of relief. She hardly knew him, after all. But perhaps it was because he'd made that first vital connection with the Charter for her, and ever since she'd crossed the Wall, albeit several hundred feet above it, Elinor had felt the immanence of the Charter, closer than it had ever been. And since arriving in the House, the Charter was explicitly all around her, she only had to touch a wall, or a book, or even taste the air to feel the Charter in its immensity, and her own connection to it, her own part in its completion.

'My arm is doing very well,' said Terciel. He tried to sound matter-of-fact and not show how frightened he was. 'A bone broken, but it is mending. I haven't exactly got a wound in my leg either. There is some sort of insidious Free Magic poison. I already can't feel my foot. It's creeping up . . .'

'Hmm,' said Mirelle. 'I'm sure Filris will be able to do something. Poke your leg out.'

Terciel grimaced and thrust his leg out from under the covers, pulling his nightshirt up. His leg looked normal enough, thought Elinor, save for a fading ring of bruising above the knee.

'What did this?' asked Mirelle. She leaned in very close and turned his foot, examining the skin.

'A serpent of glass,' said Terciel. 'A Free Magic entity called a Kerraste. I looked it up, afterwards.'

'Yes, I thought so,' said Mirelle. She tapped the base of his big toe, but Terciel didn't feel it. 'There is a tiny pinprick here, where it punctured your flesh with its sting and the veriest point broke off. That fragment of crystal, infused with Free Magic, is working its way to your heart – no, it cannot have got very far, not yet! I am sure Filris will be able to remove it, and make all well.'

'I never felt a sting,' said Terciel, after a few deep breaths to calm himself. 'The thing wound itself around my leg and struck at my face. I blocked it with my arm and its jaws were strong enough to break it. You say there is a pinprick?'

'It is minute, a dot,' said Mirelle. 'I only saw it because I suspected it was there.'

'I should have looked myself,' grumbled Terciel. 'Tizanael told me she can't see all that well any more. I should have—'

'What is the spell you're learning?' asked Elinor quickly, to change the subject.

'It's to augment my body against Free Magic, rather ironically,' replied Terciel. He gathered the papers together into a pile and put them on the side table. 'I haven't been able to focus on it, to tell you the truth.'

He looked properly at Elinor for the first time and made a kind of bow, sitting up in bed.

'But more important, what in the Charter's name brings you here? Did your house completely burn down? I still feel bad about that, but at the time I couldn't think of what else to do.'

Elinor smiled a rueful smile, and started to tell him. Terciel interjected with a few questions, nodding and then shaking his head in shared sadness as Elinor talked about Ham's death. But the laughter came soon enough as Elinor began to talk about her role at Wyverley and the rehearsals for *The Court of the Sad Prince* and she took four apples from the bowl and began to juggle with them.

Neither of them noticed Mirelle slide out of the room, leaving them talking. In the hallway outside, she saw a white cat sitting near the top of the stairs, licking his paws. A white cat with a red collar, on which swung a miniature version of Saraneth.

'You have assumed the cat form, Moregrim, Mogget, whatever your name,' said Mirelle. 'It suits you better.'

'I am hoping it will garner sufficient sympathy from you or the other visitor to fetch me a fish,' said Moregrim. 'It doesn't work on Tizanael or her idiot grand-nephew. She has forbidden me to enter her sight, and Terciel dislikes cats, apparently from having to fight over food with them in his early life.'

'I feel no sympathy,' said Mirelle. 'You are a Free Magic spirit, somehow bound imperfectly in servitude by Charter Magic, and I wonder at the ancestors who chose to do it, rather than destroying you or binding you far more rigorously.'

'But will you fetch me a fish?' asked Moregrim. 'You cannot remove my collar, so I won't bother asking *you* to do that.'

Mirelle's eyes narrowed. 'You already know Elinor also has the Abhorsen blood as well as the Clayr, do you? She will not remove your collar either, monster. She has been warned.'

Or she will be warned as soon as I can do it, Mirelle thought to herself. She rested her hand on the hilt of her poniard, though it would not be of much use if this creature got free of its binding.

'All I want from you is a fish,' said Moregrim plaintively. 'In return, I can tell you things. Knowledge lost to the Clayr, lost to everyone. But I remember.'

'I do not bargain with such as you,' said Mirelle.

'One of the river trout, just one . . .' began Moregrim, but he stopped suddenly, arched his back, and hissed. He arched higher and higher, his cat body shifting and stretching as he turned back into the broad-shouldered dwarf with the white-furred skin. This time, his ears stayed very pointy, and twitched, and a remnant tail did likewise. He turned on the spot and raced down the stairs, only seconds ahead of Tizanael, who was coming down from higher up.

She saw Mirelle, but didn't notice the departed Moregrim, confirming to Mirelle that the old Abhorsen's hearing and sight were indeed not what they had once been.

'A message-hawk, just come, has preceded Filris by mere hours,' said Tizanael. 'She is being flown down by Sazene. Doubtless she will wish to see Terciel at once, but after that, we should all gather in the hall for supper. There is other news. None of it good, and doubtless more to come.'

'I will attend her,' said Mirelle. 'I have, I think, identified the problem. The point of the Kerraste's sting broke off in Terciel's foot, and travels the bloodstream towards his heart.'

'I see,' said Tizanael slowly. 'Or rather, I should have seen it, or suspected as much. Do you think Filris will be able to take out the fragment?'

'If it is not gone too far,' said Mirelle. 'I would also have her look at the scars on Elinor's wrists. There is some remnant Free Magic there as well.'

Tizanael rubbed her watering eye in a gesture of exasperation.

'I need them both,' she said. 'Without further delay. I hope Filris is still the preeminent healer you Clayr claim.'

'She is,' said Mirelle. 'You should ask her to see to your hurts too, Abhorsen.'

Tizanael started to deny she needed any attention, but stopped herself.

'Yes,' she said. 'I need time, a little more time. Perhaps Filris can help me gain it.'

20

'I don't remember my parents at all,' said Terciel. 'They drowned before I was two. My sister, Rahi, sometimes I think I can remember her, but I'm really not sure.'

Elinor was sitting on the end of his bed now. Three of the four apples she'd been juggling had been eaten, two by Terciel and one by her. They'd been talking for hours, about all kinds of things, the topic now veering to families and relatives.

'My father died when I was ten,' said Elinor. 'But I hardly ever saw him, anyway. I didn't realise until much later that he and Mother didn't get along, and he spent a lot of time away. Well, no one got along with Mother. She was cold angry, and he was hot angry. All the time for her, and even when he wasn't angry, she would fire him up and then he'd storm out.'

'They did you a great disservice, telling you your mark was an ugly scar,' said Terciel. 'I wish I had met you sooner, to wake the mark.'

'I still would have been trapped there,' said Elinor. She tried to sound breezy, but it didn't come out that way. 'It doesn't matter. That was my past life, the chrysalid stage. Now I am here in the Old Kingdom, with the Charter, and am going to be a beautiful butterfly.'

She slipped off the end of the bed, took up the apple cores and the surviving complete apple, and juggled them, changing the order and reversing the direction. Terciel smiled, then blinked in amazement as Elinor drew a Charter mark while still juggling. It hung in the air as the apple and apple cores flew, was joined by another and then another, then the three Charter marks merged to become a golden ball that Elinor grabbed and added to the rotation. Finally she threw the golden ball straight up, almost to the ceiling, and caught the apple cores and apple, setting them down in a line on the side table before the golden ball fell. She caught that and it broke into a cloud of golden butterflies that fluttered up towards the ceiling and slowly dissipated.

'It wasn't supposed to do *that*,' said Elinor, staring.

'Where did you learn that spell?' asked Terciel.

'I, uh, made it myself,' said Elinor. 'I thought how wonderful it would be to juggle balls of light. But I could barely get them to persist for a few seconds back at the school.'

'That's very good,' said Terciel. 'Astonishing, even. Most Charter Mages cannot create *new* spells. You've learned a lot, very quickly.'

'It feels right to me,' said Elinor. 'Like this is what I was always supposed to be doing. Charter Magic. I'm looking forward to learning a lot more. Mirelle says there are thousands and thousands of books of Charter Magic in the Great Library of the Clayr, and of course, so many people to learn from.'

'Yes,' said Terciel, a little glumly. 'I forgot you were on your way to the Glacier. And the storm has passed now.'

Elinor looked out the window, over the white lawn, the stark fruit trees in the orchard; the enormously tall, snow-covered fig tree with its protruding grey-green roots where no snow stuck; the whitewashed walls; the line of mist from the waterfall beyond. She had heard its deafening roar flying in, and Terciel had explained why she couldn't any more.

'But the Paperwings usually won't fly at night,' continued Terciel. 'So you'll have to stay till tomorrow at least.'

Elinor made a noncommittal noise. Snow melting off the roof was dribbling down the windows, lines of water streaking the Charter-spelled glass, merging at the sill to form larger pools. One drop in particular attracted her gaze, because it seemed to be full of light, a softer light than from the lanterns that shone with Charter Magic, not oil, inside the room, or the weak sunshine of the early spring that was making its faltering way down through the higher cloud.

She stared at it, and the room fell away about her, or to be more accurate, reassembled itself in some slightly different guise. She felt her view shift as well, so she was somehow looking down from the ceiling and it was Terciel's room, the same room, but there was a different bedspread and a bottle of wine on the side table, not water, and no bowl of apples, and . . . Terciel was naked, mostly out of the covers, and with him was a woman and they were together in the way she had only seen in the book that Kierce had confiscated.

The woman, Elinor was shocked to see, was herself. Older, she thought. There was something about her confidence in what they were doing. Her hair was different, how she looked. It was as if Elinor was seeing an older sister, but she knew it was herself, and then she was entirely back in her own time and body staring at the water drop but she still let out a gasp and stepped back and—

Fell backwards onto the end of the bed.

'Elinor!'

Elinor sat up like a jack-in-the-box and leaped off the bed, tearing her elbow out of Terciel's tentative grasp.

'Sorry!' she exclaimed.

'Did you See something?' asked Terciel. 'In the water? I forgot you are a Clayr because they're so bossy and bright-haired, but you had the look then, when they See something . . .'

'No, I don't think so,' replied Elinor, blushing. 'Maybe. I've been reading too much, and imagination, you know, and we flew a long time so I'm a bit tired—'

'What did you See?' asked Terciel. 'Was it your own future? Or possible future, I know the Clayr always say that, because sometimes they See so many variations.'

'I'm not sure,' replied Elinor. 'I probably should go find Mirelle, see if there's something . . . I didn't mean to take up so much of your time, Terciel.'

'I'm glad you did,' said Terciel. He was still sitting forward, his arms outstretched, as if he might reach out and draw Elinor back to the bed. She took a step towards the window and turned to look out, hoping this would hide the embarrassment she was sure was evident in her expression. Or maybe it was expectation. Part of her very much wanted Terciel to draw her into his arms, onto the bed, a feeling that both alarmed and excited her, so she didn't know what to do. All she knew was she couldn't look at him right now. She needed to practise how to behave.

'I'm very glad you're here,' said Terciel softly.

As she turned, she saw the flash of movement in the sky. A red-and-gold Paperwing, no frosted snow upon it, coming down to land upon the lawn.

'A Paperwing!' she cried, pointing.

'More Clayr,' said Terciel. 'Filris, with any luck. You know, I had completely forgotten about my foot!'

'That's good,' replied Elinor. 'Oh, look!'

Spiralling down after the Paperwing came two message-hawks, brown streaks that came in over the wall, circled the fig tree once, and shot up to the western roof garden two floors above, where there was a mews built against the side of the tower, attended by several sending falconers.

'More news,' said Terciel. 'Doubtless not good.'

Elinor nodded. Terciel had told her about Kerrigor, and Lerantiel's chain, and Tizanael's plan to confront the Greater Dead wherever he was gathering his host. It sounded extremely dangerous to Elinor, and she thought

Terciel was anxious about it too, though he disguised it with talk of other Dead he and the Abhorsen had gone up against, and triumphed.

'I'd better go,' she said.

'Stay, please,' said Terciel. 'Filris is bound to want to have a bath and change and all that. It is a very long way from the Glacier.'

But Filris came straight from landing to Terciel's room. She was bright-eyed, white-haired and slight, and came into the room without knocking, a whirlwind of competence. Sendings stood aside as if for the Abhorsen herself, and Elinor jumped up from the end of the bed and made to slide out the door. Mirelle, coming up close behind, lifted her eyebrows and smiled.

'Elinor?' said Filris. 'Yes, Myrien's granddaughter. Don't go. I need to look at your wrists, gauge what is best to do there. Terciel, we have met, but you were ten or so, I doubt you recall. I am Filris, Infirmarian of the Clayr. Lie back and let's get that nightshirt off.

'I really should go,' said Elinor nervously. 'I can come back.'

'Naked men disturb you?' asked Filris. 'Or just this one?'

'Uh . . .'

'I will come and find you shortly,' said Filris, dismissing her.

Elinor fled. As she passed Mirelle, the Clayr held her elbow for a second, and said, 'You should visit the library, ground floor of the tower. I think you'll like it.'

Elinor, too flustered to answer, left the room.

'You are a wicked old woman,' scolded Mirelle.

Terciel grimaced and lifted off his nightshirt, struggling to clear his arm in the cast out of the sleeve. Filris was already lifting his foot, bending down to inspect it closely.

'By the big toe,' said Mirelle helpfully.

'I see it,' said Filris shortly. 'A Kerraste, you say?'

'I think so,' said Terciel. 'It looked just like the engraving in *Creatures by Nagy*. But that didn't mention a sting in its tail.'

'Hmm,' said Filris. She set his foot down and traced a Charter mark so close to his skin he could almost, but not quite, feel her fingertip. Her nails were carefully cut short, he noticed. She followed that mark with several more, all of them unknown to Terciel. She whispered their use-names under her breath as she spoke, and then fell silent, to sketch a master mark. It merged with the others, and a golden haze formed over the foot, before transforming into a clear pane of crystal. Terciel craned his head and saw that this pane revealed a view inside his foot, showing all the blood vessels and bones as if the skin had not only been peeled away but everything made somewhat translucent.

At the same time he felt a sudden pain halfway up the arch of his foot, and flinched. Filris's hand snapped down to hold his foot in place with a strength that surprised him.

'Hold still,' she commanded. 'I see it. Not much more than a grain of sand, but sufficient to kill you.'

'Kill me?' asked Terciel.

'If it reached your heart,' said Filris. 'But it has not got very far. I will summon it forth, back the way it went in. Mirelle, would you lay out my satchel?'

'Will I get the feeling back in my foot?' asked Terciel.

'Rather too much,' said Filris. 'I am afraid this will hurt a great deal and I cannot use Charter Magic to relieve the pain, given the nature of this fragment. Nor will a bentwhorl decoction be effective in this case. I am sorry.'

'How long will it take?' asked Terciel. He gulped.

'I will be as swift as I can,' said Filris. 'Perhaps two or three minutes.'

She took a long pair of bronze pincers from her satchel and put them by Terciel's foot, then a small silver bottle with a wired stopper, which she undid and set both pieces down.

'Mirelle, and you sendings, hold Terciel down, please.'

Mirelle put her hands on Terciel's leg above and below the knee and began to press down, but the sendings did not move, until Terciel nodded his head. Then they glided over, one on each side, and he felt the strange pressure of their magical hands upon his arms and shoulders.

'Very good,' said Filris. She handed Terciel a short piece of thick rope, knotted at the ends. 'Bite on this. All will be well, Terciel.'

She drew a mark in the air above his toe, and another, and another, in very rapid succession, her fingers leaving glowing trails of light. She brought them together and Terciel bucked rigid under Mirelle and the sending's hands, screaming as a pain like a white-hot poker shot up through his foot to his head, a line of fire along the whole side of his body.

* * *

Elinor loved the reading room. Like her bedroom, it might have been made to her own design. Bookcases of a rich, lustrous timber stretched from the floor to the very high ceiling above, all the way around, save where the stair rose to the next floor of the tower. There were four huge armchairs in the middle of the room, back to back, each with an iron-framed table that could be wheeled in place for taking notes or stacking up a to-be-read pile, but otherwise were parked besides the chairs. The whole room smelled pleasantly of books. Not a musty, tainted smell, but the clean smell of paper and parchment pages and leather and cloth bindings.

A gilded iron candelabra hung from the ceiling, a delicate construction of filigree and slim rods made in the shape of a heraldic sunburst. Charter marks for light were arrayed upon it so that it shone brighter in the centre than along the arms.

Librarian sendings drifted out from the shelves when Elinor came in. One ushered her to a lectern and indicated the massive tome on it, which was chained to the wall behind. The leather-and-gold binding had no title stamped upon it, and Elinor was reluctant to open it, until the librarian sending stepped up and did it for her, to show the title page.

'*A Catalogue of the Library of the Abhorsens Saving Those Too Secret to Mention and Sundry Others Excluded for Important Reasons,*' read Elinor aloud.

The sending bowed and indicated the books all around them, with outstretched arms, back to the catalogue, and then to itself and the two other librarians who had come to stand behind her.

'I look in the catalogue, and you fetch me books?' asked Elinor. 'I guess not any secret ones or those excluded for other important reasons?'

The sendings bowed in unison.

'Right,' said Elinor. She hesitated, then started paging through the catalogue, with no particular intent until she thought of the Breakespear play that had been put in her bedroom and then she was suddenly flipping through to the Bs.

What if there were other lost Breakespear plays?

But when Filris came to the library a scant hour later, she found Elinor fast asleep, curled up in one of the big leather armchairs. The sendings had put a blue-and-silver blanket upon her, and whatever she had been reading had already been carefully returned to the shelves.

'Elinor.'

Elinor opened one eye, remembered where she was, and sat up, dislodging the blanket. The old Clayr was looking down at her.

'Oh, I'm sorry,' said Elinor. 'It has been a very long day. We left Fort Entrance at dawn, Ancelstierran time, and then when we crossed the Wall, it was just before the dawn . . . actually I don't know how long this day has been. How is Terciel? Could you . . . could you heal his foot?'

'I have not crossed the Wall myself,' said Filris, sitting down in the chair next to her. 'But I understand it would be disorienting, and all the more so for someone coming from the south. As for Terciel, he will soon recover, though it is as well I came when I did. Now, let me see your wrists. I hear you were held by a Free Magic sorcerer, but only for a short time?'

'Seconds,' said Elinor. She pushed her sleeves back and held out her arms. 'Certainly less than a minute.'

Filris examined first Elinor's left then her right wrist carefully, and cast a spell on each featuring very tiny marks that Elinor could hardly see, which sank into her skin and vanished.

'What was that spell?' she asked curiously. 'And why were the marks so small?'

'It is a spell to clear Free Magic contamination from blood vessels,' said Filris. 'The marks begin small, because they must shrink even further to become something too small to be seen by the unaided eye, which travels the blood and eats up any trace of Free Magic.

'However,' she added, carefully replacing Elinor's right hand on the armchair. 'There was almost no contamination in you. A trace, no more. Enough that you would sense the sorcerer again, but nothing truly dangerous. It will be gone in a day or so. Now, I must see to my third patient before supper, which I admit I eagerly await.'

'Your third patient?' asked Elinor. 'Who is that?'

'Tizanael,' said Filris. 'The Abhorsen. Age wearies even those bolstered by Charter Magic, as I know myself. I will see you at supper, child.'

'Thank you,' said Elinor.

21

'Supper' was something of a misnomer, Elinor considered, as she was led into the Great Hall by a sending and saw the quantity of food on the long table, though it was sometimes difficult for her to tell if a particular highly polished dish was there for display only. The silver-crowded table caught her eye for only a second, because she was immediately distracted by the stained-glass window at the far end, which, despite it already being twilight outside, shone as if the sun was fully behind it. Nor was it glass, she realised, because the images moved, albeit very slowly. It seemed to be a scene from constructing the Wall, but Elinor found whenever she glanced away, she couldn't remember what she'd seen.

A cough behind her made Elinor turn around. Tizanael loomed above her, all craggy and dominating, made even more so by the deep blue or black dress she wore, which was dotted with the key motif in diamonds, and the diamond bracelets on her wrists, though only a single ring with a small ruby. She wore her sword, the same one Elinor had seen before: a relatively plain weapon, but its rather beaten-up leather scabbard was suspended from a belt of braided gold and silver.

'Welcome to the Abhorsen's House,' said Tizanael, and inclined her head. 'The more so, for you are yourself a distant relative.'

'What?' asked Elinor, before she remembered her manners and bowed back. 'I mean, my grandmother was a Clayr, is that what—'

'No, for all we count the Clayr as cousins of a sort, there is a more direct connection,' said Tizanael. 'Your great-great-great-grandfather was the Abhorsen Jeremiel. Though that line is no more, save for yourself, we would have had a shared ancestor a century or two ago. I have not looked into the exact genealogy.'

'I have gone from having no relatives at all to quite a number, it seems,' said Elinor, not knowing what else to say. She wondered if it was important in some way, that they had this distant connection. A great-great-great-grandfather did not seem very significant. But then people in the Old Kingdom seemed to care more about this sort of thing.

'Indeed,' replied Tizanael forbiddingly, and indicated a seat, two down on the left from the high-backed, almost throne-like chair at the head of the table. This, she unsurprisingly took herself.

Elinor sat down rather nervously. A sending immediately poured a pale red wine into one of the six crystal glasses in front of her. Rather disturbingly, there was a gold-mounted drinking horn there as well, which was as long as Elinor's forearm. She had the feeling it might be for some fermented milk or something of that nature, and hoped she wouldn't have to drink any. She'd never even had wine before arriving at Wyverley College, where they served it with dinner, and sherry afterwards.

The tap of Terciel's stick announced his arrival. He limped over and sat between Tizanael and Elinor, muttered a greeting to his great-aunt, and smiled at Elinor. She smiled back.

The three Clayr arrived together, talking quietly. Elinor was surprised to see they were all wearing the same clothes the sendings had made her change into half an hour before. Extraordinarily white, flowing robes that she was very nervous about spilling things on. The other three also had circlets of silver set with moonstones on their heads, whereas she had not been offered this particular adornment. Though a sending had brushed her hair several hundred times and set a comb of amber and red gold on the left side, which she liked. It was rather nice to be pampered, and to be given so many nice things, even though Elinor presumed they were merely lent to her for the duration of her visit. She still wore the belt of gold plaques and the bone-handled dagger.

Sazene, the Clayr who had flown the Paperwing for Filris, was older than Mirelle, but was also blonde-haired and brown-skinned, though she had very pale green eyes. She was shorter than Mirelle, and did not have the same hard look about her, so Elinor presumed she was not one of the rangers. Though, like them all, she wore a long dagger at her side.

'Sazene,' said Filris as she sat. 'That is Elinor, Myrien's granddaughter. I don't think you knew Myrien?'

'Before my time, I'm afraid,' said Sazene. She smiled, nodded to Elinor and sat down.

Mirelle sat next to her eagerly, rubbing her hands together. 'We should kidnap that sending of yours who seasons and grills the round fish, Tizanael. I have never tasted better.'

'As those fish can only be caught on this stretch of the Ratterlin, it would not help you,' replied Tizanael. 'You will have to make do with what you can eat while you're here. But before we do eat, there are important matters to discuss.'

'I saw the message-hawks flying in,' said Filris. She beckoned to a sending, and indicated the third glass along in the line in front of her, which the sending filled with a sparkling wine the colour of fresh straw.

'Four today,' said Tizanael. 'Two from Belisaere, one from Uppside, and another from the Borderer's post north of Roble's Town.'

She took a sip from her own glass, a red wine so dark it looked as if it was a black syrup quite different from everyone else's.

'Uppside is besieged. A summoned fog rolled across this morning, and beneath it, the Dead drag logs and earth to fill the canals. Gore Crows fly above the fog. Other message-hawks were sent, but only one made it here.'

'Uppside!' exclaimed Terciel. He looked stunned. 'But there must be five thousand people there, a Trained Band of hundreds, at least two dozen Charter Mages! Surely it is too strong to be attacked?'

'Kerrigor has destroyed all the villages in the Upp river valley, everything from Far Upp to Nether Upp,' said Tizanael. She spoke as calmly as ever, but Elinor noted her left hand upon the table was tightly clenched in anger. 'At least two thousand villagers, two thousand spirits reaped, two thousand bodies to be inhabited by stronger spirits drawn from Death. And he has mortal followers too, sorcerers and bandits. Against all that, I would guess Uppside can hold out only for a short time. Days, I suspect, not weeks, depending on how swiftly the water defences are breached. The message from the Borderers said the fog extends up the lower slopes of Mount Starn, where the Dead are felling the giant blackwood trees, dragging the logs down.'

'And the messages from Belisaere?' asked Mirelle.

'The Regent is suffering another fit of madness. She insists on staying in the palace, though it is known to cause these ill humours, none know why. And there is at least one necromancer in the city, within the aqueducts. I had asked for guards to be sent south, to aid us when we moved against Kerrigor, but they will not come now. I did not know he had already taken Nether Upp, three days past. I have been too slow. If we had gone against him three weeks ago, when his strength was so much less . . .'

'But you didn't have the chain then,' said Terciel awkwardly.

'Yes. I spent too long searching for it,' said Tizanael. 'And your wounding delayed us more. I should have avoided that also, known what the empty bottle meant. I grow dull with age. But late or not, we must now deal with Kerrigor. Before he can take Uppside, slay all those in the town, and swell his host even more.'

'But if there is a necromancer in Belisaere, shouldn't we—'

'No. Kerrigor is by far the greater danger. The Regent's guards can track down and slay a mortal sorcerer. There are no burial grounds, no cemeteries within the city's borders, and it has long been the practice for any corpses to be taken away and burned, whether by the Charter rite or simple fires. There are no corpses, no repository of bones and flesh, nothing for a necromancer to call upon.'

'There are a great many living people,' said Filris. 'Who might be killed.'

'One necromancer is not a significant threat there,' said Tizanael. 'Kerrigor is far more than that. He must be dealt with first.'

'How?' asked Terciel. He raised his arm and tapped his foot. 'I can use this arm, but not at my full strength. The feeling in my foot is coming back, but I'll be clumsy for a while yet. I can't carry the chain. Even if I could—'

'I need Elinor to carry the chain,' said Tizanael. She turned to look directly at the young woman. 'If you will help us.'

'No!' protested Terciel, as Elinor did not immediately reply. After his outburst, there was silence in the hall for several seconds, save for the whispery footfalls of the sendings.

'Lerantiel's chain?' asked Elinor.

Tizanael nodded gravely.

'You are an Abhorsen, in blood at least, and I believe you have the strength of will to bear the chain.'

Elinor frowned, thinking deeply. Terciel had told her about the chain. He had clearly been worried about being anywhere near the thing. He had talked of Kerrigor too, a foe far more powerful and dangerous even than the Greater Dead who had taken over her mother's body, more than Hedge who had killed Ham and burned her wrists. Yet Kerrigor was also the one ultimately responsible for what had happened to Mrs Watkins, Ham, Cook, Maria . . .

And then there were all the nice things, the beautiful bedroom, the awe-inspiring flight from the Wall, the comfort of the Charter she could feel all around, her sense of belonging as she never had before. Elinor knew there was no price as such for all this. It was a gift, freely given, but gift givers deserved to have their gifts returned in some fashion, paid in whatever coin she had.

'Yes,' she said slowly and clearly. 'I will carry the chain, and do whatever I can to help.'

'Elinor! You have no idea what you're getting into,' protested Terciel. 'You can't take my place, I—'

'I will need you too,' said Tizanael. 'Of course.'

'But—'

'Perhaps we should listen to the Abhorsen's plan, as clearly she has one,' said Filris. 'I, for one, am hungry and would like to get past the talking to the eating. It is well past my dinnertime.'

'Time is the matter that concerns me most,' said Tizanael. 'Though not for dinner. We must confront and chain Kerrigor before his forces overwhelm Uppside. That is, within the next few days.'

'It is forty leagues to Uppside,' protested Mirelle. 'Three days on horseback, at the least. If you have mounts hidden nearby. Six days on foot, for the hardy. Impossible to fly in now, in the Paperwings, if there are Gore Crows above, and a summoned fog.'

'We will fly, the Paperwings willing, but not directly to Uppside,' said Tizanael. She sketched two Charter marks in the air, closed them in her hand, and dipped her finger in her wine. Withdrawing it, she began to draw on the white linen tablecloth, ignoring the slight stir among the sendings who stood behind her chair. Her finger did not leave a spreading wine stain, but a sharp black line. She quickly drew a map of the northern end of the Red Lake, showing Uppside and its three rows of defensive canals, fed by both the Upp River and the lake; and the country around the town, particularly the lower slope of Mount Starn.

'There are still stoat fingers watching us here, and perhaps others as well. To avoid their observation we will go north along the Ratterlin, as if heading for Belisaere, until well out of sight. Then we turn to the west and fly, not directly to Uppside, but to the high plateau between Mount Starn and Mount Rewan, here. There is a sunken stream, a ravine we can follow down, into the giant blackwoods, where Kerrigor's followers are cutting timber. I have been that way several times; I know the path well.'

She sketched in this ravine and drew some trees and an X.

'According to the Borderer who reported the felling of the trees, Kerrigor has set up a kind of court in the fringe of the forest, overlooking the siege camp below and the town beyond. He has done this before, aping his living betters, thinking himself some sort of king or chieftain. We will attack him there. Terciel and I will quell the Dead, Elinor will throw the chain upon whatever living form Kerrigor inhabits, then Terciel and I will take the chained spirit deep into Death and fix him there. Once Kerrigor is gone into Death, most of the Hands will dissipate, doubtless those Dead who do not, and his mortal followers, will flee in fear.'

Silence greeted Tizanael's words.

She scowled, and continued. 'It is not as foolhardy as it might sound. We will need tonight to prepare Elinor as well to carry the chain, but we can leave tomorrow before the dawn and be at the high plateau by the end of the morning, even the roundabout way. We walk to the head of the ravine, camp there overnight, then descend in the morning. We would arrive at Kerrigor's court in the forest around noon. The weather is bound to stay clear after the storm that has passed. It always does for a few days.'

'You just told us there is a summoned fog about Uppside and the forest!' exclaimed Terciel. 'It might as well be night!'

'The Dead still feel the presence of the sun above the fog,' replied Tizanael. 'They will be weaker. The two of us can quell any number of Lesser Dead long enough to wrest Kerrigor's spirit from his body, and—'

She turned to look at Mirelle, before going on. 'I hope you will help us too, Mirelle. A ranger of the Clayr will be invaluable to keep any mortal followers of Kerrigor at bay, while we do what needs to be done.'

'You also need me to fly Elinor in our Paperwing,' said Mirelle drily.

'I do,' replied Tizanael.

Terciel shook his head.

Elinor glanced at Tizanael, and then at Terciel. She was reminded very much of the final battle scene from Breakespear's *Arbiter John*, where the aged Arbiter argued with his daughters, desperate for one final victory over the nobles to secure the constitution that even today underpinned the government of Ancelstierre. In the play, the Arbiter convinced his daughters, and they triumphantly won the battle. Elinor had a vague memory this was not the historical outcome, which had been a lot messier.

'It seems all would be staked upon a single throw of the dice,' said Filris quietly. 'Are there no alternative courses of action?'

'Unlike you, I cannot look into the future and See a hundred or a thousand paths ahead,' said Tizanael, with some bitterness. 'All I know is that if we do not move against Kerrigor now, it will become ever more difficult to do so. I would I had acted sooner, but I could not. He will grow only stronger. We will grow weaker. *I* will grow weaker. And thousands will die who place their hope in the Abhorsen, to defend them against the Dead.'

'We could bring three, maybe four score of my rangers down by boat to Qyrre, have horses waiting, ready to strike west,' said Mirelle.

'That would take a week, probably more,' replied Tizanael. 'By then Uppside will have fallen, thousands will be dead, and Kerrigor's host will be all the mightier. Besides, when have you Clayr ever moved quickly for something you have not Seen?'

'Valid criticism, on both points,' said Filris. 'I hope you are not going to ask Sazene and myself to help you, Tizanael. I believe we should go to Belisaere. I may be able to help the Regent regain her senses. I am not so sure all will be well there.'

'What have you Seen?' asked Tizanael.

'Me personally? Nothing,' replied Filris. 'But when we departed the Glacier, the Voice was calling a Watch of one thousand five hundred and sixty-eight, to try to see more clearly into the very tangled futures around the capital. That is never good, when so many paths lie ahead, and none are clear enough to find a way.'

'What do we do if it's a trap?' asked Terciel suddenly. 'If Kerrigor expects us to come, the way you plan? Or things go wrong?'

'We will do our best to defeat him anyway,' said Tizanael. 'Elinor has said she will bear the chain. Will you wield your sword and bells? Our chance of success would be greatly lessened without my Abhorsen-in-Waiting.'

Terciel looked at Elinor, who met his gaze steadily.

'I'll do my best,' she said.

'Then so will I,' said Terciel. He raised his splinted arm and flexed his fingers. 'I only wish my best was currently rather better.'

'And you, ranger?' Tizanael asked Mirelle.

The Clayr shrugged. 'I said I would bring Elinor to the Glacier. It seems we will be taking a twistier path to get there than I expected.'

'Now can we eat?' asked Filris.

Tizanael nodded, and sendings leaned in to remove the covers from the many dishes already on the table, and more sendings streamed out of the kitchen, bearing steaming platters of roast beef, ducks stuffed with sage, and at the end a confused sending stared at the platter that a few moments before had held an entire baked fish and now was empty, the fish lost somewhere between the kitchen table and the door.

Later, after the final course of a frozen ice confection of pear and rosewater that Elinor presumed must have been made with the aid of magic, because it was so delicious, she went with Tizanael and Terciel up to the Abhorsen's study. Tizanael climbed the tower stairs slowly, but Elinor was so full from dinner she was in no hurry either. As they climbed, she was thinking of the copy of *The Wise Woman* and hoping there would be time to finish reading the play before they left.

The study was a smaller version of the reading room below, the ceiling lower, with a trapdoor and ladder in one corner. It was dominated by a redwood desk with carved dragon heads at each corner and taloned feet on the legs, which Elinor noticed with interest. Were dragons real in the Old Kingdom? she wondered, and was about to ask Terciel when Tizanael spoke.

'Stand at the end of the table, Elinor.'

Elinor obeyed. Tizanael went to a glass cabinet, the only one among the otherwise open bookshelves. A single book was in the cabinet, a small tome of pale green leather with silver edges and clasp. Elinor's eye was drawn to it, but it was the kind of fascination you might have on spotting a venomous snake. She couldn't take her eyes away but she also wished it wasn't there.

Tizanael did not take the book, but a sheaf of papers from the shelf underneath. She laid these out on the table, a dozen pages covered with the symbols used to represent Charter marks. It was the guide for an immensely complicated spell, and Elinor recognised these as the pages that had been on Terciel's bed. But she only glanced at them. She couldn't tear her eyes away from the green book in the cabinet.

'That is *The Book of the Dead*,' said Tizanael, when she had finished laying out the pages. 'Do you feel a desire to read it?'

'No,' whispered Elinor. 'I do not.'

'You have been with people when they die,' continued Tizanael. 'When they did, did you feel as if you might be able to follow them? Sense they had gone somewhere you could also go?'

'No,' said Elinor. 'What do you mean?'

'Necromancers, and we Abhorsens, who are a sort of uncommon necromancer, are able to walk in Death and return to Life,' said Tizanael. 'You have heard of this?'

'A bit,' said Elinor nervously. 'But I have never felt like *I* could do that!'

Terciel cleared his throat, as if to speak, but fell silent at a quelling glance from Tizanael.

'Have you felt people or animals die?' asked Tizanael. 'That is, sensed a sudden absence, and later seen it was where someone or something died?'

'No,' said Elinor, shaking her head.

'It is difficult to explain the death sense to someone who does not have it,' said Tizanael. 'It seems you do not, or it is undeveloped. Likely the potential is there, given your heritage.'

'I don't think I want it,' said Elinor. She looked at Terciel, who grimaced. 'Sorry.'

'It is not material at this time,' said Tizanael. She hesitated, then added, 'I thought perhaps you might be a candidate as a future Abhorsen-in-Waiting.'

'What?' asked Terciel. He looked carefully at Tizanael, searching for any sign he might have missed that she was failing. She looked as indomitable and unchanged as ever, but he felt an ache in his chest, one that was part apprehension and part something else he couldn't identify. A sense of impending loss.

'It is of no matter,' said Tizanael. 'What we must do now is reinforce you against Free Magic, so you can bear the chain of Lerantiel, as we have already done for Terciel. Terciel, you are ready?'

'I am,' said Terciel. 'I still need to follow the reference for that last spell.'

He looked at Elinor, sensing her shift nervously.

'Don't worry. The spell isn't dangerous. To you, I mean. Only to us if we get it wrong, it uses a dozen master marks.'

'All right,' said Elinor. She thought of the dinner, and wondered how much wine the two Abhorsens had drunk. She hadn't really been paying attention. Terciel hadn't drunk much, but Tizanael? 'Be . . . be careful. Maybe we should wait till morning? I mean, the wine at dinner . . .'

Tizanael smiled, something Terciel had seen very rarely, and Elinor had never seen before.

'I do not drink wine in the evenings, child. I haven't for years. Only plum juice and water, with a little honey. It is quite delicious. You will need to stand still, for a quarter hour I judge. It might help to shut your eyes.'

'Can I keep them open?' asked Elinor. 'I'd like to see how you cast such a spell.'

'You may,' said Tizanael. 'Mirelle said you have surprising facility with Charter Magic, given how recently it has come to you. But you must not interfere. Do not focus too much on any one mark, or Charter forbid, try any spell yourself while we work.'

'I understand,' said Elinor gravely.

'Then I will begin,' said Tizanael. 'Terciel, you will cast the next part, after the first master mark, we will then alternate. But be ready if I falter. I will do likewise for you.'

'Yes, Abhorsen,' said Terciel. He came to stand by her side. They faced Elinor, two paces away, and Tizanael reached for the Charter and began the spell.

Elinor felt no different when the spell was done, but Terciel and Tizanael in particular were evidently exhausted. Sendings, who had not been present for the casting as far as Elinor could tell, made their silent appearance and helped the old Abhorsen downstairs to her bed. Terciel collapsed in a chair and put his leg up on the table, and Elinor stood where she'd been for the spell-casting, touching her skin to watch Charter marks she didn't know rise up like some temporary, glowing tattoo, before disappearing again.

'How long will this last?' she asked.

'Until the new moon,' said Terciel wearily. 'Maybe not so long, if you have to handle the chain for any length of time, unprotected. Or you are subjected to other Free Magic. I am sorry about this. If that snake-eel thing hadn't got me—'

'It's all right,' said Elinor. She drew out a chair and sat down opposite him. 'Gosh, these are uncomfortable.'

'They are,' agreed Terciel. He yawned and said, 'I should go to bed.'

But he did not move, and neither did Elinor. They sat in silence, together, looking at each other across the polished redwood. It was very quiet, all the sendings had gone with Tizanael. It was just the two of them.

Terciel cleared his throat and started to say something, but didn't. His eyes spoke for him, a yearning look that Elinor felt must be echoed in her own gaze, recognition that they might only have this moment, this brief bubble in time, to let each other know what they felt.

'Can I come too?' Elinor said suddenly, made brave by the knowledge that come daybreak they would be set on a path to incredible danger, quite possibly to death. There might be no second chances.

'To bed?' asked Terciel. 'With me? I wanted to ask *you* . . . uh, that is what you mean?'

'Yes. I'd like to go to bed with you,' confirmed Elinor. Her vision of them together was strong in her mind. She'd been older in that, much older, but surely that didn't mean she had to wait? 'Since I first saw you, I suppose, though I didn't know that's what it was then. The feeling, I mean.'

'I've been thinking about you too,' said Terciel. He reached across the table and their hands met with a tingling shock that made them both rise and lean forward, but the table was too broad and they laughed and edged around until they stood close together at the end, Terciel looking down, Elinor looking up, their faces very close together. 'Ever since you slammed the door on my face, I've been thinking of you, hoping I would see you, hoping I could kiss you—'

He stopped talking as that kiss became inevitable. Elinor had overheard many schoolgirls talking about kissing, but none of that stayed in her head, and she wasn't even really sure what she was doing with her mouth or her tongue, or what Terciel was doing, but she liked it and let out a small sigh as they stopped to take a very necessary breath.

'Even though I never expected to see you again,' said Terciel. He was holding her very tightly, and she was doing the same to him, Elinor realised. As if having suddenly found each other, some terrible force might break them apart.

'I didn't either,' said Elinor simply. 'But now we are here and maybe this is all the time we'll have together. Tonight. I mean, going off tomorrow to try to chain some Greater Dead . . . I wasn't going to say anything, but I remembered the Queen in *Queen Cressida* and how she regretted not taking the Duke as her lover that one night they could have and—'

'Make the best of things,' said Terciel. 'That's what Mirelle told me.'

'Oh,' said Elinor. She drew back a little, but did not let go of him. 'Do you and Mirelle have an understanding? She told me about how things work in the Glacier, I mean with men visiting and all, though I thought she—'

'No. No!' exclaimed Terciel. He quickly kissed her again, Elinor joining in enthusiastically. When once again they needed to breathe, he continued. 'No, nothing like that. Mirelle was just giving me advice. About, I don't know, not ignoring opportunities, letting myself fall in love . . .'

'I don't know much about actually *making* love, you know,' said Elinor thoughtfully into the nape of Terciel's neck, which she found herself kissing suddenly. 'I've looked at a book. I do know the Charter spells for contraception though.'

'So do I,' said Terciel. He kissed the top of Elinor's head, stepped back a fraction, and disentangled one hand to gesture at the door. 'And I think we should practise casting one *immediately*. Given our beds are almost identical, which one would you prefer?'

'The closest one,' said Elinor.

22

The morning arrived all too swiftly, with sendings coming in to wake them shortly before the dawn, bearing plates of sweet rolls and some sort of hot herbal tea with honey. Not peppermint or chamomile or anything Elinor recognised, but it smelled pleasant.

'No,' mumbled Elinor, clutching at Terciel. 'It can't be time to get up, surely?'

'The sendings will just get more emphatic,' said Terciel regretfully. He wiggled his foot, which was sticking out from under the covers. 'Hey, my foot is much better. I can feel my toes.'

'What is that smell?' asked Elinor, wrinkling her nose. Something quite different to the scent of herbal tea was assaulting her nostrils now, which were about all that was visible of her. She was almost entirely under the covers, snuggled up to Terciel, enjoying the sensation of being in bed with him, all cosy.

'Goose fat,' said Terciel. 'Being rubbed into your boots to make them more waterproof.'

The sending who had woken him touched him on the shoulder again and pointed to the door. Another one patted Elinor on the head and made a beckoning motion. The third continued to stolidly rub goose fat into her boots and the waterproof outer layer of her fur-lined cape.

Terciel reached into the Charter, invested his breath with a chosen mark, and blew it towards the ceiling, where it quickened the marks for light set in the pressed plaster. They brightened, flooding the bedroom with light. The curtains were drawn now, for privacy, not warmth, but there was a three-inch gap that showed only the faintest lightening of the sky, the sun not yet visible at all.

'It's time,' Terciel said regretfully, turning to Elinor. 'I have to go get ready. You need to as well. We'll be leaving straight away, so don't forget to eat.'

He kissed her forehead, and then as she emerged more out of the covers, kissed her on the mouth as well. Elinor kissed him back, but did not try to hold him. Their stolen time was over, she knew, and now they must get on with the serious business of being the Abhorsen-in-Waiting and whatever she was now. A chain-carrying Clayr, she supposed, which did not sound so important. But she knew it was.

'I'll see you downstairs,' said Terciel, putting on the robe offered him by the sending. He grabbed a roll from the plate, turned and bowed deeply to Elinor. 'Thank you.'

'Thank you too,' said Elinor, very seriously. She kept her face expressionless for a moment, then laughed.

Terciel smiled and went out the door, munching on the roll.

A sending turned the taps and the hint of rotten egg stench from the deep spring overcame the odour of goose fat, and steam began to rise from the basin. Elinor slid out of the bed and steeled herself for the ministrations of the sendings. She already knew they were slightly overzealous with sponge and soap.

Half an hour later, she was attired in the leather armour they'd brought the day before, with the reinforced plates at knees and elbows. Ham's three throwing knives were at her left side, a long dagger on her right. A bow made from laminated horn, roughly the size of the bow she'd practised with at Wyverley, was strapped to her pack, which contained all the clever things she'd been shown by the sendings the day before, including several spare bowstrings. A waterproof quiver with a kind of lid held a dozen arrows, and could be attached on the side of the pack.

The fur-lined, hooded, waterproof cape now redolent with goose fat completed the ensemble, but she hadn't put that on yet. It was too warm inside. A sending carried the cape, and the pack, and the quiver. Elinor looked at the load and regretted that the sending was not coming with them.

Everyone else was already outside when she came out the front door, and were all wearing their capes and packs and weapons, stamping their feet to stay warm. Elinor hastily donned her cape and pack and a sending fastened on the quiver. The backpack was not as heavy as she feared, but she knew it would grow heavier very quickly. It was icy outside, the sun just high enough to send its light into the river valley, but not high enough yet to clear the walls around the island. Her breath came out in clouds of white, and she could feel the chill on her cheeks and nose.

'We go first, as I am the superior weather-worker,' said Mirelle to Elinor, pointing. One Paperwing was already on the launching platform, the green-and-gold one Mirelle had flown Elinor in before. Another two waited below the wall, the next in line silver and dark blue, and then another in green and gold, each carried by eight sendings, the aircrafts' wings still folded. All the Paperwings had fierce yellow eyes like hawks, and every now and then Elinor thought they blinked and were full of fierce life, though at other times she was sure they were only painted.

Tizanael was holding a small ironwood chest with silver edges. A ruby shone on the lockplate.

'I have the chain here,' she said to Elinor. 'To lessen your exposure, I think it best you do not carry it until we are on foot.'

Elinor nodded. That was fine with her. She glanced at Terciel, hoping for a secret smile or a glimpse of what she'd seen in his eyes the night before, but he was looking up at the sky and holding the cast on his right arm with his left hand. He looked different to her, in his armoured coat with the bell bandolier and sword. More the Abhorsen-in-Waiting and less the young man, her young man – at least he had been and maybe would be again.

If we survive, Elinor thought again. She shivered, and tried to put that particular recurring thought out of her mind.

'Farewell,' said Filris. 'May we all meet again. I hope to see you in the Glacier, Elinor. You will be very welcome.'

Sazene smiled and nodded in affirmation of this.

'Thank you,' muttered Elinor. 'I hope I will see you there. I mean, see you, with these eyes, not with the Sight, I haven't had many visions, you know, I used to when I was little but I didn't realise what . . . I'm babbling, sorry.'

'Come on,' said Mirelle. She turned to Tizanael. 'North along the river for a league, before we two turn to the west? I will raise the wind properly behind us once we are all aloft.'

Elinor followed her up the steps, arriving on the wall at the same time the sun splashed across the parapet and lit up the waiting Paperwing, so that its green-and-gold fuselage and feathery wings shone. Elinor hadn't noticed before, or maybe the morning sun had energised them, but the whole craft was simply swarming with Charter marks.

'Stow your pack behind where you sit, bow and quiver in the pockets at the side. It will be less comfortable than when we flew up, but shorter.'

Mirelle settled her backpack in the cockpit and got in. She inhaled deeply and breathed out on the small oval mirror of silvered glass fixed in front of the cockpit, which Elinor knew was how she directed or communicated with the Paperwing. It filled with golden light, but Elinor had to stop staring at it and get her own backpack stowed away, put the bow in the pocket at the left side and the quiver on the right, and climb into the hammock-like seat. It had been pushed forward by the pack behind it, and Mirelle was right, it wasn't as comfortable.

'All ready?' asked Mirelle over her shoulder.

'Yes,' replied Elinor. She looked down to where Terciel and Tizanael were waiting for their own Paperwing to be carried up, and then to the House, to the windows of the bedrooms on the second floor. The sun was on the windows now. The whole house was lit up and looked even more warm and welcoming. She looked away, and caught the flash of something white in the vast fig tree that dominated the north lawn. An animal of some kind. It moved along a branch, and Elinor thought she saw the whisk of a tail before it disappeared into the heavier foliage.

'Do the Abhorsens have a cat?' she asked.

Mirelle half shook her head and might have given a more detailed answer, but she had already drawn breath to whistle, investing it with the Charter marks that would summon a wind. The sendings had moved along each side to hold the wings, as it was already keen to leap into the air, its eyes now fierce and fully alive.

Elinor watched and listened carefully as a beautiful, clear note came from Mirelle's pursed lips. Elinor could whistle, but she hadn't yet learned how to summon a Charter mark and incorporate it in the sound or whatever it was that made it work that way. She had learned how to breathe out a Charter mark, she figured it was some variation on that, but she also knew it would be a very bad idea to experiment. Terciel could teach her in due course. She hoped.

A wind came up from the river, even colder than the frosty air that had already chilled Elinor's face. She sank further into her furred cape, grateful that the cockpit of the Paperwing had some spells to provide warmth, or at least lessen the cold, which would be so much more intense higher in the air.

The Paperwing strained against the restraint of the sendings, wingtips shivering. Elinor gripped the sides of the cockpit, marvelling once again at the strength and solidity of the laminated paper and the feel of the Charter that was everywhere within it.

Mirelle took another breath and whistled again, this time a cheerful, uplifting jig. The wind rose with it, and the sendings let go. The Paperwing leaped from the platform and all of a sudden the crashing noise of the vast waterfall roared across them as they went beyond the protective and sound-deadening spells of the Abhorsen's enchanted isle.

The Paperwing turned north, away from the permanent mist of the waterfall, and steadily climbed. Within a minute or two, they were several hundred feet up. Elinor could see the Ratterlin stretch out ahead of them as far as she could see, and the fields and forests to either side, and distant hills and mountains. Still the Paperwing rose. It grew colder, and the roar of the waterfall behind them faded, till they flew almost in silence, as the spells in the craft for reducing the sound of the wind rushing past recovered from the battering of the waterfall's auditory assault.

'Has Tizanael launched yet?' asked Mirelle. She did not look over her shoulder, instead intent on drawing two quick marks on the breath-frosted mirror. The Paperwing's nose dipped in answer, levelling out their flight.

Elinor craned her neck around to look behind, to see Tizanael and Terciel's Paperwing launch from the platform and follow them up. The sendings were already carrying the third Paperwing up, to be readied for Filris and Sazene.

The Abhorsen's House, the whole island, in fact, looked very small now, against the broad river and the massive mistwall of the waterfall.

Elinor wondered if she would ever see it again. She turned back to the front, and tried to sound confident and cheerful.

'Yes, they're following us now.'

'Good,' replied Mirelle. 'I will keep the wind from the south, for a while.'

She drew in a breath and whistled again. Elinor could see the Charter marks coming from Mirelle's mouth, flying off into the sky, golden luminescence lost against the blue. There was almost no cloud. If that continued, the night was going to be very cold indeed.

The wind behind them strengthened in answer to Mirelle's spell. The Paperwing flew faster, the ground beneath rolling away as Elinor looked down. She had never travelled so fast in her life, not even on the train from Bain to Wyverley Halt.

They followed the river north for an hour, the sun rising above them, though it provided no noticeable warmth. The snow-dusted heath to the west slowly gave way to a dense forest, and Elinor noticed a road that came in from the west and accompanied the river, a proper paved road at least twenty feet wide, though even from on high she could see it was in disrepair, different coloured sections indicating where the pavers had gone, leaving earth behind. She didn't see anyone on the road, but she had noted a village on an island close to the western shore, with people moving around, tiny antlike figures.

An hour later still, with Elinor's legs aching from being bent up in one position, Mirelle pointed ahead and to the right.

'Qyrre!' she shouted. 'We'll turn west.'

Elinor peered down at the high-walled town on the eastern bank of the Ratterlin. It was also built on an island in the river, a swift-flowing channel fifty or sixty feet wide separating it from the mainland. A narrow bridge crossed the gap, both ends guarded by pairs of slim towers that contained apparatus to raise and lower sections.

The walls were the same whitewashed limestone as the Abhorsen's House, but higher. Most of the buildings inside the walls were of the same stone, or red brick, with wood-shingled roofs. There was a pool protected by a breakwater, half full of small boats, and a large green at the centre of the town, which was hosting a market, and there were people moving about everywhere. Living their lives, going about their usual business, unaware of Elinor watching, unaware she was part of a desperate enterprise that if it failed would affect their own futures.

Qyrre looked so safe and prosperous, it was hard to imagine anything could alter it. But it also made possible for Elinor to imagine Uppside. It was probably a similar-looking town, only now it would be fog-shrouded, its water defences being dammed and blocked, the Dead massing for an assault—

Mirelle's whistle broke through these thoughts. The Paperwing lifted one wing and turned westward, and the wind shifted too, to speed them along. Elinor looked behind, and resisted the temptation to wave at Terciel, because she didn't want to wave at Tizanael, who might think it was presumptuous or something. She was more than a little afraid of the Abhorsen.

Tizanael directed her craft to follow Mirelle's, but much further back Elinor saw a small dark shape, occasionally glinting with what she imagined was reflections of green and silver. The Paperwing of Sazene and Filris, who would keep on north to the city of Belisaere.

Soon Qyrre and the river were behind them, and there was only the vast forest ahead and below. An ancient forest of enormous oaks and beeches, so thick it was impossible to see beneath the canopy. Every now and then Elinor saw clearings, one at least evidently the result of lightning strike and fire judging by the blackened and split great tree at its centre, and several times she noted small rivers or streams, once even a small lake, frozen at the edges and dark in the middle, as if the water was very deep.

The ache in her legs was turning into cramp, so she wriggled her toes as much as she could, and bent forward to massage her calves, though neither really helped all that much. Mirelle noticed the movement, and glanced back.

'Another hour, hour and a half,' she said. 'The forest is thinning ahead.'

Sure enough, the forest was opening out, the trees shorter and further apart, the lesser shrubs and saplings beneath the giants' cover now visible. Elinor saw several animals she thought were deer, though the bucks had horns that didn't look quite right. But she was still high up, and the Paperwing moving fast, so she couldn't really tell.

There were former pastures beyond the forest, or so Elinor presumed, from her own experience of the abandoned fields at Coldhallow. She could see drystone walls, many fallen. The grass was very high, and there were no visible livestock.

As they flew further west, this picture grew no better. There were only abandoned fields, fallen walls, ruined farmhouses. At one point they flew over a very straight north–south road, even wider than the one Elinor had seen by the Ratterlin. But it too had long sections where it was overgrown or returned to dirt.

The ground started to rise past the road, with rocky hills and heather-clad slopes. There were no stone walls to delineate fields here, but Elinor saw a few fallen pens, where sheep or the like might have been counted or kept safe.

Soon, the ground was covered in snow again, as it rose still higher. There were hills ahead, all white, and beyond them mountains, vertical faces of bare grey stone where the snow and ice could not hold, between peaks of pure white.

Mirelle whistled again and turned the Paperwing into a slow, rising loop. Elinor wondered why until she saw Tizanael fly their Paperwing ahead, and begin to ascend still higher, leading the way towards one of the peaks, still several leagues away.

At this point, Elinor started to think she needed to go to the toilet, distracting her from the ache in her legs and the small of her back. The Paperwing suddenly did not seem to be flying as fast as it had before.

The feeling intensified as they rose higher and Elinor wanted to cross her legs, but that was too difficult in the cramped cockpit. She also wished she hadn't drunk Terciel's cup of tea as well as her own.

The Paperwing suddenly bucked and dropped twenty or thirty feet, sending Elinor's stomach into her throat. She forgot about needing to go to the toilet as the craft rocked again and rose as suddenly as it had fallen, and tilted down on its left wing, making Elinor clutch at the sides.

Mirelle whistled urgently, and the craft stabilised.

'Air currents around the mountains,' she shouted. 'Always tricky. But we'll be landing soon. Tizanael is descending. We'll see how she goes and land once they're down safe. Be ready to fight.'

'What?' asked Elinor. She looked over the side of the Paperwing, trying to see enemies.

'In case,' shouted Mirelle. 'I can't see anything, but best to be cautious.'

The Paperwing angled down. Elinor half drew and then replaced one of her throwing knives, loosening it in the scabbard. She could draw and throw in an instant, from her sitting position. Which given the way her legs were feeling, would be likely, Elinor thought. She hoped it wouldn't be necessary.

They flew lower, down towards a saddle between two mountains, a long flat stretch of snow several hundred feet below the icy peaks to either side. Tizanael's Paperwing was ahead and below them. It flew past the ridge of the saddle, turned into the wind, and came back to land near the southern edge, on a flat area the size of a cricket pitch, nestled between outthrust grey-green rocks, only the tops capped with snow and ice.

'All well,' said Mirelle. She whistled and drew marks on the mirror, turned much more sharply than Tizanael had done, and they rocketed down, far too fast as far as Elinor was concerned. Mirelle whistled again, the wind against them intensified, and the Paperwing reared back on its tail to slow down, before levelling out to make a very gentle landing, hardly sliding over the snow at all.

Tizanael and Terciel were already out of their Paperwing, standing and stretching in knee-deep snow. Terciel waved, but Tizanael turned away and clambered through the snow towards the nearest pile of upthrust rocks, disappearing behind it.

Mirelle hopped out of the aircraft, apparently none the worse for being cramped up for hours, and helped Elinor out. She needed it, and would have fallen into the snow without Mirelle's assistance.

'How come your legs are all right?' asked Elinor.

'Practice and small exercises,' said Mirelle quietly, taking out her sword and buckling it on, before grabbing her pack, bow and quiver. 'Speak softly. Sound travels a long way here. Get your pack and bow.'

'Uh, I need to go—'

'Get your things first,' said Mirelle sternly.

Elinor stretched quickly, grabbed her pack, attached the quiver to the side, and swung it to her back before grabbing her bow. Mirelle reached over and undid the lid of the quiver, flipping it back.

'Only fasten that if there's rain, or moisture in the air,' she said. 'You might need an arrow in a hurry. Go where Tizanael went, throw snow over whatever you have to do.'

Elinor nodded, and hurried off to the rocks.

When she came back out, Mirelle's Paperwing was moving, with no one in it. The Paperwing slid along the snow for twenty or thirty feet before launching into the air. A few seconds later it was followed by Tizanael's Paperwing.

The two aircraft climbed steadily before turning to the north and speeding away, up into the clear blue sky. Elinor watched them go with a sinking feeling in her stomach. She hadn't thought about what would come after chaining Kerrigor, but had half thought it would include climbing back in the Paperwings and flying off to the Glacier, a comforting daydream, particularly if you didn't think about what had to be done before that could happen.

'Mirelle has gone ahead to scout the way,' said Terciel quietly, coming up next to her. 'Tizanael would like you to carry the chain from here, to be ready. She is going to leave the chest. Are you all right?'

'Yes,' said Elinor. 'How is your foot and arm?'

'Good,' said Terciel immediately. 'Well, not exactly good. But serviceable. Come on.'

She followed him, stepping in his sunken footprints in the snow, over to where Tizanael crouched on a low flat-topped rock. Her bell bandolier was carefully laid out on another rock a dozen paces away. She had opened the chest. Elinor could smell the faint stench of hot metal, the same smell she had caught back at Coldhallow, though less intense. She wrinkled her nose and tried to ignore it.

Tizanael held out a pair of gauntlets. Elinor slipped them on. They were made out of some dull, off-white metal cloth and reached almost to her elbows. Charter marks moved in the coarse weave, a great sea of roiling marks, thousands and thousands of them. Elinor gulped, reminded unpleasantly how dangerous the chain must be, if the gauntlets were laden with such an array of protective spells.

'The chain is in a bag of the same material as the gauntlets. It offers some measure of protection,' said Tizanael. 'It has a simple flap that can be secured with a ribbon. Don the gloves and take the bag, take a look at the chain. Do not touch it, not until you have to use it.'

'Do I throw it or something?' asked Elinor as she took up the gloves. She felt the touch of the Charter as she slid them on, a warm buzz of recognition. 'I mean, how exactly do I use the chain?'

'We will hold Kerrigor in place with the bells, in whatever body he is wearing,' said Tizanael. 'The chain has a loop on one end. You need simply drop the loop over his head, and keep hold of the free end. That is very important. You must hold it until we have fastened the chain in Death. At that point it will disappear from your hands. Do you understand?'

'Yes,' said Elinor. 'I drop the loop of the chain over Kerrigor's head and hold on until the chain disappears.'

'Once you carry the chain, you must not come any closer than four paces to Terciel or myself, we had better say six to be safe,' said Tizanael. 'The resonance with the bells may wake it untimely. When we do use the bells, the chain will definitely wake and it will want to be used and will become unruly. You will feel its eagerness in your mind, and must maintain control.'

'Uh, right,' replied Elinor doubtfully. 'How do I do that?'

'Speak to it,' said Tizanael. 'As if it were an unruly child, or a dog. But your words must be backed by the full concentration of your will.'

'I can do that,' said Elinor. She thought of the younger girls in the chorus in *The Court of the Sad Prince*, who alternately supported the Fool or Roger Cardamom in their duel. There was always one or two of them she had to bark commands at, and wrangle back into doing what they were told.

'Also, from this point on, we must all cast no Charter Magic, unless we are under attack. The Dead and others can sense it from afar.'

Elinor nodded.

'Good luck,' said Tizanael. She surprised Elinor by resting her hands on her shoulders for a moment, squeezing lightly. 'And thank you.'

Tizanael stepped off the stone and went to retrieve her bells.

Elinor looked down into the open chest, bent over and picked up the bag. It was warm to the touch, even through the gauntlets. Elinor hesitated as Charter marks flared on glove fingertips and the bag, and the stench of Free Magic grew stronger. But only for a moment. Moving swiftly, she lifted the bag and slung the strap over her shoulder, adjusting the backpack's straps so it sat more easily. The bag hung over the poniard on her right side, so she slid it more to the front, loosened the ribbon and peeked inside.

The chain looked surprisingly flimsy, not much more than a chunkier version of the kind someone might wear as jewellery. The links were black iron, but strangely joined together by golden flowers, which it took Elinor a moment to recognise were daisies. There was an intense density of Charter marks on the golden flowers, and none at all on the iron links. When Elinor looked away, the afterimage of red fire within the iron links persisted in her version.

She closed the flap and tied the ribbon in a bow, shifting the bag so it rode on the outside of her poniard, so that it provided her with some extra separation from the chain inside.

Terciel and Tizanael were waiting about ten yards ahead, on the downslope. Beyond them there were tracks in the snow where Mirelle had gone before them.

'Remember, cast no Charter Magic,' said Tizanael quietly. Her words carried easily across to Elinor in the still, crisp air. 'Don't get too close, and remember to stay quiet.'

She turned and stumped off through the snow. Terciel smiled at Elinor, and followed Tizanael. Elinor let him go ahead, listening to the crunch of his boots breaking the snow crust, wanting to run after him and take his hand, to be close, to feel the comfort of his hand wrapped around her own. But her hand was gloved in metal cloth now, and she felt the presence of the chain. She knew she could not get close. Elinor waited, and did not follow until Terciel was more than a dozen paces away.

She walked in his footsteps, and despite the good boots, the extra goose fat and two pairs of socks, her feet were cold, and growing colder.

23

The snow cover began to thin as they descended, and Mirelle found a track that initially wound its way through spotty snow over rocky ground before continuing on through waist-high, windswept heather, which seemed to go on for miles. But after another hour of slow descent through the heather, Mirelle gestured for them to stop. She came back to talk quietly to Tizanael and Terciel, gesturing for Elinor to come close enough to hear.

'There is a path down into the head of the ravine a little way on. Elinor, have you been watching our back?'

'Um, no,' said Elinor. 'No one told me I should.'

'Stop and look back and listen every thirty or forty paces or so. You are our rear guard. Be aware you are the last in line. We had best cut heather here for our beds, before we descend into the ravine.'

Elinor opened her mouth to say something, but Mirelle was already quietly padding up the track, bow in hand, with an arrow held vertically alongside the bow. Terciel and Tizanael walked ahead a little, and started to cut the heather, lying it down to be tied into bunches. She knew there was a groundsheet in her pack, and she had a furred cape, so wasn't sure why the heather gathering was necessary, but she started cutting her own.

Mirelle returned when Elinor had several large bunches and helped her tie the heather with leather thongs she took from her own pack, before gathering more for herself. She also answered Elinor's unspoken question.

'The ground is so cold it will leach the heat out of you, so we'll put down a layer of heather to sleep on,' she explained, loading the tightly wrapped bunches of heather on top of Elinor's pack so they towered up well behind her head. Elinor noticed the Clayr was careful to stay on the side away from the chain in its bag. 'It's going to be a very cold night in general, down a ravine, on a clear night, without a fire. Though we're lucky we're already seeing signs of spring. Ready?'

'Yes,' agreed Elinor. Mirelle dropped her own pack, tied her bunches of heather on, and swung it back up, all very swiftly, before loping ahead. She did not stop to talk to Tizanael and Terciel, merely waving them on as she passed.

The ravine was a rocky scar that split the mountainside. Up here it was shallow, and narrow, but looking down along it, Elinor saw it ran for miles, growing deeper and wider. She could see the forest two thousand feet or more below, a vast green swath on both sides of the ravine. Maybe nine or ten miles away the green became a swirl of greyish-white. Low cloud, or as Elinor suddenly realised, the summoned fog of Kerrigor.

She stared for a few seconds longer, thinking about what lay ahead, then followed Terciel out of the heather, across the rocky ground to a depression that must mark the beginning of the way down into the ravine. Mirelle was already disappearing into it, only the high stack of heather on her pack visible for a moment.

The rocky track down into the ravine was uneven, very steep and narrow, with a long fall to the icy stream below. It also got much darker, very quickly, so Elinor had to really concentrate on where she put her feet and on her balance. She was grateful for the wire-walking Ham had taught her, in a disused Coldhallow barn, with a rope stretched from front to back. She also noticed that Mirelle had somehow managed to overtake Tizanael on the narrow path and was ahead again. The old Abhorsen was moving slowly, so that Terciel often had to stop and wait, and then Elinor had to as well, to maintain the distance. She was all too aware of the chain in the bag at her side.

By the time they reached the bottom, where a deep stream rushed along too fast for much ice to form, it was as if night had come, though Elinor could see the sky was still light high above. The ravine here was perhaps fifty feet wide, but they were down three or four hundred feet.

It was also already colder, at least on Elinor's exposed face, and the gauntlets, while they might protect her from Free Magic, did little to ward off the cold. The rest of her was sweaty and hot under armour and fur-lined cape, but she knew that wouldn't last.

Mirelle led them on a little further, to an expansive hollow carved into the side of the gorge, almost a cave.

It didn't go very far back, but it was sheltered overhead, had a sandy floor, and was big enough that Elinor could make her bed of heather on one side and the others some dozen feet away. Terciel smiled at her as they all set about making camp, such as it was, but it was already so dark it was almost impossible to see him.

The Clayr ranger lit a small metal oil lamp she took from her pack, using a clockwork firestarter and a pinch of tinder rather than a spell, and set it far back in the cavern. It shed very little light and could not be seen from the outside. Next to it she dug a narrow trench in the sand, using a metal mug. Coming over to Elinor, she leaned in close to explain the lamp marked where they should go to the toilet, the trench dug for that purpose. The lamp would also provide a point of reference in the dark.

'You, Terciel, and I will take four-hour watches,' she said very quietly, handing Elinor a cheese and pickle sandwich out of a package carefully wrapped in waxed cloth by the kitchen sendings. 'Terciel will take the first, you the second, and I the third. Tizanael needs to sleep, though she denies it. She accepts I command this part of our journey and will do as she is told.'

'What do I have to do on watch?' asked Elinor anxiously. She also kept her voice as low as she could, but their whispers in the dark still felt loud. It was all too easy in this darkness to imagine enemies already creeping in on them, even this whispering enough to obscure the sound of their stealthy approach. Also she didn't have a watch or a clock or anything. 'And how will I know when it's time to wake you up?'

'I will wake at each watch change, to oversee the change,' whispered Mirelle. 'All you have to do is stay awake, keep quiet and listen. If you hear anything, come over and wake me, without making noise. You see where the lamp is? Put it to your left at a right angle and take twelve steps. I do not sleep deeply in the wild.'

'I can do that,' muttered Elinor.

'I will help you arrange your bed,' said Mirelle softly. 'It is a pity we could not carry more heather to cover ourselves as well, but lay it out so. You have your groundsheet? Put it over the heather and weigh the corners with these stones. Your pack will make a pillow of sorts. Lie on your back and keep your weapons on, your boots too. We are effectively in enemy territory. Yes, I know it is uncomfortable, but you will have rest, if not sleep.'

'The bag with the chain is warm,' said Elinor. 'And sometimes I think I can smell that awful stench, the hot metal . . .'

'I do too, from time to time,' said Mirelle. 'Keep the strap over your shoulder, but put the bag out as far as it will go to one side. Do not be tempted by the warmth, and do not open it. Free magic will draw some of our enemies as much as the hint of Charter Magic. Sorcerers, tempted to test their strength, hoping to overcome a rival or a Free Magic entity and take their power for themselves.'

'I see,' said Elinor, her whisper so quiet Mirelle leaned even closer.

'Are you all right?' asked Mirelle, clasping Elinor's shoulder, an encouraging contact. 'It is strange for you, I know, and unusual in that we must keep our distance. If not for the chain and the bells, we would be best huddled together for warmth. I am sorry you must be alone.'

'Me too,' said Elinor. 'When do we go on? At dawn again?'

'No,' said Mirelle. 'Later in the morning. We need to wait for light to reach the depths, it is too dangerous to follow the path in the dark. It will be a long night. Finish your food, and rest. And Terciel asked me to tell you he will be thinking of you, just over there.'

'Oh,' said Elinor. She smiled, a small smile, and glanced over to where she knew Terciel and Tizanael were, though she couldn't see them. 'Tell him I will think of him also. When I'm not being too frightened to think.'

'You are not that frightened,' said Mirelle decisively. 'Only the right amount, I would say. Enough to be careful, not so much you cannot do what must be done. Do not be slow to wake me later, if you feel the need. Better to be woken for something that turns out to be nothing than not to be woken at all.'

She gave Elinor's shoulder a final pat, and went to her own bed. Elinor could now only just make out the shape of her, if she turned her head to look out the corner of her eye. Otherwise it was completely dark, save for the faint glow from the lamp well back in the cave.

Moving by feel, she lay back on her bed, the heather crunching under her at first, before it was broken enough to be quiet. She pulled her cape together and hood forward and thought she would never go to sleep, despite feeling very tired.

Some time later, she jerked up with a start, her hand going to the hilt of her upper throwing knife. A whispered voice near her made her fingers relax, the panicked drive to draw the weapon fading away.

'It's Mirelle. Your turn for the watch. Four hours. Stand up, but don't move more than a few steps unless you have to. Don't stamp your feet or make unnecessary noise. Are you awake?'

'Yes,' muttered Elinor, shaking her head. She stood up and stretched. Her back and shoulders ached.

'Who am I?'

She couldn't see the Clayr. She was simply a voice, close in the darkness.

'Mirelle.'

'And what are you going to do now?'

'Keep watch.'

'Good. You are awake. It has been quiet so far. Not even animals passing by. Stay alert. I will tell you when your time is done.'

Elinor took a deep breath in and let it out slowly. She felt wide awake now, and freighted with responsibility. She heard Mirelle softly tread back to her bed, and movement near her, which she supposed was Terciel settling down. It would have been good to talk to him, even those same few words as she had exchanged with Mirelle, but she accepted that he must keep the bells on and her the chain . . .

She had a momentary panic the chain might be gone, and felt for the strap of the bag. It was there, and when she followed it down she felt the top of the bag, and lifting it, the weight of the chain.

It wasn't very heavy. It should be much heavier, she thought, given what it was.

The stream in the ravine was much louder now everything else was quiet. Or the darkness made Elinor's hearing better. The water was burbling away steadily out there, a constant, almost reassuring sound.

Soon, Elinor wished she did have a watch, or some means of keeping track of time, which seemed to stretch on and on. For a while she counted in her head – one elephant, two elephants, three elephants and so on – but that made her sleepy and distracted, too much focused on getting the numbers right.

Next she thought about the night with Terciel, but that was distracting as well. Eventually, she settled on focusing on the burble of the stream and any other small noises she heard. This at least had the virtue of keeping her awake, because every small variation in the natural noises of the night made her heart jump and her hand go to the topmost of her throwing knives.

But none of the errant sounds were repeated, none resolved into steps or footfalls or more sinister movement. There was only the darkness, the constant rush of the stream, the occasional small noise from the others moving in their sleep: the crackle of some unbroken heather, a slight exhalation, something that was almost a snore but did not become one.

Wariness and exhaustion and cold warred in Elinor. She took a few steps, forward and back, stood on one foot, then the other. She rubbed her face energetically, to warm both her cheeks and her hands, the sound of it astonishingly loud. The gloves felt strange upon her skin, neither cloth, metal or skin, like nothing she knew. An unpleasant feeling, and not worth the momentary warmth it delivered.

She hugged herself and swayed on the spot, the small movements helping a little to keep the cold at bay.

Finally, long, long after she was sure she had spent far more than the four hours allotted to her, she heard Mirelle get up. Another sound that at first made her jolt into full alertness, before she realised what it was. But even listening carefully, she was surprised when Mirelle spoke to her from only a few paces away.

'Lie down now, try to sleep. The day will be hard.'

'Have you Seen something?' whispered Elinor anxiously.

'No,' answered Mirelle. There was more than a trace of amusement in her reply. 'No vision of the future is needed to predict that! Rest now.'

Elinor lay back down, adjusting the bag with the chain, her poniard, her throwing knives. There was no way to get properly comfortable, only to reduce exactly how uncomfortable she was. Nevertheless, she soon felt herself dropping off to sleep and—

Woke suddenly, she didn't know how much later. It was still completely dark, save for the tiny glow at the back of the cave. She heard something, the pop and ripple of a stone dropped in the stream, or something like that, and then it came again. She sat up, reaching for her knife, sucking in the kind of desperate breath needed for fight or flight.

'It's only river otters,' said Mirelle quietly, not far away, though Elinor could not see her. 'Fishing. It will be dawn soon. Sleep again, if you can.'

Elinor lay back down. She heard rustling over to the side, the sound of Terciel and Tizanael settling back as well. She was oddly comforted that they also woke at the noise. It wasn't her being irrational, the novice scared in the dark.

She shut her eyes and listened to the sounds in the stream. River otters, fishing. She'd like to see them, she thought, but in other, easier circumstances. She pictured otters playing in a stream, in sunshine, and her and Terciel picnicking on the bank. Slowly, sleep overcame her and her head slid sideways so her nose poked into her pack.

Some time later, the chain rattled in the bag. A strange, clattering sound, as if made by a living animal, not an inanimate object.

Elinor shot completely out of her bed this time and stood up, taking a pace before she got control of herself. Instinctively she held the bag out from her body, but she could hear the chain moving inside, like a trapped snake.

'What is it?' asked Mirelle.

'The chain, it's moving in the bag,' said Elinor tremulously.

'Tizanael?' asked Mirelle conversationally. 'I note the otters are also fleeing downstream.'

Heather crackled, footsteps scuffed the sandy floor. Elinor heard three slow, deliberate sniffs. She couldn't smell anything much herself, certainly not the acrid, metallic reek of Free Magic she feared. Then she caught a smell, the faint whiff of some pleasant smoke, as if from a fire of aromatic wood. Not anything she recognised. It lingered for a moment, then it was gone.

'Is the chain still moving?' asked Tizanael.

'A little,' said Elinor anxiously.

'Tell it to be still,' said Tizanael. 'As I said before, as if speaking to a child or a dog. Think it as well.'

Elinor cleared her throat and thought for a moment, putting herself back on stage with the unruly choir.

'Be still!' she said. Not loud or annoyed, but forceful. She concentrated hard on those two words, infusing them with her will.

The bag stopped trembling in her hand.

'It was answering to something that has passed down the ravine,' said Tizanael. She sounded very weary. 'A kind of echo or remnant of a Free Magic entity. One of the myriad lesser beings that gave itself to the Charter, but some fragment remained. It is harmless, unless you are directly in its path. I had forgotten it would walk here, in the spring, as a herald of the dawn.'

'What would it do if you *are* directly in its path?' asked Elinor.

'Take you with it, out of time,' said Tizanael. 'It is not entirely of the here and now.'

'What does that mean?'

'You would return unchanged and unharmed, on some spring day, weeks or months or even years hence,' said Tizanael drily. 'Not something to be desired at the present.'

'The sun has risen, above,' said Mirelle. Elinor had no notion how she could tell. It was still entirely dark. 'In another hour it will be light enough to move on. Eat and drink something, stay alert. I will take a look along the stream.'

Elinor heard her moving off, though she didn't make the sound of footsteps. It was more a slight scuffing noise.

'How can she see *anything*?' she asked.

'There is Charter Magic to alter one's body,' said Tizanael. Elinor could hear her settling back down. 'Senses may be augmented permanently, reflexes enhanced, and so on, and all these are employed by the Rangers. It is a magic closely related to healing, and the spells for ensuring health against the ravages of age. Though all such have their costs, and their limits, as is only right.'

Terciel made a slight noise, which Elinor correctly interpreted as surprise that Tizanael had answered a question without additional prompting.

'Well, breakfast time,' said Terciel, in a tone that was meant to be cheery but didn't come out quite that way. 'More cheese and pickle sandwiches. Still better than hard biscuit.'

Elinor got her own wax-paper package out of the top of her pack, and her water bottle, by feel, and they ate in silence, companionably thirty feet apart. As she finished eating, Elinor noted that she could now see the outline of the cave entrance, and the faint shapes of the two Abhorsens, and her pack was a differentiated lump of darkness.

A few minutes later, Mirelle returned. Elinor saw the movement first, before she heard her.

'It will soon be light enough to go on,' said Mirelle. 'I will eat and then we will depart. I think we will reach the fog an hour before noon. Tizanael, you said there are several places we can climb out of the ravine?'

Tizanael did not immediately answer. Mirelle repeated the question.

'Yes. I am thinking. There are numerous re-entrants along the way, lesser cracks in the earth that join this one. We can follow any one of them up. On the eastern side, that is. Kerrigor's court will be closer to Uppside. The trick will be to find the closest, to give us the greatest element of surprise.'

'What do we do if the way out is guarded?' asked Terciel. 'If we are to use neither bells nor magic until we can close on Kerrigor?'

'At noon, even in fog, any guards should be mortal,' said Tizanael. 'We kill them as quietly as possible and go on.'

'There may still be Dead alert enough to function,' continued Terciel. 'Noon or not. They cannot be dealt with without magic.'

'If we must, we will use bells and Charter Magic,' said Tizanael. 'And *press on*, without delay. That is most important. We forge ahead, no matter what, even if the alarm is raised. We must confront and defeat Kerrigor as quickly as possible.'

24

The track alongside the stream became broader and somewhat easier as the rift widened and descended, but there were still sections where it became more difficult and they had to climb up and over huge falls of rock, with Mirelle finding the best way forward.

But they made steady progress, getting faster as the morning light made its way into the depths. It was a sunny day, up above. Elinor felt her heart lift when she caught actual sight of the sun, a blinding dot framed between the stony walls of the rift. It made up a little for being tired, and clammy from yesterday's sweat having frozen on her only to be thawed by new sweat, and having aching shoulders and numb toes.

As the sun continued its rise, Mirelle ranged further ahead, reconnoitring the smaller re-entrant ravines on the eastern side of the gorge. Elinor marvelled at how quickly Mirelle climbed up and down very narrow, difficult paths. As she also went ahead along the stream and back again, to check up on everyone, she easily covered twice as much ground as everyone else, but showed no signs of fatigue.

The fourth time Mirelle came back down from one of these narrow adjoining gulleys that rose up to the forest above, the sun was beginning to descend from its high point and soon would fall out of sight from where they were down the bottom of the rift. Elinor watched it anxiously, knowing the presence of the sun was an important part of their planned attack.

Mirelle signalled them to stop, and they all gratefully sat on boulders, or in Elinor's case a ledge of rock that might almost have been purposefully shaped like a bench rather than simply being the result of erosion.

'There is a conjured fog above this next side ravine,' said the Clayr, speaking quietly but clearly, so they all could hear, despite maintaining their distance. 'This is where we need to ascend. But it is already almost an hour past noon, and it will take another hour to climb to the forest, and from there it may take an hour or more to find Kerrigor's court. Will the sun be strong enough above the fog to diminish the Dead, if we are so late? Tizanael?'

The Abhorsen frowned.

'I had hoped to be earlier, but I believe it is not too late. We must hurry.'

'We should drop our packs here,' said Mirelle.

'Not at the top, where we might retrieve them more easily?' asked Terciel.

'The path up is arduous,' said Mirelle. 'If we are victorious, we can survive a night in the forest and walk down to Uppside. If we are not, we would retreat back down here anyway, to the stream, to gain the protection of running water. Unless you know of somewhere defensible above, Tizanael?'

'There are small watercourses that run through the forest, down to the Upp,' said Tizanael. 'They are not as swift or deep as this stream, and would offer little protection. None against Kerrigor himself. But then neither would this. We must, and we will, chain him in Death.'

She started to take off her pack, gesturing Terciel to stay back as he moved in to help. After a moment, he took his own pack off, leaning it up against the rock he'd been sitting on. Elinor swung her pack off and set it on the ledge. It was a relief to have the weight off her back, but at the same time it was also a dread kind of punctuation. She might not ever come back to it.

'Take your quiver and your water bottle,' said Mirelle. 'It will hook on your belt.'

Elinor slung quiver and bow on her back, and fixed the water bottle on next to her poniard, just behind her hip. She noticed Terciel was having some sort of low-voiced argument with Tizanael. The Abhorsen was saying something crossly, but very contained, when Terciel simply turned his back. Taking off his bell bandolier, he laid it on the ground and hurried over to Elinor, ignoring Tizanael's hissed, 'Terciel! There is no time.'

He came right up to Elinor and hugged her, though he did so slightly at an angle so he didn't touch the bag with the chain. After a moment's hesitation, Elinor hugged him back. She was surprised to find that she was shaking a little, and had to take a slow breath to keep still. Or maybe it was Terciel who was shaking, and the tremors came from him? Either way, after a few seconds they were completely still, deep in an embrace.

'Elinor, if by some chance we are all slain, you can escape,' he said, his breath warm on her ear. 'The best chance is to come back here and go downstream. Cross as soon as you can, and follow the stream down to the Upp. It is a big river. Find a boat or make a raft, whatever you can do, and take the river south, to the Red Lake. There are some villages along the shore. They may survive some time even if Uppside has fallen. Seek help there, if you can see people, if there is sunshine. If not, keep going south. Head for the Wall, cross it, go back to Ancelstierre.'

'I hadn't even thought I might survive and no one else,' said Elinor, turning her head so her face was in his neck, just above his armoured coat. Experimentally, she dug her nose in, and was surprised she didn't mind the smell. Maybe it was because she smelled just as bad.

'It doesn't seem very likely, does it? I think we will live or die together, Terciel. Preferably live, of course. Put your bells back on. Like Tizanael says, there is no time.'

'I know,' said Terciel, his voice full of regret. 'I know.'

He eased off a little, and bent down, and she looked up, and they kissed. A gentle kiss, almost a goodbye kiss with only the hint there might one day be another. Then he spun about on his heel and ran to put his bandolier back over his shoulder. Tizanael was already starting up the path, with Mirelle a good thirty to forty yards in front.

Elinor followed, wondering why she felt so sanguine about what was to come. Clearly Terciel thought there was a very good chance they would die. That had been clear from the outset. Mirelle was more restrained, but had not discounted the danger. Tizanael – it was difficult to know what Tizanael thought, she showed so little in her face, or in her voice.

I am afraid, Elinor thought to herself. But I am not terrified. And if I am to die, it will be doing something, something important. The sort of thing that could become a story, a song, even a play. *The Binding of Kerrigor.*

She wouldn't be the main character herself, Elinor thought. But an important supporting one. The bearer of the chain. If Breakespear was writing it, she would have a short soliloquy perhaps. To tell the small story within the big story, about how a little girl who thinks she is disfigured and without family grows up to discover she has a magical heritage, and despite loss and pain along the way finds a path to a new life, the potential of new love as well, and meaning and significance. Even if it might not be for very long.

But the play was not written, the story still unfolding. Elinor took a deep breath and started up the track, not forgetting to pause after a dozen steps and glance backwards, as Mirelle had told her to make sure no one and nothing was creeping up on them from behind.

They moved more swiftly without the packs, but the climb up was difficult, and Tizanael was slow.

Some two thirds of the way up the re-entrant, it became less of a ravine and more of a narrow valley, the rocky ground giving way to luxuriant grass growing from rich earth, as if a great deal of mud had slid down in the distant past and stuck there. There were wildflowers among the grass, primroses and daffodils, visible signs of the spring, and it was warmer too, though it could still only be described as cold.

Right at the top, they even came into a narrow band of direct sunshine. Elinor turned her face up to the light and warmth, revelling in the thawing of her nose. She'd have liked to take her strange gloves off to get sunshine on her hands as well, but did not do so. While the sunshine, the vibrant grass and the wildflowers gave an air of peacefulness and calm, it could not quell the fear and anxiety that was steadily rising in Elinor, the sense that something terrible was about to happen.

Fifty yards away the giant blackwood forest began. Huge trees, with trunks twenty or thirty or forty feet in diameter, rising up several hundred feet, each standing like some lonely monarch, their outstretched branches not quite reaching to their neighbours, as if each tree had come to an agreement they would not touch.

Usually, the separation of the giant trees would allow the sunshine to illuminate the forest, to relieve the shade immediately under the trees. But not now. Fog cloaked the giants and swirled along the avenues. White, wet fog that looked as if a massive cloud had drifted down from the mountainside above and taken up permanent residence over the forest. The great trees became more and more indistinct, black streaks against the fog, until they were subsumed into blank whiteness.

Tizanael pointed into the forest.

'Kerrigor is there, with many other Dead things,' she said. 'Less than a half a league away.'

'And little affected by the sun above, it seems to me,' added Terciel. 'Or is what I sense Kerrigor alone? Is it the strength of many lesser revenants I feel, or just the one?'

'Something of both,' said Tizanael.

Terciel craned his neck to look up at the blue sky, his face brightly lit. He lowered his head and looked at the fog-wreathed forest ahead, then back at Elinor for a long moment before he fully faced Tizanael again.

'We are fortunate to have this moment of sunshine, before we go on.'

Tizanael nodded slowly. She drew a deep breath and spoke with a sudden new energy, casting off the weariness that Elinor had noted and Terciel feared.

'We will get as close as we can, then both of us wielding Ranna will put as many of the Dead into slumber as possible,' she said. 'Though Ranna will not be strong enough to make Kerrigor sleep. Then I will use Saraneth and Terciel Kibeth. I will concentrate on Kerrigor. Terciel, you will force any Dead who have not slept to walk away. Into sunlight, if possible. Mirelle, slay any mortal opponents. They are likely sorcerers, and will need to be shot several times with Charter-spelled arrows, preferably in the head. There are so many Dead here, I think Kerrigor will not sense any new deaths, unless they are very close to him. Elinor, as soon as we use the bells you close with me, stay by my side. You will need to dominate the chain and keep it ready for immediate use.'

'A bowshot will not be any great distance in that fog,' said Mirelle. 'I do need to be able to see my targets, to some degree.'

'There is a spell that will clear the fog somewhat, immediately about us,' said Tizanael. 'But it will not last long, not if Kerrigor maintains his effort.'

'Even a minute or two of better visibility would make a difference,' said Mirelle.

'Very well,' said Tizanael. 'I will cast it upon our assault. Is everyone ready?'

She did not wait for a reply, but strode off towards the closest avenue between the vast blackwood trees, the fog billowing about her. The others followed, Terciel and Mirelle close, Elinor still hanging back a little. She could feel the chain shivering in the bag, as if it already knew what was to come.

Elinor loosened all three of her knives as she followed the others. It was like stepping into another world as they left the sunshine behind. The fog was all-enveloping, obscuring even the vast trunks on either side. Elinor could see only twenty or thirty feet and twice she almost panicked as the trio ahead of her disappeared from sight for a moment, and she had to quicken her pace to catch up.

The fog seemed natural enough at first, until Elinor realised she could hear none of the natural sounds one might expect in a forest. There were no birdcalls, no rustles in the undergrowth. Nothing. Only the quiet tread of her companions on the carpet of fallen needles from the trees, and alarmingly, her own breath, which seemed to have become ridiculously loud.

Then, all too soon, there was the smell. Not the reek of Free Magic, that corrosive hot-metal tang. This was the stench of corruption, of something rotting. For a few moments Elinor though it was simply the forest, the smell of decomposing leaves or vegetation, till it grew stronger and stronger and she knew the stink came from the Dead. Rotting meat, a miasma woven into the fog, so foul she started to breathe only through her mouth, hoping this would help. It didn't.

There had been no such smell from the Dead at Coldhallow House, but they had been ancient bodies, long preserved in a bog. The ones who lurked ahead inhabited newer corpses, slain only days or weeks before, the bodies not desiccated and leathery but bloated and ripe, in the early stages of decomposition.

Mirelle suddenly moved, leaping ahead, and Elinor heard the twang of her bowstring, quickly repeated, then a low cry and the thud of something hitting the thick detritus of the forest floor. She started to run forward, but Tizanael turned and held up her hand, signalling her to stop, while Terciel moved ahead, his hand on his sword hilt, but the weapon not drawn.

Elinor stopped, but not before she got too close to Tizanael and her bells, and the chain began to thrash and jiggle, only quieting when Elinor quickly stepped back, lifted the bag near her face and hissed at it, 'Be quiet!'

When she lowered the bag and looked ahead, the Abhorsen was gone. Elinor couldn't see anyone, only fog and the dim outline of the great trees to either side. She almost cried out, suppressing it as Tizanael came back out of the fog and made a half gesture for her to come along, a signal Elinor interpreted meant for her to follow but maintain the safe distance. Elinor started after Tizanael, slowly, one hand on a knife hilt, the other resting on the flap of the bag that held the chain.

A little further on, she saw a body lying in blackwood needle litter by the side of the path, fresh blood pooling under her head, indicating she had been mortal, not a Dead Hand. Mirelle had already removed her arrows, but it was clear from the wounds that the dead woman had been shot in the left eye and through the throat. Elinor wanted to look away and hurry on, but she found herself staring. The dead woman was perhaps thirty, and looked quite ordinary. She had short hair, very roughly cut, and was wearing similar leather armour to Elinor, though hers was more roughly worked and dyed or painted a dark red. She had a curved sword at her belt, still in its scabbard.

Feeling a strange fascination, Elinor stopped to look, intending to only take a second. But as she stepped closer, the woman's empty eye socket suddenly filled with fire, the terrible dark fire Elinor had seen in the Greater Dead creature at Coldhallow. Worse, the skin on her forehead erupted into an ugly, wormlike scar, the same as she'd seen on Hedge, and suddenly Lerantiel's chain thrashed wildly, sending the bag swinging. Elinor clamped it to her side and through gritted teeth whispered, 'I've told you already! Be still!'

The chain stopped moving, and to Elinor's surprise, the fire in the dead woman's eye socket blinked out like a snuffed candle, and the mark of Kerrigor faded on the corpse's skin.

Elinor jumped, but this was because Mirelle had suddenly appeared at her side.

'Do not linger!' hissed the ranger. 'Do not pay attention to dead sorcerers! Come on!'

Mirelle didn't wait, but ran ahead. Elinor followed, not quite running, fog swirling about her. She saw Tizanael, her face unreadable as ever, and Terciel, who looked at her with deep concern, but only for a fraction of a second as they both spun about and continued on. They walked faster now, little short of a jog, with Mirelle even swifter in front. Elinor matched their pace, closing in as much as she dared, six paces, maybe seven, slowing a little as the bag shivered, or maybe it was her hand gripping it that shivered, she could not tell.

They moved on along the avenue, the ground continually sloping down, but the way easy between the great trees. But they had not gone much further when Mirelle's bow sang out again, this time three times, and then there was the unmistakable clash of metal upon metal and a moment later Charter Magic flared, a great golden explosion that separated the fog and sent it spinning away to reveal a clearing ahead, where the giant blackwoods had been felled, leaving only jagged stumps as high as a person and thirty or forty feet in diameter, save one of the true ancients, which had been easily sixty feet across.

That huge stump had been transformed into a platform, decorated to be a vicious parody of a throne room. The carpets and curtains of the half dozen villages destroyed along the Upp had been strewn across the half-sawn, half-broken surface of the stump, and hung from the tall, six-inch-thick jagged stalagmites of broken bark that remained.

In the middle of this platform, there was a pile of broken stone. Shaped stone, once menhirs or obelisks, snapped into pieces like carrots broken by children. The surfaces of these stones were pitted with trails like those made by woodworm, dark, meaningless scribbles that Elinor instinctively understood had once been Charter marks, now somehow immobile and broken, mere shadows of what they had once meant.

Atop the stone, there was a gilded chair with one broken armrest, and several torn and bloodied banners draped over it. Something that had the general shape of a man sat upon it, dressed only in a leather apron stained white from flour and red from blood. The body had been a miller, huge in life, easily seven feet tall, with shoulders and muscle built to scale and hardened by years of lifting great sacks of wheat and flour. But the Dead spirit inside had eroded the flesh, so bones protruded from his fingers and thumbs, the flesh had receded around his mouth and eye sockets and only sad, scattered tendrils of hair hung from his exposed skull. His feet were bare, and had hard usage, so were now almost completely skeletal. Tiny tendrils of dark fire licked away at every border between skin and exposed bone, and roared up and out when he opened his mouth to speak.

'Guests,' said Kerrigor, rising up, the body of the miller mirrored by a dark shadow that moved within it, but was not entirely confined by the rotten flesh. His voice seemed to come from all around, not from his mouth, which continued to roar with fire, and his voice was painful to the ears and mind. 'Make them welcome.'

He gestured, and all around the broken stump the Dead rose from the ground where they had lain. Hundreds and hundreds of Dead Hands, the slain villagers and farmers of the valley, their innocent spirits gone, replaced by dread things who had lingered long in Death, who had given their allegiance to Kerrigor for their chance to walk in Life again. Even if it should be in broken, torn, limbless, and damaged bodies, who could not stand under the sun.

Kerrigor gestured again, and the fog swirled back in, even as Mirelle's bow sang in swift time; and Tizanael's and Terciel's arms moved as one, swinging up and down, and the sweet sound of Ranna rang out everywhere, calling all the Dead who heard it into sleep.

25

Dead Hands tumbled down in their scores like windswept grass, Ranna sending them into slumber. But not all of them, and the tide of revenants flowed forward even as the attackers ran towards the great stump where Kerrigor held court, the Abhorsens ringing their bells, Mirelle shooting her bow, Elinor wrestling with the chain, which had burst forth from the bag and writhed in her hands like an enraged snake, the loop at the end trying to flip itself over *her* head, and she was shouting at it to be still and using every part of her juggling expertise to keep it away.

Kerrigor himself was entirely unaffected by the Sleeper. He stepped down from his makeshift throne and strode to meet them, fire flaring and smoke billowing under his skeletal feet. A kind of honour guard shuffled and squelched and scraped along behind him, Dead Hands in the bodies from the Trained Bands who had tried to defend the villages, or the Regent's Guards sent to investigate. Rotten, damaged corpses in tattered, broken armour, their bony or bloated hands clutching the weapons they had wielded when they were living soldiers.

Tizanael and Terciel rang their bells again, a sweet, restful peal of notes that sang a lullaby and sent more Dead to their sleep, the Hands dropping as they marched.

But it was not enough. The tide of Dead came on, rank upon rank through the billowing fog. Diminished, but not stopped. Mirelle tried an arrow at Kerrigor's eye, her best arrow, spelled in point and shaft to fly true and deal destruction. It fled her bow like a golden spark, but the spark died as it hit the shadowy outline around the miller's body, and the arrow turned instantly to ash, yew and steel and magic vanquished in an instant.

Kerrigor ripped a vertical splinter from the blackwood stump as he jumped down, a long spear of tough timber. Dark flames spread from his hand to the wood, enveloping it entirely, but it did not burn.

Tizanael stopped and replaced Ranna and drew Saraneth, all in one quick motion, as next to her Terciel did the same, though he took out the bell Kibeth. Binder for the Abhorsen, Walker for the Abhorsen-in-Waiting.

They rang the bells together, the two distinct voices somehow sounding at once but remaining separate: the deep, demanding voice of Saraneth underlying the sharper, leaping and bounding notes of Kibeth. Elinor could feel the power of the bells, almost see their voices shimmer in the air, along with the still-lingering sigh of Ranna, and was relieved it was all directed forward, else she would have already been asleep, or walking away, or bound to Tizanael's will.

The chain she held desperately with both hands heard the bells too, and thrashed and turned, resisting Elinor's efforts to keep it under control. Its black links burned now, with the same sort of dark fire as limned Kerrigor's form, but the flames were contained by the glow of Charter Magic, and the golden daisies that joined the links were bright as the sun, too bright for Elinor to look upon. Even now Ham's teaching helped her, and she instinctively took the chain's erratic energy and shaped it, sending the loop spinning over her head, just like the rope trick the old juggler had taught her. Spinning, the chain could not strike of its own accord.

The advancing Dead turned in answer to Kibeth's call, stumbling and falling over those asleep, gobbling and screeching in protest as best they could with dried-out mouths and desiccated tongues and lungs that were now little more than leather bellows. Desperately they tried to evade the bell's command to walk away, but none could resist.

Only Kerrigor. He laughed, a great gout of flame bursting from his mouth, his jaw unhinging to drop almost to his breastbone, and he strode forward, straight at Tizanael, who stood before him wielding the bell that was supposed to have already stripped the Greater Dead's will and made him obey.

'Stand!' called Tizanael, and she rang Saraneth again, in a complicated peal that Elinor, even behind her, felt deep inside the marrow of her bones.

'Stand still!'

Kerrigor did not stand still. He rushed forward, astonishingly and terrifyingly fast, and thrust his burning splinter-spear at Tizanael's heart with inhuman force. Though the wooden weapon could not pierce her armoured coat, she was hurled at least ten feet backwards with terrible force, striking the ground with the sickening crack of broken bone. Though she kept her grip on the sword in her left hand, the bell in her right slipped from her grasp. Tizanael made one last despairing snatch as it tumbled and gripped the clapper, but not before it had struck once against the side.

Saraneth's single discordant note struck everyone like a savage, physical blow to the head. Elinor staggered away, screaming, but somehow managed to keep spinning the chain; Mirelle dropped her bow, clapped her hands to her ears and fell to her knees; only Terciel withstood the shriek of the errant bell. With the speed and ease of years of practice he replaced Kibeth, drew his own Saraneth and rang it with perfect technique and grim deliberation, investing it with all his will.

'Stand!' he roared. 'Stand still!'

For a second, two seconds, Kerrigor was held by the power of the bell.

It was enough for Elinor to send the loop of the chain sailing over his head and upthrust arm, so it settled diagonally across the barrel chest of the miller's body. Elinor pulled on the end she held, stepped back, and the loop drew tight. A storm of silver sparks flashed where the golden daisies touched the shadow-stuff that lurked beneath the decaying skin, and flames roared out around the black iron links.

'What is this!' roared Kerrigor. He raised his splinter-spear but it was smashed from his hand with a blow from

Terciel's sword, the stroke shearing off the finger bones, so that only shadowy tendrils remained, with little fires where fingernails had once been.

Elinor yanked on the chain again, and it tightened further, cutting through flesh and bone into the shadow-stuff beneath. Kerrigor lunged towards her, to grip and rend, but she skipped away, keeping tight hold of the chain.

Terciel rang Saraneth again, close and purposeful, while Kerrigor was distracted chasing Elinor.

'Go!' he commanded. 'Go! Into Death!'

Kerrigor stumbled, the huge miller's body twisting, more bones protruding from the flesh. Sparks blew out from the chain. Fire roared skyward. The shadow within writhed and twisted and turned back towards Terciel, even as the physical body faced the other way.

'Go!' spat Terciel through clenched teeth. 'Into. Death.'

The shadow vanished, the fires went out, the sparks faded. The chain was only black iron links and golden daisies now, and all it held was the corpse of a huge man, which fell forward on its face.

'Do not let go of the chain!' shouted Terciel. 'Do not let go until it vanishes of its own accord!'

He rushed to Tizanael's side, a few paces away, but did not check to see if she still lived. He already knew she was dead, her skull fractured, her back broken. He had felt her spirit go, a scant moment after she stilled the bell with the last of her strength. He pried her fingers from her sword, the Abhorsen's sword, and took it in place of his own.

Then he replaced the bell Saraneth in his bandolier and with sword held ready in his right hand, the fifty-second Abhorsen stepped over to Elinor and put his hand over hers and tightened his fingers, so he too held the chain, via her grasp.

'What happens now?' asked Elinor.

Terciel did not answer. He had become completely still. Frost rimed his skin, and then actual ice formed, so he became a frozen statue. Elinor stared down at the frozen hand that held hers in place on the chain, at Terciel's face, now blurred behind the coat of ice, his eyelashes a fence of icicles.

'What, what is he . . .'

'He has gone into Death,' said Mirelle, staggering to her feet. She reclaimed her bow and started to help herself to arrows from Elinor's quiver. 'May the Charter grant he is strong enough alone to fix Kerrigor in place.'

She looked around at the multitude of sleeping Dead and added, 'And he comes back here very quickly!'

'Tizanael?'

'She's dead,' said Mirelle.

Elinor looked around fearfully. There were Dead Hands everywhere, lying in piles, but they only slept, she knew, and there were far more back in the fog. If they woke up . . .

'Can we burn them somehow?' she asked. 'All of them, I mean, at once?'

'No,' said Mirelle. She was turning slowly in place, an arrow nocked and ready. She did not seem quite herself, and Elinor noticed there was a thin line of blood trickling from her left ear, the side that had been closest to the fallen bell.

'The fog!' exclaimed Elinor. 'Can you summon a wind, blow the fog away? The sun—'

'I . . . I don't know,' replied Mirelle. 'My ears are ringing. If I can't hear myself whistle I'll get it wrong and – look out!'

She shoved Elinor aside as a bolt of fire sped overhead, missing Elinor's head by inches, the hot-metal stench of its passage making her gag.

Ice cracked from the sudden movement, but Terciel's hand stayed on Elinor's and hers on the chain. She steadied herself, and with her free hand she drew a knife and sent it flying back where the bolt had come from: a man on the fringe of the fog, standing on the edge of the massive stump that had been Kerrigor's throne room.

A man Elinor had seen twice before and wished never to see again.

Hedge.

Terciel stepped into the intensely cold river of Death and the current immediately grabbed him and tried to wrestle him under and take him away. He set his legs wide, steadying himself against the flow, and swiftly looked around. The chain blinded him. It was still bright here, a thing of fire and white light, the black iron links dripping with red flames and the golden daisies that joined them small suns made of brilliant Charter marks, which shed fountains of sparks.

At the end of the chain Kerrigor also braced himself against the current. A massive shape of darkness even bigger than the miller's body he had occupied in Life. His eyes burned deep with fire, and flames licked about his mouth.

Terciel flicked the chain in the manner instructed by *On the Making of Necromantic Bells and Other Devices* and strode away, deeper into Death. He could already see the line of mist that marked the First Gate, and could hear the roar of its waterfall, deeper and louder than the rush of the river.

'Fool,' said Kerrigor, his voice loud and frightening, redolent with power. The huge mass of shadow leaned back, making the chain come taut, so it was a tight horizontal line of brightness between them, so strange in the grey light of Death. 'You are too weak! *You* can take me no further. Flee now, and I will allow you a little grace. You might even escape.'

Terciel flicked the chain again.

'Move!' he commanded. But the chain stayed taut, and Kerrigor did *not* move.

The Greater Dead creature chuckled, a horrible, wet laugh that made Terciel shiver. He forced himself to stay calm, to think about the book and the instructions in it. He couldn't use the bells on Kerrigor now, not while holding the chain. He shouldn't have to. Lerantiel's book said a spirit bound by the chain would be forced by the chain's power alone to walk deeper into Death.

Charter help me, thought Terciel. He couldn't think, he was on the verge of panic, that awful chuckling sound was eating at his mind. I cannot move him, and Elinor and Mirelle are in Life, surrounded by Dead who will wake all too soon.

Doubt was fatal in Death. It was strength of will alone that kept the river from taking a spirit onward. Terciel felt the current growing stronger, felt his knees weakening. His arm ached where it had been broken, his foot was numb again, he wasn't as strong as he should be, he couldn't hold the chain . . .

Kerrigor stopped chuckling. Terciel heard the sound of something wading towards him, the change in the river's rushing noise. He spun about, keeping a tight hold on the chain, and saw—

The sorcerer dodged aside and the knife missed. Hedge flung another bolt of Free Magic fire, this time straight at the frozen figure of Terciel. Elinor, about to throw a second knife at him, saw his hand move and without even thinking swung herself in front of the Abhorsen, pivoting around their joined grip on the chain.

The bolt struck her on the shoulder. Elinor felt an intense stab of pain that felt like it went all the way through her chest and came out her back. For a moment she thought that was it, this was the moment of her death. She looked down, expecting to see, just for that last elongated second of life, a hole like the one Hedge had blasted through the poor soldier back at Wyverley College.

But her shoulder was intact. The leather armour was singed and blackened, but it was whole. The pain was fading, and was already not much worse than being struck with one of Ham's juggling balls, as had happened to her many times in her early training.

Mirelle's bowstring thrummed. Elinor snapped her head up to see the arrow fly straight and true, into and through the sorcerer's neck. Horrifyingly, no blood spurted forth, and he did not fall or falter. He dodged aside as another arrow sped through the air where he had stood, then slowly retreated, brushing another arrow away from his face as he backed off, as easily as if it might have been a fly. He did not have the air of someone defeated. It was rather a calculated withdrawal, and he took something that flashed silver from his belt as he disappeared back into the fog.

'Elinor! How badly—'

Mirelle's question faltered as she saw Elinor was not mortally wounded, her mouth dropping for a moment before she realised what had happened.

'The spells to reinforce you against the chain!'

'I guess so,' said Elinor. She flexed her fingers a little, more ice cracking on Terciel's hand above her own, though it instantly refroze. She wondered if the bolt had stripped her of the augmentation against the chain, and how she would know. The chain was warm, perhaps warmer than it had been before. But at least it was quiescent now.

'The sorcerer will be back, with help, I gauge,' said Mirelle, looking out into the fog. 'At least I made him fear for his eyes.'

'That was Hedge,' said Elinor, shivering. She forced herself to stop the shivers, taking a deep, slow breath. She must not panic, she told herself, must not even think about running away or anything like that. All she had to do was hold the chain. Hold the chain until it disappeared, then

Terciel would come back and all would be well. She had to keep hold of that, thought Elinor. Terciel would imprison Kerrigor in Death and come back into Life himself.

'Hedge?' said Mirelle. 'Sword-work, then. I'll have to get close enough to take off his head.'

'Maybe he won't come back,' said Elinor, very hopefully.

Mirelle didn't answer.

Elinor looked at the chain again. It was definitely warmer, almost hot now, even through the protective glove, though the links no longer burned, and the Charter marks on the daisies that joined them were no brighter than the sheen of the gold.

She took another long, slow breath and let it out over a dozen seconds.

As she exhaled, she heard an uncanny whistle. Not someone whistling a Charter mark to summon a breeze, this was more . . . metallic. It took her only a moment more to realise the sound was from necromantic panpipes like Terciel had used at Coldhallow House, the lesser instrument akin to the bells.

'Hedge is waking the Dead!' she exclaimed. 'We have to clear the fog! We need the sun!'

'I still can't hear well enough,' said Mirelle, very matter-of-fact. 'You'll have to do it. Do you remember, when I flew the Paperwing, taking off from the Abhorsen's House? That spell, that whistle, that's the one you need.'

'I'm not sure,' said Elinor, shaking her head. She cast her mind back, pushing aside her fear that the chain was growing ever warmer, the piercing note of the pipe that made her skin crawl and her hair lift with static electricity.

All that had to be ignored. She remembered the bright, cold morning she was in the Paperwing with Mirelle, and that whistle, and the marks that came out her mouth, she fixed them in her mind.

Taking a breath, she held it. If she called the wrong marks, miscast the spell, then she would likely burn out her throat and mouth, maybe die on the spot. But that fierce note from the pipe was waking the Dead, the *hundreds* of Dead Hands, and there was nothing she or Mirelle could do against so many, save banish the fog and let in the sun.

Elinor pursed her lips, reached deep into the Charter, and blew a pure note infused with magic.

Tizanael stood next to the staring, open-mouthed Terciel. Her spirit form, at least. She looked different now in Death to how Terciel had seen her here before, because she had no living body to return to any more. She was less vivid, her skin translucent rather than merely pale, her hair not black streaked with silver but a luminous white. Her eyes were deep pools of starlight, without white or pupil.

She reached out and gripped the chain, flicking it as Terciel had done, and called out, 'Move!'

Her voice was strong and vigorous, more commanding than it had been in recent years. It reminded Terciel of when he had first met Tizanael, long ago in the fish hall of Grynhold.

Kerrigor looked up, up into the grey mist that swirled perpetually above and shouted, a wordless howl that sent a vicious jet of flame from his mouth. But as it faded, he bent his head and moved, reluctantly stepping forward, the river sizzling and steaming about his legs.

The chain grew slack, until Tizanael tapped Terciel's elbow, a touch that was colder even than the river. He moved too, striding with the current, careful to set each footfall so it could not trick him and carry him under and away. Kerrigor shambled after, led by the chain all too like some temporarily quiescent bear who the bearward feared might attack at any moment.

'How are you . . .' said Terciel. 'How are you still here, Great-Aunt?'

'It is a grace given to all Abhorsens, at the end, that we may tarry on the way,' she replied. 'But we must not waste what little time I have. Kerrigor has summoned his minions and allies with that shout. We must hurry. Be on your guard.'

She flicked the chain again. Kerrigor growled in response, and tried to rear back, but the chain tightened and he could not resist. Terciel pulled hard, felt Tizanael adding her strength, and they picked up the pace.

The veil of mist that marked the First Gate was close now. Terciel glanced at Tizanael, who inclined her head, telling him he must speak the words of the Free Magic spell that would open the way for them.

Terciel thought of the page from *The Book of the Dead*, saw the spell there. He had done this before, many times, gone through the First Gate and beyond. He spoke the words, feeling their heat in his mouth, the sparking on his lips.

The mist parted in answer, revealing a series of waterfalls that fell away forever, into some impossible depths. Terciel continued the spell, gesturing to the left and right with his sword, the Abhorsen's sword, the emerald in the pommel now glowing with an eerie green light. Behind him, the chain still lit the rushing waters, a light that was somehow absorbed into the darkness that was Kerrigor.

A path appeared between the waterfalls, a gentle incline between the waters. It did not seem to extend far, but it was impossible to look along it, mind and eye unable to process what it saw.

A narrow path, where a false footfall would send the traveller over the edge, down into the falling waters and onward, without control or any chance of return.

Terciel stepped onto the path, Tizanael's spirit close behind him, her with two translucent hands on one of the golden daisies, the light shining through her fingers, his own left hand clenched about the iron link he held as if it had been fixed there by a smith.

Together, they flicked the chain again, and Kerrigor followed. The mist closed up after his massive, shadowy form, and the path itself faded behind his last footfall.

26

Charter marks flew from Elinor's pursed lips, rising up to the white-shrouded, foggy sky, cutting through it like sparks through paper, boring light-streaked tunnels through the cloud as they continued to climb.

But her whistle did not drown out the call of the necromancer's pipe. Mosrael the Waker called out to those pushed into slumber, and though the pipe was less powerful than the bell, Ranna no longer sounded and its influence waned by the minute. The Dead Hands stirred, bones clicking, dry tendons tightening, broken jaws grinding, dribbling out splintered teeth.

Wind lifted Elinor's hair, the faintest hint of a breeze. The fog swirled and shifted, but showed no signs of breaking, as she continued to summon marks and send them into her breath, which was coming to an end, the last recesses of her lungs emptying.

Mirelle started forward and picked up Terciel's sword, a lesser sword than Tizanael's, but one still imbued with spells for the sundering of Dead flesh and the breaking of Dead bones. Charter marks flared as she lifted it, the steel of the blade surrounded with golden light.

The pipe's harsh, waking call stopped at almost the same time Elinor's breath failed and her whistling ceased. She was sure she had the spell right, but no wind came in answer, though at least she had not burned out her throat and mouth, or killed herself. In fact, she felt invigorated, closer to the Charter than ever. Not that this would be much help, not without the sun to banish the Dead.

She glanced at Terciel, still covered in ice, and at their hands together on the chain, and knew she was not alone, and never would be again, no matter what happened.

In the sudden silence, the Dead moved. Creaking and hissing, clicking and rasping, they came forward between the huge stumps of the sawn-down blackwoods, the protective fog wreathing their advance. Hands distorted into skeletal talons readied to rend, jaws snapped and those who still held weapons made stabbing or slashing motions, trying to recall how it was done.

'We have to try to keep them off Terciel,' said Elinor. She was surprised to hear how calm she sounded. 'And I have to keep hold of the chain. For as long as we can. I'm sorry I couldn't summon the wind. I did my best.'

Mirelle did not answer. Instead she suddenly charged forward, towards the closest Dead Hands, sword held high.

Elinor drew her poniard and leaped around on the pivot of her and Terciel's handfast, to put herself between him and the Dead, the chain sliding in the blackwood needles behind her till it grew taut, anchored by the miller's fallen body. With the blade she drew three Charter marks in the air, whispering the use-names to herself, before pointing the weapon at a Hand who was charging towards her, vanguard of many more to come. It was a misshapen thing, more skeleton than flesh, already distorted by the spirit inside, its arms lengthened and its fleshless hands fused into shearing blades of bone.

'Anet! Calew! Ferhan!'

Charter marks joined to become silver blades that flashed through the air. One smote the Hand's head entirely from the body, one took off its left arm, and the third struck its right hip, so it fell over backwards. It lay on its back like a headless insect for a moment, then flipped up and began to crawl forward, while the decapitated head chattered its teeth in rage.

A dozen Dead creatures overtook the crawling, dismembered thing and came on, straight for Elinor.

The path was of indeterminate length, and passage along it seemed to take both forever and no time at all, but they emerged into the Second Precinct, another flat and endless expanse, with the impossibly wide river flowing onward, ever on.

It was different from the First Precinct in some ways. The grey light was softer and weaker. It was difficult to see very far, and the river was even more dangerous because there were deep holes and sudden drops.

There was a safe way though, dependent on counting steps on leaving the path, and making memorised turns to get around the hidden depths. Or you could probe the river ahead with sword or staff, and go with the flow, slowly skirting any holes found with this probing method. That way was slow, if sure.

Terciel counted the steps, and did not probe ahead with his sword. It was more difficult than usual, because Kerrigor moved slowly and Terciel had to look back and make sure he made the correct turns as well, flicking the chain to ensure his obedience. Theoretically, since he was actually dead, Kerrigor had even more to lose if he fell in one of the deep holes and the current got hold of him properly, but Terciel didn't know how the Greater Dead creature had kept himself from the river's clutches so long anyway, or how he had got back into Life. Perhaps he could fall in a hole and somehow resist the pull of the river and return to Life, while Terciel and Tizanael would be swept away.

'Five steps,' he said to Tizanael as they neared the Second Gate and then without warning the chain snapped tight. Kerrigor strained against it in an explosion of fire and sparks from the iron and gold links, and at the same time something burst from the river ahead. A creature that had spent too long lurking beyond the Fifth Gate. A human now transformed into something that was a horrific mixture of pallid insect and ancient crone, a massively wrinkled, totally bald woman's head atop a shrivelled human torso, but with chitin-armoured arms that ended in serrated claws, and a multiplicity of quadruple-jointed legs thrashing at the river to keep it in place.

Terciel kept hold of the chain and struck with the Abhorsen's sword, slicing off a pincer aimed for his throat, twisting his wrist around to take off the other in a circular stroke to use the back edge of the blade. The creature still sprang at him, the apparently human head unhinging to show the whole head was all a single jaw full of rows of teeth. Terciel dodged and struck again, but before his sword landed, Tizanael used the slack in the chain, whipping it across that gaping maw. The chain smashed into the creature's head, and the whole monster suddenly disintegrated in an explosion of red fire and silver sparks, its fragments falling into the river.

'Your servants are inferior,' said Tizanael to Kerrigor. She snapped the chain again, Terciel joining in a fraction of a second later. 'Terciel, the gate.'

Terciel took two steps forward, and then three more, and the Second Gate formed immediately in front of his feet. A vast sinkhole, unseen until that moment, the waters of the river swirling around and down in silent frenzy.

He looked down into it, and spoke the Free Magic spell that would allow the passage, smoke billowing from his mouth as he did so. The words echoed back to him, and the waters of the sinkhole began to slow. A few seconds later, they stopped moving completely, as if the whirlpool had been snap frozen. There was a spiralling, downward path now, which Terciel took, he and Tizanael tugging on the chain, the reluctant Kerrigor coming after them. The fires in his eyes and mouth were banked now, little more than glowing coals, and his shadowy shape was more diffuse, less human in shape.

'Hurry,' said Tizanael. 'We must hurry.'

Mirelle swung low, shearing through the knees of two Dead Hands, Terciel's sword parting decayed flesh with a dazzling flash of Charter marks and silver and gold sparks. The Hands fell and she jumped back, turning to repeat the blow on two more Hands who sought to outflank her, before retreating several more steps. The crippled Hands on the ground scrabbled towards her, sending up great gouts of blackwood needles and dirt as they pulled themselves forward.

Elinor pivoted around Terciel's hand where they both gripped the chain and cast the spell of the silver blades again, knocking over the closest Hand, only a dozen paces away. But there were more behind it, scores or hundreds more in seemingly never-ending waves.

All the Dead that had been put to sleep by Ranna were now awake. Bereft of Kerrigor's instruction, they knew only to attack the nearest living creatures: Elinor and Mirelle.

Mirelle hacked more down, and retreated again, almost back to Elinor and Terciel. She was panting from the effort, and blood trickled down her arm from where one of the Hands had managed to get close enough to scratch her with a sharpened finger bone before she chopped its legs off.

Something touched the back of Elinor's neck. She whirled around, poniard ready, knowing it could not do much, that this was the end.

There was no one there. She felt the touch again, this time on her face, and knew it and cried aloud in relief and wonder, for it was the caress of a soft spring breeze, a warm wind from the west. She looked up and saw the fog suddenly rolling back, the constant swirling straightened to become a widespread retreat across the sky.

The wind gusted, lifting her hair, picking up blackwood needles and small sticks to send them flying across the ranks of Dead Hands, who had halted. They sensed what was to come and were already fearful. Their lust to consume Life was always lesser than their dread of banishment, a return to Death that this time would be final.

Thin rays of sunshine began to penetrate the fog, which was no longer a heavy blanket of white lying upon the earth, but already scattered skeins of gauze, swiftly being torn apart by the wind.

Croaks of fear and anguish rose from hundreds of broken, twisted throats, and the Hands began to scurry away like ants disturbed by sudden rain, fighting each other as they tried to escape, to find hidey-holes that would save them from the sun. But there were none close enough, and as the sun struck down, so the spirits within the Dead Hands were sent back to Death, bodies dropping everywhere with a finality quite different to the slower, stumbling fall to sleep caused by Ranna.

The wind blew stronger still, and the last wisps of fog disappeared as if they had never hugged the ground. Sunshine spread across the slope, lighting up the barren desecration of the forest, revealing the logging that had been done to get timber to fill the water defences of Uppside. There were hundreds of mighty blackwood stumps and fallen trunks, some not yet stripped of branches, some roped for dragging, many laid out along the long scar of raw earth, the road that Kerrigor had ordered to be made to bring the timber to his siege works.

The road, with stumps and cut trees either side, extended all the way down to the broad blue waters of the Upp river. With the fog gone, in the far distance Elinor saw the towers of Uppside, red-tiled roofs gleaming and white walls shining. Very faintly, carried by the wind, she heard the peal of trumpets and hunting horns, sounding a most unexpected salvation.

'Slow,' said Mirelle, a small smile curving up the corner of her mouth. 'But you did it.'

The smile disappeared as one figure came towards them, one man moving through the fallen bodies. He had an arrow through his neck, and was carrying a forester's great axe, though this one dripped with flames as black as tar, and though a normal man would need both hands, he wielded it easily in one.

Hedge was coming back.

It was necessary to run across the Third Precinct, to evade the wave that came soon after leaving the Second Gate behind. For a moment or two Terciel thought Kerrigor would not do so, dooming them all to be taken. But if the Greater Dead had some secret for evading the river's clutch elsewhere, he evidently did not here, for no sooner had they stepped off the path than the chain grew slack and the creature rushed forward, without prompting or command.

'Run, fools!' boomed Kerrigor, and then they were all sprinting, lifting their legs high out of the river, sending great splashes of water up as the current tried to twist them aside, take them down, or at least delay them long enough for the following wave.

Terciel heard the boom of the wave begin and redoubled his efforts, all too aware he had to stay ahead of Kerrigor as well as the wave. The chain was supposed to prevent the Greater Dead attacking him, but he was not fully confident it would.

So he ran, and tried to draw the deepest of deep breaths, for he needed the wind to speak the spell that would open the Third Gate, and soon, and it didn't feel like he had the lung capacity to do so.

'Now,' said Tizanael, even as Terciel began to speak the words. He could barely hear himself, the crashing wave sounded so close behind, but the spell worked. All of a sudden there was a wall of mist ahead, and then a doorway in the mist, a broad, arched gate. Terciel and Tizanael stepped within it and moved aside to allow Kerrigor entry also. As the Greater Dead creature crossed the threshold, the wave passed by, breaking to either side of the doorway so that only a thin ripple of froth washed about Terciel's knees. In the wave, he saw flailing spirits, hundreds of them to either side, hurried on their way to a final death.

The Fourth Precinct was akin to the First, though the current was even stronger. Terciel and Tizanael pushed forward, flicking the chain every now and then to encourage Kerrigor. Terciel was wary of the creature's passivity, and presumed he was only waiting for some chance to try to free himself. If Tizanael was unable to continue to resist the pull of the river, for example. He looked across at her for signs she might be fading, giving in. But she strode on firmly, and though clearly the spirit of someone dead rather than a living person temporarily trespassing, Terciel was heartened by how much she looked like she always had before in Death: an Abhorsen totally in command of the situation.

The Fourth Gate was not cloaked in mist, and soon became visible. It looked like a shallow fall, something that could be stepped down, with the river continuing on past it. But Terciel knew this was a trap for the unwary or untrained.

He stopped a dozen paces back and spoke the spell to summon the dark bridge that was not only the Fourth Gate, but the only way to safely cross the Fifth Precinct beyond. A narrow bridge, only three feet wide, it was as night-black as the shadow-flesh of Kerrigor.

Flicking the chain, Terciel stepped onto the bridge, Tizanael close behind, Kerrigor shuffling more reluctantly. Another attack was likely here, Terciel knew, for there were Dead beyond who waited desperately for a necromancer to summon such a bridge, lacking the art to do so themselves. When one appeared they would rush down, and any Dead who could do so would be by definition among the strongest, or they would already have gone on.

But no attack came. Maybe it was the presence of two Abhorsens, albeit one of them a spirit, Terciel thought. Or perhaps it was the chain, or Kerrigor himself, a great ruler of the Dead who lesser entities might hope was removed from contention for supremacy among them.

Ahead, the river suddenly rose in front of them, falling up. A reverse waterfall, which was the Fifth Gate. The path ended short of it, leaving a gap. Terciel stopped at the edge and looked at Tizanael.

'We have to bring him close,' he said nervously. 'In the book, it mentioned an extra loop?'

'Yes,' said Tizanael. She flicked the chain, bringing Kerrigor closer and then as he stepped in, twisted her hand so that an extra loop formed and fell over the creature's head, so there was the original loop diagonally across his body and another smaller and tighter loop around his neck. Flames shot higher all along the chain, and sparks sizzled in the shadow stuff.

Kerrigor growled, a deep, menacing growl.

'You know not what you do,' he said. 'You delay me, annoy me, that is all. And one day you will pay the price.'

The Abhorsens ignored him. Terciel spoke the spell, and the rising water ahead broke apart, and a tongue-like formation thrust out and wrapped itself around the three of them, though it never quite touched. Then it began to rise up the reverse waterfall, higher and higher, till the river below disappeared into a grey blur.

Then it flung them in a half circle, depositing them in the Sixth Precinct, even as the water around continued to rise, to some limitless height.

The river was still here, the water pooled, and because it was so, many Dead were gathered. Those who had found the strength to prevent themselves being taken on, and those even stronger who had managed to struggle back from even deeper in Death.

Terciel looked at them, saw shadowy spirits standing in the water, hundreds of them, all watching the new arrivals, knowing one at least of them was a living person, who if they could devour his spirit would help them return to Life. But they also saw the burning, sparking chain, the dense shape of Kerrigor, and the spirit form of Tizanael.

She spoke now, calling out across the still waters.

'I am the Abhorsen Tizanael, and with me the Abhorsen Terciel. Let none stand in our way, lest they be sent onward *at once* to the Ninth Gate and the final death!'

For a moment, there was no response, then the Dead turned and slowly waded away, the closest first and then the rest, like the spreading ripples from a dropped stone. Terciel saw no Greater Dead who might have been more inclined to dispute their passage, but he did not pause to wonder at their absence. He flicked the chain and they walked on, deeper into Death.

The Sixth Gate was in no fixed place. It opened randomly from time to time within the precinct, or it could be summoned anywhere a suitable distance from the previous gate.

Terciel had never gone so far in Death before, but *The Book of the Dead* was imprinted in his mind from countless readings. He knew the spell to call the gate, and he began it as soon as they reached a suitable point. As he spoke the words, the water began to drain away beneath the trio, until they stood in a circle ten feet in diameter, pitted grey stone beneath their feet. Dry stone.

The disc of dry ground began to sink and the water around them rose. It sank faster and faster, the watery walls around them grew ever higher. Within a minute they were in a circular shaft sunk hundreds of feet deep in turbid, thrashing water.

Then, with a mighty roar, the watery walls collapsed outward. Nothing fell inside, but they were surrounded by a mass of froth and spray. When it cleared, they stood in the river again, the current grabbing their legs, the constant grey light all around.

The Seventh Precinct, and in the distance, a line of red fire that burned eerily on the water. An endless line stretching to either side as far as Terciel could see, the flames rising up perhaps a hundred feet before the fierce light of the fire merged with the strange grey light that otherwise pervaded Death.

Terciel stared at the fire, mesmerised by it for a moment. It marked their destination. The Seventh Gate was in the line of fire. Beyond it, they could secure Kerrigor, and Terciel could turn about and rush back to Life before it was too late for Elinor and Mirelle.

'We should run,' said Tizanael calmly. 'My time can be measured in heartbeats now, a score or two, no more.'

Terciel flicked the chain, once, twice. Kerrigor resisted, rearing back, until Tizanael joined in, and then he lumbered forward in answer to the chain, and they ran to the line of the fire, Terciel already preparing the words to open the archway that would allow them passage to the precinct beyond. It sprang into being, and they passed through, Kerrigor roaring in rage as he was unable to resist the power of the chain and the two Abhorsens.

'Here,' said Tizanael, only a dozen paces beyond the gate. The Eighth Precinct was very dangerous, for the river was lit by moving patches of fire – dark, oily fires that slid across the river as if they might be alive, even against the current. None were close, but Terciel knew they would soon come if he lingered in one spot.

He knelt down, a dangerous manoeuvre anywhere in the river of Death, and felt the current strengthen as it contacted more of his body. He was rocked back by it, but steeled himself to resist with body and mind. This was the final act, the thing he must do. He took the end of the chain and plunged it into the water. Steam geysered up all around, but it had no heat. He kept pushing down, forcing the end of the chain into whatever strange ground lay beneath the river. It resisted at first, as if he tried to push an arrow through an iron plate, but then it suddenly gave way and four links of chain sank straight into it, like a tent peg into mud, up to the first of the golden daisies.

Kerrigor lunged forward, snarling. But Tizanael stood against him and kept him back from Terciel. Unarmed, wielding no bell, she merely pushed her hands against the chain where it bound the shadowed bulk of the beast, sinking the burning links and the shining golden daisies deeper into his strange flesh. Kerrigor roared, flames jetting from his mouth, and he struck viciously at Tizanael. His clawed hands cut deep rents into the Abhorsen's spirit form, sending glowing ribbons out across the water. But she held on.

Terciel visualised the necessary page of *On the Making of Necromantic Bells and Other Devices*, got it clear in his mind, and spoke the spell that would fix the chain in place for eternity – or at least until the prisoner's spirit was eroded away, and the remnants taken on by the river.

As the words fell burning from his lips he felt the chain slide through his hand, going deeper into the riverbed. Kerrigor roared and hauled back on the links, but he could not hold the chain as it dragged him down. Terciel let go and moved away. A moment later, Tizanael too jumped clear.

Landing, she stumbled once . . . twice . . . and fell backwards into the river. Terciel ran to her, reached out. Even as he did so, he knew it would be too late, and in any case the inevitable end could not be delayed. Everything he had ever learned as the Abhorsen told him so. For everyone and everything there is a time to die.

Tizanael struggled up, got her head out of the water, long enough to look at Terciel and speak her final words.

'Farewell, Terciel!' she said quietly. A small, uncharacteristic smile spread across her face. 'May you be ever spared from salt fish!'

The river curled up around her head, dragged her back down, and Tizanael was gone. Taken onward to the Ninth Gate, from which there was no return.

Terciel looked back to Kerrigor. The chain had tightened more, dragging the monster onto his back, so he was almost entirely submerged. The river rushed around him, only his broad shoulders and massive head above the surface, like a shadowy rock. His inner fires were quenched now, his eyes mere candlelights, and his mouth a void without fire.

'One Abhorsen less, at the least,' he rumbled. 'And soon enough you too will go to the Ninth Gate, and beyond.'

'One day,' agreed Terciel. There was a final spell to cast, a variation to be used or not at the chain-wielder's pleasure. He chose to do so, speaking the words quickly, eager to be on his way. The Free Magic burned particularly hot in his throat and mouth, and he thought he might temporarily lose his voice from it. It was a small price to pay.

The chain answered to the spell, dragging Kerrigor entirely under the surface. Within a few seconds, Terciel could no longer see him at all, nor the chain, though he presumed it still burned and the Charter marks still shone. There was only the swirling, chill waters of the river of Death. He stared for a moment, then had to swiftly move away as a floating patch of fire began to drift towards him, moving against the current like some riverine predator sensing its prey.

Terciel moved against the current too, as fast as he could wade, eager to return to Life – and Elinor – as quickly as possible.

27

Out in Life, the chain suddenly vanished. Elinor blinked twice, unable to believe it had disappeared. She had hoped Terciel would succeed, but had been far from certain he would.

But she didn't pause to think about him. Swiftly, she pulled her hand out from under Terciel's icy grasp, and ran forward to snatch up the long splinter Kerrigor had used as a spear. It had reverted to mere wood when it was cut from the Dead creature's grasp, but as Elinor picked it up the red fire rekindled along its length, oily black smoke coiling up from the point. She felt a jolt of intense pain through her gloves as she lifted it, but ignored this as she moved closer to Mirelle, though not too close. She knew the Free Magic on the spear might be harmful to the Clayr. She hoped it would be harmful to Hedge.

Hedge had stopped some twenty yards away. He looked old and worn in the bright sunshine, his skin puffy and sallow, his leather armour loose on his scrawny frame. But he held the heavy axe high, and the fire burned darkly on the blade.

'Go,' said Elinor. 'Before the Abhorsen returns.'

'I should have killed you in that greenhouse,' spat Hedge. 'My master was ever too greedy.'

'Your master is vanquished, sorcerer,' said Mirelle. 'You are fortunate my sister is merciful and gives you leave to depart. I doubt Terciel will do so.'

Hedge didn't answer. He shifted the axe a little, and for a moment Elinor thought he was about to charge forward. But at that moment, ice cracked behind Elinor and Mirelle, a sharp sound in the silence. They both started to turn before snapping their eyes back to the front, to their enemy.

But Hedge did not charge. Instead he dropped the axe and started to back away, around the edge of the huge stump.

'I will go now, but I will return,' he called. 'As will my master!'

When he was covered by one of the tall vertical splinters projecting from the rim of the stump, he turned about and walked faster, not looking back. Mirelle and Elinor watched him carefully. More ice cracked behind them, but they did not look. The sorcerer skirted the first stump and crossed to the next, jumped up on it, and broke into a scuttling run, all too like a spider seeking the shelter of a gap between floorboards.

'Thank the Charter,' muttered Mirelle wearily. 'I am spent.'

The ranger let her sword drop, and leaned on the hilt. Elinor threw the wooden spear away, as far as she could. As it left her hands, the oily fire upon it guttered out.

'Me too,' said Elinor. She looked at her hands and grimaced.

'Elinor? Mirelle?' said Terciel, his voice so hoarse from the use of Free Magic that for a moment they did not recognise him, and steeled themselves again for some new enemy, until they saw it really was Terciel stumbling towards them. He went to embrace Elinor, but she quickly stepped back.

'What?'

'I am . . . I am not sure,' said Elinor shakily. 'But I think the Free Magic from the chain has got into me. The gloves have melted on my hands. You had best stay away.'

Her hands really hurt now. She'd felt the heat and the burgeoning pain, but had been able to put both aside in the tumult of battle. Now, in bright sunshine, with no enemies in sight, it was hard to think of anything else. She looked at Terciel.

'You did it. Chained Kerrigor in Death, all by yourself!'

'Tizanael helped,' said Terciel.

'What? How could she——?'

He didn't answer, instead he just looked at Elinor as if he had never seen her before, and wanted to fix her in his memory in case she disappeared. 'I'll tell you later. Hold your hands out in front. I was reinforced to bear the chain before you, remember. The Free Magic won't hurt me.'

Elinor obeyed. She flinched as he took her hands, the pain intensifying with every small movement. The palms of the gloves were shredded, and no Charter Magic flared under Terciel's touch. Elinor shut her eyes and tried to think of pleasant things, but for some reason images of Coldhallow House burning came into her head, the roar of the fire, the smell of the smoke—

She felt another, much sharper pain and gasped, then a gentle coolness spread across her hands. Elinor bit back a sob and opened her eyes. Terciel had ripped the gauntlets off and now from his own cupped hand was pouring a stream of golden light made from dozens of Charter marks across her palms, a complex healing spell she did not know.

'That will help for a while,' he said. He hesitated, then added, 'I do not think there will be any permanent harm. There are healers in Uppside who will be able to do more. But we cannot go there yet, because all these bodies must be burned before nightfall, and that will be no small task, even if they do come to assist us. I expect they will send a force out to see what has happened here. Can you help until they get here?'

'Yes,' said Elinor, without hesitation. She felt the presence of the Charter very strongly, and knew she would be able to call upon it at her need.

'We will begin with Tizanael,' said Terciel. 'She should have that honour, and more. Even death could not keep her from doing what had to be done.'

'Something of an Abhorsen trait, I think,' said Mirelle. She straightened up and lifted her sword. 'I will keep watch for a little longer, should Hedge come back.'

'Hedge was here?' asked Terciel, suddenly alert. 'The sorcerer who attacked you, Elinor?'

'He has fled,' said Elinor. 'Mirelle put an arrow through this throat, which I think at least discouraged him.'

400

'And he didn't like the sun,' added Mirelle. 'That was Elinor's doing.'

'Uh, good,' said Terciel.

He crooked his forefinger around Elinor's, very gently. Together they walked to Tizanael's body and looked down.

'Her bells!' exclaimed Elinor. 'They're gone! But how?'

The bell bandolier was missing entirely, but nothing else, save the sword Terciel had already taken. Tizanael lay on her back. She looked as if she might be asleep, save for the blood that stained the ground behind her head, and the surcoat over her armour was torn where Kerrigor's spear had struck. Her face was less harsh than it had been while she lived, the discipline that had infused it and every aspect of her life vanished.

'The bells move mysteriously at times,' said Terciel. 'Mine came to me between the chimneys of the fish hall of Grynhold. I suppose Tizanael's have gone to whoever will be my Abhorsen-in-Waiting, or will go, in time. I had hoped it might be you, Elinor.'

Elinor shook her head.

'I am no Abhorsen, nor wish to be one,' she said. 'Even if I have the blood. I had wondered if perhaps you wanted to lay your own bells down?'

'It has crossed my mind more than once,' admitted Terciel. 'But not now. I *am* the Abhorsen, whether I wish it or not. This is my path. But I have also learned I need not live my entire life as Tizanael did, at least in later times, as the Abhorsen and nothing else. It is possible to let others into my life. The office I hold, the necessary work I do, it should not keep all else at bay. Or so I hope.'

He knelt down to touch his free hand to Tizanael's head, Elinor kneeling with him. He drew a mark above the baptismal mark on the old Abhorsen's forehead, the new one shining above the old, faded sign that was now no more than a faint discoloration on the skin. The next mark he drew above her navel, and the third mark he kept in his closed hand.

He and Elinor stood up and bowed their heads.

'Farewell, Great-Great-Aunt Tizanael,' said Terciel. 'I know you have gone already, beyond the Ninth Gate. You did look back, to stay your journey, and I stand here because of it. You were a true Abhorsen.'

He let the third mark fall. There was a flash, a whoosh of contained fire, and then there was nothing but a line of ashes, which the breeze picked up and began to spread among the blackwood needles and the bare earth.

They stood in silence for a moment, then Terciel turned to face Elinor.

'So *I* am to carry on as the Abhorsen,' he said. She could feel the tension in his finger where it held her own. 'What will you do?'

'First, I will go to the Glacier of the Clayr,' replied Elinor. 'As was always my intention. To discover my vast, extended family, which I am already somewhat horrified about, from hearing Mirelle's tales. There, I will join a troupe of entertainers – the Clayr have several, apparently – and put on plays. When we are not all looking into the future, of course.'

Terciel nodded dumbly. His breath caught and he swallowed.

'A good plan,' he said finally, looking away. 'Well, we had best get on—'

Elinor smacked him on the shoulder, forgetting her burned hand. She yelped and he stared at her, until she managed to stop sobbing out 'ow' and talk.

'Secondly, I hope to spend at least part of every year with my lover at the Abhorsen's House, and I hope that he will likewise spend time with me in the Glacier, his duties permitting. Idiot.'

EPILOGUE

I t was midsummer, and the Glacier of the Clayr bustled with preparations for the traditional celebrations. Not only was there to be the dance led by the Bird of Dawning through the major tunnels and avenues, there was also a performance of Breakespear's *The Court of the Sad Prince*, a play not performed in the Old Kingdom for a hundred years or more, according to First Assistant Librarian Werone, who was an expert in the field. Moreover, the player who was performing the role of the Fool was apparently the most astonishing juggler and tumbler, and the excited talk from those privileged enough to be part of the production or to see rehearsals had meant the long-disused theatre between the main spiral and the Third Back Stair had to be set to rights, and it looked like there would be a dozen performances at least, rather than the originally mooted four.

Word of the play had spread far beyond the Glacier, and many more visitors than usual had come for the midsummer festival. Visitors from all over the Old Kingdom, making the Rangers even more short-handed and taciturn than ever as they investigated them at the waystations and led those who were allowed to pass through twisty ways to the guest quarters.

One special visitor flew in by Paperwing, and was greeted, as was only proper for someone of his eminence, by the Voice of the Nine Day Watch; the Captain of Rangers; the Chief Librarian; the Banker and Coiner; the Steam-Mistress; and Filris the Infirmarian, who embarrassed him by looking at his arm and foot immediately after the official welcoming.

But the high and mighty eventually left, leaving Terciel the fifty-second Abhorsen with only one slight, somewhat short Clayr, who took him by the hand and led him to her chambers.

They stopped along the way at the Zally Memorial Fountain, and sat on one of the benches and drank to each other from the crystal glasses, as had swiftly become their tradition, as much as climbing the great fig in the Abhorsen's House, which Elinor had also adopted as her own. She had forgotten she meant to ask Terciel about the white cat she was sure she had seen there.

'I have been wondering what kind of play Breakespear might write about us,' said Elinor, replacing the glasses under the rim of the fountain, where the returning water would wash them clean. 'I mean, if she was writing now.'

'What do you mean?'

'A comedy, a tragedy or a history?'

'A history, surely, since it's actually happened?'

'Breakespear's histories do not necessarily follow what actually happened,' continued Elinor.

'I don't really know any of Breakespear's plays,' said Terciel. 'Or any plays, in fact. I've only ever seen two. One in Belisaere, that was all music and clowning and didn't make any sense, and the other one I saw here years ago and it was gloomy and confusing, with too many characters and very long speeches. I can't wait to see yours tonight. Everyone's talking about it. What's the difference, anyway? Is it simply a comedy is funny, and a tragedy is sad?'

'For Breakespear, the comedies end happily, usually with a wedding. In the tragedies everybody dies. Or almost everybody.'

'Everybody does die,' said Terciel quietly. 'Or they should.'

'Yes, but preferably at the right time,' said Elinor. 'The tragedy is when it is too soon.'

As she spoke, her eye caught a glistening bead on the lip of the fountain, a single drop of water. In it she Saw a woman stumbling up a hillside at dusk. She was heavily pregnant, and badly hurt. There was a wound in her shoulder, too close to her heart. Her hand was pressed against it, red to the wrist with bright new blood. More gushed through her fingers with every pace, with every beat of her heart. Too much blood, flowing too fast. She would not live for more than a few minutes.

Elinor knew it was herself. Older. Her hair was different, her face fuller. There were some lines around her eyes. She was perhaps thirty years old, and very soon to die.

The vision changed, the world turning. She saw Terciel. He was older too, and bearded, and she incongruously thought, Oh, I like that. He knelt by the side of a dead woman. Elinor. He was by *her* side, and Elinor's heart stopped as she heard someone unseen say:

'The child is dead, Abhorsen.'

Then her heart stuttered back to life as the vision swirled and there was Terciel again, his face close to the baby now, a baby whose bottom lip quivered and eyes looked furiously at the world, a baby alive and literally kicking, and Terciel's face was filled with both wonder and sorrow and he said:

'Father of Sabriel.'

The drop fell, taking the vision with it.

Elinor blinked and looked away. Terciel was talking about tragedies and timing. She half listened to him, her thoughts leaping ahead. The vision might not be a true one. Even if it was, it could be forestalled. Not being pregnant would do that. Or avoiding hillsides . . . and in any case, she had looked thirty or even more ancient. A decade at least in the future.

And they would have a baby. A little girl called Sabriel.

'So what would it be?' asked Terciel. 'A comedy certainly doesn't fit. Too much death, for a start.'

'Not a tragedy,' said Elinor firmly. Nor would it be, she decided. However much time she had to live, however much time she had with Terciel. She shrugged and added, 'Some plays defy categorisation, as do lives.'

Terciel smiled fondly at her, unsure where she was headed.

'What was it Mirelle said to you again?' Elinor asked, tucking her arm in his. 'You told me, that day in the House, when I sat on the end of your sickbed. Her philosophy. Make the best of things?'

'Yes,' said Terciel.

'Hmm,' Elinor said slowly. 'Good advice. We should follow it. How long are you going to stay this time?'

'As long as I can,' said Terciel. 'Several weeks, at the least, I hope. There seems less trouble in general, now Kerrigor is gone. Though the Regent continues to wander in her mind occasionally, there have been no new reports of Dead within Belisaere itself. And as you doubtless know, the Clayr are still bothered by their inability to See around the Red Lake. But I am hopeful we might be entering the better times Tizanael always wished for.'

'Good,' said Elinor. 'After *The Court of the Sad Prince*, which is clearly going to be an absolute knockout, the next play I am to put on is *The Wise Woman*. One of Breakespear's comedies, as it happens. There is a part you are perfect to play.'

Terciel looked shifty.

'I've never acted,' he said. 'I'm not sure I could do it. Is it a major part?'

'One of the biggest,' said Elinor. 'The Wise Woman's Doting Suitor.'

Terciel frowned.

'Why did you think of me for that?'

'Because I am to play the Wise Woman,' said Elinor. 'One wise enough to know that if you really can't act, I'll get someone else for the play. You'll have to keep the role outside it though.'

Terciel gathered her in, and their noses touched.

'In that case,' he whispered, 'count me in.'

ACKNOWLEDGEMENTS

Returning to the Old Kingdom once again is a reminder to me of all the people who have helped me along the way. There are too many to list here. If I attempted it this would become a book of thanks rather than a novel, and no one would publish it. But I do want to say thank you to everyone who has worked in any capacity on the Old Kingdom books, all the way back to *Sabriel* in 1995. This has included agents, publishers, editors, copy editors, designers, illustrators, translators, production managers, printers, publicists, marketers, sales representatives, warehouse staff, booksellers and more. I am grateful to everyone who has helped so many readers around the world visit the Old Kingdom, and return again and again.

More specifically, for *Terciel & Elinor* I owe particular thanks to my agent, Jill Grinberg, and her wonderful team at Jill Grinberg Literary Management in New York; to my Australian agent, Fiona Inglis, and the crew at

Curtis Brown Australia in Sydney (where in the far-off past I was an agent myself); and to Matthew Snyder at CAA in Los Angeles, who looks after my film and TV representation.

I am similarly fortunate to continue to work with tremendously supportive, experienced and talented publishers: Katherine Tegen and her team at Katherine Tegen Books, an imprint of HarperCollins, in New York; with Eva Mills and the Allen & Unwin gang in Melbourne and Sydney; and Emma Matthewson and her band of publishing professionals at Hot Key Books, part of Bonnier, in London. On the audio side, Rebecca Waugh and crew at Random House Audio continue to make my books worth listening to, ably supported by Bolinda Australia. I am also always very grateful to the publishers who publish my books in translation, transcending my limitation of only being able to write in English.

I do not think the Old Kingdom books could have lasted so long, or that I would have written *six* of them, without the enthusiasm and support of readers. Not simply the purchasing and reading of the books (though that is *very* significant, please keep it up), but also the creation of fan art, and cosplay, and making wikis, and talking about the books and characters and settings and might-have-beens, and generally investing time and love and energy in an imagined world, making it all the more real to everyone, including me.

Finally, as always, I am extremely grateful to my wife, Anna, and my sons, Thomas and Edward, and our dog,

Snufkin, who in a difficult year all supported me and each other. I could not have written this book without the solidity of my home life, a strong bubble of kindness and calm in an uncertain world.

Venture further into the Old Kingdom.

SABR(EL

The bandoleer was designed to be worn across the chest, with the pouches hanging down. Sabriel opened the smallest and pulled out a tiny silver bell . . .

Read on for more.

PROLOGUE

It was little more than three miles from the Wall into the Old Kingdom, but that was enough. Noonday sunshine could be seen on the other side of the Wall in Ancelstierre and not a cloud in sight. Here, there was a clouded sunset and a steady rain had just begun to fall, coming faster than the tents could be raised.

The midwife shrugged her cloak higher up against her neck and bent over the woman again, raindrops spilling from her nose on to the upturned face below. The midwife's breath blew out in a cloud of white, but there was no answering billow of air from her patient.

The midwife sighed and slowly straightened up, that single movement telling the watchers everything they needed to know. The woman who had staggered into their forest camp was dead, only holding on to life long enough to pass it on to the baby at her side. But even as the midwife picked up the pathetically small form beside the dead woman, it shuddered within its wrappings and was still.

'The child, too?' asked one of the watchers, a man who wore the mark of the Charter fresh-drawn in wood ash upon his brow. 'Then there shall be no need for baptism.'

His hand went up to brush the mark from his forehead then suddenly stopped, as a pale, white hand gripped his and forced it down in a single, swift motion.

'Peace!' said a calm voice. 'I wish you no harm.'

The white hand released its grip and the speaker stepped into the ring of firelight. The others watched him without welcome and the hands that had half sketched Charter marks, or gone to bowstrings and hilts, did not relax.

The man strode towards the bodies and looked upon them. Then he turned to face the watchers, pushing his hood back to reveal the face of someone who had taken paths far from sunlight, for his skin was a deathly white.

'I am called Abhorsen,' he said and his words sent ripples through the people about him, as if he had cast a large and weighty stone into a pool of stagnant water. 'And there will be a baptism tonight.'

The Charter Mage looked down on the bundle in the midwife's hands and said: 'The child is dead, Abhorsen. We are travellers, our life lived under the sky, and it is often harsh. We know death, lord.'

'Not as I do,' replied Abhorsen, smiling so his paper-white face crinkled at the corners and drew back from his equally white teeth. 'And I say the child is not yet dead.'

The man tried to meet Abhorsen's gaze, but faltered and looked away at his fellows. None moved, or made any sign, till a woman said, 'So. It is easily done. Sign the child, Arrenil. We will make a new camp at Leovi's Ford. Join us when you are finished here.'

The Charter Mage inclined his head in assent and the others drifted away to pack up their half-made camp, slow with the reluctance of having to move, but filled with a greater reluctance to remain near Abhorsen, for his name was one of secrets and unspoken fears.

When the midwife went to lay the child down and leave, Abhorsen spoke: 'Wait. You will be needed.'

The midwife looked down on the baby and saw that it was a girl child and, save for its stillness, could be merely sleeping. She had heard of Abhorsen, and if the girl could live . . . warily she picked up the child again and held her out to the Charter Mage. 'If the Charter does not—' began the man, but Abhorsen held up a pallid hand and interrupted.

'Let us see what the Charter wills.'

The man looked at the child again and sighed. Then he took a small bottle from his pouch and held it aloft, crying out a chant that was the beginning of a Charter; one that listed all things that lived or grew, or once lived, or would live again, and the bonds that held them all together. As he spoke, a light came to the bottle, pulsing with the rhythm of the chant. Then the chanter was silent. He touched the bottle to the earth, then to the sign of wood ash on his forehead, and then upended it over the child.

A great flash lit the surrounding woods as the glowing liquid splashed over the child's head, and the priest cried: 'By the Charter that binds all things, we name thee—'

Normally, the parents of the child would then speak the name. Here, only Abhorsen spoke and he said: 'Sabriel.'

As he uttered the word, the wood ash disappeared from the priest's forehead and slowly formed on the child's. The Charter had accepted the baptism.

'But . . . but she is dead!' exclaimed the Charter Mage, gingerly touching his forehead to make sure the ash was truly gone.

He got no answer, for the midwife was staring across the fire at Abhorsen, and Abhorsen was staring at – nothing. His eyes reflected the dancing flames, but did not see them.

Slowly, a chill mist began to rise from his body, spreading towards the man and midwife, who scuttled to the other side of the fire – wanting to get away, but now too afraid to run.

He could hear the child crying, which was good. If she had gone beyond the first gateway he could not bring her back without more stringent preparations and a subsequent dilution of her spirit.

The current was strong, but he knew this branch of the river and waded past pools and eddies that hoped to drag him under. Already, he could feel the waters leeching his spirit, but his will was strong, so they took only the colour, not the substance.

He paused to listen and, hearing the crying diminish, hastened forward. Perhaps she was already at the gateway and about to pass.

The First Gate was a veil of mist, with a single dark opening, where the river poured into the silence beyond. Abhorsen hurried towards it and then stopped. The baby had not yet passed through, but only because something had caught her and picked her up. Standing there, looming up out of the black waters, was a shadow darker than the gate.

It was several feet higher than Abhorsen and there were pale marsh-lights burning where you would expect to see eyes, and the fetid stench of carrion rolled off it – a warm stench that relieved the chill of the river.

Abhorsen advanced on the thing slowly, watching the child it held loosely in the crook of a shadowed arm. The baby was asleep, but restless, and it squirmed towards the creature, seeking a mother's breast, but it only held her away from itself, as if the child were hot or caustic.

Slowly, Abhorsen drew a small, silver handbell from the bandoleer of bells across his chest and cocked his wrist to ring it. But the shadow-thing held the baby up and spoke in a dry, slithery voice, like a snake on gravel.

'Spirit of your spirit, Abhorsen. You can't spell me while I hold her. And perhaps I shall take her beyond the gate, as her mother has already gone.'

Abhorsen frowned, in recognition, and replaced the bell. 'You have a new shape, Kerrigor. And you are now this side of the First Gate. Who was foolish enough to assist you so far?'

Kerrigor smiled widely and Abhorsen caught a glimpse of fires burning deep inside his mouth.

'One of the usual calling,' he croaked. 'But unskilled.

He didn't realise it would be in the nature of an exchange. Alas, his life was not sufficient for me to pass the last portal. But now, you have come to help me.'

'I, who chained you beyond the Seventh Gate?'

'Yes,' whispered Kerrigor. 'The irony does not, I think, escape you. But if you want the child . . .'

He made as if to throw the baby into the stream and, with that jerk, woke her. Immediately, she began to cry and her little fists reached out to gather up the shadow-stuff of Kerrigor like the folds of a robe. He cried out, tried to detach her, but the tiny hands held tightly and he was forced to over-use his strength, and threw her from him. She landed, squalling, and was instantly caught up in the flow of the river, but Abhorsen lunged forward, snatching her from both the river and Kerrigor's grasping hands.

Stepping back, he drew the silver bell one-handed and swung it so it sounded twice. The sound was curiously muffled, but true, and the clear chime hung in the air, fresh and cutting, alive. Kerrigor flinched at the sound and fell backwards to the darkness that was the gate.

'Some fool will soon bring me back and then . . .' he cried out, as the river took him under. The waters swirled and gurgled and then resumed their steady flow.

Abhorsen stared at the gate for a time, then sighed and, placing the bell back in his belt, looked at the baby held in his arm. She stared back at him, dark eyes matching his own.

Already, the colour had been drained from her skin. Nervously, Abhorsen laid a hand across the brand on her forehead and felt the glow of her spirit within. The Charter mark had kept her life contained when the river should have drained it. It was her life-spirit that had so burned Kerrigor.

She smiled up at him and gurgled a little, and Abhorsen felt a smile tilting the corner of his own mouth. Still smiling, he turned and began the long wade back up the river, to the gate that would return them both to their living flesh.

The baby wailed a scant second before Abhorsen opened his eyes, so that the midwife was already halfway around the dying fire, ready to pick her up. Frost crackled on the ground and icicles hung from Abhorsen's nose. He wiped them off with a sleeve and leaned over the child, much as any anxious father does after a birth.

'How is the babe?' he asked and the midwife stared at him wonderingly, for the dead child was now loudly alive and as deathly white as he.

'As you hear, lord,' she answered. 'She is very well. It is perhaps a little cold for her—'

He gestured at the fire and spoke a word, and it roared into life, the frost melting at once, the raindrops sizzling into steam.

'That will do till morning,' said Abhorsen. 'Then I shall take her to my house. I shall have need of a nurse. Will you come?' The midwife hesitated and looked to the Charter Mage, who still lingered on the far side of the fire. He refused to meet her glance and she looked down once more at the little girl bawling in her arms.

'You are . . . you are . . .' whispered the midwife.

'A necromancer?' said Abhorsen. 'Only of a sort. I loved the woman who lies here. She would have lived if she had loved another, but she did not. Sabriel is our child. Can you not see the kinship?'

The midwife looked at him as he leant forward and took Sabriel from her, rocking her on his chest. The baby quietened and, in a few seconds, was asleep.

'Yes,' said the midwife. 'I shall come with you and look after Sabriel. But you must find a wet-nurse . . .'

'And I daresay much else besides,' mused Abhorsen. 'But my house is not a place for—'

The Charter Mage cleared his throat and moved around the fire.

'If you seek a man who knows a little of the Charter,' he said hesitantly, 'I should wish to serve, for I have seen its work in you, lord, though I am loath to leave my fellow wanderers.'

'Perhaps you will not have to,' replied Abhorsen, smiling at a sudden thought. 'I wonder if your leader will object to two new members joining her band. For my work means I must travel and there is no part of the Kingdom that has not felt the imprint of my feet.'

'Your work?' asked the man, shivering a little, though it was no longer cold.

'Yes,' said Abhorsen. 'I am a necromancer, but not of the common kind. Where others of the art raise the dead, I lay them back to rest. And those that will not rest, I bind – or try to. I am Abhorsen . . .'

He looked at the baby again and added, almost with a note of surprise, 'Father of Sabriel.'

1

The rabbit had been run over minutes before. Its pink eyes were glazed and blood stained its clean white fur. Unnaturally clean fur, for it had just escaped from a bath. It still smelt faintly of lavender water.

A tall, curiously pale young woman stood over the rabbit. Her night-black hair, fashionably bobbed, was hanging slightly over her face. She wore no makeup or jewellery, save for an enamelled school badge pinned to her regulation navy blazer. That, coupled with her long skirt, stockings and sensible shoes, identified her as a schoolgirl. A nameplate under the badge read 'Sabriel' and the Roman 'VI' and gilt crown proclaimed her to be both a member of the Sixth Form and a prefect.

The rabbit was, unquestionably, dead. Sabriel looked up from it and back along the bricked drive that left the road and curved up to an imposing pair of wrought-iron gates. A sign above the gate, in gilt letters of mock Gothic, announced that they were the gates to Wyverley College.

Smaller letters added that the school was 'Established in 1652 for Young Ladies of Quality'.

A small figure was busy climbing over the gate, nimbly avoiding the spikes that were supposed to stop such activities. She dropped the last few feet and started running, her pigtails flying, shoes clacking on the bricks. Her head was down to gain momentum, but as cruising speed was established, she looked up, saw Sabriel and the dead rabbit, and screamed.

'Bunny!'

Sabriel flinched as the girl screamed, hesitated for a moment, then bent down by the rabbit's side and reached out with one pale hand to touch it between its long ears. Her eyes closed and her face set as if she had suddenly turned to stone. A faint whistling sound came from her slightly parted lips, like the wind heard from far away. Frost formed on her fingertips and rimed the asphalt beneath her feet and knees.

The other girl, running, saw her suddenly tip forward over the rabbit and topple towards the road, but at the last minute her hand came out and she caught herself. A second later, she had regained her balance and was using both hands to restrain the rabbit – a rabbit now inexplicably lively again, its eyes bright and shiny, as eager to be off as when it escaped from its bath.

'Bunny!' shrieked the younger girl again, as Sabriel stood up, holding the rabbit by the scruff of its neck. 'Oh, thank you, Sabriel! When I heard the car skidding I thought . . .'

She faltered as Sabriel handed the rabbit over and blood stained her expectant hands.

'He'll be fine, Jacinth,' Sabriel replied wearily. 'A scratch. It's already closed up.'

Jacinth examined Bunny carefully, then looked up at Sabriel, the beginnings of a wriggling fear showing at the back of her eyes.

'There isn't anything under the blood,' stammered Jacinth. 'What did you . . .'

'I didn't,' snapped Sabriel. 'But perhaps you can tell me what you are doing out of bounds?'

'Chasing Bunny,' replied Jacinth, her eyes clearing as life reverted to a more normal situation. 'You see . . .'

'No excuses,' recited Sabriel. 'Remember what Mrs Umbrade said at Assembly on Monday.'

'It's not an excuse,' insisted Jacinth. 'It's a reason.'

'You can explain it to Mrs Umbrade then.'

'Oh, Sabriel! You wouldn't! You know I was only chasing Bunny. I'd never have come out—'

Sabriel held up her hands in mock defeat and gestured back to the gates.

'If you're back inside within three minutes, I won't have seen you. And open the gate this time. They won't be locked till I go back inside.'

Jacinth smiled, her whole face beaming, whirled around and sped back up the drive, Bunny clutched against her neck. Sabriel watched till she had gone through the gate, then let the tremors take her till she was bent over, shaking with cold. A moment of weakness and she had broken the promise she had made both to herself and her father. It was only a rabbit and Jacinth did love it so much – but what would that lead to? It was no great step from bringing back a rabbit to bringing back a person.

Worse, it had been so easy. She had caught the spirit right at the wellspring of the river and had returned it with barely a gesture of power, patching the body with simple Charter symbols as they stepped from death to life. She hadn't even needed bells or the other apparatus of a necromancer. Only a whistle and her will.

Death and what came after death was no great mystery to Sabriel. She just wished it was.

It was Sabriel's last term at Wyverley – the last three weeks, in fact. She had graduated already, coming first in English, equal first in Music, third in Mathematics, seventh in Science, second in Fighting Arts and fourth in Etiquette. She had also been a runaway first in Magic, but that wasn't printed on the certificate. Magic only worked in those regions of Ancelstierre close to the Wall which marked the border with the Old Kingdom. Farther away, it was considered to be quite beyond the pale, if it existed at all, and persons of repute did not mention it. Wyverley College was only forty miles from the Wall, had a good all-round reputation, and taught Magic to those students who could obtain special permission from their parents.

Sabriel's father had chosen it for that reason when he had emerged from the Old Kingdom with a five-year-old girl in tow to seek a boarding school. He had paid in advance for that first year, in Old Kingdom silver deniers that stood up to surreptitious touches with cold iron. Thereafter, he had come to visit his daughter twice a year, at Midsummer and Midwinter, staying for several days on each occasion and always bringing more silver.

Understandably, the Headmistress was very fond of Sabriel. Particularly since she never seemed troubled by her father's rare visitations, as most other girls would be. Once Mrs Umbrade had asked Sabriel if she minded and had been troubled by the answer that Sabriel saw her father far more often than when he was actually there. Mrs Umbrade didn't teach Magic and didn't want to know any more about it other than the pleasant fact that some parents would pay considerable sums to have their daughters schooled in the basics of sorcery and enchantment.

Mrs Umbrade certainly didn't want to know how Sabriel saw her father. Sabriel, on the other hand, always looked forward to his unofficial visits and watched the moon, tracing its movements from the leather-bound almanac which listed the phases of the moon in both Kingdoms and gave valuable insights into the seasons, tides and other ephemerae that were never the same at any one time on both sides of the Wall. Abhorsen's sending of himself always appeared at dark of the moon.

On these nights, Sabriel would lock herself into her study (a privilege of the Sixth Form – previously she'd had to sneak into the library), put the kettle on the fire, drink tea and read a book until the characteristic wind rose up, extinguished the fire, put out the electric light and rattled the shutters – all necessary preparations, it seemed, for her father's phosphorescent sending to appear in the spare armchair.

Sabriel was particularly looking forward to her father's visit that November. It would be his last, because college was about to end and she wanted to discuss her future. Mrs Umbrade wanted her to go to university, but that meant moving further away from the Old Kingdom. Her magic would wane and parental visitations would be limited to actual physical appearances, and those might well become even less frequent. On the other hand, going to university would mean staying with some of the friends she'd had virtually all her life, girls she'd started school with at the age of five. There would also be a much greater world of social interaction, particularly with young men, of which commodity there was a distinct shortage around Wyverley College.

And the disadvantage of losing her magic could possibly be offset by a lessening of her affinity for death and the dead . . . Sabriel was thinking of this as she waited, book in hand, half-drunk cup of tea balanced precariously on the arm of her chair. It was almost midnight and Abhorsen hadn't appeared. Sabriel had checked the almanac twice and had even opened the shutters to peer out through the glass at the sky. It was definitely dark of the moon, but there was no sign of him. It was the first time in her life that he hadn't appeared and she felt suddenly uneasy.

Sabriel rarely thought about what life was really like in the Old Kingdom, but now old stories came to mind and dim memories of when she'd lived there with the Travellers. Abhorsen was a powerful sorcerer, but even then . . .

'Sabriel! Sabriel!'

ABOUT THE AUTHOR

GARTH NIX has been a full-time writer since 2001, but has also worked as a literary agent, marketing consultant, book editor, book publicist, book sales representative, bookseller and as a part-time soldier in the Australian Army Reserve.

Garth's books include the Old Kingdom fantasy series: *Terciel & Elinor, Sabriel, Lirael, Abhorsen, Goldenhand and Clariel*; SF novels *Shades Children* and *A Confusion of Princes*; fantasy novels *Angel Mage* and *The Left-Handed Booksellers of London*; and a Regency romance with magic, *Newt's Emerald*. His novels for children include *The Ragwitch*; the six books of *The Seventh Tower* sequence; *The Keys to the Kingdom* series; and *Frogkisser!* His short fiction includes more than sixty published stories, some of them collected in *Across the Wall* and *To Hold the Bridge*.

He has co-written several books with Sean Williams, including the Troubletwisters series; *Spirit Animals Book*

Three: Blood Ties; *Have Sword, Will Travel* and *Let Sleeping Dragons Lie*.

More than six million copies of Garth's books have been sold around the world, they have appeared on the bestseller lists of the *New York Times*, *Publishers Weekly*, the *Bookseller* and others and his work has been translated into forty-two languages. He has won multiple Aurealis Awards, the Ditmar Award, the Mythopoeic Award, CBCA Honour Book, and has been shortlisted for the Locus Awards, the Shirley Jackson Award and others.

www.garthnix.com
Twitter @garthnix
facebook.com/garthnix

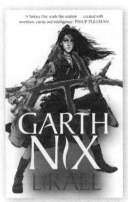
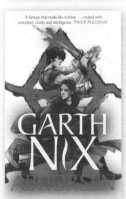
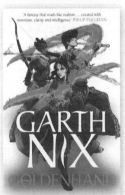
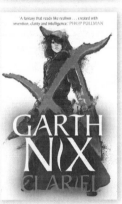

Thank you for choosing a Hot Key book.

If you want to know more about our authors and what we publish, you can find us online.

You can start at our website

www.hotkeybooks.com

And you can also find us on:

We hope to see you soon!